Three Stories of Second-Chance Love
Will Delight at Any Season

A PATCHWORK
Christmas
COLLECTION

JUDITH MILLER ✳ NANCY MOSER
STEPHANIE GRACE WHITSON

BARBOUR BOOKS
An Imprint of Barbour Publishing, Inc.

Print ISBN 978-1-63409-022-3

eBook Editions:
Adobe Digital Edition (.epub) 978-1-62029-096-5
Kindle and MobiPocket Edition (.prc) 978-1-62029-097-2

Cover photography by iofoto

Published by Barbour Books, an imprint of Barbour Publishing, Inc., P.O. Box 719, Uhrichsville, Ohio 44683, www.barbourbooks.com

Our mission is to publish and distribute inspirational products offering exceptional value and biblical encouragement to the masses.

Member of the
Evangelical Christian
Publishers Association

Printed in the United States of America.

A PATCHWORK
Christmas
COLLECTION

Seams Like Love

Judith Miller

Acknowledgments

Special thanks to Karen Jenkins for development
and use of the Homestead Rose mitten pattern.

Special thanks to Caroline Trumpold for her willingness to meet with me
and share a wealth of valuable knowledge regarding Amana quilts.

Special thanks to the staff of the Amana Heritage
Museum for their valuable research assistance.

Chapter 1

Upper South Village, Amana, Iowa, 1890

O uch!" Karla Stuke dropped her quilting needle and stuck the tip of her index finger into her mouth. Leaning forward, she examined the pale blue fabric for any red droplets. She wrinkled her nose as the metallic taste of blood assaulted her taste buds. How often must she prick her fingers before she no longer startled every time the front bell jangled or someone called her name?

Her self-recrimination continued as she pushed away from the quilting frame. Her family had been living in the Upper South Amana Hotel for most of her twenty-four years, yet the bell still managed to surprise her at least once a week—and always when she had a needle in her hand. With so many tiny pricks in her fingers, she should be described as a human pincushion rather than an expert quilter.

Still holding the tip of her finger between her lips, she hurried toward the hotel lobby. Who could be arriving at this time of day? The train had stopped at the depot an hour ago, and she'd registered only one guest, a salesman who'd said he was going up to his room to rest until time for the evening meal. Perhaps he, or one of the guests who had arrived on the earlier train, had decided on a bit of fresh air. At the thought of going for a stroll, Karla shivered and drew her woolen shawl tight around her shoulders. With the freezing temperatures, she couldn't imagine anyone going outdoors unless absolutely necessary.

She removed a white handkerchief from the pocket of her dark blue wool skirt and wrapped it around her finger. "*Guten Tag!* May I help. . ." She stopped short as the man at the front desk turned to face her.

"Guten Tag to you, Sister Karla. It's *gut* to see you."

"Brother Frank! I didn't know you had returned to the Colonies. It is gut to see you as well." She glanced toward the small gladstone bag sitting near his feet. "Or are you here for only a visit?"

His gray eyes sparkled, and a broad, easy smile stretched across his face. "I'm finally home to stay." He chuckled. "Well, not exactly home yet. I'm going to be living here at the hotel for a while."

Karla arched a brow. "And why is that?"

Had she not known Frank so well, Karla wouldn't have indulged in such inquisitiveness, but she and Frank were childhood friends who had skipped rocks at the pond, caught fish near the dam, and ice-skated with the other young people during the winter months. Those fun-filled childhood days had been many years ago—back before the elders sent Frank away to college and pharmaceutical school. Yet his easy manner and smiling presence took her back as if it had been only weeks ago.

"The elders thought it would be wise for me to spend some time working at the apothecary with Brother Hueber here in South for a few months before I take charge of the apothecary in Middle Amana—a type of apprenticeship, they called it," he said, his German returning with apparent ease. "And since my parents are now living in Middle, they suggested the hotel here in South would be a gut choice during my stay." He grinned. "Even though I graduated from apothecary school, I'm thinking they want Brother Hueber to make certain I know what I'm doing before they assign me to work alone at the apothecary in Middle."

A few months after Frank had departed for college, the elders moved his parents to Middle Amana, where his father's talents as a mechanic had been needed in the woolen mill. After the family moved, Karla had seen little of Frank.

She stepped behind the desk and opened the leather-bound guest register. "And does it bother you that the elders have made this decision?"

"*Nein*. I've missed life in the Colonies." He moved to the desk and met her gaze. "To be honest, I grew weary of explaining I was not Amish. Even after hearing my lengthy explanations, I don't think most people understood the difference between the Amish and Inspirationists. And living in a large city was much different than our communal way of life. I even missed attending daily prayer services."

Karla met his steady gaze. "I remember when you were a little boy and you told me you didn't want to belong to the Community of True Inspiration because Inspirationists attended church every day."

He nodded. "*Ja*, I remember that, but now I am grown and happy to be living in the Colonies." He rested one hand atop the desk. "Besides, once I discovered I would be staying here at the hotel, I didn't mind. I decided it was probably God's way of letting us renew our friendship."

Heat crawled up the back of Karla's neck. She didn't dare look into his eyes. Swallowing hard, she dipped the nib of her pen into the ink bottle and handed it to Frank. "You should sign here."

When he reached for the pen, Frank's fingers brushed against her hand and an unexpected shiver raced up her arm. She watched as he signed his name in the register, remembering how he'd printed their names in the sand along the river's edge years ago. Back then they'd developed a close friendship, but early on she realized a plain girl like her could never win the heart of a good-looking man like Frank Lehner. Yet he had continued to keep company with her. Had it not been for Antje, Karla's beautiful sister, she probably never would have understood why Frank maintained their friendship.

All those years ago, Antje had sat her down and made it quite clear: pretty girls didn't view Karla as a threat because of her plain looks. And Frank sought her out because she was willing to bait her own hook and because she wanted to ice-skate rather than sit by the fire and hold hands. Back when Antje had explained all of this, Karla had been only fourteen and hadn't quite grasped the importance of outward beauty. Ten years later, the value of physical attributes had become painfully clear.

Frank placed the pen atop the metal rack of the inkstand before he assumed a nonchalant stance and rested his forearms across the counter. She took a backward step. Had he heard about her engagement? Surely he must have—that must be why he mentioned renewing their friendship. A single man would never suggest a friendship with a married woman. He'd returned to the Colonies, and now he planned to take pity on her by once again offering his friendship.

"How have you been, Karla?" He glanced over his shoulder. "I suppose I should address you as Sister Karla, but it seems strange on my tongue. I wondered if you would be living at the hotel or if the elders moved you to another house when you and Oskar married." He stretched across the counter and lowered his voice. "How does he like working at the hotel? I cannot imagine him greeting guests and carrying luggage upstairs." He directed a fleeting look toward the steps. "And what about your parents? Do they continue to live in the hotel?"

At the mention of Oskar's name, Karla's lips tightened into a frozen smile. Determination surged through her. She would not reveal the pain that surfaced every time someone directed a pitying look at her or uttered Oskar Freitag's name. Especially not in front of Frank Lehner, her childhood friend who'd always considered her brave and strong. She was the girl who could take a fish off a hook with greater speed than any of the boys, the girl who raced her sled down the highest hill, the girl who could outrun any boy in a footrace. She was supposed to be made of sterner stuff.

"Let me see if I can remember all of your questions. I'm fine. Yes, you should address me as Sister Karla, for we are both much older than when we played children's games." She inhaled a shallow breath and hoped he couldn't hear the pounding of her heart. Before Frank had left for college, he'd been a handsome young man with dark brown hair and gray eyes. But now, broad shoulders and a strong jawline enhanced his good looks.

She took a deep, steadying breath. "My parents and I continue to live here in the hotel, as does my sister, Antje—at least until her wedding in February. Oskar does not work at the hotel, so you need not worry about whether he is content carrying luggage. He and his wife live in West Amana, where he now works at the flour mill. I continue to help at the hotel, and the elders have also assigned me to teach knitting and crocheting in the *strickschule* classes for several hours each day." She could feel her smile beginning to droop and forced her lips back into position. "I think that was everything, was it not?"

His brow furrowed and the sparkle in his eyes diminished. "I thought. . .I mean, I was told you were. . ." He shook his head as if to clear his thoughts. "So you and Oskar never married?"

"Nein." Her throat squeezed and the all-too-familiar ache returned to her chest. She hoped he wouldn't expect her to detail the failed marriage plans, but her hopes were dashed when he pushed up from the counter and folded his arms across his chest.

"But the last I heard, the two of you had entered your year of separation in order to marry." He hesitated, and then his jaw dropped. "Are you telling me that Oskar fell in love with someone else during *your* year of separation, and that he's already married to her?"

"Ja." Karla looked away from him, unable to meet his intense stare. Sunlight shone through the front window and cut thick vertical patterns across the striped rug that covered a large square of pine floor in the lobby. "You've been gone more than long enough for all of that to happen, Brother Frank. I'm surprised someone in Middle didn't mention it when you were home for a visit. The truth is, Oskar hadn't been gone more than six weeks when he told me and the elders that he had changed his mind."

Frank unfolded his arms and placed his palms on the counter. "I never heard a word, but my *Mutter* has never been one to carry gossip, and you know word doesn't spread quickly between the villages."

He leaned forward—as if lessening the distance between them made his account more believable. Or had he drawn closer because he expected a more detailed answer from her? If so, he would be sorely disappointed. She'd given him all the answer she could manage right now.

Moments later, Frank straightened and inhaled a deep breath. "For whatever it's worth, I would say that Oskar Freitag is a fool. But maybe his foolishness will be a very gut thing for me."

The kindness of his words and the sweetness of his tone were enough to give most any woman hope—but Karla had heard sweet words before. Frank had been a dear friend for many years. She would continue to offer her friendship, but she would not offer him her heart. The scars of being rebuffed by Oskar had left enough pain for a lifetime. Besides, once the attractive young women learned Frank had returned to the Colonies for good, he would have more than enough women seeking his attention.

Frank tucked the room key into the pocket of his suit jacket. Karla had suggested he might want to unpack before supper, but he didn't plan to heed her recommendation. If he remained near the front desk, she might be willing at least to visit with him. As much as he wanted to learn more about her broken engagement, he decided against pressing that topic right at the moment. When he'd lived in Upper South, they'd spent hour after hour talking and laughing when they'd gone fishing on long summer afternoons. He wanted to believe their friendship had weathered the test of time and that Karla felt the same way—that she would be pleased to reignite the easy camaraderie they had shared during their youth.

With hopeful expectations, Frank strolled toward the overstuffed chairs not far from the front desk, but by the time he settled into position, Karla had stuffed the ledger beneath the counter and disappeared. Tapping his foot, he glanced around the empty lobby and wondered why she seemed intent on avoiding him. Had he said or done something to offend her? Perhaps he was assuming far too much. Because they'd been close friends during their youth, he'd expected her to welcome him with a show of enthusiasm. Her lack of excitement had surprised him, and the disappointment stung.

She'd probably been right: he should go upstairs and unpack. But until his trunk arrived, he didn't have many clothes to hang. If he went upstairs and unpacked the few belongings in his bag, he would still have time for a brief visit with Brother Hueber before time for supper. He pushed to his feet, but as he neared the foot of the staircase, he changed directions. The unpacking could wait, and so could his visit to the apothecary. Right now, he wanted to know why Karla seemed so determined to avoid him.

He'd been in this hotel many times during his youth. Had she gone upstairs, he would have seen her. Perhaps she was in the kitchen preparing for the evening meal that would be served to the hotel guests, but he hadn't heard the rattle of pans or the clinking of dishes. In that case, she must be in the room adjacent to the lobby. The door remained slightly ajar, though no sound came from within. Feeling a bit like an intruder, Frank stepped to the doorway and peered inside.

Karla sat at a quilting frame with her back to the doorway. From his vantage point, Frank gained a good view of her as she dipped her needle into the taut fabric and pulled it through the layers. The quilt top was one solid piece of fabric—pale blue in color—much the same as one he'd had on his bed at home. Moving a little closer, he watched as she continued making the tiny stitches.

"Looks like a pretty pattern you're quilting." She startled and glanced at her finger. "I hope I didn't cause you to stick yourself again."

She shook her head. "My finger is fine, but you shouldn't be in here when I'm alone."

He tipped his head to one side and considered her words. She'd been friendly when he first arrived, but after he mentioned Oskar, she had become distant. "The door is open, Kar. . .*Sister* Karla, and I'm standing in the doorway, not inside the room. You're acting as though I'm a traveling salesman or visitor rather than an old friend who lives in the Colonies."

"We are no longer children, Brother Frank. We need to abide by the rules." Her eyes softened, but her tone remained cool. "You should go up to your room and unpack."

He leaned against the doorjamb and pointed toward the quilt. "Are you making that for yourself or someone else? I thought the women usually got together and quilted. Has that changed while I've been gone?" He moved closer to the quilting frame. "My Mutter and some of the women made wedding quilts for me years ago when my Mutter was hoping I would marry." Confusion shone in Karla's eyes. Long ago it had become a custom in the Colonies for both a bride and groom to bring two wedding quilts to the marriage, but Frank had never been engaged. To learn his mother had already stitched quilts for him had obviously raised questions in Karla's mind.

He wished she would look at him, but she kept her gaze fastened on her stitching. "I think she believed the quilts would encourage me to find a wife. No doubt she fears she will never have any grandchildren. Maybe you remember how much my Mutter enjoyed children."

Karla gave a slight nod. "I do recall she loved children." After poking her needle into the fabric, she glanced up at him. "I don't mean to be unwelcoming, Brother Frank, but. . ."

He nodded. "I promise to go away if you'll tell me about the quilt."

"I'm not sure I believe you. You used to make promises when we were young, and then you would tell me you'd crossed your fingers behind your back, so it didn't count. Do you remember?"

"Of course I remember. But I always kept my word. You can't blame me for teasing you all those years ago." He extended his arms and spread his fingers. "You can see for yourself. My fingers aren't crossed."

She gave him a guarded look that told him she wasn't totally convinced he was trustworthy. "The quilt is for my sister, Antje— one of her wedding quilts. She asked if Mutter and I would help her make her two wedding quilts."

"Without help from the other women?"

Karla bobbed her head. "Ja. She didn't want to hurt any feelings, but sometimes Sister Wilda's stitches are uneven. Her eyesight isn't so gut anymore. Rather than exclude Sister Wilda, we decided the quilting would be a family project. Besides, the rest of the women have another quilt they're working on right now, so there is more than enough sewing for everyone."

Frank had forgotten Antje's ability to persuade others to do her bidding. Karla's younger sister had always been a sweet girl. And combined with her natural beauty, charming personality, and stunning smile, she could win her way at most anything. And usually did. With the exclusion of Paul Meister and himself, she'd won the hearts of all the unmarried young men in the village at some point during her growing-up years, but Frank wasn't certain whom she'd finally agreed to marry.

He didn't move a muscle for fear Karla would again tell him he should go to his room. "So who did Antje decide to marry? As I recall, she could have chosen one of several."

"Paul Meister."

"Paul!" He clapped his palm over his lips and glanced around. "I'm sorry. I didn't mean to shout, but Paul's name was the last one I expected to hear. Paul never appeared to be interested in Antje— at least not. . ."

Her blue eyes sparkled. "At least not as a wife?"

"Ja. I'm surprised to hear it is Paul."

She shrugged one shoulder. "Perhaps she viewed him as a challenge. His disinterest always appeared to intrigue her."

"Intrigued or annoyed?" He quickly gave a dismissive wave. "You don't need to answer. If they're happy, then I'm pleased for both of them. I've not seen Paul for some time now. Where is he living during their separation?"

"Lower South—he wasn't sent too far away, which pleased my sister a great deal. They're able to see each other every Sunday afternoon."

He wasn't surprised by her answer. It seemed everything fell into place for Antje. He wished the same would happen in Karla's life. Though she never spoke of feeling inferior, Karla had always played second fiddle to her sister. Not only was Antje pretty, but she was full of life and always managed to make herself the center of attention. Yet Karla had the attributes he found captivating. Although her loyalty, honesty, and kindness had won him years ago, she'd never flirted with him like the other girls. Even now, with no plans to wed, she didn't show any sign of interest in him. And heaven knew he was trying to gain her attention.

Before he could ask another question, the front door opened and a cold breeze chased across the floor. Frank shivered as he turned around. "Sister Stuke! It is gut to see you."

The older woman squinted as she crossed the room. "Brother Frank? Is it really you?" She lifted the woven market basket from her arm and placed it atop the front desk. "Come here and let me have a gut look at you." She shook her head as Frank approached. "You have grown three inches taller since the last time I saw you."

Frank forced his features into a mock frown and planted his hands on his hips. "Now, Sister Stuke, don't try to convince me that you didn't know it was me standing in front of you."

"Ja, I knew it was you. The elders told me you would be coming to stay in the hotel for a few months, but I didn't think you were going to arrive until next week." She patted his arm. "It is gut to see you, and I'm glad you will be staying with us. It will be like old times having you in South. And you should call me Sister Irma. You're a grown man now, and we are friends."

"Danke." He reached for the market basket but turned at the sound of footsteps behind him. Karla had closed the distance between the quilting frame and the front desk in record time.

The bodice of her dress rose as she inhaled a deep breath, and her blue eyes flashed at her mother. "You said nothing to me about Brother Frank returning to South and living in the hotel."

Sister Irma hiked one shoulder as she tapped the counter with her index finger. "If you had checked the record book in the top drawer, you would have seen Brother Frank's name listed as an arriving guest." Her features softened as she shifted her eyes toward Frank. "Of course, you aren't really a guest—more like returning family."

He beamed and nodded toward the basket. "Would you like me to take this to the kitchen?"

"Ja, that would be very nice." She wiggled her finger at Karla. "And you should join us, too. No more time for quilting until later. We need to begin supper preparations." She pointed to a tall wooden stool near the back door. "You can sit over there and visit with us, Brother Frank. I'm eager to hear about your schooling and plans for the future."

Sister Irma's offer to remain in the kitchen pleased Frank, but from the frown on Karla's face, he could tell she was less than pleased. Still, he tried to memorize her features as she peeled the potatoes. While he'd been away at apothecary school, he had often tried to remember the way Karla held her lips when trying to bait a hook or the intensity of her blue eyes when she prepared to race across the ice. More often than not, his memory couldn't capture the exact image. And now, seeing her lips set in that same tight line and her eyelashes fanned across her cheeks, he took pleasure in the sight.

As if magnetically drawn, Karla looked up and met his gaze. She stared for a moment before returning to her work. Her eyes had carried a message—one that appeared to say she wished he would leave the room. Discouragement slithered around him and squeezed the air from his lungs.

Frank jarred to attention when Sister Irma banged a pot onto the top of the stove. "So tell us about your time at school." She gave her earlobe an enthusiastic tug. "I'm ready to hear."

He glanced at Karla. He had hoped she, too, would express some eagerness to hear a few of his stories. Instead, she looked everywhere but at him.

Chapter 2

Karla still couldn't believe her mother had invited Frank to join them in the kitchen. In the past, she had always shooed everyone but the kitchen workers from the room during meal preparations. Yet this afternoon, she'd welcomed Frank into the kitchen as though it were an everyday occurrence to have a man sit and watch them peel potatoes. And when he became silent for more than a moment, her mother would ask another question. With each response, her mother beamed approval and encouraged him to tell her more.

Karla grabbed the handle of a metal pail and headed toward the door. They would need water to wash dishes after supper, and she preferred pumping it before rather than after the meal.

Frank jumped up from the stool. "Let me do that." His hand connected with hers, and she drew in a sharp breath.

Looking up, she met his gaze, and the softness in the depth of his eyes kindled an unexpected longing deep within her—a longing she had promised herself she would never succumb to again. Just when she believed she'd finally overcome Oskar's rejection and the desire for marriage and children, Frank's presence had proved a fresh reminder of what she had lost.

As Frank tugged on the bucket handle, she realized her fingers remained entwined beneath his hand. With a start, she dropped her hold and took a backward step. "I won't argue. It is cold outside."

"I don't think I'll turn into an icicle." With his free hand, Frank lifted the collar of his suit jacket.

Karla's mother pointed to the row of pegs near the door where they hung their cloaks and scarves. "Wrap one of those woolen scarves around your neck, Frank. You'll catch a cold, and we'll have to ask Brother Hueber to mix you some medicine before you even begin your work in the apothecary." He grabbed one of the scarves and flung it around his neck in an exaggerated gesture. Sister Irma laughed. "When you get outside, you will be glad for the warmth."

The moment he opened the door, a gust of cold air burst into the room. Karla shivered and hurried back to the worktable. She stood opposite her mother while the two of them shaped the sausage patties they would fry for supper.

"I cannot believe you invited Frank to sit in the kitchen while we are cooking. You never permit visitors."

Her words bore a harsh tone, but she didn't want to experience the emotions Frank's presence stirred up—feelings that could once again lead to pain. After Oskar canceled their marriage plans, Karla had resolved to safeguard herself against future heartbreak—and she intended to keep that commitment. But she already knew that Frank's arrival was going to prove a difficult test.

Her mother's features pinched into a frown. "Frank isn't a visitor. He is like family."

"Family? He hasn't lived in South Amana for years. I've seen him only once since he left for school, and that was during the first year after he went away." Karla reached into the bowl and scooped up another handful of the meat mixture. "And I think this is the first time you've seen him since he departed."

"Ja, it is. And that is reason enough to want to talk to him and find out what he has learned and how he has been."

Karla sighed. "He has learned to be a pharmacist, and he appears to be in very good health."

"And you appear to be in very bad humor. You and Frank were gut friends. You say you're surprised I invited him into the kitchen. Well, I'm surprised by your. . ."

Her mother glanced up and stopped midsentence when the back door opened and Frank reappeared. Another gust of cold air burst into the room with him. He placed the pail of water on the floor and unwrapped the scarf from around his neck.

"You were right about the scarf, Sister Irma. That wind has turned colder than when I first arrived. I wouldn't be surprised if it begins to snow."

Her mother nodded. "Ja, well, it is the time of year when we expect snow and cold weather. Soon Christmas will arrive, and it would not be Christmas without snow."

Frank agreed. "Tell me about your favorite Christmas when you were a little girl, Sister Irma."

Sister Irma's lips curved in a slow smile, and Karla immediately knew what story Frank would hear. Before her mother began the tale, she pointed at the stove and signaled Karla to begin frying the potatoes. "My family wasn't among the first groups to move here from the settlement in Ebenezer in New York. We didn't come to Iowa until 1859, but my best friend, Marta, and her family moved a year before me. I was so lonely, and even though my Mutter told me we would be moving, too, I began to think I would never again see my friend."

Karla turned the potatoes with the metal spatula and glanced at her mother. This was the part of the story when she usually became teary-eyed. Sure enough, Karla could see the glisten of tears as her mother touched her handkerchief to her eye.

Her mother drew a ragged breath. "It was on Christmas Eve that my *Vater* said he had a very special present for me."

Frank scooted so far forward on the stool, Karla thought he might topple. "What was it?"

"A note from the *Grossebruderrat* telling my Vater that our family had been selected to depart with the next group in the spring." Karla's mother clasped a hand to her chest. "Our Christmas pyramid was on a table in the center of the parlor, and I danced around the table until I was dizzy." She glanced at Frank. "That was the best Christmas present I ever received."

"For sure that is a wonderful Christmas story, Sister Irma."

"Ja, and she tells it to us every Christmas." They all turned to see Karla's sister standing in the doorway between the kitchen and dining room. Antje narrowed her blue eyes and took a step forward. "Brother Frank? Is it really you I'm seeing?"

"Ja, it is really me." As if to prove he was real, Frank stood and turned in a circle.

Antje hurried toward him and clasped his hand. "What a wonderful surprise." She turned to her mother. "Did you know he was going to visit? You should have told me. I would have come home earlier. Now I've missed all the fun." Antje's lower lip protruded in a tiny pout. "It's not fair that the two of you have had the pleasure of Frank's company while I was filling in for Karla at the strickschule classes for the children."

Karla tapped the metal utensil on the frying pan. "I'm remembering that it was you who asked to take my place with the knitting lessons at the strickschule so that I could sew on your quilt." She arched her brows and looked at her sister. "Is that not true?"

"Ja, it is true, but. . ."

"With you there is always a 'but,'" their mother said while

gesturing for Antje to remove her cloak. "You don't need to worry further. Brother Frank will be staying here until he finishes his training at the apothecary with Brother Hueber."

"We are for sure going to enjoy having you with us, Brother Frank." Eyes sparkling, Antje looked at Karla. "Isn't that true, Karla?"

All three of them stared in Karla's direction. She bobbed her head. What else could she do? To disagree would have been an insult to Frank and an embarrassment to her family. It wasn't Frank's presence that bothered her as much as the fact that he was a reminder that she wasn't good enough—not for Oskar and certainly not for Frank Lehner.

❧

Before dinner began, Karla met the hotel guests outside the dining room. "Since none of you have stayed at our hotel before, I want to explain that our dining room is set up just as the dining rooms in the kitchen houses throughout all of the villages."

Mrs. Wilson, one of the guests who had registered with her husband earlier in the afternoon, waved at Karla. "What is a kitchen house?"

Karla was accustomed to answering the many questions of guests who visited the Colonies, but generally any inquiries were made during registration. These visitors, however, had been eager to settle in their rooms and rest before supper, so they had inquired only about what time supper would be served.

After a quick glance toward the kitchen, Karla offered the guests a bright smile and weighed her choices. If she spoke quickly, her response wouldn't take long, but her thick German accent would make the explanation difficult to understand. If she spoke in a slow and distinct voice, the guests would understand, but the food would get cold—and her mother detested serving cold food. Better to keep her mother happy and give Mrs. Wilson a hurried response.

Karla inhaled a deep breath. "A *Küche* or kitchen house is where the residents eat their meals. Each neighborhood has a kitchen house, and we are assigned to the one that is closest to where we live. Since my family operates the hotel and we serve meals to our guests, we prepare meals and eat here as well."

From the confused looks on several faces, Karla wasn't certain the guests had understood, but she waved them toward the large dining room before anyone could ask her to repeat the explanation.

Once they had gathered behind her in the dining room doorway, she turned to face them. "The men will sit together at the tables to the left and the women to the right." She didn't miss the look of surprise that washed over Mrs. Wilson's face.

"Why would we do that? My husband and I always sit together for our meals."

Karla sighed. Now she wished she would have insisted on explaining their customs earlier, before the guests had gone upstairs to their rooms. "It is our way of life to sit at separate tables, Mrs. Wilson, and we ask our guests to observe the practice when they're our guests in the Colonies."

The older woman tugged on her husband's arm and looked up at him. From the frown on her face, she appeared to be communicating a private message to him. Mr. Wilson frowned in return but cleared his throat and held up his index finger. "I believe we would rather be seated at the same table."

"Think of your visit here as an adventure where you're able to learn by experiencing the lifestyle of other people."

Everyone but Karla turned to see who had spoken. Though she hadn't seen him standing in the shadows, she had immediately recognized Frank's voice. "Come and follow me, gentlemen." He stepped forward and wove his way through the small group. "You should also know that we don't converse during our meals, though there is ample time to do so afterward in the parlor."

Although Mrs. Wilson had been slow to release her husband's arm, Frank had managed to shepherd all of the men into the dining room. Karla straightened her shoulders and gestured to the two women. "Please follow me, ladies." She hoped the women would pay heed to Frank's comment about conversation. That seemed to be the most difficult rule for outsiders to follow when they visited the hotel dining room.

Mrs. Wilson's frown deepened when Karla directed her toward the wooden benches that lined both sides of the well-scrubbed pine tables. She stared at the backless benches and peered across the room at her husband. "I'm accustomed to sitting in a chair during my meals. I like to rest my back when I dine."

Frank tapped his hand on one shoulder. "The benches are gut for your posture and help the digestion when you eat." As soon as he replied, he touched his index finger to his lips.

Mrs. Wilson's eyebrows dipped low on her forehead. "Is he shushing me?"

Karla nodded. "I don't think you heard Brother Frank explain that we don't converse unless necessary during our meals." She whispered the response and hoped the older woman would follow suit.

Mrs. Wilson slid onto one of the benches that faced the men's table. "Well, I've been told that conversation during a meal aids in digestion."

Undeterred, Frank shook his head. "That may be true in other places, but since we are accustomed to silence during our meals, conversation tends to upset our stomachs. I feel certain you will honor our request, since I don't believe you would want any of us to become ill."

Mrs. Wilson glared across the room before she picked up her napkin and then slapped it onto her lap with a vengeance. Not wanting Mrs. Wilson to hear her giggle, Karla escaped to the kitchen, where her mother and Antje were filling the remaining bowls and platters.

Her mother nodded toward the fried potatoes. "Take those. Antje and I will bring the rest. Your Vater is at the table?"

Karla picked up the dishes and gave a nod. "Ja. He is ready to pray once the food is on the tables."

The three women arranged bowls and platters on the tables in short order. Karla's father stood and quietly explained that he would offer a prayer of thanks for their meal. All heads bowed in unison. When her father had finished offering thanks, Karla offered a silent prayer of thanks that Mrs. Wilson hadn't interrupted him.

The woman's silence was short-lived. The minute Karla passed her the bowl of green beans, her questions resumed. Karla peeked at her mother from beneath her thick lashes and waited. Mrs. Wilson leaned forward as if her movement would encourage an answer. Karla's mother picked up the plate of bread and passed it to Antje.

"One of us will be most pleased to answer your questions in the parlor after supper, Mrs. Wilson. If you feel it is necessary to talk during the meal, please visit with Mrs. Fuller."

Mrs. Fuller perked to attention and shook her head. "Don't talk to me. I'm trying to experience your ways, just like the gentleman suggested." She lifted her fingers to her mouth and pretended to lock her lips.

"If you truly lock your lips, you won't be able to eat, Mrs. Fuller." Mrs. Wilson leaned a little closer. "And I find your actions somewhat childish."

Mrs. Fuller straightened her shoulders and glowered. "And I

find your behavior extremely rude."

The haughty exchange between the two guests caused Karla's stomach to ripple with discomfort, but the banter had at least accomplished the requested quiet. For the remainder of the meal, a tense silence reigned over the room.

છ

Antje bustled into the kitchen, her arms laden with dirty dishes. "I'll wash and dry the dishes tonight. You go into the parlor and visit."

Karla wrinkled her nose and shook her head. "No, thank you. Mutter will join the guests and answer their questions. I'm happy to be out here."

Propping her hands on her hips, Antje gave her sister a scowl. "It isn't the guests I'm thinking about. You need to go in there and talk to Brother Frank."

"Why do I need to do that? He was out here in the kitchen the whole time we were preparing supper. I've already heard about his years in school and how pleased he was when the Grossebruder-rat assigned him to work in South Amana for a while—though I would think he'd have preferred to be in Middle with his parents."

"I thought you would be pleased to have him here."

Karla shrugged. "Where Frank lives isn't something of great importance to me. What is truly important right now is that we finish your quilt and that the girls and boys in strickschule complete the mittens they're making for Christmas gifts. How did they do today? Louisa Neffbaum was having the most trouble with her stitches—did she accomplish much today?"

"You aren't fooling me. You don't want me to talk about Frank, so you ask questions about the knitting classes." Antje lifted the pot of boiling water from the stove and poured it into the large metal dishpan before she scraped shards of soap into the dishwater. "The knitting and quilting can wait when there is a handsome, single man of our faith living in the hotel. You need to go into the parlor and visit with him. I don't know why you're acting like he's a stranger—or like you aren't interested in him."

A flash of anger sparked deep in the pit of Karla's stomach. She didn't need her little sister telling her whom she cared for or what she should do. Karla added several cups of cold water to the dishpan before she lowered a stack of plates into the dishwater. Before she withdrew her hand, she flitted a spray of water at her sister.

"Look what you did!" Antje grabbed a linen towel and jumped away from the sink. "The top of my dress is wet, and I won't have time to change before prayer meeting! I should tell Mutter."

"Suit yourself, but she will probably say you should have been wearing an apron." Karla surveyed the bodice of her sister's dress. "It will be dry before time to leave. Go and stand by the stove while I wash the dishes."

"You did that on purpose—so you wouldn't have to go into the parlor."

Karla shrugged as she dipped her hands into the water and began scrubbing the plates. "Nein." She lifted her soapy finger to her nose. "I did it so you would keep your nose out of my business. If I want to talk to Brother Frank, I will do so, but I don't need you to meddle."

Antje wheeled around, her eyes dark with anger. "After Oskar ended your engagement, you were the one who told me that all you had ever wanted was a happy marriage and children. Am I to think that has now changed? I was only trying to help."

Karla grasped the submerged dishrag and squeezed until her fingers ached. "Danke, Antje, but I will tell you when I want help."

She turned away before her sister could see the tears that

29

threatened to overflow. It seemed Antje had forgotten that, many years ago, she had issued a warning that Frank would never be interested in a plain girl.

Chapter 3

A week had passed and Frank remained baffled by Karla's detached behavior. He'd taken every opportunity to regain a friendship that had deteriorated without his awareness. And though he tried, he still couldn't comprehend what had happened. Each time he approached her, she'd been as cold as the December weather.

Granted, Karla had been hurt by Oskar, but what did that have to do with him? He had never betrayed her friendship or her trust. In the past, he'd never faced such a situation. Though he didn't consider himself vain, he knew that girls had always thought him good-looking, for they had been quick to seek out his attention without much effort on his part.

Since his return, several young women had stopped by the apothecary or the hotel to welcome him back to South and offer him an assortment of invitations. He'd been invited to attend a taffy pull at the Swensons' home, an ice-skating party, as well as a sledding party in the coming weeks. He had asked Karla to join a group going ice-skating after prayer service this evening, but she had declined, saying she needed to finish Antje's wedding quilt so they could begin work on the second one.

His attempts to persuade her had fallen on deaf ears. Though Karla's earlier refusal had been disheartening, Frank hoped to convince her before the skaters headed off to the slough located in the forest between the villages of South and West Amana. Once there, he planned to clamp his skates onto his shoes and fly across the ice for as long as his legs would hold him or until the cold became unbearable—whichever occurred first. Of course, he planned for Karla to be at his side. Together they'd skate until she recalled all the fond memories they'd shared on the ice, and her coldness toward him would melt away.

With his skates in hand, he stopped by the door to the side parlor, where Karla sat at the quilting frame. Doing his best to sound happy, he nodded toward the front door. "Why don't you come along? You don't have to skate for very long. I promise to escort you back home as soon as you say you're ready to return." He wanted to skate by her side, if only for a few minutes.

She shook her head. "Not today. I want to finish the quilt. There isn't much time until the wedding."

His stomach churned with disappointment. How could he break through her reserve? What had he done to make her dislike him?

Unable to maintain any semblance of cheerfulness, Frank turned and strode from the house, his skates in one hand and a lantern in the other. He hadn't gone far before the flicker of kerosene lanterns beckoned to him in the outlying darkness. Holding his lantern high, he swung it back and forth so the group wouldn't depart without him.

Laughter and shouts for him to hurry echoed in the still night air as he picked up his pace. His chest expanded and then tightened as he inhaled deep breaths of the freezing air—air as cold as Karla.

"What took you so long?" Henry Jenkins called as he neared

the group. "Sister Antje managed to get here on time, and you both live in the same house."

Frank raised his lantern to gain a better view of the group. Henry had spoken the truth. Along the outside fringes of the group, Antje stood beside Paul Meister, the two of them deep in conversation. How could Antje be here enjoying herself while Karla remained at home to work on her wedding quilt? Why hadn't Antje insisted on staying home to work on it herself?

Henry shouted for the group to head out. "Those with lanterns scatter among the group so everyone can see."

Frank worked his way forward until he came alongside Paul. "It is gut to see you, Paul. I hear congratulations are in order."

Paul flashed a wide grin and bobbed his head. "Ja. Antje has made me the happiest man in the Colonies. The year cannot end soon enough." He turned toward Antje. "Isn't that right?"

She nodded and leaned closer. "And I'm the happiest woman in all the Colonies."

"I'm pleased to be surrounded by such cheerfulness, but I'm curious about something, Sister Antje."

She pulled the hood of her cloak tight beneath her chin. "Ja? What is that?"

"I asked your sister to come ice-skating and she refused. Do you know why?"

"Nein. I didn't even know you had asked her. I wish she would have come. We would have had great fun."

Frank breathed a loud sigh, and a ghostlike whorl ascended overhead. "I think so, too, but Karla said she needed to finish stitching on your wedding quilt so she could begin on your second quilt tomorrow. That does not seem right to me."

A brisk wind tugged at Paul's scarf, and he tucked it beneath the collar of his wool coat. "What does not seem right? That Karla is helping to make the quilt? The women work on each other's quilts all the time."

Frank swallowed his irritation. How could the two of them be so blind to the situation? "How is it that the quilt isn't important enough for Antje to remain at home and sew, but Karla feels she cannot quit working on it? It's Antje's wedding quilt, not Karla's."

"Ach!" Paul nudged Frank's arm. "They're sisters, and I'm sure Karla understood that Antje wanted to spend time with me." He grinned and reached to hold Antje closer to his side. "Or maybe she thought the sewing was more enjoyable than your company." Paul's laughter echoed in the crisp night air.

"What is so funny? Tell us the joke," Henry hollered.

Paul cupped his hands to his mouth. "I told Frank that I think Sister Karla has decided that quilting is more enjoyable than his company. She refused to come ice-skating with him."

Noisy guffaws and hoots disturbed the quietude of the secluded setting. Determined not to cause Karla's family any grief, Frank tightened his jaw and kept his clenched fists anchored at his side. Paul was joking with him, but still the words stung—mostly because he feared Paul had hit on the truth. A truth Frank didn't want to accept.

Matthew Olson, one of the fellows Frank had attended school with, stepped a little closer and clapped him on the shoulder. "You aren't used to being turned down by the young women, but now you know what the rest of us single fellows have to contend with all the time."

Just like Henry, Matthew had spoken loud enough for everyone to hear. It seemed Frank would be the one to bear the brunt of the jokes this evening. Had their banter been about anything else, he would have laughed and shrugged off the comments, but for over a week, he'd been unable to melt Karla's icy attitude. Now he wondered if he ever would.

Matthew chuckled as he matched Frank's stride. "For sure, I think you may have to work a little harder to get the attention of the ladies. You will find most of the ones we went to school with are now married." He gave Frank a playful shove. "And when I was in the apothecary yesterday, I noticed your hair isn't as thick as it used to be. I'm told the ladies don't like bald men very well." He grabbed for Frank's wool cap.

Frank twisted out of his reach. "They must not like men with a headful of unruly hair either. Otherwise, you would already be married."

The joking continued until they neared the slough. Frank joined several others collecting wood for a fire near the frozen pond. Once he had an armful of small branches, he carried them to an area near the ice where he discovered the charred remains of wood from previous fires.

He waved to Paul. "You want to build the fire in this same place?"

"Ja. The trees give a little protection from the wind." Moments later, Paul joined him. Soon the kindling crackled and popped as the fire gained strength and sparked to life. Paul clapped Frank on the shoulder. "Stay with it and make sure it doesn't go out. I'm going to go and help Antje with her skates."

There wasn't much chance the fire would go out, but Frank sat down on a nearby log. He would watch the fire until he'd fastened on his skates. After that, someone else could worry about whether it went out. As he clamped on his second skate, a tap on his shoulder caused him to glance over his shoulder.

❦

Nearly cross-eyed from stitching, Karla stood and stretched. She needed a break. If she hurried, maybe she could catch up with Frank and the others after all. Once she'd told her parents where she was going, Karla donned her coat, grabbed her skates from the hook, and lit a lantern.

The others had tramped a clear path in the crunchy snow to the pond. The crisp air reminded her of when she and Frank used to go skating. They'd race one another until they were too tired to move, and then they'd sit by the fire and talk for what seemed like hours. How she'd missed those times.

Would Frank be excited to see her now? She shouldn't let her hopes grow that way. She was setting herself up for more heartache, but his carefree grin came into her mind unbidden.

Friends. We are simply old friends.

Nothing more.

But what if there was an inkling of romance between them? A corner of her heart longed to take a chance, but she was afraid. The pain of what happened with Oskar ached like it had happened yesterday. The Frank she used to know wouldn't hurt her, but would this worldly, college-educated Frank be the same? How much had he changed? And could he ever be content with someone as plain as her?

With only one way to find out, Karla followed the trail toward the fire, but she stopped short at the end of the path.

Tears pricked her eyes. Apparently, it hadn't taken Frank long to replace her.

❧

"Could you help me, Brother Frank?" Gerta Schiffer held out her skates to him. "I always have trouble getting my skates tight enough. Only last week one of them came off while I was out on the ice, and I fell."

Before Frank could answer, she dropped to the log beside him and placed her skates in front of his feet. He didn't know Gerta well. Her family had moved to South the year before he departed for college, and she lived at the other end of the village, so he'd never seen much of her. He picked up one of the skates and unfastened the leather strap. He scooted off the log, knelt in front of her, and lifted her foot into the skate. "Push down and be sure your heel is tight into the back of the skate."

Once he'd helped her into both of the skates, she held out her hand. He helped her to her feet, but when he attempted to loosen his hold on her hand, she grasped tighter. "Aren't you going to skate with me? That way you'll be with me if one of my skates should come loose." In one swift movement, she tucked her gloved hand into the crook of his arm.

"We'll take one turn around the pond to test your skates, Sister Gerta. After that, you should have no trouble." He didn't want to be impolite, but he'd met other girls like Gerta at college. And none of those girls had piqued his interest in the least.

Lantern light flickered across the frozen pond and reflected on the sparkling rime clinging to the low-hanging tree branches. Frank settled into his normal easy pattern, enjoying the swooshing sound of his blades as they cut across the ice.

Gerta pulled on his sleeve. "Why don't we slow down?"

Though he truly wanted to bend low and fly across the ice by himself, Frank slowed his pace until Gerta said she'd like to warm herself by the fire. After they arrived at the edge of the frozen slough, he escorted her to the fire. He had hoped to return and challenge Matthew, Henry, or Paul to a race, but Gerta maintained a tight hold on his hand.

"Do sit down and warm yourself by the fire with me, Brother Frank. I'm eager to know more about your training at apothecary school."

Nothing about this evening had turned out as he'd hoped. He

hadn't wanted to sit and visit with Gerta, but she'd stared at him with such anticipation, he'd been unable to refuse her request. Short of being rude to the girl, he wasn't sure what to do. Girls in the world had acted like this, but he'd not seen it in the young women of Amana. If only Karla would show him such interest. When he grew weary of Gerta's questions, he suggested they take to the ice one final time before the group returned to the village.

They'd skated a short distance from the others when Gerta turned and began to skate backward. She offered a sweet smile and reached for his hands. "I know you will think me forward, but I would be pleased to have you escort me to the taffy pull next week." She waited a moment. Light from the full moon and a shimmer of illumination from the lantern flickered across Gerta's face. "Unless you've already invited someone else."

In spite of himself, her features revealed an eager anticipation that caused a tightening in his stomach. He didn't want to hurt her, yet to encourage her attention would be wrong. "I have not invited anyone, but I have interest in only one woman, and I'm determined to win her heart." He hadn't meant to be so blunt, but Gerta's forwardness had spurred his own honesty.

Her lips drooped into a frown as she turned and once again skated alongside him. "Who is the fortunate woman? Lydia? Or perhaps Renate?"

He shook his head. "Nein. It's someone I've known since childhood."

"Sister Karla? Karla Stuke?"

He didn't miss the disbelief in Gerta's voice. Anger surged through him. "I didn't say it was her, but Sister Karla is a fine woman and a dear friend."

She giggled. "I know one thing. Since she refused your invitation to come skating tonight, maybe you should start looking elsewhere."

The words hit him with the force of a snowball in the face. Perhaps Karla was trying to discourage him in a kind way just as he'd been trying to discourage Gerta. But he'd been praying about Karla and felt like God was leading him to pursue her. Could he be misinterpreting the feelings he thought God had pressed on his heart?

She leaned close and tightened her hold on his arm. "I want you to know that if Sister Kar—or whoever your mystery interest is—continues to refuse your invitations, I would be pleased to receive your attention."

Frank glared at Gerta, her presence like salt in an open wound. He shook her hand from his arm and stomped his cold feet. "Let's go." Frozen twigs crunched beneath their feet as the group headed off toward the village a short time later. Lantern light spilled through the trees and cast dancing shadows along the path through the dense woods. Gerta pushed past him and grabbed the arm of Vicktor Krutsfelt. She laughed loudly at Vicktor's jokes and glanced back at Frank, apparently wanting to make sure he'd noticed. The lantern light shimmered in the darkness and revealed a daring glimmer in Gerta's brown eyes. Did she think her behavior would make him jealous? Didn't she realize that unless he had romantic feelings for her, it mattered little to him if she was with another man?

He had to admit Gerta was quite pretty, but she didn't possess Karla's beauty. Gerta's brown eyes lacked the depth he saw in Karla's clear blue ones. And Gerta's lips seemed tightened in a permanent pout, while Karla's lips blessed those around her with kind words. Where Gerta was self-seeking, Karla was self-sacrificing. When Gerta walked into a room, she wanted to be the center of attention. When Karla walked into a room, even the air itself seemed sweeter.

Still, in one way Gerta possessed an advantage. Gerta saw

herself as a prize to be won, while Karla refused to see herself as an amazing creation of God.

If she would only give him a chance, Frank would spend the rest of his life making sure Karla knew just how special she was.

Chapter 4

At the sound of sleigh bells in the distance, Karla poured a steaming cup of coffee into a heavy tin cup and set it on the counter near the back door before she donned her cloak. "I'm guessing Brother Schermer wasn't pleased he had to put runners on the wagon this morning before he started the bread deliveries."

Irma shrugged. "Ja, well, maybe he anticipated the snow and got the runners on last night. Even your Vater predicted we would have snow when we got up this morning." She glanced up from the stove. "Your Vater was also pleased to see that Frank had risen earlier than him and cleared the porch and walkway of snow." When Karla didn't immediately comment, her mother frowned. "You don't think it was nice of him?"

"Ja, of course it was nice of him, Mutter."

The curt reply caused her mother's frown to deepen. "You got up on the wrong side of the bed, ja?"

"Nein." She forced a grin and tapped a finger to her lips while pulling her hood atop her crown of soft brown hair, which still bore a few stubborn streaks of sun-kissed blond. "See? I'm happy."

Her mother flitted her hand in a dismissive gesture. "You don't fool me. Something makes you unhappy."

Without waiting for any further comment, Karla pushed down on the heavy metal door latch and picked up the cup of coffee with her other hand. All thoughts of her mother's comments about Frank left her mind as a blast of cold air whipped at her cloak and tossed her hood backward. The freezing wind cut through her clothing, and she quickened her step. Brother Schermer had already jumped down from the bread wagon and opened the back doors.

"Guten Morgen, Sister Karla. It is a cold morning, for sure." He slapped his gloved hands together in an effort to ward off the freezing temperatures. "You need help to carry the bread?"

She didn't miss the look in his eye. He wanted to be on his way as much as she wanted to return inside. "Nein, but thank you for the offer." She extended the cup of coffee. "I hope it isn't already cold."

He took a quick gulp then placed the cup on the bed of the wagon. "It is still gut and warm. Danke." Arching forward, he leaned inside the wagon and removed one of the bread trays and placed the empty tin cup from yesterday beside one of the crusty loaves. After handing her the tray, he picked up the cup of coffee and downed another gulp. "Warms the insides." He grinned and patted his stomach. The wool fabric stretched taut between the coat buttons and exaggerated his expansive girth. "You're kind to always bring me my coffee—and to remember that I like it with a little sugar. I think you're the sweetest girl in all of South. Some man will be lucky to take you for a wife."

His words warmed Karla as much as any cup of coffee on this cold winter morning. "It is my pleasure, Brother Schermer." A bittersweet feeling poured over her. She'd never be anyone's wife—especially Frank's. He had moved on with Gerta. She'd seen it with her own eyes.

He grinned and tipped his hat before he hoisted himself onto the wagon seat and took up the leather reins. Before she'd opened the kitchen door, the sound of sleigh bells jangled their tune in the still morning air. Keeping her attention focused on the braided rug inside the kitchen door, she wiped the snow from her shoes. Slick soles that could cause her to fall and send the bread flying across the kitchen floor would not fare well with her mother.

Her hands tightened on the tray when a pair of men's shoes suddenly appeared just beyond the edge of the braided rug—shoes that were all too familiar. In fact, she didn't need to look up—she knew both the shoes and the outstretched hands offering to take the tray of bread belonged to Frank. Apparently he was determined to further endear himself to her mother. After last night, she refused to believe it had anything to do with her.

Without asking, he took the bread tray from her arms. "We missed you skating at the pond." He placed the tray on the wooden worktable as she removed her cloak. "I was surprised that Antje decided to attend rather than work on her wedding quilt."

Several strands of graying hair slipped from beneath her mother's dark cap when she shook her head. "Karla didn't need to remain behind, but she has decided she should no longer take pleasure in life. She wants to be like some of the men in the Bible—what is that word?"

Frank arched his brows. "Holy?"

Her mother laughed. "Nein, not holy." She slapped her palm to her head. "Martyr. That's the word. Karla wants to behave like a martyr and never have any fun."

Anger and embarrassment joined together and formed a tight knot in the pit of Karla's stomach. She crossed the kitchen in long strides and rested her palms on her hips. "That isn't true, Mutter. I agreed to help Antje finish her quilts, and that's what I'm doing.

I don't think of myself as a martyr, but as someone who's keeping her word."

Frank cleared his throat. "I apologize. I didn't mean for my comment to cause a problem."

"No need to blame yourself, Frank. Karla and I have had this same talk before. She never wants to have any fun."

"That isn't true, Mutter. I enjoy having fun as much as anyone else." Karla tightened her jaw as she began to slice thick pieces of bread. "Besides, you know that I went down to the pond after all."

"You did?" Frank followed her to the table. "Why didn't you come find me? I was all alone."

"You didn't seem alone to me," Karla whispered.

Frank answered in low tones. "Are you talking about Gerta? She latched onto me, but I made it clear I'm not interested in her." Frank held out his hands, palms upward. "You believe me, ja?"

"It makes no difference if I believe you or not. You can do as you want."

"In that case—" Frank folded his arms across his chest. "Since you still like to have fun, Sister Karla, you should happily agree to attend the taffy pull with me next week."

"I—I—it depends on how much work must be completed on the quilt, and there are the Christmas decorations that must be unpacked, and baking for the holiday, and. . ."

"We have always managed to accomplish all of those things in the past, Karla," her mother said. "If you go to the taffy pull, I'm sure we will still be able to celebrate Christmas. And if the quilt isn't finished in time for the wedding, Antje will need to permit some of the other ladies to help complete the task, or better yet, work on it herself."

"I will help with the Christmas decorations if that will convince you to join us." Frank leaned his tall frame against one of the worktables and looked down at her. "What do you say? Will you attend?"

Between her mother and Frank, she'd been artfully cornered. There seemed to be no excuse—yet she might think of something between now and then. She offered a broad smile. "I hope you won't mind if I ask you to wait until next Monday for my answer. You would still have more than enough time to invite someone else, like Sister Gerta, if I cannot attend."

He uncrossed his arms and moved away from the worktable. "I have no interest in asking someone else, but if it will make you happy to wait until Monday before you answer, then I will wait until Monday."

"Guten Morgen, Brother Frank." Antje strolled into the kitchen and casually poured herself a cup of coffee.

"And what have you been doing all this time?" Irma asked. "Did you forget we have breakfast to serve?"

Antje glanced at her mother. "I went to look at my quilt. Did you know Karla finished it last evening?"

Irma quirked an eyebrow at Karla. "Truly? Then it seems you have no more excuses."

"I was speaking of Antje's second quilt. We haven't even begun to work on it yet."

"There is more than enough time to complete it before Antje's wedding. If not, she will have only one quilt and that will be her concern, not yours, ja?" Without waiting for an answer, her mother turned toward Karla's sister and pointed to the stove. "Antje, you should begin to fry the bacon, or breakfast will be late. Your Vater won't be happy and neither will our guests."

Frank's gaze lingered on Karla. "If you decide you want to attend the taffy pull, please don't think you must wait until Monday to tell me." He gestured toward the dining room. "I think I should move out of the kitchen. I don't want to be in the way."

Her sister did a skipping sidestep across the kitchen. "What is this I'm hearing? Frank has invited you to the taffy pull?"

Karla sighed. Now that Antje knew of Frank's invitation, she would be like a dog after a bone—determined to convince Karla she should go with Frank. Trying to distance herself from the possibility, Karla started toward the dining room to set the table but stopped short when she caught sight of Frank visiting with one of the hotel guests. What if he spoke of the taffy pull in front of the guest?

Antje gently tapped Karla's arm. "You're keeping secrets from me."

Karla swiped at her sister's hand. "I am not keeping secrets. You already know Frank invited me. You heard what he said."

"Antje! The bacon!" Their mother pointed to the stove. "While you two argue, the bacon is burning."

Karla stepped to the worktable, where she picked up the sharp bread knife and cut thick slices of the crusty white and rye loaves.

Her moment of thankfulness was short-lived however. Once their mother was out of earshot, Antje glanced over her shoulder and pointed the meat fork in Karla's direction. "Tell me why Frank must wait until Monday for an answer from you."

"Because there may be other things I need to do other than go to a taffy pull. Christmas will soon be here. If you must know, I have gifts I need to complete."

"I would rather have you attend the taffy pull than worry over a Christmas gift for me."

"I didn't say the gift was for you, and I don't need you to make my decisions."

Antje forked the bacon onto a platter. "Well, I can tell you that there is at least one other young woman who would be pleased to have Frank escort her to the taffy pull."

"I'm sure there are plenty of single women who would be pleased to have his company. I'm not competing with any of them."

The grease popped and sizzled as Antje placed strips of raw bacon in the hot skillet. "If you're wise, you will go to that taffy pull. You should have been ice-skating with us last night. Gerta Schiffer couldn't get close enough to Frank the whole evening. Every time I looked around, she was either sitting beside him near the fire or skating with him."

Jealousy pinged through Karla's chest. Should she tell Antje she had seen Frank with Gerta last night? For a moment, Karla considered confiding in her sister but stopped herself. Right now, she wasn't sure she wanted to admit how she was feeling—not even to Antje. "I'm sure they had a nice time. Gerta is a sweet young lady, and it sounds as though Frank found her to be gut company. Otherwise he would not have pursued her attention."

The bacon grease popped, and Antje jumped backward, but not in time to miss being spattered. She swiped the back of her hand down her apron. "Frank didn't pursue her! When did I ever say that? You're putting words in my mouth. I said that Gerta clung to Frank's side all evening. But mark my words, some girl will sweep him up sooner or later, and if you love him, you'll start encouraging his attentions."

Love him? The thought made her insides turn to jelly. She didn't—she couldn't possibly—she didn't dare let herself—love him. Loving someone could eventually lead to being hurt, and she couldn't let that happen again.

The bacon popped again, and Antje cried out while shaking her hand in the air.

"I will take care of the bacon. You need to dip your hand in cold water before it blisters." Karla stepped to the stove and took the meat fork from her sister.

"You would not believe what else Gerta did." Antje looked over her shoulder at Karla while she submerged her hand in a pan of cold water.

Karla lifted the pieces of bacon onto the platter. "If you intend to keep up this talk of Gerta and Frank, maybe you should go outside and put your hand in the snow. That would for sure prevent blisters, and it would give my ears a rest from your constant chatter."

"What are you doing over at the sink, Antje? You're supposed to be frying the bacon." Mother sighed and shook her head. "I cannot leave this kitchen for a minute."

"I burned my hand, Mutter. I have been telling Karla she should go to the taffy pull with Frank before Sister Gerta wins his heart."

"I don't think we need to worry about such things while we are cooking breakfast."

"Danke, Mutter. I couldn't agree more." Karla gave her sister a smug grin.

Her mother nodded but then stopped short. "What has Frank said that makes you think he is interested in Sister Gerta?"

Karla wanted to run from the room. Just when she thought her mother had taken her side, she asked a question about Frank and Gerta. "It isn't important, Mutter."

"Ja, it is important." Antje dried her hand on a soft towel as she crossed the room. "Sister Gerta invited Frank to the taffy pull. I heard her with my own ears. Can you believe she would do such a thing?"

"Nein—that is not proper." Their mother perched her hands on her hips and shook her head. "Sister Gerta knows better than to ask a man to escort her. What was she thinking?"

"I'll tell you what she was thinking." Antje directed a stern look at her sister. "She was thinking she has no competition for

Frank and that he most likely hopes to marry soon. Unlike Karla, Gerta wanted to make sure Frank knew she was interested in his attention."

Their mother turned toward Karla. "Well, he must not be too interested in her since he invited our Karla to go with him."

Karla's stomach lurched. The pride in her mother's voice set off a warning signal as loud as a rumbling train. This conversation needed to stop before her mother and Antje began plans for a double wedding. "Enough! If I hear another word about Frank, Gerta, or taffy, I'm leaving, and you'll have to serve breakfast without my help."

❧

Frank had hoped Karla would have a change of heart and tell him she would be pleased to accompany him to the taffy pull. Instead, she did everything possible to keep distance between them. After going to bed the past several nights, he'd tried to recall what he might have done to cause an even greater chasm in their friendship.

He turned when the bell over the apothecary door jangled and was surprised to see Antje step inside. She shivered and shook the light layer of snow from her cloak before she crossed the room.

Frank tensed, immediately concerned Karla might be ill. "Someone is sick at the hotel?"

Antje shook her head. "Nein. One of the guests asked for headache powders, and we didn't have any. Mutter asked if I would stop and get some from you."

As the tension in his shoulders eased, he smiled. "I wish your Mutter would have sent Karla. Not that I don't enjoy visiting with you, but. . ."

"You don't need to explain, Brother Frank. I know you're waiting for my sister to accept your invitation. I've done everything

I can to encourage her," Antje said. "Unfortunately, I think my efforts have had the opposite effect."

He lifted an amber-colored bottle from the shelf and placed it on the counter. "What do you mean? What could you say that would discourage her from accepting?"

Antje inhaled a deep breath and related the conversation they'd had in the kitchen the day after they'd gone ice-skating. "I thought if I told Karla about Sister Gerta being interested in you, she would be jealous and agree to go with you."

His stomach clenched and his fingers trembled while he poured some of the powder onto a small white paper and folded the edges together. How he wished Antje hadn't interfered—and yet he knew her intentions were good. She wanted nothing more than to help him win her sister's heart. "I don't think trying to make Karla jealous will work. She has been hurt once, and if she believes I could be swayed by someone else, she will never trust me."

"It seems you know her better than me. She said that Sister Gerta is a very nice young woman and that the two of you would make a gut match." Antje slapped her gloved hand on the counter. "Sometimes she makes me furious. I'm sure she cares for you, but she is afraid of being hurt again. I've tried and tried to think of something that will change her way of thinking, but I'm at a loss."

"Only God can help me."

"But the Lord helps those who help themselves, ja? How will she learn to trust you if she will not spend time with you?"

Frank handed Antje the packet of headache powders. "Don't worry, Antje. I won't let her go that easily."

Chapter 5

On Sunday afternoon, Karla was alone in the kitchen after the dishes from the noonday meal had been washed. Her mother and father had gone upstairs to rest, and her sister had departed to enjoy an outing with Paul. Karla donned her heavy wool cloak and lifted a lantern from a nail near the back door. For several days now, she'd been attempting to locate the large china plate they used for cookies each Christmas. Since those in Amana owned few personal possessions, the plate was dear to her mother, and Karla had been unable to find it in the upstairs china cabinet. Her mother thought it must have been packed away in the cellar with their other Christmas decorations, and this afternoon she decided she'd do her best to locate it. Her mother would be delighted when the missing plate was finally found.

The deep snow crunched beneath her feet as she pulled her cloak tight against the frigid wind. A bright winter sun shone on ice-laden tree branches that crackled overhead like corn popping over a hot fire. The temperature had warmed just enough to melt some of the ice. When several drops of cold water splattered on the hood of her woolen cloak, she quickened her pace.

An unladylike grunt escaped her lips as she leaned down and lifted the heavy cellar door that lay flush with the ground and slanted away from the side of the house. After descending a few steps, Karla turned her back to the wind, lit the lantern wick, and continued down the cellar steps. An uneasy shiver raced along her arms as the dank smell of clammy earth rose up to greet her. Through the years, Karla had done her share of retrieving jars of canned goods, milk, and any of the other staples stored in the cellar beneath the house. In her early years, she'd thought the cellar an adventure, but after being locked down there for several hours when she was twelve, the cellar had become a formidable place. A couple of boys had seen her go in, and they'd wedged the cellar door closed behind her. No amount of pounding, yelling, or crying had made the boys open the door. Each time she descended the steps, thoughts of that horrid day washed over her.

Even now, she wasn't certain what she disliked the most—the frightening shadows created by the lantern light or the cobwebs that hung from the wooden beams and brushed against her body and clung to her hair and clothing.

Trying to push her worries aside, Karla held the lantern high and carefully edged her way into the adjacent room where her father stored the Christmas decorations. After scanning the shelves, Karla's spirits plummeted when her gaze settled on two large boxes, one of them on an upper shelf. Could she possibly get either of them down without mishap?

The lantern sputtered as she lifted it onto a slightly protruding nail in one of the overhead beams. She waited until the flame once again burned steady, then reached for the box on the lowest shelf. Using the side of her hand, she inched the container toward the edge. When it propelled forward and landed against her chest, Karla gasped and took a backward step to gain her balance. Bending forward, she carefully placed the box on the floor and then retrieved the lantern. Once again, the flame flickered and dimmed. She tried to settle her nerves as she placed the lantern on the floor and waited for the wick to glimmer with a fixed stream of light. What if it went out and she was left down here in the dark?

Her stomach churned at the thought, and without waiting any longer, she stooped and opened the container. "Please let the platter be in here." Her whispered plea sounded eerily hollow to her own ears. She swallowed hard as she lifted the Christmas pyramid and slid her fingers beneath the cardboard crèche and some of the other decorations. The platter would not be found—at least not in this container.

She sighed, closed the box, and stared at the shelf. If she could find something to stand on, the box on the upper shelf would be much easier to handle. Holding the lantern high, she surveyed the room. *Nothing.* Perhaps she'd find something in one of the other rooms. Her old fears escalated as she continued into first one small room and then another. She was about to give up when she spotted an old washtub in a far corner of the room. If she could turn it over, it would give her the necessary height to reach the shelf—as long as she didn't fall—but first she would need to get it into the other room.

If she placed the lantern at a distance, it would provide enough light to aid her while she carried the washtub back to the other room. But before she picked up the tub, Karla held the lantern overhead and peered inside to make certain it was empty. She didn't want to be surprised by some unsuspecting creature that had taken up residence and now considered the washtub its home. Though she was pleased when she didn't see anything inside, her mood quickly changed when she noted there were no handles on the tub. She groaned. So much for trying to carry it into the other room.

Her arms certainly wouldn't fit around the circumference. With a heavy sigh, she carried the lantern to the entrance of the room, then returned and hoisted the tub up and onto its side. After catching her breath, she carefully rolled the tub toward the lantern.

She continued the process of moving the lantern and rolling the tub forward, although rounding the corner into the final room proved more difficult than she'd anticipated. She hesitated for a moment when she thought she heard a noise near the steps but soon decided her imagination was playing tricks on her. She wouldn't mind a mouse, but the thought of a weasel or rat caused her hands to tremble as she turned the washtub upside down in front of the shelf. Oh, how she disliked this place!

Lifting her skirts, she raised one foot onto the center of the tub. Satisfied it was stable enough to hold her weight, Karla grasped the edge of the shelf with her left hand as she lifted her other foot onto the tub. It wobbled, and she grasped the edge of the shelf for several moments before finally feeling secure enough to turn loose and reach for the box. She smiled, pleased that she wouldn't have to push up on her toes in order to gain a good hold on the box. Too late, she realized it would have been easier if she'd placed the washtub a little farther away from the shelf. Still, if she was careful, this would work. She held the box in her arms and was preparing to step down when a large shadow moved across the room.

She jolted. The uneven tub tipped. She let out a short squeal and landed squarely in Frank's arms as the box slipped from her hands and landed on the dirt floor.

Stepping away from him, she shook her head. "What were you thinking? You nearly frightened the life out of me." She hadn't meant to sound harsh, but Frank's actions could have caused her to end up nose-first on the cellar floor. Her heart squeezed, and she silently chastised herself for her stern words.

"I'm sorry I frightened you, but I looked inside the house, and when I didn't see you, I thought you might be outside at the pump. But once I saw the cellar door open, I was sure you had come down here." He pulled a piece of cobweb from her hair. "I remembered how much you disliked this place and decided to follow you and see what you were doing. His gaze settled on the two boxes. "What were you doing?"

"Trying to find Mutter's Christmas cookie platter. The box was too high for me to reach, and I decided to stand on that old washtub. It was working fine until. . ."

"Until I came down here and frightened you." Lamplight danced in his eyes.

"I might have fallen anyway. Perhaps you saved me." She shivered.

"Are you cold?" He reached for her, running his hands over her cloak. "Or is it the bad memories of being down here?"

"Both," she admitted.

The room suddenly felt much warmer. On the day she'd been locked inside, it had been Frank who'd come to find her. He'd heard his friend bragging about what they'd done, and after giving him a fat lip, he'd come to let her out. She'd never been happier to see anyone in her life.

"Do you remember how you rewarded me for rescuing you?" He pulled her closer.

She placed her hands on his chest. Beneath her palms, his heart hammered strong and sure. "I kissed your cheek."

"What is my reward for catching you today?"

Her cheeks grew hot under his gaze.

"We aren't children anymore."

"Nein." He cupped her face, running his thumb over her cheek. "We certainly aren't."

The light sputtered, and she jumped. Her foot hit the upturned box lying on the floor, and the contents rattled. "The plate! How could I have forgotten?" She dropped to the floor and reached for the box.

Frank knelt beside her and moved her hands away. "Let me. If something is broken, I don't want you to get cut." He carefully lifted and set the box upright. Shifting around, Karla turned up the lantern's wick and lifted it closer while Frank opened the container. Near the middle of the box he discovered the platter snugly wrapped in an old towel. Pulling back the cloth, he looked at her. "All is well—it didn't break. Now I think we should take the boxes and return upstairs."

Before she lost her nerve, she leaned over and kissed his cheek. "Danke."

When they reached the top of the stairs, the sun shone bright on the blanket of white snow, and Karla hurried inside while Frank closed the cellar door and followed behind. It wasn't until he entered the house that she noticed his injury.

She pointed to his forehead. "You're bleeding. When did that happen?"

"The wind caught the cellar door."

"Come over to the sink and let me see to your wound."

Frank followed behind her. "It isn't so bad." She ripped a strip of cloth from one of the linen towels, poured water into a bowl, and wet the cloth. After wringing out the water, she traced her fingers through his hair and pushed it from his forehead, surprised by the pleasure the simple act evoked. Being careful to hold his hair away from the wound, she dabbed his forehead. When she first saw the blood, she had thought it was only a scrape. Now, as the bleeding continued, her concern mounted.

Lifting the cloth away from his head, she once again dipped it into the water. "I may need to go for the doctor. I'm not certain this is going to stop bleeding without a stitch or two."

Once again she placed the cloth to his head. He lifted his hand and laid it atop hers. "Sometimes it takes more pressure."

He pressed against her hand, and the look in his eyes sent tight quivers racing through her belly. She shuddered and inhaled a deep breath. What was his mere touch doing to her? How could he cause this deep, undesired longing? She thought she might swoon, but scolded herself.

No fainting, she silently reprimanded herself. That would add another layer of embarrassment—one she couldn't possibly bear.

He grinned down at her. "Since I was severely wounded in your service, can I at least know why you didn't ask for help getting those boxes?"

She inhaled a sharp breath. "Do you truly think it's severe? I'm going for the doctor right now." She attempted to lift her fingers from his forehead, but he held her hand tight.

"I don't need a doctor. Your touch is enough to heal my forehead." His words sent a flame of warmth coursing through her body and up her neck. She could feel the heat spread across her cheeks. Hoping Frank wouldn't notice, she turned away.

"My healing powers aren't as great as you seem to think." She attempted to lift her hand. "Let me remove the cloth so I can see if the cut is still bleeding." He dropped his hand away from his forehead, and she gently lifted the corner of the cloth and peeked at the cut. "I think it has stopped bleeding, but it would be best if you keep pressure on the wound." She reached for his hand and lifted it to his forehead.

"I think I would like it much better if you held the cloth in place and I sat down on a chair."

Her earlier fear returned in a rush, and she reached for his arm. "Do you feel weak?"

"I would like to tell you I'm feeling faint, but that would be unfair." He grinned. "I was enjoying your attention, but from the look in your eyes, I can see that I've already caused you far too much worry." He walked into the lobby.

Karla followed behind him and watched as he removed the cloth and looked in the mirror. "Ach! It looks fine. Wrap the bandage around my head and it will be like new in no time." He turned and looked deep into her eyes. "Will you tie the bandage for me?"

"Ja, of course. Sit down in the kitchen, and I will take care of it."

Holding a long strip of cloth in one hand, Karla returned, and after cleaning the cut, she wound the bandage around his head. She traced her fingers through his hair and pulled it over the cloth. "I think your hair might hide the bandage." She stood back and looked at him, giggled, and then shook her head. "I spoke out of turn. The bandage can be easily seen."

He touched his hand to his forehead. "If others see the bandage, it is fine. I will simply tell them that you tripped me."

"Frank!" She perched her hands on her hips. "You should not even think about saying such a thing. There are some who might believe you."

He shook his head. "There is no one in all of South Amana who would believe you capable of such an unkind act. Throughout this village you are known to be a sweet and considerate young woman."

Upon hearing Frank's words of praise, heat climbed up Karla's neck. Hoping he wouldn't see the blush that had begun to warm her cheeks, she ducked her head and stepped across the kitchen. Stooping down, she picked up one of the boxes. Frank jumped up from the chair and in three long strides was by her side. He reached for the container.

Keeping her head bowed, she pointed toward the chair with her free hand. "Go and sit down before your head begins to bleed again."

"I will not sit here and watch you carry heavy boxes around the kitchen." He frowned and reached around her.

"I'm perfectly capable of moving this box. You're the one who is injured. Please sit down." She reached inside the box and removed the cookie platter in a triumphant salute. After placing it on the counter, she stacked one box on top of the other. "I'm going to carry these upstairs so we'll have the decorations in the parlor when it's time to decorate the room for Christmas."

Frank stood and shook his head. "I don't think it's wise to stack the boxes. You won't be able to see where you're going."

"No need for worry. I can find my way through this house with my eyes closed."

Though she insisted he sit down, he followed her to the stairs. She tapped the toe of her shoe against the first step to make certain she was in position. Lifting one foot, she teetered slightly.

"Stop, Karla. Let me help you."

She kept her gaze fastened on the steps. "I am fine. I don't need help, and you need to sit down."

"Maybe you don't need my help, but my head is fine, and it gives me pleasure to help you. I'll carry the boxes."

As he reached forward and brushed her arm, the boxes swayed, and she faltered. Frank grasped her around the waist, and the warmth of his hands fanned to an unsettling fiery flame that took up residence in the pit of her stomach.

"What are you doing?"

"What I do best. Taking care of you."

"I'm fine, Frank. I don't need you to hold on to me." His hands remained around her waist, and she glanced down at him. "Didn't you hear me? I'm fine."

He winked. "Ja, I heard you, but I quite enjoy helping you."

"It isn't proper, Frank."

He shot her a look of disbelief. "Is it improper for a man to help a woman when he fears she will injure herself?" He shook his head. "I don't think so."

"I can assure you I'm not going to injure myself, and it's quite safe to remove your hold."

He shook his head. "It is the least I can do after you did such a fine job of bandaging my head. Either put the boxes on the steps and I will carry them up for you or accept me holding on to you. It's for your own safety." She twisted her head and stared down at him, certain he was enjoying her discomfort. The boxes began to grow heavy, and she knew she couldn't continue to hold them forever. His hands remained firmly on her waist as she placed the boxes on the step. If she turned and stepped down, it would be impossible to escape if he attempted to embrace her. Then again, she was being silly. Frank wouldn't embrace her up here where her family or a guest might see them.

Yet maybe he would. He was showing true interest in her. He'd asked to be her escort—twice. And he'd just made it clear that he had feelings for her. And in the cellar. . .

Why was that so hard to fathom?

And if he did embrace her. . .why would she want to escape?

She turned toward him. "I've placed the boxes on the steps. What else must I do in order to have you turn loose of me?"

"Agree to attend the taffy pull with me." His smile was as sweet as the taffy the group intended to make next week.

She could either agree or stand on the steps until one of her parents came out of the parlor, but that could be another hour. Remaining on these steps for another hour was completely out of the question.

Or was it? Karla was struck by an odd thought, that standing near Frank for an hour might be a wonderful experience. Even two hours. Or three.

"It seems you've left me no other choice than to agree to go with you." Though she attempted to give him a stern look, she could feel the edges of her lips bowing. And she couldn't deny the unexpected surge of delight that bubbled deep within.

When his hands slipped from her waist, she immediately missed the warmth and security of his hold.

She looked into his gray eyes, and her heart skipped. Clearly he was quite pleased with coercing her into joining him. Hope that had budded in her heart began to flower. Frank truly was interested in more than friendship.

She blinked. Even if he was interested, she'd not forgotten the burn of rejection. And as it was with most burns, the scar that had formed over her heart was a constant reminder of what could happen when one trusted a man. She needed to be careful.

Squaring her shoulders, she stepped around him and heard his wistful sigh.

No, she wouldn't let her guard down.

She simply couldn't.

❧

Frank waited in the lobby, his foot tapping a nervous beat on the braided rug. Antje and Paul had departed for the taffy pull fifteen minutes ago, yet there had been no sign of Karla. Before she'd scurried out the door, Antje had promised Karla would be right down. If they didn't leave soon, the candy would be cooked, cooled, and pulled before they arrived. At the sound of footsteps in the upper hallway, he stood and walked toward the stairs. But instead of Karla, it was her father who appeared.

When he reached the bottom of the stairway, he clapped Frank on the shoulder and nodded toward the chairs in the lobby. "Why don't we sit down? I don't think Karla is ready yet."

A sick feeling settled in the pit of Frank's stomach. Had Brother Johann come downstairs to tell him Karla wasn't going to attend the party? Did she decide it would be easier to have her father deliver the message rather than try to argue with him? He chose a chair facing the steps and let his eyes stray in that direction as he sat down. If only she realized how much he wanted her to appear— and how he longed to earn both her trust and her love. Yet if she wouldn't even go to a party with him, how would he ever succeed?

"I was surprised when Karla told me she had agreed to attend the party with you, Frank." Brother Johann dropped to the chair and pulled his pipe from his pocket. "You do understand how her engagement to Oskar Freitag came to an end? I would be most unhappy to see her hurt again." He looked at Frank from beneath hooded eyes while he cupped his hand around the bowl of his pipe and filled it with tobacco. "Karla is a sweet and kind young woman. A girl who loves the Lord and follows His teachings, but she has come to believe her inner beauty isn't enough to gain her a husband. What happened with Oskar has further convinced her that it is outer beauty that matters to most men."

"But I'm not most. . ."

Brother Johann waved his pipe. "Let me finish, and then you may talk." Using slow, precise movements, he tamped the tobacco in the bowl of his pipe. "You and Karla were gut friends until you went away to school, and that means you knew each other very well—back then." He held the pipe stem between his lips, struck a match, and held it to the bowl of his pipe while he drew in several quick breaths. "You have been gone to college and apothecary school, and during those years you and Karla have not been around each other."

The tobacco-spiced air circled above Frank's head. "When I came home for visits, I went to Middle because my family had moved. And later, Karla was promised to Oskar. You know it's difficult to—"

Once again, Brother Johann motioned Frank to silence. "I'm not condemning you for going to visit your family. I'm simply trying to make things very clear—for Karla's sake as well as your own. To do that, I must be sure you understand how her Mutter and I feel about this attention you have been directing toward her."

Dread flooded over him, and his stomach clenched in a painful spasm. Did her parents now believe Karla should never marry? Did they fear she couldn't withstand the possibility of being hurt again? Surely they knew him well enough to realize his intentions were honorable and that he would never deliberately hurt their daughter. With damp palms, he leaned back in the chair and prepared to hear what else Brother Johann had to say.

"Although she tries to hide her pain, her Mutter and I know that what happened changed her in some ways. She isn't the same trusting young woman."

Brother Johann puffed on his pipe, and a curl of smoke circled above his head. Frank waited a moment and was about to respond when Brother Johann inhaled a deep breath. He looked deep into Frank's eyes. "From the time she was a little girl, Karla thought she was never as pretty as the other girls—probably because everyone complimented Antje on her beauty. Her Mutter and I never compared the girls—they're both special in their own way. But you spent a great deal of time with her in your early years, and I think you probably know she didn't feel equal to some of the other girls. Then when this thing happened with Oskar. *Ach!*" Brother

Johann shook his head.

Frank scooted forward on his chair. "I would never betray Karla. I've always cared deeply for her. We were dear friends, but I now realize my feelings for her run much deeper than friendship, Brother Johann. You've known me all of my life. I hope you know you can trust me."

The older man rubbed his palm along his jaw and shook his head. "Here is the problem, Frank: I knew Oskar all of his life, too. He always appeared to be a kind and trustworthy young man. We trusted him as much as Karla did. When the news arrived that he wished to break his engagement, I was as surprised as Karla. For sure, the hurt wasn't the same as for her—but I'd never imagined Oskar would do such a thing."

"What am I to do other than tell you my intentions are pure, and I'll not hurt your daughter? I've prayed and believe it's God's will for us to be together, Brother Johann."

"Gut! If you have earnestly prayed and believe you're following His will for your life, then I can't argue with you." He pointed the stem of his pipe at Frank. "But that does not mean that you've won my complete trust—or Karla's."

"How am I supposed to do that? Please tell me. I will do anything."

"Only your actions will prove yourself to me—and to her."

Frank nodded. With God's help, he would demonstrate he was a man worthy of Karla's trust, but right now he remained uncertain who would prove his bigger challenge—Brother Johann or Karla.

Chapter 6

Karla wasn't sure what her father had discussed with Frank, but when she came downstairs to meet him, he appeared drawn and pale. His winter coat was draped across his arm. "Are you not feeling well? If you're sick, we don't need to attend the party. I can remain at home and quilt or knit."

If he was ill, it would be an answer to her prayers. Guilt jabbed her. What a shameful way to think! But after yesterday, she'd spent more time in thought and realized they'd both been swept away by memories. Frank had always come to her rescue, and now he wanted to do so again. But that was not enough reason for either of them to pursue a relationship.

Frank straightened his shoulders and shook his head. "I feel quite well, and I don't intend to let you sit at home while there is taffy to be pulled—and eaten." He winked, and a flood of warmth raced up her neck and spread across her cheeks.

She hoped he hadn't noticed her embarrassment. "I need to get my cloak from the kitchen."

Instead of remaining in the lobby, Frank followed behind her while shrugging into his coat. She reached for her cloak, but before she could lift it from the hook, he covered her hand with his own. "Let me help you."

She nodded and withdrew her hand from beneath his. "Danke."

"My pleasure."

He lifted the cloak onto her shoulders and gently squeezed her upper arms in a soft caress. His touch fanned the warmth in her cheeks, and her face blazed hotter. She didn't dare let him see her. For him to know the effect his touch had on her would only make matters worse. Antje said men enjoyed knowing when a woman cared for them. If that was the case, she must be very careful.

She hurried out the door, where she could blame the cold air for the heightened color in her cheeks. Frank offered his arm, but when she didn't take hold, he reached out and grasped her gloved hand within his own. To pull away would give rise to questions she didn't want to answer. It would be easier simply to let him hold her hand. After all, they were both wearing gloves, and though she would never tell him, she enjoyed the warmth that radiated from his hand to her own.

"Am I walking too fast?"

A bright moon shone overhead, and when she looked up, her gaze collided with his. The kindness that shone in his eyes urged her to let down her guard—to trust him—to believe him. *Be careful. Don't fall into his trap.*

"Did you say I'm walking too fast? We can slow down." His smile broadened, and she looked away.

"No, we should hurry. I've already made us late."

"It isn't your fault. Your father wanted to talk to me—about us."

She stopped in her tracks. "Us? There is no 'us.' Did you tell him we are merely friends, and you invited me to the taffy pull because you feel sorry for me?"

"What?" He turned to face her. "Who gave you such an idea? I invited you because I care for you and enjoy your company—surely you realize that." He reached forward and lifted her chin. "Why do you continually insist on pushing me away? It will not change my feelings for you, Karla."

She moved his hand away from her chin. "I don't wish to discuss this further. It is cold, and we are already late for the party."

"Nein. We are going to discuss this now."

"Frank, please. Don't be ridiculous."

"Why shouldn't I be? You certainly are." He glared at her. "After yesterday, you can pretend nothing passed between us?"

"I didn't say that."

"Karla, I know Oskar hurt you. I know it is going to be hard for you to learn to trust again, and I'm willing to earn your trust. All I'm asking for is a chance."

"I want to, Frank, but—" She rubbed her chilled hands together.

He covered her hands with his own. "One chance. What will it cost you?"

He had no idea. Already he had more of a hold on her heart than she could admit to anyone, including herself. Could he see the terror in her eyes?

If she agreed, she would have to risk her heart.

She swallowed. "I'll try."

He squeezed her hands. "That's good enough for me."

The sweet aroma of warm molasses greeted Karla as they entered the house. They were the last ones to arrive at the party. That fact might have gone unnoticed, except Gerta hurried to Frank's side and grasped his arm the moment they entered the door. "I was beginning to think you weren't going to appear." She tugged on his arm. "Come to the kitchen. There is a batch of candy that is almost cool enough to begin pulling."

Frank appeared momentarily stunned by Gerta's unseemly behavior. He gently pulled away from her. "We have not yet removed our coats." He glanced at Karla. "And I'm Sister Karla's escort, so we will be pulling taffy together this evening."

Discomfort washed over Karla when Gerta frowned at her. "I'm surprised to see you here tonight, Sister Karla. When Brother Frank and I went ice-skating last week, he mentioned you were determined to complete a wedding quilt for Sister Antje."

Frank's jaw twitched. "You make it sound as though we attended the skating party together, Sister Gerta." He inched closer to Karla.

Gerta hiked one shoulder and smiled. "Nein, but we did spend most of the evening together, and I found your company most pleasant." She hesitated a moment and let her gaze rest on Frank's lips. "I hope you're able to say the same."

The air was thick with discomfort, and Karla breathed a sigh of relief when Antje spotted her. "Karla! Frank! Take off your coats and come to the kitchen. We're ready to begin pulling the candy."

Gerta turned and headed for the kitchen as Frank lifted Karla's cloak from her shoulders. "I'm sorry, but I did nothing to encourage her attention while I was at the pond. You can ask your sister."

Karla reached for her cloak and hung it atop several other wraps on the metal hooks near the door. "You don't owe me any explanation, Frank. If you wish to ice-skate with Gerta or any other woman, it is your decision. It isn't my concern." Hot tears stung her eyes, and she turned away. She swallowed the lump that had formed in her throat, determined to hide her true feelings.

Frank shrugged out of his coat and gently grasped her hand. "But I want it to be your concern. And I want what happens with you to be my concern."

She withdrew her hand and tucked a loose strand of hair behind her ear. "You're talking nonsense." She stepped around him. "We should go to the kitchen before Antje comes out here and hollers at us again."

Antje motioned to her as she entered the kitchen. "You and Frank are just in time. The taffy has cooled, and we're dividing it." She looked at Frank. "Karla is excellent at pulling taffy when she has a gut partner. I hope you have skills to match hers."

Frank straightened his shoulders and rubbed his hands together. "I will do my best."

Karla picked up a piece of the candy and quickly passed it back and forth between her hands. "It is still quite warm." Frank extended his arm, and Karla tossed the candy the short distance into his outstretched hand. "Don't be too brave. You will end up with burned fingers."

Frank flipped the piece of candy a little higher in the air and continued moving it from hand to hand. "Better that my hands are burned than yours."

"Frank is a fine gentleman, ja?" Antje gave Karla a gentle nudge and winked.

Karla pinned her sister with a warning look. Why couldn't Antje keep her thoughts to herself? Instead of helping, Antje's comments made Karla even more uncomfortable. She turned toward Frank and reached for the candy.

"I think it has cooled enough." She quickly tossed the candy to her other hand. "We can't wait too long before we begin." She nodded toward her sister and Paul. "They've already started, so it must be fine."

Laughter and chatter, along with the tantalizing smell of candy, filled the room. Frank took the candy in his hands and stretched until he had the piece long enough for Karla to hold one end while he held the other.

Their hands touched as he passed the candy to her. "I think this taffy is almost as smooth as your hands."

"I think you should concentrate on pulling the taffy so we don't end up with bulging lumps that are impossible to chew."

Over and over, they stretched and folded the rope of taffy. As the taffy started to harden and became more difficult to pull, their chatter and laughter diminished, and from the strained facial expressions in the room, Karla could see most of the candy would soon be ready.

"I forgot how much work this can be." Frank folded the taffy, and he and Karla once again stretched the candy into a long, thin rope.

"My hands and arms are beginning to ache, so it is gut that the candy has begun to cool and is just about right." She folded the long rope. "See how the color has changed to a perfect buttery shade?"

"I'll take your word for when it's done. I'm no expert on taffy— except when it's time to eat it," Frank said.

Karla gave one final pull and then handed the rope to him. "You can put it on one of the plates."

Several of the couples had already placed their ropes onto plates, and Frank did the same. He didn't allow much time for the candy to harden before cutting off several pieces. He picked up a small piece of the taffy. "You taste it first. I want to be sure it is gut enough to eat." Karla opened her lips, and Frank popped the candy into her mouth. He watched as she chewed the candy for several moments and swallowed. He arched his brows. "Well? Is it gut?"

Karla shook her head. "I don't think you will like it. I should suffer and eat all of it."

Frank laughed, stuck a piece of candy in his mouth, and chewed. Soon he pointed to his mouth. "Very gut." His cheek protruded around the lump of candy. "Sorry, but you'll have to share."

All thoughts of an early departure escaped Karla's thoughts when one of the girls announced there was another batch of taffy ready to be pulled. Frank immediately volunteered.

Gerta pushed her way through the group and drew close to Frank's side as he stood at the table. "I think I heard Sister Karla say her arms were tired. I'd be happy to help you this time, Frank."

Karla stood nearby and waited to hear what Frank would say. She half expected him to accept Gerta's offer. Instead, he shook his head. "I told you that I'm Sister Karla's escort, and if her arms are too tired, we will sit and watch." He glanced over his shoulder at Karla and winked. "Are you ready to begin again?" He tossed a warm piece of taffy from one hand to the other.

Karla gestured for him to hand her the candy. His eyes twinkled as he gently squeezed her hand before giving her the taffy. Every nerve in her body sprang to life at his touch. *Stop it! You will be hurt again.* The warning screamed in her head like a whistling wind. For the remainder of the evening, she did everything in her power to temper her feelings for Frank while it seemed *he* was doing everything in his power to win her heart.

When all of the taffy had been pulled and divided, he gathered their portion into a paper sack and handed it to her. "I did my best to get only the candy we pulled. I know it is the sweetest because you helped make it."

Warmth flooded her heart. She should ignore the comment. Offering kind words was easy. Commitment was much more difficult. Yet if she was honest with herself, Frank seemed to be offering her both.

While Frank and Paul went to the other room to retrieve their coats, Antje drew near. "You and Frank were having a gut time. It pleases me to see you laugh and enjoy yourself again." She glanced toward the other side of the room, where Gerta was standing among several young men. "She is very interested in Frank, but he cares for you, Karla. Don't give her the opportunity to win his heart."

Karla followed her sister's eyes. "It appears Sister Gerta is interested in any number of young men. You should remember that I don't control Frank's heart. Just like with Oskar, it is his for the giving and taking."

"Frank isn't anything like Oskar. He is gut and true."

Karla smoothed the front of her skirt. "Ja, but he is also a man, and men are attracted to the pretty girls. We both know there are many girls in the Colonies who are much more attractive than me." She forced a feeble smile. "I remind myself that beauty is a gift from God. He blessed Queen Esther with beauty, and He has blessed you in the same way. But my gift from Him isn't one of outward beauty."

Antje's blue eyes glimmered in the dim light. "So what? Beauty fades. Inner beauty endures. Any man would be proud to call you his wife."

Disbelief washed over Karla. "What are you saying? Do you not remember what you told me years ago?"

Her sister frowned and shook her head. "I don't know what you're talking about. What did I say?"

"You told me the pretty girls didn't view me as a threat because of my plain looks." She swallowed hard. "And the reason Frank took me fishing was because I would bait my own hook and that he would never consider me any more than a friend."

Antje's eyes widened to huge proportion. "I said *that*? Are you certain? I cannot believe I would say such things to you. When was this?"

"I was fourteen and you were twelve, but it seems like only yesterday. I remember every word." Karla's voice faltered, and she looked away.

Antje grasped her arm. "We were children. I was probably

jealous because Frank took you somewhere and I couldn't go." She tipped her head to look into her sister's eyes. "I'm truly sorry I caused you this pain. To know you believed such terrible words for all these years breaks my heart." She shook her head. "I can't change the harm I did, Karla, but please believe me when I tell you that nothing I said back then is true. I hope you can forgive me."

Karla swiped a tear from her cheek. "You're my sister, and I love you. How could I do anything less than forgive you?"

Antje pulled her into a tight embrace. "You're beautiful, both inside and out—you always have been. I hope you won't let anything that has happened in the past keep you from a wonderful future with Frank."

"I need to give it time. We will see what happens," Karla said.

Antje sighed. "I could stand here and tell you how beautiful you are until my breath ran out, but you are the one who must believe it is true. I think you're leaning on your own understanding, dear sister, and not on God's, ja?" Antje pressed close to Karla's ear as Frank and Paul returned with their cloaks. "Put your trust in God and in the plans He has for you."

Karla bit her lip. How easy it was for beautiful Antje to say such things. She'd never been teased or taunted or disregarded for someone else. But did she have a point? Had Karla been leaning on her own understanding?

They bid the others good night, and the foursome was soon on their way back to the hotel. Frank and Karla took the lead. A short time later, when Karla glanced over her shoulder, Antje and Paul had fallen a good distance behind. "We should wait for them—or tell them to hurry. After we get to the hotel, Paul still must travel to Lower South."

Frank tenderly grasped her hand and tucked it into the crook of his arm. "Let Paul worry about when and how he will return home. I think he and Antje purposely dropped back so they could be alone." A shaft of moonlight played hopscotch across Frank's strong jawline and revealed a twinkle in his eyes. "Or maybe they were being kind and wanted to give us time to be alone."

She waited a long, aching moment. Frank's words and behavior were inviting, yet it was so hard to even think of giving her heart to another man. She couldn't survive being hurt again. "Frank, I've tried to make it clear that I—"

He gently tugged her to a halt and placed his finger against her lips. "Please listen carefully to what I'm going to tell you, Karla." Taking hold of her shoulders, he turned her toward him and stared deep into her eyes. "I promise you that I will always keep my word, and no matter the circumstance, I will do anything I can to help you feel good about life again." Longing poured from his voice, and he inhaled a ragged breath. "Unless you give me a chance, I can never prove that I'm a man you can trust. Please say you will drop these barriers you've built around your heart." He lifted his hand and trailed his fingers across her cheekbone, then cupped her chin in his palm. "If it will ease your fears, you may test me. I'm a man of my word."

At the touch of his hand, her heart pulsed a furious beat. Could she trust him? Should she give him a chance? Her head said no, but her heart—oh, how deeply her heart wanted to say yes.

Chapter 7

Even though Karla hadn't promised to give him a chance the night of the taffy pull, she'd been less guarded around him, and Frank decided that was a good sign. He would continue to pray that God would work in her heart to reveal that he should not be judged based upon the behavior of another man. If he continued to treat her with love, kindness, and affection, surely the walls she had built around her heart would drop like the walls that had surrounded Jericho.

As a young boy, Frank had learned the Bible story of Joshua and the Israelite army circling the city of Jericho with the priests blowing their trumpets until, on the seventh day, the walls fell. He grinned as he arranged several bottles on the shelf of the apothecary. Maybe he should circle around Karla, blowing on a horn until the walls around her heart came down. Now that would be something, for sure!

"What's so funny, Brother Frank?" Leaning heavily on his cane, Brother Hueber hobbled from the back room.

Frank tapped his finger on the side of his head. "I was just thinking about something. I doubt anyone else would find it amusing." He pointed to the older man's cane. "You're having more trouble walking today, ja?"

Brother Hueber rested his cane against the walnut counter, where an old balance with generous brass pans awaited the weighing of compounds to heal the sick and ailing. "A little, but not so much that I can't do my job." An array of colored and clear glass bottles filled with tinctures, powders, and herbs lined the many shelves of the apothecary. The scent of burning pine and oak radiated from the heating stove and mingled with the familiar herbal and medicinal odors as Brother Hueber gazed around the shop. "You have done a gut job keeping everything in order for me." The old man reached forward and rearranged two of the bottles. "There, that is better."

Frank grinned. No matter how perfectly he aligned the bottles, Brother Hueber always moved one or two. "Are you feeling gut enough that I can leave and go to the school?"

"Ja, ja." He gestured toward the front door. "Be on your way, and be sure to tell the boys how they should do gut in their studies so they can go to college and become a doctor, pharmacist, or schoolteacher."

Frank was eager to go and talk to the boys, but more than that, he hoped to catch a glimpse of Karla teaching her knitting classes at strickschule.

With a shuddering groan, the older man eased into the chair and pointed his cane toward the wall of brass-handled drawers that filled a cabinet below the shelves. "If you would bring me my Bible, I can read until I have a customer."

Frank handed him the Bible before shrugging into his coat. "I should not be gone more than an hour."

Brother Hueber opened the leather cover of his Bible. "Any suggestions on what I should read while you're gone?"

"I've been thinking about Joshua a great deal this morning. Maybe you would enjoy reading about the battle he fought at Jericho."

The older man scratched his balding head. "Joshua it will be, then." He pushed his glasses against the bridge of his nose and thumbed through the feathery pages of his Bible. "Take all the time you need."

Frank pushed down on the heavy metal latch and stepped outside. He'd gone only a few steps when he turned up his collar and bent his head against the north wind. Already, he missed the cozy wood-burning stove, but talking to Karla would be worth suffering the cold temperatures. Though his fingers remained stiff and cold, the thought of her warmed his heart.

If he picked up his pace to a jog, he would keep warmer and be inside the school much sooner. At least that was his hope as he propelled himself toward the school, all the time being mindful of slippery patches of ice. When the school came into view, he returned to his familiar long stride. He gulped air, each breath stinging his lungs as he inhaled. Maybe jogging hadn't been such a grand idea after all. Outside the door of the schoolhouse, he leaned forward and rested his gloved hands on his knees. He'd wait outside long enough for his breathing to steady.

He didn't want to walk into the classroom and collapse. What a sight that would be. Instead of helping Brother Reichman with the children, Frank would become another burden for the old schoolteacher.

"Frank! Are you ill?"

Surprised, he jerked upright and turned. "Karla! I didn't hear you." He clasped a gloved hand to his chest. "I'm fine."

"Truly? You don't look fine." She arched her eyebrows and stared at him.

From the look in her eyes, she appeared both confused and

concerned. And he couldn't blame her. No doubt he'd made quite a spectacle of himself. He pointed a thumb toward the door. "I'm going to talk to Brother Reichman's class about studying hard and making gut grades in school."

"So why were you bent over? I thought you might be having chest pains."

"Nein. My heart is beating fine." He patted his chest. "I was out of breath from running. The cold air made it hard for me to breathe."

Karla turned toward the small building where she taught handwork to the children. "My class will begin soon. I should go inside." She pulled her cloak tighter. "Besides, it is cold."

He reached forward and placed his hand on her arm. "I thought I would stop in the strickschule when I finish my talk at the school."

She tipped her head to the side and looked up at him. "For what reason?"

His frustration pulsed to life. He sighed. "Because I would like to see you work with the children and because I enjoy your company. Is that reason enough?"

She giggled, and he stopped. She'd been teasing him. Finally.

"I'm not sure it is proper, and the children might find it hard to concentrate with you there."

"They will or you will?" He folded his arms across his chest and shook his head. "I will prove that you're wrong about the children." He grinned and tapped his finger on the tip of her nose. "Just wait and see."

❧

Karla sat down beside young Louisa Neffbaum and covered the girl's hands with her own. "Let's try this, Louisa. While holding your hands, I will guide your fingers through several of the stitches and see if that will help."

When the little girl looked up, Karla noticed a tear forming in one of her cornflower-blue eyes. "Danke, but I don't think I will ever learn." Her lower lip trembled as the tear slipped down her plump, rosy cheek. "What will I give my Mutter for Christmas if I cannot finish the mittens?"

"You will finish in time. If necessary, I will stay late and help you. There is no need to cry, Louisa."

"But the rest of the class have already finished and are knitting or crocheting other gifts."

"You should not compare yourself to others, Louisa. God gives each of us special talents. While some of the other girls may knit at a faster pace than you, I'm sure there are things you can do better than them. It is best if we are thankful for however we look and whatever talents God gives us, don't you think?"

"Ja, I think that is right, Sister Karla." Both Karla and Louisa twisted around to see Frank standing behind them. "That is a gut lesson to always remember—even for big people like me and Sister Karla." He smiled at Louisa and pointed to a completed mitten resting on Karla's lap. "If that is the mitten you're making, I think it looks like a very difficult pattern for such a young girl. I'm pretty gut at knitting, and I'm not sure I could knit that pretty pattern."

Louisa's eyes sparkled. "Sister Stuke made the pattern for us. She called it the Homestead Rose." Louisa pointed to the pattern. "See how it looks like a rose?"

Frank nodded. "It does. But why did she call it the Homestead Rose when we live in South Amana?" He lifted his gaze and looked at the boys and girls sitting across from him. A woven knitting basket rested on the floor beside each child, and lengths of yarn draped from the numerous knitting needles or crochet hooks to the colorful balls of yarn inside their baskets. "Do any of you boys or girls know the answer?" Wide-eyed, they all looked at Karla and shook their heads.

Louisa frowned. "Why did you name it after Homestead, Sister Stuke?"

"Sister Karen brought it with her when her family moved here from Homestead. They were the caretakers at the Homestead meetinghouse, and she found the mitten one day when she was cleaning."

Several of the other children drew near to hear the story as Karla continued. "For a number of years, she tried to find the owner, but no one ever claimed it. After Sister Karen's family moved to South, she found it in one of her trunks and showed it to me. I created the pattern from looking at the one Sister Karen found, and I named it the Homestead Rose because it was found in their meetinghouse."

"Then I would say that is a very gut reason for the name." Frank sat down on the bench beside her and pointed to Louisa's mitten. "Maybe I should see if I can knit this pattern."

The children applauded and urged him on.

"Don't encourage him, children. If he takes up Louisa's needles, I fear I will have to rip out all the stitches and replace them."

"You have no confidence in me?" Frank leaned around Karla and faced Louisa. "Do you trust me with your mitten, Sister Louisa?"

The little girl's forehead creased, and her eyebrows drooped low as she considered his question. "If Sister Stuke will fix it when you're done. I have to be finished in time for Christmas."

He grinned at Louisa. "That does not sound as though you have great belief in my knitting ability, but let me see what I can do."

Frank looped the yarn around his index finger and dug the needle into the stitch. When he wrapped the yarn below the needle, Louisa jumped up and squealed. "You're supposed to purl, not knit. On this row, the yarn goes over the top, not underneath."

"Ja, ja, I see now. Danke, Sister Louisa." He had been pretty good at knitting as a boy, but his large hands and years away from the craft revealed he'd lost a great deal of his ability. "I think it is beginning to come back to me now."

Louisa sighed and shook her head. "That stitch is too loose. It must come out, right, Sister Stuke?"

Karla gave a firm nod. "She is right—it is much too loose."

"Maybe you should teach him the way you were showing me. That way you won't have to rip out too much." Louisa beamed a proud look at both of them.

Frank scooted closer to Karla. "That is a gut idea, Sister Louisa. I don't know why I didn't think of it myself."

"I'm not sure Brother Lehner truly needs knitting lessons since he has no need to knit, Louisa. Perhaps he should give you back your mitten so that you may work on it yourself."

Frank grinned at her. "I may want to knit someone a pair of mittens for Christmas, and unless you help me, I will not be able to complete my gift. It has been a long time since I was taught to knit in strickschule."

For a moment, she considered arguing with him. But with the children listening, it would be best to do as he asked so he would be on his way. She gestured to the group of children. "All of you must get your yarn baskets and return to work. You already know how to knit. There is no need to stand here and watch while I help Brother Lehner."

Still holding a knitting needle in each hand and with the partially knitted mitten dangling between the needles, he extended his arms toward her. "I'm at your command."

He looked so silly that she couldn't help but smile at him. "First, you need to bend your elbows. You know it is impossible to knit with your arms extended like that."

Frank dutifully bent his elbows. "I only wanted to make certain you could reach my hands. I think it might be easier if you stood behind me."

Karla shook her head. "We will do it the same way I helped Louisa." She reached sideways and covered his hands. Her fingers trembled as she guided him through the first stitch. The warmth of his breath tickled her cheek as she leaned closer to check the stitch. "I cannot see when you move the mitten so far away."

As he turned toward her, his gaze settled on her lips, and he leaned in. Her breath caught, and she pulled back. A burning quiver traveled from the pit of her stomach, spread up her neck, and radiated across her cheeks. "Not so close."

"You said you couldn't see, so I leaned closer."

She cleared her throat and removed her hold on his hands. "I think we've had enough for today. Louisa needs to complete her Christmas gift, and I'm sure you need to return to the apothecary."

"Perhaps you'd consider giving me another lesson this evening."

She arched a brow. "So you intend to knit a Christmas gift, and you need help?"

"You could say that."

Karla crossed the room and picked up one of the knitting baskets. "Then let me give this to you to take to the apothecary with you. In your spare time, you can begin practicing. Tonight I will be pleased to see what you've accomplished."

Frank donned his coat and lifted the knitting basket from her hands. "You know I enjoy a challenge, Karla. Otherwise, I would never have set my sights on you, ja?"

Chapter 8

Aweek had passed since Frank's visit to the knitting class. He had continued his practice stitches, and Karla had been impressed when, after only a few days, he had resumed his childhood speed and ability. Though she'd deemed further lessons unnecessary, Frank continued to join her in the downstairs room used for quilting after prayer service each evening. He would knit, or at least hold the needles in his hands, while she worked on Antje's second wedding quilt.

Some evenings both Antje and her mother would join them, but usually only their mother appeared. Given Antje's dislike of quilting, she would often seek out something else to fill her time. Tonight, only Frank and Karla had come to the parlor.

Frank sat a short distance away from the quilting frame with yarn and knitting needles in hand, while Karla had settled close to the frame on the other side. She held her quilting needle close to the lamp, expertly threaded the eye, and momentarily studied her stitching.

"Your Mutter isn't joining us tonight?" Frank poked his knitting needle into what appeared to be lengthening into a scarf of some sort.

"Nein. She isn't feeling well. I was surprised she attended prayer meeting with us. All day she has complained of stomach pain. Before I came downstairs, she said the pain had lessened, but now she has a headache and said she was going to bed."

Karla dipped her needle into the buttercup-yellow fabric that had been stretched tight on the quilting frame and tried to set aside her worries. It wasn't like her mother to surrender and take to her bed. Still, it would be only a few hours until bedtime, and it did make sense for her mother to rest. And with Christmas approaching, they all needed to be in good health. They had much to accomplish over the next few days.

"I'm sorry to hear she isn't well, but I'm always pleased to have a little time alone with you." Frank picked up the knitting basket and carried his chair to the other side of the quilting frame.

Before he could set the chair beside her, Karla held up her palm. "No closer than the end of the frame. I like to have room when I'm quilting."

Frank raised a brow and blew out a long breath. "Is that the only reason?"

His eyes shone with sadness, but Karla detected a hint of resentment in his tone. "To be alone isn't proper. My parents trust you to behave as a gentleman, and I think that includes sitting at a distance while we visit, ja?"

He placed the chair at the end of the frame and dropped to the chair with a thud. "What about you, Karla? Have I gained your trust in me?"

She couldn't tell him that he had won her heart and she'd come to believe he would never intentionally hurt her. To tell him such a thing would be improper—and embarrassing. And to say the words out loud would make her far too vulnerable. What if he should change his mind about her? As much as she wanted to, she wasn't yet prepared to take such a chance.

"You're a fine man, Frank, and I remember everything you have told me since your return." She withdrew a handkerchief from her pocket and swiped the dampness from her palms.

His brow inched higher. "But?"

"Give me a little more time. Trust can be quickly destroyed, but restoration takes much longer."

"But I've done nothing to lose your trust." His voice rose. "Your issue is with someone else. I'm not him. I don't make promises and take them back."

"Frank, I'm trying. I just need more time."

"How much time will it take for you to forget the pain? Am I truly expecting too much too soon? I had hoped that our friendship would prove a strong enough foundation to build on." He shoved the piece of knitting into the basket. "I think I will go upstairs." He pushed up from the chair and walked to her side. Her heart quickened when he touched her cheek. "I've been praying that God will give you the ability to trust me. I don't plan to stop asking until He grants the desire of my heart." He slid his hand down her cheek and lifted her chin until their eyes met. "I love you, Karla. You can trust me to be at your side and not leave you."

The moment he removed his hand from her face, she longed for the warmth of his touch. Why didn't she tell him? Why did she permit him to leave without saying a word?

Coward! The accusation echoed in her head long after Frank had departed the room.

❧

Karla stared into the mirror in her bedroom, and the same homely face stared back at her. *Lord, why couldn't You have made me beautiful like Antje?*

She recalled her talk with her sister about leaning on God's understanding and not her own. Frank loved her. Could she ever see herself as he saw her? He'd complimented her on her soul-filled eyes and her sweet disposition. And more than once, he'd brushed his fingers across her cheek. She mimicked the gesture. Her cheek felt soft against the back of her fingers.

But how did God see beauty? She remembered the verse that said beauty came from a gentle and quiet spirit. Was her spirit gentle? Deep inside she knew it was gentle, even if that hadn't always been the case lately. A quiet spirit? No. Her spirit had not been quiet. She'd questioned everything since the day Oskar had chosen another. Trust and faith eluded her. Could she find them again? Could she become the woman Frank saw?

After breakfast Karla cleared the plates and bowls from the dining tables while her mother returned to the kitchen. Her father had checked out the two remaining hotel customers before heading to one of the forested areas outside the village to help cut wood. Keeping houses and businesses supplied with firewood was an ongoing task that was shared by the men in the village, and her father helped as often as possible. Today the men would be gone until supper time, so both Karla and her mother would register any new guests who might arrive.

Frank stopped by the dining room before he departed for the pharmacy. "I think I may need help with my knitting tonight. I cannot determine for sure, but I think I dropped a stitch several rows back."

"If you want to bring it downstairs, I can check it later this morning."

He shook his head and winked. "I'll bring it downstairs this evening."

Did he realize that each time he winked in her direction, her stomach formed a knot and her heart pounded a new beat? She ducked her head as heat inched up her neck.

Before she could reply, Antje burst into the room. She came to a screeching halt when she caught sight of Frank. "I'm sorry. I didn't mean to interrupt." She lifted the wool cloak from her arm and dropped it across her shoulders as she turned toward her sister. "I'm leaving. I will try to be back to help with supper." Since Sister Margaret Brewster had given birth to twins two weeks ago, Antje had been assigned to help her on the other side of the village. The difficult birth had left Sister Margaret abed, and with another child only eighteen months old, the woman needed as much help as possible.

"You didn't interrupt, Antje. Brother Frank stopped to say good-bye before he departs for work." Karla reached across one of the long wooden tables and picked up a stack of dirty plates. "I'm sure you both need to leave for work, and I must wash the breakfast dishes." Karla entered the kitchen shortly after Frank and Antje departed.

She lowered the plates into the hot, sudsy water her mother had prepared. "Are you sure you're better, Mutter? Your color appeared fine earlier, but now you're pale. Maybe you should go upstairs and lie down."

"Nein. I'm just a little weak." She dipped her hands into the water. "Once we have finished the dishes, we will start on the marzipan. Then tomorrow we need to begin the Christmas cookies." She lifted the corner of her white apron and dabbed perspiration from her forehead.

Her mother might think they would make marzipan today, but Karla had her doubts. Once they finished the dishes, she was going to insist her mother rest. Whether her mother wanted to admit it or not, she had a fever and should be in bed. After gathering the last of the breakfast dishes and returning to the kitchen, Karla placed them on the worktable. "Let me finish, Mutter."

Her mother started to offer a weak protest, but before she'd completed the objection, her knees buckled. An involuntary squeal escaped Karla's lips as she lunged around the worktable and caught her mother as she slipped to the floor. Fear pulsed through Karla's veins in unmerciful, gushing surges as she stooped beside her mother.

"Mutter! Please answer me!"

Her mother remained silent, her eyes closed, her complexion pale and clammy. Karla jumped to her feet, dipped a clean dishcloth into the bucket of cold water, and placed it across her mother's forehead. Her fingers trembled as she loosened the top button of her mother's dress before applying a wet cloth to her cheeks and neck. The tightness in her chest relaxed a modicum when her mother's eyelids fluttered open and a groan escaped her lips.

"Mutter? You're ill and you fainted. When you feel strong enough, I need to help you to bed and go for the doctor."

"I will be fine. Help me to my feet."

Karla placed her arm beneath her mother's shoulders and helped her to a sitting position. "Sit for a minute and see how you feel before you try to stand." She was pleased her mother didn't argue, but after a few moments, she motioned for Karla to help her to her feet.

"There, you see? I'm. . ." Her mother faltered and reached for the worktable.

Karla tightened her hold around her mother's waist. "Let's see if you can make it upstairs to bed. If not, you must lie down on the sofa in the lobby, and I will go for the doctor."

"I will not do such a thing. What if a guest should arrive and see me?"

"It will be at least another hour before a train arrives. And what do you care what anyone thinks if you're ill?"

Her mother leaned heavily on Karla but insisted they go upstairs. With each step, Karla worried her mother might faint once again. What if she couldn't hold her and they tumbled down the stairs? Her mother's breath sounded labored with each step, and by the time they arrived at the upper hallway, Karla's fear had escalated to new heights.

"Only a little farther, Mutter, and you will be in bed." Karla's arm ached, yet she dared not change positions.

Step-by-step, they slowly crossed the parlor. Once they entered the bedroom and her mother caught sight of the bed, she took two long steps and dropped onto the mattress. With legs akimbo and her lifeless arms dangling in awkward positions, she looked like a rag doll that had been carelessly tossed aside.

Panic began to take hold of Karla, but she forced it down. *Lord, let me have a quiet spirit. I trust You. I trust You. I trust You.* Karla gently lifted her mother's arms and then her legs into more comfortable positions. After another quick assessment of her mother's condition, she covered her with a quilt. "I'm going for the doctor, Mutter. Don't move from the bed. Do you hear me?"

She didn't answer, but Karla couldn't wait any longer to fetch help. Racing down the steps, she grabbed her cloak from the hook and yanked open the door. Sleet pelted her face, and she instinctively pulled her hood tight beneath her chin. When had it started to snow? She hadn't even noticed. Her feet slipped on the icy wood sidewalk, and frustration soon turned to anger. Why had her father gone to cut wood today? Why was Antje off helping Sister Margaret with her new twins? Her mother should not be at home alone right now. As if to taunt her, the sleet turned to heavy, wet snow, making it difficult to see. The cold slush penetrated her leather shoes, but she trudged on until she arrived at the doctor's office. She tapped on the door and entered, thankful for a bit of warmth.

Neither of the kerosene lamps was lit, and there was no sign of the doctor. Fear seized her as she crossed the room. "Dr. Neilson? Are you here?"

At the sound of approaching footsteps, relief swept over her. "I'm so happy. . ."

"Guten Morgen, Sister Karla."

"Guten Morgen, Sister Neilson." Karla stretched to the side, hoping Dr. Neilson would appear behind his wife. "My Mutter is ill, and I need Dr. Neilson to come to the hotel."

"He isn't here. The elders sent him to Chicago to learn some new procedures at the teaching hospital. He left on the train yesterday and will not return for two more days." She glanced toward the window. "Maybe your Vater should go to Middle for the doctor, ja?"

"He's not at the hotel. He went out with a group of men to cut wood this morning."

"With this heavy snowfall, I think they will soon return." Sister Neilson frowned. "Promise you will not try to go yourself."

Reluctantly, Karla nodded. Her mother needed a doctor, and she couldn't be certain her father would return anytime soon. If they thought the storm might subside, they wouldn't be so quick to come home. The ground was already covered in a thick blanket of white, and the sky remained heavy with snow.

Karla stepped outside and glanced across the street. Through the blinding whiteness of snowfall, she was drawn to the flicker of light shining through the window of the apothecary.

Frank! He would help her.

Treading with a careful step, she crossed the road. A bell jangled overhead as she opened the door, and a welcome rush of heat from the woodstove greeted her as she entered. She inhaled the aroma of dried herbs that mingled with the burning pine to create a special scent all their own.

"Frank! Frank! Where are you?"

Lifting a mittened hand to her face, she wiped the wet snow from her eyelashes and rushed to the counter.

Frank emerged from a back room, and delight momentarily shone in his eyes. It was quickly replaced with a frown. "Karla! What are you doing out in this blizzard?"

"Mutter is ill, and Vater went with the men to cut wood. I've no idea when he will get back. I went to fetch the doctor, but Sister Neilson said he has gone to some medical school. I need to return home and see to Mutter." Fear knotted deep inside at the mention of her mother's condition. "With this terrible blizzard, it isn't safe for anyone to go to Middle, so I was hoping that you would give me some medicine for her that will help. You remember she wasn't feeling well last night, but this morning she seemed better. Then a short time after you and Antje departed, she fainted. She has a fever and—"

"I can't just give you medicine, Karla. Maybe you can give her some headache powders that you have at the house, but I'm not a doctor, and I'm not permitted to administer medicine without a prescription from the doctor."

Tears formed in her eyes and anger rose in her chest. He'd said that he would do anything she asked—that she could trust him. "I'm asking for your help, Frank." When he hesitated, she glanced toward the doorway that led to Brother Hueber's living quarters. "Where is Brother Hueber? Maybe he can give her something."

"Brother Hueber isn't well and is resting, but I can tell you that he would not prescribe medicine for your Mutter either. It is against everything we are taught as pharmacists. Besides, I have no idea what is wrong with her. What if I gave her the wrong thing and her condition worsened?"

"Then come to the house. Check her and see what you think it is."

He nodded. "Let me get my coat."

ॐ

Grasping Karla's arm to keep her upright against the blustering wind, Frank urged her toward the hotel. Once inside, he ordered her to get warm by the stove while he checked on her mother.

Rushing upstairs, he found Sister Irma curled on her side in her bed. He pressed his hand against her forehead and pulled it back when he felt the searing heat beneath it. Fear shot through him. He didn't need to be a doctor to know Karla's mother was very ill.

"Sister Irma?" He sat down in the chair beside the bed. "Can you hear me?"

She nodded but didn't open her eyes.

"Where does it hurt?"

"Stomach." She grimaced.

Moments later Karla bolted into the room. "See how sick she is? Now that you've seen her, what can you give her?"

"Karla, I'm not a doctor. This is one thing I can't do."

She glared at him. "Cannot or will not? You went to college. You understand medicine. I'm sure you could help her if only you would. I can't trust you any more than I could Oskar."

The words stung as much as the biting sleet, but he understood her words were coming from her fear. "All we can do is keep her as cool as possible."

"That's it?"

He wrapped his scarf around his neck and moved toward the door.

"And where are you going?"

"To get what she needs. I'll be back." He squeezed her shoulder. "Trust me."

Chapter 9

As the remainder of the day wore on, so did the blizzard. Karla's father had safely returned home by early afternoon, though Antje would likely remain at the Brewster home until tomorrow. The early train had arrived far behind schedule and without any guests for the hotel. For that, Karla was thankful. She wished to give her mother undivided attention. But where was Frank? He'd been gone for hours and hadn't returned with medicine.

Realization hit her like a gust of cold wind. He must have gone for the doctor. *Oh Lord, what have I done?*

Despite her trembling hands, Karla carried a bowl of broth and a cup of tea upstairs to her mother and placed them on a small bedside table. "Go and eat, Vater. There is a warm plate on the table in the kitchen. I will sit with Mutter and see if she will take some broth when she wakens."

Her father pushed up from his chair and stood alongside the bed. "She is still warm, but I've been using the cool cloths on her forehead, so I don't think her fever is as high." He leaned down and placed a kiss on her mother's forehead, then walked toward the bedroom door. "Frank is home from the apothecary?"

"Nein. He said he was going to help. I thought he went for medicine, but he hasn't returned."

"How long ago was this?"

"Hours."

"That isn't like him."

"I fear he went to Middle for the doctor."

Her father shook his head. "That would not be a smart thing to do, and Frank is a smart man—and a gut man, too. It is my hope that he decided to spend the night at the apothecary. But just in case he went for the doctor, we should pray for him."

❧

Snow slashed at Frank's cheeks and ice crystals crusted around his eyes. How could he have gotten the sled stuck?

He put his shoulder to the sled and called to the team of horses. "Get up!"

They strained forward.

"Whoa!"

He repositioned himself and called to them again. After more tries than he cared to count, the sled finally lunged forward. He didn't want to risk getting stuck again, so he didn't halt the team. He struggled through snow up to his knees until he finally managed to jump inside the sled. Thankfully the team of horses had been slowed down by the same deep snow.

Fingers barely working, he untied the reins from the front of the sleigh and gave them a slap. Never had the distance between South and Middle seemed so great. Using one hand, he pressed his scarf against his lips. The bite in the air was freezing cold, making it hard to breathe.

Lights!

The dim glow rose over the hill. The tired horses quickened

their pace. Perhaps they, too, knew a warm place waited for them at the end of this journey.

He drove the sled straight to Dr. Morrow's, forced his weary body from the sled, and vaulted up the front steps.

Pounding on the door, he called for the doctor. After what seemed an eternity, the man appeared at the door. Without a word, he grabbed Frank's arm and hauled him inside. "Frank Lehner, what are you doing out in a storm like this? You, of all people, should know better." He pushed him toward the fireplace. "Let me see your hands. You've probably got frostbite."

"No, I'm not the patient. Get your bag. Sister Irma Stuke over in South is terribly ill. She needs you right away."

Dr. Morrow pressed Frank into a chair and took hold of his wrist. He pulled off one of Frank's ice-encrusted mittens and dropped it to the floor. The tips of Frank's fingers glowed white. "You're not going anywhere until you get warmed up."

"But—" Frank started to stand.

The doctor laid a hand on his shoulder. "As soon as the storm eases, we'll go. We can't be of help if we get stuck out in this storm."

❧

Karla stiffened at her father's final remark. Frank might be smart, but if he'd gone for the doctor, he'd placed himself and the doctor at risk. If anything happened, though, she had only one person to blame. Herself. How could she have said those horrible things to him?

"Vater, go rest in one of the guest rooms. I know you're tired. You can spell me later. Mutter needs for both of us to remain well."

"You'll come get me if she worsens?"

She nodded and dipped a cloth in the basin of water and placed the cool, damp rag across her mother's forehead.

The bedside lamp flickered as Karla pulled the rocking chair close to the bedside. Tears flooded her eyes as worry consumed her. Tears for her Mutter and for Frank as well. At last she sat down, lifted the Bible from the table, and began to pray. She didn't know how long she'd been asleep before she awakened to the sound of men's voices and the echo of stomping feet downstairs. She jumped to her feet, the Bible slipping to the floor. The train must have arrived with passengers seeking rooms at the hotel.

Wiping the sleep from her eyes, Karla stopped only long enough to touch her mother's cheek. Warmer. Much, much warmer. What was she going to do?

Snow! Snow would bring down her mother's fever. She raced for the stairs and came to a halt at the top of the steps, blinking at the approaching figure.

She squinted, certain she must be wrong. "Dr. Morrow?"

"Ja." He bobbed his head and lifted his black medical case as if to further affirm his identity. "You have forgotten me?"

Karla shook her head. "Nein, I remember you." She'd met the doctor from Middle on several occasions when he'd come to the hotel to care for visitors before Dr. Neilson had moved to South. "Did Frank fetch you in the sleigh?"

"Ja." He raked his fingers through his thick white hair. "He got stuck in the snow on the way. It is a wonder he made it at all. I know he was unhappy with me, but I insisted we wait until the blizzard let up before I would return with him." He glanced over his shoulder and lowered his voice. "I don't know who is colder, the horses or Brother Frank. I'm sure he would be thankful for something warm to drink. I'm worried about his frostbite, but I think he will be fine." His eyes sparkled in the dim light. "Now let me go and check on your Mutter. And tell your Vater to please come upstairs."

Karla's father appeared at the bottom of the stairway. "I'm right behind you, Doctor." His gaze rested on Karla. "Go now and see to Frank. He needs you." Once the two men had entered the upstairs parlor, Karla hurried downstairs.

One look at Frank standing near the stove warming his hands and guilt assaulted her. Tears ran down her cheeks unchecked. How wrong she had been. He'd risked his own life to show her he could be trusted—that he was a man of his word. What if he had frozen to death out in the blizzard? Her actions could have cost Frank his life.

"Frank, I was wrong. I never should have. . ."

He closed the distance between them in two long strides and placed his finger against her lips. "It hurt me to think you didn't trust me. I was angry, but I understood your deep concern for your Mutter. Fear makes us do many foolish things."

She gently stroked his fingers. "Look what has happened because of my foolishness and anger." A tear rolled down her cheek.

"There is no need for tears. My hands are fine. I went because it was my deep desire to help you, and I was pleased that you came to me in your time of need." He grinned down at her. "But I wasn't so pleased that you didn't understand when I told you I couldn't give medicine to your Mutter without a doctor's order."

"I'm so sorry." She lowered her gaze. "I knew what you said was true, but in my desperation I was unwilling to believe you couldn't help. My anger took hold, and I'm ashamed I acted in such a manner. I hope you will forgive me. I wish there was some way I could show you how grateful I am for what you've done."

He crooked his finger beneath her chin and lifted her face. Smoldering warmth spread through her stomach as he traced his finger across her lips. "There is one thing that you can do, Karla." His finger continued to glide across her lips. "You can trust me."

"I do, Frank. With my whole heart."

Leaning in, he kissed her. At the gentle touch of his lips, her heart pattered an exciting new rhythm. She gazed into his eyes. Never had she felt so cherished. "I do trust you, Frank. Comparing you to Oskar was unfair. You aren't anything like him."

"He wasn't a gut kisser?" He quirked a teasing grin.

"Frank! I'm trying to be serious. You could have died in that blizzard, and it would have been my fault. You know better than to go out in a storm like this, and I'm surprised Brother Roth gave you permission to take a horse and sleigh in such weather."

Frank hiked a shoulder. "He wasn't at the barn when I arrived, so I suppose you could say that I took the sleigh without permission."

"Ach!" She clapped her hand over her lips. "You should not have done such a thing." She hesitated for only a moment. "But I'm thankful you cared enough to help—and I'm even more thankful that God protected you."

He nodded his agreement. "Ja! I did a lot of praying on the way to Middle. Without God's grace and protection, I don't think I would have made it to Dr. Morrow's office."

They jumped apart at the sound of footsteps on the stairway. "Did you get Frank warmed up, Karla?" Her father entered the kitchen.

"What?" Her stomach knotted as she whirled around. Had her father seen them embrace? What would he say to such improper behavior?

Her father picked up a cup and pointed to the coffeepot. "Did you feed him some soup and give him some coffee?" He patted his belly. "Hot food warms the body, don't you think, Frank?"

Karla stepped between the two men, concern for her mother mounting when Dr. Morrow didn't follow her father into the kitchen. "What does the doctor say about Mutter?"

"He thinks she may be suffering from an inflammation of the

stomach. He believes once the inflammation subsides, her temperature will go down as well." He handed Frank a piece of paper and grinned. "Once you have warmed yourself, he would like for you to go to the apothecary. I couldn't remember what the doctor told me, so he wrote it down for you."

Frank scanned the note and then stepped to the window. Using his shirtsleeve, he wiped a patch of light frost from the window and peered outside. "It looks like it has quit snowing. I think I would rather go now and enjoy my soup and coffee when I return. The sooner Sister Irma has the medicine, the sooner she will be feeling better."

A lump settled in Karla's throat. How could she ever have doubted this sweet, kind man who had shown her nothing but friendship and love for all these years? Ever since Oskar had broken their engagement, she had worn invisible blinders, but Frank's determination had forced her to examine him with clear eyes. She'd let fear and not faith rule her life. She whispered a prayer of thanks as he donned his boots and heavy coat.

She walked to the door with him. "The soup will be waiting for you when you return."

His eyes sparkled in the kerosene lamplight. "And I hope you will be waiting for me as well."

Frank strode into the kitchen and rubbed his hands together. Though the doctor's concern about frostbite had been unfounded, the cold continued to bother his fingers more than usual. Three days had passed since he'd gone to Middle Amana for the doctor, and though the condition of Karla's mother had improved, she still remained abed. Dr. Morrow had warned that until all signs of the illness passed, he didn't want her working in the kitchen or near any hotel guests. "Just in case her disease is contagious—you can never be too careful when it comes to illness."

Frank glanced around the kitchen and spotted Karla stirring a pot on the stove. "What can I do to help you?"

"After the mess you made the other day while helping me, maybe it would be best for you to set the tables in the dining room, and I will take care of the food, ja?"

"So you no longer trust me?" He winked, and when her lips curved in a slow smile, his heart warmed.

"I trust you. It's those rambunctious hot kettles of food that I don't trust." The spunky girl he'd known years ago had finally returned.

She pointed a wooden spoon in his direction. "I think maybe you spilled that pot of potatoes just so you could avoid further kitchen duty."

He clasped his hand on his chest. "How could you ever think such a thing?" Scanning the kitchen, he pointed to a pan of hot gravy. "Maybe I should pour the gravy into a bowl for you, ja?"

"Nein." She waved him toward the dining room. "I think it would be safest for both of us if you help in the dining room. Things seem to heat up in the kitchen whenever you're around." Her cheeks blossomed pink. "I didn't mean for that to sound like it did."

"You're simply telling the truth." He kissed her cheek. "Does that mean you don't want me in the kitchen when you're baking Christmas cookies this evening?" He tipped her chin and looked into her eyes. "Just remember, I'm willing to taste each batch to make certain they're gut. I thought you would be happy for such an offer."

"I think my Vater has already filled the position of cookie taster. He has been doing it for years, and I don't think he will easily give up the job. And I don't think I will bake the cookies until tomorrow."

"Then I will for sure miss out on tasting the cookies." He waited a moment, hoping she would ask why, and was pleased when she hurried to his side.

"Why? Where will you be?" Her voice trembled, and he quickly reached for her hand.

He shouldn't have teased her. He'd just won her trust. If he wasn't careful, he'd destroy the progress he'd worked so hard to foster over these past weeks. "I'm going to go and visit my parents. Brother Hueber agreed that I could be gone from the apothecary."

Once he explained why he would be gone, Frank expected to see Karla's fear dissipate, but she withdrew her hand and shot him a look of apprehension.

"Of course you want to spend Christmas with your parents, but I didn't expect you to leave two days before Christmas. I'm sure I sound like a selfish child, but I had hoped to at least spend Christmas Eve with you. I don't even have your gift. . ." She stopped short.

"I'm going to take gifts to my parents tomorrow, and then I will return by nightfall." He tried to hide his excitement. "I will be here to celebrate Christmas Eve and Christmas Day. I will be here to help you put up the Christmas pyramid, and I will be here to see you open my gifts to you." As some of the sparkle returned to her eyes, Frank relaxed his shoulders.

"Do you think your parents will be unhappy if you aren't at home with them for Christmas?"

He lifted her hand to his lips. "Trust me. They will be delighted to know I'm spending Christmas with you."

Favoring him with a smile that affected his heart like fire on ice, she whispered, "I do trust you, Frank."

Chapter 10

December 24

Throughout the seven colonies, the celebration of Christ's birth held special meaning. Like all of the families that lived in the villages, Karla and her relatives attended church on Christmas Eve, where they joined their voices together in familiar carols and listened to the Christmas story from the Bible. Afterward they returned to their homes where families continued their celebration by presenting gifts to one another. This year would be the same—except that Karla's mother would be unable to attend meeting with them.

Earlier in the day, Frank had helped Karla place a pasteboard nativity, complete with stand-up cutouts of Mary and Joseph and a three-dimensional manger, on a table in the hotel lobby, and she had tied red ribbon around several bunches of greens and placed them around the room. Warmth from the heating stove mingled with the fir and pine branches, scenting the room with the fragrances of the season. Before departing for church this evening, they'd unpacked the handmade Christmas pyramid her grandparents brought from

Germany many years ago and placed it on a walnut side table in the parlor.

The pyramid had been created by her grandfather and consisted of three graduated wooden tiers. A hand-carved nativity bedecked the first tier; farm animals and shepherds adorned the second level; and angels blowing their trumpets stood within the top tier. Candles surrounded the base of the pyramid, and once lit, the heat caused the propeller on top to turn. Though some families owned pyramids with four or five levels, Karla much preferred the one carved by her grandfather.

Her excitement mounted as she walked home from meeting beside Frank. "Since your Mutter couldn't attend meeting with us," her father said while hanging up his coat, "I think we will read from the Bible after we light the candles on the pyramid. She said she is feeling up to joining us for a bit tonight."

Her father's thoughtfulness reminded her of Frank. She'd never before connected how much the two men she loved had in common. It seemed a special gift from God that she should recognize they shared so many wonderful attributes on this wondrous night. Karla squeezed her father's arm. "I think Mutter would like that very much."

Stomping the snow from her feet, Karla called from the kitchen, "Mutter! We are home." She continued through the house and ran upstairs.

Her mother greeted her as she entered the room. "Church was gut?"

"Ja. Very gut, as usual." She gathered her mother's shawl from the back of the straight-back chair in the bedroom. "Vater will be up to help you to the parlor, and I will bring some hot tea and cookies upstairs. We will celebrate like always."

"You and Frank and Antje stay downstairs until your Vater calls to you." Her brows furrowed. "Is Paul downstairs with Antje?"

"Ja. He arrived as we were returning from church."

"Gut. All four of you should wait in the kitchen until your Vater says you may come upstairs."

Karla grinned. "Ja, Mutter, I know the rule." From the time they had been little children, they had waited in the kitchen until their father called them upstairs. He would open the parlor doors with a flourish, and they would gasp at the beauty of the lighted pyramid and the gifts that surrounded the pyramid table. Sometimes the presents would be covered with a sheet, and other times they would be wrapped in pieces of fabric their Mutter would later stitch into curtains or a shirtwaist.

While Karla brewed the tea and arranged cookies on the large platter, Frank watched from across the room. He picked up one of the cookies, took a bite, and gave a nod of approval. "I was wondering if you would like to receive your Christmas gift from me when we go upstairs or if you might like to open it down here while we're alone."

Karla pointed to the other room, where Antje and Paul were sitting on the couch in the lobby. "We're not exactly alone."

"I don't think we need to worry about Antje or Paul interrupting us." He rubbed his hands together with childlike anticipation.

"I'm guessing you want to give me your gift now, but the present I have for you is upstairs, and I cannot go up and get it. Mutter has already given me instructions that I'm not to come up there until Vater calls for us."

Frank crossed the room and removed a large package he had hidden in one of the cabinets where the family stored extra dishes and serving pieces. "I can wait for my gift until we go upstairs, but I want you to have this now." The package was wrapped in a large piece of dark fabric with tiny white dots arranged in triangles. "My

Mutter chose the fabric and thought you could make it into a new waist."

"It is lovely. Danke."

"The fabric is a gift from my Mutter and Vater."

Karla gasped. "Why would they give me a present?" She had sent a plate of marzipan with Frank when he went to visit his parents, but she had not expected them to send her a gift, especially something so costly.

"They had to use some of their credit at the store for this fabric." She ran her hand over the soft material, touched by their sacrifice. "But before you open that large package, I have another gift for you."

He handed her a small paper sack that had been carefully creased to keep the contents hidden. She unfolded the edges of the sack and slipped her hand inside. "Oh, Frank! I cannot believe this." She held a pair of mittens in her hand and stepped closer to the lamp. A red rose had been knitted into the center of each black mitten. "You made these? From the Homestead Rose pattern?"

His eyes shone with delight. "Ja, but don't look too close for mistakes. I had to have Brother Hueber help me with a few of the stitches in your Homestead Rose."

She slid the mittens onto her hands and held them up for him to see. "They fit just like they were made for me. But when did you have time to knit these mittens? They aren't what you were working on while I was quilting in the evenings."

"It isn't so busy in the apothecary with two of us to fill prescriptions. And Brother Hueber took great delight in watching me knit. He said that I could begin a pair of mittens for him once I had finished yours." Frank shook his head. "I told him I didn't think I wanted to make any more right away. That's when he demonstrated his own knitting abilities. He must have paid attention in strickschule better than I."

He motioned to the paper bag. "There is a note in there, too. I should have put it inside one of the mittens so you didn't miss it."

She reached inside the sack, withdrew the piece of paper, and read the carefully scripted note.

My dearest Karla,
I knitted these mittens to warm your hands, but I hope it
is my love that will warm your heart.

Merry Christmas,
with all my love,
Frank

Her breath caught as she read the words. "Danke, Frank. You could not have given me a gift that would have been any more special to me."

He extended his hand toward the fabric-wrapped gift. "I hope you will find this one a little more special than the mittens."

She truly didn't know how he could give her anything more special than the mittens, but when he extended the package toward her, she again traced her hand across the soft cotton fabric. She guessed that Frank's mother had tied the piece of red ribbon around the package. She had even tied a small sprig of pine into the bow. The extra gesture pleased Karla almost as much as the lovely piece of fabric that had been woven in the Amana cotton mill.

She carefully untied the ribbon and lifted away the fabric. Her fingers trembled as she examined what lay underneath the dark fabric. Beneath the bodice of her dress, her heart pounded an erratic beat. "Is this?" She couldn't bring herself to finish the question. It appeared to be a wedding quilt, but why would Frank give it to her?

"It is one of the wedding quilts my Mutter made for me years ago." He stepped closer and lifted her chin. "I want to marry you, Karla. Giving you the wedding quilt was my way of asking if you would consider having me as your husband."

Her chest constricted until she could barely breathe. "You want me to marry you?"

"Ja. I didn't think it would come as a great surprise. If so, I have been a miserable failure as a suitor." He gave her a heart-tilting smile.

Was this really happening?

"I didn't permit myself to dream I could be enough for you. I feared there were pretty girls who would be much better suited for someone such as you." Frank started to protest, but she touched her finger to his lips.

"It has taken me a while to learn that I am God's creation— exactly as He intended. I thought I didn't trust you, but I now know I hadn't fully placed my trust in God."

After inhaling a deep breath, he said, "So? I have already spoken to your Vater and asked permission to marry you. All that remains is for you to agree, and I will go before the elders and ask their permission."

In the other room, she could hear her sister's laughter. The aroma of the freshly brewed tea filled the kitchen, and the floorboards creaked overhead as her father moved about. She leaned against the worktable to gain her balance. Everything seemed completely normal—but it wasn't. Frank had already declared his love for her and now proposed marriage.

He grasped her hand. "We will trust each other, and together we will place our trust in God to help us build a strong marriage."

Karla inhaled a ragged breath and looked into his eyes. "How could I refuse such a proposal?"

A wide grin spread across Frank's face, and the spark returned to his eyes. "So you're saying ja?"

She squeezed his hand. "I'm saying ja."

With his hands on her waist, he lifted her until her feet no longer touched the wooden floor. "You have made my Christmas complete." Slowly he lowered her and captured her lips in a lingering kiss. "I'm the happiest man in all the Colonies."

"Karla! Antje! All of you! Bring the tea and come upstairs."

At the sound of her father's voice, Karla jumped. "I haven't gathered everything. They're going to wonder what I've been doing all this time."

Frank laughed. "I'm guessing they'll know."

Discussion Questions

1. Karla allowed herself to be defined by a fleeting remark made to her years ago. Have you personally struggled with overcoming a negative comment that was once made to or about you?

2. Do you struggle to see yourself as God's special creation with specific gifts He has given you to glorify Him? Is it because you haven't yet identified those gifts? Will you ask God to show you those gifts and then use them for Him? If you aren't using your gifts for Him, what is stopping you?

3. The comment that created Karla's insecurity was about her outward appearance. In today's world, appearance has become very important. What messages does the "world" send us about our appearance? How does this affect us? How do you overcome those feelings and push forward or counteract those messages to help a young person?

4. This story is set in the Amana Colonies where the people lived a communal lifestyle. Though many lived in separate housing with their families, everything was owned by the Society. In Amana, the residents were permitted to leave if they didn't want to remain a member of the community. What do you think the advantages of living in a communal society were? What were the disadvantages? Would you be happy or unhappy in such a community? Why?

5. Karla compares herself to her sister and some of the other young women in the community and finds herself lacking. What is the danger in comparing yourself to others? What circumstances cause these feelings, and how can you overcome them?

6. Karla feels Frank has betrayed her when he doesn't do as she asks when her mother becomes ill. Have you ever felt betrayed by a friend, coworker, or family member? How difficult was it to begin trusting after that incident? What tools did you use to once again open yourself to trusting others?

7. Karla overhears a bit of conversation between Frank and Gerta when she sees them at the pond. Karla makes some incorrect assumptions. Have you ever overheard a snippet of conversation and misconstrued what was said? If so, how did that incident affect you? How did it affect the other person or persons involved?

8. Did the Amana lifestyle make you long for a simpler life? What things could you do in your own life that would fulfill those longings?

9. You are the casting director for the film version of *Seams Like Love*. Who would you cast to play Karla? Frank? Gerta?

10. If you were in charge of writing epitaphs for these characters, what would you say about them?

Homestead Rose Mittens

In cleaning out the old Homestead General Store, built in 1863, a pair of moth-eaten black-and-red woolen mittens bearing an exquisite rose pattern was found in a discarded box. A summer was spent transcribing the pattern onto paper, line by line, by Karen Jenkins who lives in the Amana Colonies. The following is a slightly edited version of that original pair, which is currently on display at the Amana Heritage Museum Bookstore, Amana, Iowa.

LEVEL: Intermediate

MATERIALS: (2 sets) 4 double-pointed needles (sm/med adult mittens: cuff 2.25 mm/mitten 2.75 mm; med/lg: cuff 2.75 mm/ mitten 3.25 mm). Sport weight wool yarn, 75–100 grams.

GAUGE: 8 sts = 1"

Abbreviations: k2tog—knit 2 together; psso—pass slipped stitch over; rnd(s)—round(s); sl—slip; st(s)—stich(s)

Right Mitten

Cuff:

Using smaller needles, cast on 51 stitches. Divide among three needles. Pattern for cuff is K2, P1. 3 rnds color B, 3 rnds color A, 2 rnds color B, 2 rnds color A, 1 round each (B, A, B, A, B), 2 rnds color A, 2 rnds color B, 3 rnds color A, 3 rnds color B.

Body of Mitten:

Switch to larger needles while knitting Rnd 1.

Rnd 1: Knit entire round in color A.

Rnd 2: Knit 1A, 1B, 10A, 1B, 11A, 1B, 2A, (1B, 1A) 2 times, cast on 1A, 1A, 1B, 2A, 1B, (3A, 1B) 3X, 2A, 1B—(52 sts).

Rnd 3: Knit 1A, 1B, 4A, 4B, 2A, 1B, 4A, 3B, 3A, (1B, 1A) 3X, 1B, 3A, 1B, 1A, (3B, 1A) 4 times, 1B.

Rnd 4: Knit 1A, 2B, 2A, 1B, 1A, 4B, 2A, 1B, 2A, 3B, 5A, 1B, 2A, (1B, 1A) 2 times, cast on 1A, 1A, cast on 1A, 1A, 1B, 2A, (1B, 3A) 3 times, 1B, 2A, 1B—(54 sts).

Rnd 5: Knit 1A, 2B, 5A, 4B, 1A, 1B, 1A, 4B, 5A, 1B, 2A, 1B, 1A, 1B, 5A, 2B, (3A, 1B) 3 times, 3A, 2B.

Rnd 6: Knit 1A, 2B, 9A, 2B, 1A, 3B, 4A, 3B, 2A, 1B, 1A, 1B, 5A, 3B, (1A, 3B) 4 times.

Rnd 7: Knit 1A, 2B, 1A, 1B, 5A, 1B, 3A, 3B, 4A, 3B, 3A, (1B, 1A) 2 times, cast on 1A, 3A, cast on 1A, 1A, 2B, 3A, (1B, 3A) 3 times, 2B—(56 sts).

Rnd 8: Knit 1A, 2B, 1A, 1B, 3A, 2B, 5A, 1B, 4A, 4B, 3A, 1B, 1A, 1B, (3A, 1B) 2 times, 2A, 1B, (3A, 1B) 3 times, 2A, 1B.

Rnd 9: Knit 1A, 1B, 2A, 1B, 1A, 1B, 2A, 1B, 1A, 4B, 5A, 4B, 3A, (1B, 1A) 2 times, cast on 1A, 1A, 3B, 1A, cast on 1A, 1A, 1B, 1A, (3B, 1A) 4 times, 1B—(58 sts).

Rnd10: Knit 1A, 1B, 1A, 2B, 1A, 1B, 3A, 1B, 1A, 5B, 1A,

1B, 1A, 3B, 4A, 1B, 1A, (1B, 4A) 2 times, 1B, 2A, 1B, (3A, 1B) 3 times, 2A, 1B.

Rnd 11: Knit 1A, 4B, (1A, 1B) 2 times, 4A, 6B, 1A, 3B, 4A, (1B, 1A) 2 times, cast on 1A, 1A, 1B, 3A, 1B, 1A, cast on 1A, 1A, 2B, 3A, (1B, 3A) 3 times, 2B—(60 sts).

Rnd 12: Knit 1A, 1B, 3A, 2B, 1A, 1B, 2A, 1B, 6A, 1B, 1A, 2B, 5A, 1B, 1A, 1B, 2A, 3B, 1A, 3B, 2A, 3B, (1A, 3B) 4 times.

Rnd 13: Knit 1A, 1B, 4A, (1B, 1A) 3 times, 1B, 6A, 1B, 7A, (1B, 1A) 2 times, cast on 1A, 2A, 1B, 3A, 1B, 2A, cast on 1A, 1A, 2B, 3A, (1B, 3A) 3 times, 2B—(62sts).

Rnd 14: Knit 1A, 1B, 5A, 2B, 2A, 1B, 7A, 1B, 6A, 2B, 1A, 1B, 2A, 1B, (3A, 1B) 2 times, (2A, 1B) 2 times, (3A, 1B) 3 times, 2A, 1B.

Rnd 15: Knit 1A, 1B, 2A, 5B, 2A, 1B, 7A, 1B, 6A, 2B, 1A, 1B, 1A, cast on 1A, 3B, (1A, 3B) 2 times, 1A, cast on 1A, 1B, 1A, (3B, 1A) 4 times, 1B—(64 sts).

Rnd 16: Knit 1A, 1B, 9A, 1B, 8A, 1B, 3A, 1B, 1A, 2B, 1A, 1B, (3A, 1B) 4 times, 2A, 1B, (3A, 1B) 3 times, 2A, 1B.

Rnd 17: Knit 1A, 1B, 11A, 4B, (3A, 1B) 2 times, 1A, 2B, 1A, 1B, 1A, cast on 1A, (1B, 3A) 3 times, 1B, 1A, cast on 1A, 2B, (3A, 1B) 3 times, 3A, 2B—(66 sts).

Rnd 18: Knit 1A, 1B, 3A, 1B, 4A, 2B, 1A, 5B, 2A, 1B, 3A, 1B, 1A, 2B, 1A, 1B, (1A, 3B) 9 times.

Rnd 19: Knit 1A, (1B, 3A) 2 times, 10B, 1A, 1B, 3A, 1B, 2A, 1B, 1A, 1B, 2A, (1B, 3A) 3 times, 1B, 2A, 2B, (3A, 1B) 3 times, 3A, 2B.

Rnd 20: Knit 1A, 1B, 3A, 1B, 2A, 12B, 4A, 1B, 2A, 1B, 1A, 1B, slip next 18 sts onto stitch holder, (cast on 2A, 1B, 3A, 1B, 1A), finish round with 2A, 1B, (3A, 1B) 3 times, 2A, 1B—(56 sts).

Rnd 21: Knit 1A, 1B, 3A, 1B, 2A, 2B, 5A, 5B, 4A, 1B, 2A, (1B, 1A) 2 times, (3B, 1A) 6 times, 1B.

Rnd 22: Knit 1A, 1B, 3A, 1B, 2A, 1B, 1A, 5B, 1A, 6B, 5A, 1B, 1A, 1B, 2A, 1B, (3A, 1B) 5 times, 2A, 1B.

Rnd 23: Knit 1A, 1B, 3A, (1B, 1A) 2 times, 7B, 1A, 5B, 5A, 1B, 1A, 2B, 3A, (1B, 3A) 5 times, 2B.

Rnd 24: Knit 1A, 1B, 5A, 1B, 1A, 8B, 1A, 2B, 3A, (1B, 1A) 3 times, (3B, 1A) 6 times, 3B.

Rnd 25: Knit 1A, 1B, 6A, 9B, 1A, 3B, 3A, 1B, 2A, 1B, 1A, 2B, (3A, 1B) 5 times, 3A, 2B.

Rnd 26: Knit 1A, 1B, 6A, 9B, 1A, 3B, 3A, 1B, 2A, 1B, 1A, 1B, 2A, (1B, 3A) 5 times, 1B, 2A, 1B.

Rnd 27: Knit 1A, 2B, 5A, 2B, 2A, 5B, 1A, 3B, 5A, 2B, 1A, 1B, (1A, 3B) 6 times, 1A, 1B.

Rnd 28: Knit 1A, 2B, 6A, 1B, 2A, 4B, 1A, 3B, 6A, 2B, 1A, 1B, 2A, (1B, 3A) 5 times, 1B, 2A, 1B.

Rnd 29: Knit 1A, 2B, 2A, 1B, 4A, 4B, 2A, 3B, 5A, 1B, (1A, 2B) 2 times, (3A, 1B) 5 times, 3A, 2B.

Rnd 30: Knit 1A, 2B, (2A, 1B) 2 times, 15A, 1B, 1A, 2B, (1A, 3B) 7 times.

Rnd 31: Knit 1A, 2B, (1A, 1B) 3 times, 13A, (1B, 1A) 2 times, 2B, 1A, 2B, (3A, 1B) 5 times, 3A, 2B.

Rnd 32: Knit 1A, 1B, 6A, 1B, 13A, 1B, 1A, 2B, (1A, 1B) 2 times, 2A, (1B, 3A) 5 times, 1B, 2A, 1B.

Rnd 33: Knit 1A, 1B, 6A, 1B, 11A, (1B, 1A) 2 times, 4B, 1A, 1B, (1A, 3B) 6 times, 1A, 1B.

Rnd 34: Knit 1A, 1B, 7A, 1B, 10A, 1B, 1A, 2B, 3A, 1B, 1A, 1B, 2A, (1B, 3A) 5 times, 1B, 2A, 1B.

Rnd 35: Knit (1A, 1B) 2 times, 5A, 1B, 10A, 1B, 1A, 6B, 1A, 2B, (3A, 1B) 5 times, 3A, 2B.

Rnd 36: Knit (1A, 1B) 2 times, 5A, 2B, 9A, 2B, 5A, 1B, (1A, 3B) 7 times.

Rnd 37: Knit 1A, 2B, 1A, 1B, 2A, 2B, 1A, 6B, 4A, 5B, 2A, 1B,

1A, 2B, (3A, 1B) 5 times, 3A, 2B.

Rnd 38: Knit 1A, 1B, 4A, 3B, 1A, 1B, 1A, 5B, 1A, 1B, 8A, 1B, 1A, 1B, 2A, (1B, 3A) 5 times, 1B, 2A, 1B.

Rnd 39: Knit 1A, 1B, 4A, 3B, 2A, 1B, 2A, 4B, 9A, (1B, 1A) 2 times, (3B, 1A) 6 times, 1B.

Rnd 40: Knit 1A, 1B, 3A, 4B, 3A, 1B, 14A, 1B, 1A, 1B, 2A, (1B, 3A) 5 times, 1B, 2A, 1B.

Rnd 41: Knit 1A, 1B, 3A, 3B, 5A, 1B, 13A, 1B, 1A, 2B, (3A, 1B) 5 times, 3A, 2B.

Rnd 42: Knit 1A, 1B, 2A, 3B, 5A, 3B, 12A, 1B, 1A, (3B, 1A) 6 times, 3B.

Rnd 43: Knit 1A, 1B, 9A, 3B, 1A, 2B, 10A, 1B, 1A, 2B, (3A, 1B) 5 times, 3A, 2B.

Rnd 44: Knit 1A, 1B, 2A, 1B, 6A, 3B, 1A, 1B, 1A, 4B, 6A, 1B, 1A, 1B, 2A, (1B, 3A) 5 times, 1B, 2A, 1B.

Rnd 45: Knit 1A, 1B, 2A, 1B, 5A, 3B, 2A, 1B, 2A, 4B, 1A, 1B, 3A, (1B, 1A) 2 times, (3B, 1A) 6 times, 1B.

Rnd 46: Knit (1A, 1B) 3 times, 3A, 3B, 4A, 1B, 2A, 4B, 4A, 1B, 1A, 1B, 2A, (1B, 3A) 5 times, 1B, 2A, 1B.

Rnd 47: Knit 1A, 1B, 7A, 3B, 3A, 1B, 1A, 1B, 2A, 2B, 5A, 1B, 1A, 2B, (3A, 1B) 5 times, 3A, 2B.

Slip end stitch from 1st needle to 3rd needle.

Rnd 48: Sl 1, knit 1B, psso, 4A, 3B, 10A, 1B, 5A, k2tog B, sl 1, knit 1A, psso, 2B, (1A, 3B) 5 times, 1A, 2B, k2tog A—(52 sts).

Rnd 49: Sl 1, knit 1B, psso, 21A, k2tog B, sl 1, knit 1A, psso, (3A, 1B) 5 times, 3A, k2tog A—(48 sts).

Rnd 50: Sl 1, knit 1B, psso, 19A, k2og B, sl 1, knit 1A, psso, (1B, 3A) 5 times, 1B, k2tog A—(44 sts).

Rnd 51: Sl 1, knit 1B, psso, 4A, 1B, 12A, k2tog B, sl 1, knit 1A, psso, 1B, (1A, 3B) 4 times, 1A, 1B, k2tog A—(40 sts).

Rnd 52: Sl 1, knit 1B, psso, 3A, 1B, 11A, k2tog B, sl 1, knit

1A, psso, 2A, (1B, 3A) 3 times, 1B, 2A, k2tog A—(36 sts).

Rnd 53: Sl 1, knit 1B, psso, (1A, 1B) 2 times, 9A, k2tog B, sl 1, knit 1A, psso, (3A, 1B) 3 times, 3A, k2tog A—(32 sts).

Rnd 54: Sl 1, knit 1B, psso, 4A, 1B, 6A, k2tog B, sl 1, knit 1A, psso, (1A, 3B) 3 times, 1A, k2tog A—(28 sts).

Rnd 55: Sl 1, knit 1B, psso, 3A, 1B, 5A, k2tog B, sl 1, knit 1A, psso, 1A, (1B, 3A) 2 times, 1B, 1A, k2tog A—(24 sts).

Rnd 56: Sl 1, knit 1B, psso, (1A, 1B) 2 times, 3A, k2tog B, sl 1, knit 1A, psso, 2A, 1B, 3A, 1B, 2A, k2tog A—(20 sts).

Rnd 57: Sl 1, knit 1B, psso, 5A, k2tog B, sl 1, knit 1A, psso, 3B, 1A, 3B, k2tog A—(16 sts).

Rnd 58: Sl 1, knit 1B, psso, 3A, k2tog B, sl 1, knit 1A, psso, 1B, 3A, 1B, k2tog A—(12 sts).

Rnd 59: Sl 1, knit 1B, psso, 1B, k2tog B, sl 1, knit 1A, psso, 3A, k2tog A—(8 sts).

Cut yarn with enough length to draw through final 8 stitches with crochet hook, pulling yarn through top into mitten's interior and gently tightening.

Thumb:

Continue using larger needles. Divide 18 held stitches evenly onto 2 needles. Pick up 8 stitches from cast-on edge onto 3rd needle using crochet hook. End with color B.

Rnd 1: (1B, 3A) 4 times, k2tog B, 3A, 1B, k2tog A, 2A—(24 sts).

Rnd 2: 2B, (1A, 3B) 5 times, 1A, 1B.

Rnd 3: (1B, 3A) 6 times.

Rnd 4: 2A, (1B, 3A) 5 times, 1B, 1A.

Rnd 5: (1A, 3B) 6 times.

Rnd 6: Repeat Rnd 4.

Rnd 7: Repeat Rnd 3.

Rnd 8: Repeat Rnd 2.

Rnd 9: Repeat Rnd 3.

Rnd 10: Repeat Rnd 4.

Rnd 11: Repeat Rnd 5.

Rnd 12: Repeat Rnd 4.

Rnd 13: Repeat Rnd 3.

Rnd 14: Repeat Rnd 2.

Rnd 15: Repeat Rnd 3.

Rnd 16: (k2tog A, 1B, 1A) 6 times—(18 sts).

Rnd 17: (k2tog A, 1B) 6 times—(12 sts).

Rnd 18: (k2tog A) 6 times—(6 sts).

Cut yarn with enough length to draw through final 6 stitches with crochet hook, pulling yarn through top into thumb's interior and gently tightening.

Left Mitten

Cuff: Same as for right mitten.

Body of Mitten: Reverse all of the above, including sl, k, psso vs. k2tog. Slip last stitch from 3rd needle to 1st needle after Rnd 47.

Thumb: Same as for right mitten. Begin with k2tog in B and continue as above, making adjustment to end Rnd 1 with 24 sts.

Prune Drop Cookies

(Zwetchen Kecks)

⅔ cup shortening or butter
1 cup brown sugar
1 cup white sugar
2 eggs, beaten
½ cup milk, mix in ½ teaspoon soda
1 cup prunes, chopped and cooked
3½ cups flour
1 teaspoon baking powder
1 teaspoon cinnamon
¼ teaspoon salt
½ cup nuts, chopped

Cream shortening and sugars. Add beaten eggs and mix well. Add milk and remaining ingredients. Mix and drop by teaspoonfuls on greased cookie sheet. Bake 15 minutes at 350 degrees.

Date Cookies

(*Dattel Kecks*)

3 eggs
1 cup sugar
1 cup flour
1 teaspoon baking powder
⅛ teaspoon salt
¼ teaspoon cinnamon
4 tablespoons butter, melted
1 teaspoon vanilla
2 cups dates, chopped
1 cup nuts, chopped
Confectioners' sugar

Beat eggs until light. Gradually add sugar and blend well. Add flour, baking powder, salt, and cinnamon to egg mixture, beating well. Add melted butter and beat well. Stir in vanilla. Fold in dates and nuts. Pour into greased and floured 9x13-inch pan. Bake 25 minutes at 350 degrees. When cool, cut into bars and sift confectioners' sugar over all.

 Judith Miller is an award-winning author whose avid research and love for history are reflected in her novels, many of which have appeared on the CBA bestseller lists. Judy makes her home in Topeka, Kansas.

A Patchwork Love

Stephanie Grace Whitson

Acknowledgments

Special thanks to the amazing Jo Morton (jomortonquilts.com)
for providing the Four Patch doll quilt pattern.

Chapter 1

Omaha, Nebraska, 1875

It took every ounce of Jane McClure's waning faith to put her last two coins into the horse-drawn trolley driver's hand. Normally she and ten-year-old Molly would have walked to the train station this evening. But Molly had developed a slight cough as the temperature plummeted, and Jane was determined that she not "come down with anything." Mr. Huggins was kind but a bit remote when it came to Molly, and nothing must stand in the way of their enjoying a pleasant holiday together—as if they were a family. He'd enclosed two tickets in his recent letter—a letter that sounded. . .*hopeful.* He'd even mentioned how much Molly would enjoy seeing the Christmas decorations in Denver's department store windows. For Mr. Huggins to be thinking of how to please Molly was a good sign. And so Jane was spending the last of her money for a ride to the train station. Out of the cold. For Molly's sake.

The driver waved them on board the empty car with a teasing comment about the chilly fog descending over the city. "Just look at it, won't you?" He waved around them. "The perfect atmosphere for magic!" He winked at Molly. "Tell the truth now, miss. You're a princess and this old car is soon to become a golden coach." He called out to the gray horse. "Hear that, yer majesty? It's a golden harness for ye, and a velvet cape for myself!" The horse shook its head and whickered, as if answering the old man in the battered top hat.

Molly giggled and led the way on board, sliding into a seat near the driver. Jane plopped their two carpetbags on an empty seat and sat down, tugging Molly's knit cap down over her ears.

"All right, ladies," the driver called out, "next stop, Omaha City's train station—with stops along the way for other fares, of course." With a tip of his hat and a curious smacking sound to the horse, he took up the reins, and they were off.

When Molly put a mittened hand to her mouth to suppress a cough, Jane scolded herself, even as she concentrated on the familiar scenery passing by the plodding car. *I should have put the last of that wood in the stove this afternoon.* Why couldn't she seem to conquer her fear at the prospect of using up the last of things? It had wound itself into the fabric of her every day in recent weeks. Three bits of wood in the woodbox meant they wouldn't freeze. Even one coin in her threadbare change purse meant they weren't destitute. And as long as there was a bit of cheese and a package of biscuits in the cupboard, hunger couldn't win.

But the cupboard's bare now. That's the last of the cheese and biscuits in your bag. Of course using the last of the food made sense today. They wouldn't be back for at least a week, and food must not go to waste. But wood for the stove was different. She'd be able to build a fire when they got back. On the other hand. . .if things went perfectly, perhaps they wouldn't have to come back. Should Mr. Huggins's hopeful tone bear fruit, perhaps they'd be wiring

Mrs. Abernathy to pack up the few things in their rooms and ship them to Denver.

Molly coughed again and snuggled close. Jane hugged her bony shoulders. "Quite the adventure we're having, isn't it? Money for a ride to the station *and* passage to Denver." She forced anticipation into her voice. "Mrs. Abernathy says Denver is 'big and bustling.' And Mr. Huggins said he's looking forward to showing you the Christmas displays in the department store windows."

Molly sniffed. "Wicked," she said, and shrugged a bit of distance between herself and her mother.

"I beg your pardon?"

Molly repeated the word. "Mrs. Abernathy said that Denver is big and bustling. . .and *wicked*." She cleared her throat. "I don't know why we have to go."

The ever-present knot in Jane's stomach tightened. She hadn't realized just how worried she'd been of late, until Howard Huggins sent those train tickets, and she nearly cried with relief. "Well. . ." She paused. "It would be rude not to accept such a generous gift. And won't it be nice to see someplace new? Someplace. . .exciting?"

"I suppose so." Molly sat back, then murmured, "I wish Sarah hadn't moved away. She said she'd write." She peered up at Jane. "What if her letter comes and we're gone?"

"Mrs. Abernathy will save it, and it'll be waiting when we get back. Probably tucked under the door." *If we come back.*

With a "Whoa" and a tug on the reins, the driver pulled the team up alongside the walkway leading to the train station entrance. Grabbing hers and Molly's bags, Jane thanked the driver and headed down the steps with Molly close behind. She'd just let go of the bar by the step when she realized that the evening mist was beginning to freeze. One foot found purchase. The other did not. Grabbing for something—anything—to keep from falling,

Jane turned back toward the horse car, but she was too far away. As she fell, she shouted a warning at Molly. Molly took care, but Jane lost the battle to stay upright.

For a moment, everything faded away. When things began to unscramble, Jane realized she was sitting in a most unladylike position, legs sprawled, bonnet askew. Molly crouched next to her, frightened tears shining in her blue eyes. Blinking, Jane concentrated on Molly's terrified "Mama! Mama!"

"It's all right. . .I–I'm. . .all right." Jane reached up to straighten her bonnet, grateful to see that Molly was holding on to both their bags. It wouldn't do to lose the only decent things they owned to some thief taking advantage of the ice and the evening shadows.

"Here now, miss."

A hand cupped her elbow, and the aroma of stale tobacco smoke wafted down as the driver tried to help her up. Kind eyes shone from beneath his bushy white eyebrows as he asked, "You all right?"

"I—I think so," she said. But when she tried to stand, she wasn't sure what hurt more, her right knee. . .her left ankle. . .or the elbow the driver held while helping her back to her feet.

"I told one of the porters they needed to spread sand out here. I could feel the temperature dropping long before it did. My knees always give warning, and they've been killing me all day. But did anyone listen? And now. . .now they've caused a lovely lady to be injured."

"Really. . .I'm all right." Was she bleeding through her last pair of good stockings? Had she torn anything? She wasn't bent on deceiving anyone, but she saw no need to let Mr. Huggins see *destitution* when she and Molly stepped off the train. Thank goodness she'd packed a mending kit. Mr. Huggins had to know she wasn't well off. He'd insisted on seeing her back to the boardinghouse one evening during his brief visit to Omaha a few weeks ago. It was obvious from her lodging that Jane had suffered a setback. Still, Mr. Huggins had continued to write. And as the weeks wore on and their situation grew more and more desperate. . .well. This trip simply had to work out.

Her heart pounding, Jane suppressed a groan as pain shot up both legs. She forced a bright smile. "Thank you for being so kind. Please don't let me make you late for your next fare. We'll be fine." She reached for the larger of the two bags and forced another smile for Molly's sake. *Please, God, You know I don't have the fare to pay for a ride back to the boardinghouse. We have to get on that train.*

The driver looked doubtfully toward the station, then back at the trolley, where three people had now taken seats.

"I'll be fine," Jane repeated as she reached for Molly's hand. "We'll take our time."

"See that you do," the old man said, sliding the sole of one boot across the pavement. "It's slick enough to go coasting without the sled." With a nod and a tip of his hat, he climbed aboard.

Jane let go of Molly's hand long enough to straighten her bruised elbow. "Did I tear my sleeve?" she asked, grateful when Molly inspected it, then shook her head. She shifted her weight to her right leg and tested her left ankle. The ankle seemed all right. The knee was another matter. In fact, it nearly gave way. With a quick little gasp, she put her hand on Molly's shoulder to steady herself. The look of panic on the child's face strengthened her resolve.

"A twisted knee is *not* going to keep us from our adventure." Jane took a deep breath, noticing for the first time the pools of light dotting the slick surface as night fell and the new city gaslights lit up. "We have to take small steps on the ice anyway. Just go slow. I'm sure I'll feel better once I've loosened it up a little. It'll be warmer inside. That will help, too." Leading with her left foot, she clenched her teeth and limped her way toward the station.

Once inside, she was afraid to pause. They had to get on that train. She could ice her knee and wrap it and do whatever else might be required once they rolled out of the station, but she could not let a little thing like a silly fall keep her from the promise represented by Mr. Howard Huggins. If this trip worked out, it could mean an end to Jane's constant worries. They'd have enough. Enough food. Enough fuel. No more days struggling to keep Molly from realizing her mother had skipped a meal to feed her. No more excuses about being tired and needing to turn in early, when the real reason for heading for bed was a lack of fuel and a need to get warm.

Mr. Huggins might be a bit shorter than Jane and a bit portly and a bit—well—*quite* bald, but he was forward-thinking enough to believe in education for women. In fact, he'd said there was a very good boarding school they could visit with Molly in mind "if things worked out." And Jane was determined to see that "things worked out." Mr. Huggins might not be a knight in shining armor, but he seemed kind, and a woman could learn to love. Friendship was more important than passion anyway.

Pushing against the pain, Jane led the way through the station and to the track, pausing just long enough to look up at the board indicating that the train to Denver was on—of course—the far track. She peered in that direction. Less than a city block. Surely she could walk that far.

"We shouldn't go," Molly said. "You're hurt, and Mr. Huggins doesn't even *like* me." Her voice wavered. She tugged at her scarf, then used it to cover her mouth while she coughed.

"Mr. Huggins," Jane said with more certainty than she felt, "is actually rather fond of you. It's just that he hasn't been around ten-year-old girls. He doesn't quite know how to— Well, he's a bit shy."

Molly tipped her head and met Jane's gaze with a doubtful eye.

"You aren't the only one in the world who's shy, Molly. Even grown-ups can be shy."

"I'm not *shy*," Molly protested. "I'm just. . .quiet around people I don't know."

"Well, then. You should be even more excited about this trip, because once you've had the opportunity to get to know him, I'm quite certain you'll discover that Mr. Huggins has many admirable traits. And he will discover that *you*"—Jane tapped the tip of the freckled nose—"are *wondermous*." When Molly giggled, Jane smiled and nodded at the far track. "Let's make our way to the train before you turn into a *frozen* wondermous." She clenched her teeth and willed herself to walk.

Somehow they made it onto the train, although Jane couldn't help letting out a grunt or two with the effort of climbing aboard. To make it up the last step, she placed her carpetbag at the top of the stairs, grasped the railing with both hands, and hopped up so she could land on her good—or at least her less injured—leg. She managed to make a joke that put a smile on Molly's troubled face and then hobbled to the first seat they came to in the emigrant car, where they'd be until night after next.

Mr. Huggins might want them to come, but he hadn't seen his way to providing berths in the sleeping car. That had been a disappointment, but Jane reminded herself that thrift was an admirable quality. After all, if Stephen had been a bit thriftier, his widow and child might not have found themselves pinching pennies until they— *Stop resenting poor Stephen, God rest his soul. He thought that investment was a good idea.*

As passengers filtered onto the car and settled in for the long ride ahead, Jane entertained Molly by whispering stories. The tall man with the ridiculous mustache was a prince in disguise. The portly middle-aged woman had once trained elephants in the circus. As for the gentleman across the aisle who had tipped his hat and made

Jane blush—well. Jane didn't know what to say about him, until Molly nudged her and offered the opinion that he seemed much friendlier than Mr. Huggins. By then Jane's throbbing knee was challenging her forced good cheer.

"You are simply going to have to trust me in the matter of Mr. Huggins. I've said all I'm going to say on that subject." As the train whistle blew, announcing their departure, she reached into her bag and withdrew the book she'd been saving for the long trip. "Would you like me to read to you?"

Molly shrugged. "I guess."

"I beg your pardon?"

"Yes, ma'am."

"That's better." Jane traced the gilt oval on the dark cover. "I've been saving this until you were old enough to enjoy it."

Molly gazed down at the book. "Where's it been?"

Jane smiled. "At the very bottom of the little trunk I keep under my bed." She paused. "I was seventeen when this book was new." She cleared her throat. "Your grandmother and I took turns reading it to one another through a very long winter when the snow piled up against the windows and we huddled next to the stove trying to keep warm." The memory of that horrible, hungry, snowbound winter still made her shiver.

The train picked up speed, and finally they were leaving the bluffs along the river and heading out onto the Nebraska prairie. The flickering light in the train car and the rhythmic rocking helped Jane ignore her throbbing knee. She'd check it later when Molly was asleep.

Opening the book, she began to read. "'Christmas won't be Christmas without any presents, grumbled Jo. . . .'"

Chapter 2

Molly dozed off somewhere in the middle of the March girls' Christmas performance of an "Operatic Tragedy." Jane realized the child had fallen asleep only when a soft snore sounded and was then punctuated by yet another cough—this one accompanied by a significant amount of rumbling in Molly's chest. A woman a few seats away glanced at Jane with a frown. Closing *Little Women*, Jane slipped it into her carpetbag, then slid over and pulled Molly closer, offering her lap as a pillow.

She glanced around the train car. Most of the passengers who hadn't disembarked at various stops along the way had headed for the dining car with murmured comments about the roast beef or a "nice cup of tea." When Molly coughed again, Jane wished tea were an option for them. Mrs. Abernathy had given them an early supper at the boardinghouse. If they were very careful about portioning out the cheese and crackers, they'd be only hungry and not ravenous when the train finally pulled into the station in Denver. Jane could only hope that Mr. Huggins would be amenable to a late welcome supper. In the meantime. . .there would be no hot tea. . .and no real treatment for her swollen knee either. She could, however, get a look at it in the necessary.

Tucking her carpet bag beneath Molly's head for a makeshift pillow, Jane grasped the edge of the seat to keep her balance, then hopped the few feet to the necessary, hoping the handful of passengers still in the car wouldn't notice the ridiculous performance. Once inside, she lifted her foot and braced it on the rim of the commode as she leaned back against the wall and pulled her skirt up to see. . . *Oh dear.* She hadn't bled through her stockings. She'd ripped a hole large enough to expose her entire knee. Not only had it ballooned in the last couple of hours; it was also beginning to turn several shades of purple and green. Try as she would, Jane couldn't straighten it. *Probably the swelling.* Looking at it seemed to make the pain worse. Trembling, she closed her eyes and leaned against the wall, moistening her lips and closing her eyes. *All you have to do is make it to Denver.*

Somehow she managed to hobble back to her seat and retrieve her mending kit. She was trying to gather courage to move again when a porter came into the car. His mellow voice was kind as he held out a pillow and blanket "for the young lady."

Jane shook her head. "That's very kind, but we can't—"

"Courtesy of the Union Pacific," he said with a wink.

Jane could have hugged him. Instead, she snuggled the blanket around Molly.

"Name's Henry, ma'am," the porter said. "You need anything else, you let me know. I'm on all the way to Denver." When Molly stirred and coughed, he glanced her way, then back at Jane. "Tea with lemon and honey? Be happy to bring some on my way through next time."

"That's very kind of you, but we—"She swallowed the words

don't have any money and forced a smile. "We'll be fine." She busied herself smoothing Molly's blanket and blinked away desperate tears. The porter went on his way.

As the evening wore on, Jane learned that most of the people in the car had rented sleeping berths. Only one seedy-looking couple at the far end of the car had unfolded their seats to arrange makeshift sleeping quarters on the train car. Once again, Jane fought the temptation to wonder about the extent of Mr. Huggins's devotion. Why couldn't he have arranged for a berth? She and Molly would be on the train for two nights.

As the train swayed and the lamp the porter had turned down on his way through the car cast only the faintest glow, Jane once again made her way into the necessary. Removing her gloves, she laid them on the edge of the wash basin and lifted her skirt, fumbling beneath her bustle in a vain attempt to untie the ribbon holding her petticoat up.

The train swayed and she nearly lost her balance. She finally gave up and, taking her mending scissors, felt her way to cutting off one leg of her drawers, which she then cut into strips. Tying the strips together, she bound her injured knee as best she could, happy that the effort did seem to ease the pain a bit. It would help keep the swelling down. At least she hoped so.

Sacrificing her drawers was humiliating. But then, who would know? She supposed it was better to sacrifice drawers than a petticoat. Now that she thought about it, the drawers were definitely the way to go. An observant man might notice the absence of a petticoat. Was Mr. Huggins observant? The thought made Jane blush.

Someone knocked on the door. "You baking a cake in there? There's other people on the train, ya know."

Jane opened the door and apologized. It took all her willpower not to cry out in pain as she attempted to take a normal step into the aisle. The other woman didn't notice, merely brushed past Jane and slammed the door, quite literally almost in her face. Blinking back more tears, Jane hobbled back to her seat. Grabbing the pillow the porter had left behind, she used it to cushion her knee as she settled opposite Molly on the bench vacated by passengers who'd disembarked at the last stop. Leaning her head against the frosted window, she closed her eyes and fell instantly asleep.

❧

Jane started awake. *Gray light.* She glanced over at Molly, still fast asleep, only the top of her head showing from beneath the blanket supplied by the kindly porter. What time could it be? She gazed about the car. Had the others gone to breakfast? Her stomach growled at the thought. She moved gingerly, all thought on her injured knee as she lowered her feet to the floor. Was it her imagination, or did her knee hurt less? *Please let it be better. Please.*

She swiped at the window, wondering what stop they were at now. *Snow.* Bending low, she whispered at Molly's still form, "Someone is frosting the world with white, princess. It's snowing!"

Molly stirred. With an audible sigh, she tugged the blanket down and peered over the edge at Jane, croaking, "Snow?"

Jane nodded as she reached for the carpetbag tucked beneath their seat. "Snow and breakfast, if you're hungry."

Molly shook her head. Turning onto her side, she snuggled back out of sight. Jane broke off a bit of bread and had popped it into her mouth just as the porter made his appearance, bearing a steaming mug of tea.

"For the little lady," he said, then offered it to Jane. "Or her mama, since the little lady is obviously not ready for breakfast." He nodded toward Molly. "I was glad to note a distinct absence of coughing as I passed through in the night."

Jane nodded, even as she declined the tea.

"Might as well drink it. You'll be doing me a favor, actually. Someone in the next car ordered it, then changed their mind and decided to head up to the dining car. Said to just toss it out." He looked down at the cup. Shook his head. "Never did understand how a body could add cream to a perfectly good cup of black tea." He held it out. "Shame to let it go to waste." When Jane finally relented, the porter nodded. "Next stop is Grand Island. They put on a good breakfast if you're interested."

"Thank you, but we've brought everything we need."

The porter nodded again and continued on his way. Jane settled back to stare out the window at the empty landscape and the swirling snow, sighing with pleasure as the warm tea coursed down her parched throat.

❧

Molly was still asleep when the train stopped at the place called Grand Island. Peering through the snow, Jane could see evidence of neither an island nor anything grand. When she said as much to the porter, he laughed.

"Can't speak to the idea of 'grand,' but there is an island in the middle of the river. Lovely when it's warm." He cocked his head at the still-sleeping Molly. "That little miss is quite the little bedbug, isn't she?"

"She was coming down with a cold when we left home. Hopefully she's mending so she can enjoy the sights in Denver."

The porter nodded. "I might ask you to move up to the Pullman if no one climbs aboard at the next stop. There's no reason for the two of you to be back here all alone, and to tell the truth, it'll lighten my load if I only have to keep one car warm. Word from up ahead is we're headed into quite a storm. Thermometer's dropping

137

fast at Kearney Junction."

Jane glanced out at the snow drifting softly to the earth.

"I know. It doesn't look like much, but there's nothing to stop the wind out here, and things can change fast." The porter smiled. "Nothing to worry about. Even if we have to stop over at one of the stations and wait for the storm to blow by, the UP takes good care of its folks." With a tip of his cap, he was on his way.

The train headed into the storm.

❧

Molly woke not long after the snow began to fall in earnest, grimacing as she stretched her arms above her head.

"It's about time you woke up." Jane smiled and nodded outside. "It's still snowing."

Molly swiped a hand across the window to clear the steam away. "Wow." She looked back at Jane, her cheeks red, her eyes bright with. . .something besides excitement.

Instinctively, Jane pressed her palm to Molly's forehead. "Tell me how you feel."

Molly frowned. When she opened her mouth to answer, her words were cut off by a dry, raspy cough. She grimaced. "My throat hurts. And. . .everything."

"Everything?"

Molly nodded. "Everything hurts."

And just like that, money and Mr. Huggins and the snowstorm became the least of Jane's worries.

❧

True to his word, the porter checked back with them after two more stops and suggested they move to the Pullman. "We've only two more passengers," he explained, "and they're getting off at Gibbon. Shame to have that big fancy car and no one enjoying it."

"I appreciate it," Jane said. "Really, I do. But Molly isn't feeling well, and I—well, I slipped on the ice at Omaha, and I'm afraid I'm about as useful as a lame horse at the moment. I'm sorry to make you walk the length of the train just because of us, but I don't think—"

"How about I carry the young miss, and you lean on my arm?" The man didn't wait for Jane's reply before scooping Molly up. "She's light as a feather. Reminds me of my little gal waiting at home." With obvious practice, he shifted Molly to his right shoulder so that his left arm was free to assist Jane. He smiled. "I guarantee you'll love the Pullman."

Clutching their bags with her left hand, Jane tucked her right hand beneath the man's arm and hung on. When they traversed the open space between the cars, she shivered. The thermometer was most definitely dropping. She glanced at the landscape, but swirling snow obscured everything.

The porter opened the door to the Pullman. Jane stared in amazement at the opulence— the brass fittings, the plush seats, the velvet drapes, the painted murals up above. Molly barely woke as the porter settled her in one of the overstuffed chairs while he made up a berth, then moved her once he had it ready. With Molly settled in, he stood back with a satisfied smile. "That's better, don't you think?"

"It's wonderful," Jane agreed. "I don't know how to thank you."

The porter smiled as he moved a chair close to Molly's berth so Jane could stay close. "You just did, ma'am. If my wife and child were headed into a blizzard alone, I'd hope someone would see to their needs. 'Do unto others'—isn't that what the Good Book says?"

A stern male voice sounded from the front of the car, someone demanding the coffee he'd asked for "long ago."

With a little salute, the porter headed off, leaving Jane to wonder at her good fortune, even as she worried over Molly's red cheeks, the fringe of damp curls about her face, and the occasional whimper that sounded as she slept.

Chapter 3

The grumpy passenger who'd demanded so much of Henry's attention disembarked at Kearney Junction midmorning. From where Jane sat by Molly's berth, all she could see of the train station was a dark smudge in a world of white. Moments after the train headed out, Molly began to toss and turn. The porter brought more tea with honey, insisting that the UP would have his head if he didn't offer comfort for an ailing child. "So please, ma'am, let's not have any more arguments about the matter," he said, and Jane relented. When Molly grimaced with each swallow, Jane's stomach clenched a little more.

A few minutes later Molly whimpered for Katie, and Jane produced the rumpled rag doll with growing concern. Molly had been going through an I'm-too-grown-up-for-dolls phase. They'd only stuffed the doll in her carpetbag at the last minute. Now Jane sighed, alternately grateful for the comfort the beloved doll could give and worried over just how sick Molly was going to get.

Moments later, when Jane handed Molly's empty teacup over,

Henry said, "Next stop is Elm Creek. There's not much there save the store and the railroad eating house. But we can wire ahead for you and have the doctor at Plum Creek meet us. We'll pull in there about 1:30 this afternoon if the storm doesn't cause any delays."

Jane shook her head. "I haven't any way to pay a doctor. Unless—" Did she dare presume on Mr. Huggins to wire money? She swallowed and looked into the porter's kind, dark eyes. "Surely she'll be feeling better by then."

Henry nodded. "The young ones have a way of bouncing back. I'm sure the good Lord can be trusted to undertake for the little miss."

How Jane longed to be as certain as the porter seemed to be of God's taking notice of one child on an empty train. She settled back in her chair, newly aware of her throbbing knee as she fought her fear with prayer. *I haven't asked You for anything in a long while. But this—this is important. Please let Molly get better quickly. Let us find a doctor who won't take advantage. And let Mr. Huggins understand. We need his help. Please let him see that. Let him care.*

Molly coughed again. Jane began to hum, then to sing, directing the words of a favorite lullaby toward Molly, who opened her eyes for a moment and smiled. "I like that one," she croaked, then closed her eyes.

Jane's stomach roiled with hunger. Breaking off another crust of bread from the increasingly stale loaf in her bag, she chewed and washed it down with the rest of the lukewarm tea Henry had brought her when he brought Molly's. She'd just reached for the copy of *Little Women*, thinking to calm her own nerves by reading ahead, when, with the screeching of metal on metal, the train ground to a halt.

Frowning, Jane set the book aside and leaned toward the window, looking first this way and then that. Seeing nothing but a wall of white, she rose and limped to the door. She'd only cracked it open when the roar of the wind and a blast of snow made her yank it shut. With a shiver, she rubbed her arms and sat back down, but not before pulling her coat down to use as a lap robe.

Molly stirred. "Are we there?" She lifted her head, frowning as she glanced at the window.

"It's snowing even harder," Jane said. "I think we must be at the next stop, but I can't tell."

"I'm c–cold."

"I'll see if I can get you another blanket." Jane rose and hobbled toward the front of the car, searching the compartments overhead as she moved along. Finally she located a thick red-and-black-striped blanket. Shaking it out, she made her way back to Molly. She'd just tucked it around when someone stepped into the car—someone new, Jane thought. He was taller than the porter, his face obscured by a turned-up collar, a bushy mustache, and the flaps of his hat pulled down to cover his cheeks.

His black eyes glittered as he glanced to where Molly lay, peering at him above the edge of the blankets. He nodded at Molly, then turned to Jane. "S. C. Parr, ma'am. Henry's readying a place for you and the little miss up in the dining car. Sorry to make you move again. Won't be as comfortable up there, but we'll do our best. Crew's on its way to clear the tracks, but it could be awhile. Soon as the storm stops, I expect the stationmaster at Elm Creek will get word as to what to expect. Until then, we've enough food to get by for a few days. Fuel's scarce, but we won't freeze. Henry'll be back to fetch you soon as we're ready to hunker down."

Jane frowned. She glanced out the window. "Hunker. . .down?"

"Yes, ma'am. We've hit a wall. Of snow, that is. Drifted up so high there's no way through. At least not right now. As soon as the storm blows past, we'll get out with our shovels and get to digging out. Crews will be heading our way from the west as well. I don't imagine we'll be stuck longer than a day or two. Hopefully not even that long."

Jane's heart began to pound. "But—my daughter—the porter was going to see about a doctor at Elm Creek."

"I know, ma'am. And we'll do what we can about that as soon as possible. In the meantime, you enjoy whatever accommodations the UP can provide—*gratis*."

Jane thanked him, just as Henry stepped into the car with an armful of blankets. With a nod, the other man was gone.

"Got things set up for you," he said, and handed Jane two more blankets. "Wrap yourself up good. Thermometer's dropping faster than a frog falling down a well. Don't you worry, though. We'll be toasty up in the dining car." He grinned. "Toasty and well fed. Mr. Parr said to use up whatever we want." He scooped Molly up and headed for the door. "I'll come back for your bags, ma'am. Soon as we get the little miss and you settled up by the best stove on the train—aside from the boiler, that is." Before opening the door, he put a blanket over Molly's head.

Jane hobbled after Henry as best she could. When the car door opened, snow blasted into the Pullman. The wind roared. Henry didn't have to tell Jane to hold on tight. Even so, she felt compelled to lean against the wind whistling between the two stalled cars. Once in the dining car, she ventured another look outside, shivering at the thought of anyone caught out in the blizzard.

As promised, the dining car was warm and inviting. Henry stretched across a table to lay Molly as gently as possible on one of the cushioned benches. Jane thanked him and slid onto the opposite bench as Henry retreated to get their bags. It wasn't quite noon yet, but as soon as Henry returned, he began to light the elegant brass lamps hanging overhead. The glow of lamplight did little to make it feel warmer. Jane pulled her own blanket around her shoulders, newly aware of her numb feet and fingers. How far had the thermometer dropped? How cold would it get? Molly whimpered, and Jane moved to her bench, doing her best to gather the child in her arms, all the while trying to ignore the frisson of fear that ran up her spine.

&

As the storm raged and Molly slept, Jane alternately worried and read. When the wind finally died down, she limped to the doorway and peered out, gasping at the realization that the train was virtually buried in a drift. It was impossible to see beyond the edge of the platform connecting the dining car to the coal car ahead.

The crew worked to dig them out, and as the afternoon wore on into evening, they managed to clear away the snow so that Jane and Molly could see out the windows on the north side of the car. Only an occasional shadow stained the white surface of the earth, albeit without giving a hint of what might lay beneath the drift. As the light faded, snow began to fall again.

Molly woke and croaked a request that Jane read to her, but as Jane opened the book, she cocked her head. "You hear that?" She sat up and swiped at the frosted window, peering outside.

Could it be? Jane slid over to the window on her side of the table and squinted into the distance.

Molly coughed even as she smiled. "Sleigh bells!"

A dark dot of something came into view, gliding across the snow like a low-hovering raven flying toward the stranded train. As Jane peered at the spot, it grew, transforming into the discernible outline of a sleigh pulled by a massive black horse. The driver could have been animal, vegetable, or mineral, so swathed was he—or she—in a fur coat and hat. It was hard to tell where the coat left off and the hat began, thanks to a wide gray scarf wrapped 'round and 'round the driver's neck and head. Jane wondered at the driver's ability to see much through the narrow slit at what Jane presumed to be eye level.

Molly waved as the sleigh slid past the dining car. A pile of blankets next to the driver moved, and one red-mittened hand returned the wave. Apparently the driver wasn't alone.

ॐ

The car door opened, and Henry stepped inside, followed by a woman with merry blue eyes shining above the scarf she was pulling down from her face as Henry spoke. "Looks like the good Lord has answered our prayers for the little one." He nodded at the woman. "Mrs. Gruber's son was at a neighbor's when the storm hit. He saw the stranded train on his way home—"

"—and so," the woman said as she plopped a basket on the table, "I bake." She pulled a blue and white cloth aside to reveal three loaves of bread.

The driver—presumably Mrs. Gruber's son—stomped in behind them, still swathed in the gray scarf.

"My son, Peter," the woman said as she reached for the basket he was carrying. Relieved of his burden, the man said something to Henry about talking to the engineer and retreated back outside, leaving his mother to reveal the contents of the other basket—a pie of some kind and a plate of cookies. Pulling off one red mitten, the old woman reached for a cookie. She hesitated, looking to Jane for approval. "Is all right, *ja*?" She nodded at Molly.

Jane nodded. "Yes, of course."

But Molly had already hunkered back down beneath her blankets. When Mrs. Gruber held the cookie out, Molly shook her head. "Thank you," she coughed, "but I'm not hungry."

The old woman tilted her head and stared down at Molly. Depositing the cookie back on the plate, she stepped closer and leaned down, putting her palm to Molly's forehead. She turned back to Jane. "To the house you must come." She paused. "Better I make the child. Ve haf tea. And herbs." She pointed at the horizon to the north. "Just there. Is warm, Peter's house. We bring you back when the train is ready." She glanced at the porter. "The whistle you blow, and Peter brings back. Is gut, ja?"

Jane didn't give Henry time to answer. "That's very kind of you, Mrs. Gruber, but we should stay with the train. We'll be fine." She nodded at the baskets of food. "Especially now that you've brought supper." The aroma of whatever was in that pie was making her mouth water.

"Is nothing," the old woman said with a wave. "Better I have at home." She looked at Henry. "You should all come. Eat." She went to the door and shouted for Peter. Her son reappeared, tugging at his gray scarf as Mrs. Gruber waved him into the train car. She babbled in German and gestured toward Molly and Jane.

The man's voice rumbled through his scarf. "We don't live far. Come where it's warm, Mrs.—?"

"McClure," Jane said. "Jane McClure." She glanced at Molly. "And this is Molly."

The man chuckled and glanced at his mother, who smiled and said, "Is good name, Molly."

Mr. Gruber's voice warmed with obvious pride as he said, "Mother's brought several hundred children into this world. She's an excellent nurse." His dark eyes crinkled at the corners as he said to Jane, "She already has an onion plaster planned to break the fever. And there's syrup for the cough." He shrugged. "It tastes terrible. But it works."

The old woman broke in. "When train whistles, Peter brings

you back in sleigh." She patted Molly on the head. "Your Molly will be better."

Jane cleared her throat. "I. . .I don't have. . ." She swallowed. Shook her head. "I can't pay for medical care."

The old woman put her palm to her chest. Sighed. Shook her head. "Not to pay." She tucked gray curls back beneath her knit cap, then pulled her mittens back on as she appealed to Henry. "You must to say. Ja?"

Henry spoke up. "I've been riding these rails a few years now, ma'am. Porters hear things, just as a routine part of the job." He smiled. "Mrs. Gruber has quite the reputation in Buffalo County. Healing hands, folks say."

As if on cue, Molly coughed. And coughed. And coughed, whimpering with the effort and murmuring about a sore throat. Jane swallowed. Was it her imagination, or was her own throat a little sore as well? The woman smiled and nodded. And her son— what little of him Jane could see—he had kind eyes, at least. She relented with a nod. "All right then. Thank you." When she reached for her coat, her knee twinged. With a soft grunt and a grimace, she shifted her weight.

Mrs. Gruber caught her hand. *"Vas ist?"*

"It's nothing," Jane lied. "I slipped on the ice at the train station."

The old woman arched one eyebrow. "Also ve vill see to this 'nothing.'" She spoke again to her son. Jane helped Molly don her coat and then shrugged into hers. While they gathered their things, Henry reassured Mrs. Gruber that the train crew would gather soon and enjoy the feast she'd provided before the pie got cold.

As Jane reached for their carpetbags, she twisted her knee just the wrong way. Pain shot up her thigh, and though she pressed her lips together to prevent it, Mrs. Gruber apparently heard her soft cry, for she said something to her son, and before Jane could utter a protest, the man had swept her off her feet and headed up the aisle of the train and out to the sleigh. Over his shoulder, Jane saw Henry scoop Molly up and follow in their wake. Mrs. Gruber trundled behind them with the two carpetbags.

In no time, Jane and Molly were settled behind the driver's seat, swaddled in layers of fur hides and comforters. Mr. Gruber helped his mother aboard and then climbed up beside her, even as Henry called out reassurance from the platform between the train cars. "You rest well, ma'am. Soon as the snow stops, we'll start digging out. There's sure to be a crew on the way to help. You'll be in Denver before you know it."

Denver. Jane gazed back at the train as the sleigh glided across the snow to the rhythmic jangle of the sleigh bells attached to the black horse's harness. She should have asked to send word to Mr. Huggins. Would the Union Pacific give notice to people coming to meet the train in Denver? Surely they would. Still, Jane wished she'd asked Henry about sending Mr. Huggins a telegram. Then again, telegrams cost money. And she had none.

Chapter 4

With a whimper about her head hurting, Molly climbed into Jane's lap as Mr. Gruber drove the horse across the frozen landscape. Not until the sleigh came to a stop did Jane take note of anything but Molly's whimpers, her restlessness, and the heat from her feverish body. Mr. Gruber helped his mother down first, then came to the side of the sleigh where Jane was seated. When he opened his arms, Jane handed Molly over.

As the man headed for the house, Jane took note of what little of the place she could see. Did these people live in a cave? Snow obscured nearly everything, save a length of pipe emerging from a drift and the shoveled path to what appeared to be a very heavy wooden door. There had to be a barn, but Jane couldn't see it. The world around them was a blank slate of white.

❧

The child was too thin—just like her mother. They both had that pinched look about their eyes, the look he'd seen on too many faces in the cities he'd marched through on that fabled "March to the Sea" masterminded by General Sherman. Peter had been little more than a boy all those years ago, but some of the things he'd seen still haunted him. There'd been so much hunger. So much need.

Peter offered to carry the woman inside if she would just wait while he took the child in, but she shook her head and climbed down with a soft grunt. As she followed him inside, Peter wondered what lay hidden behind those gray eyes of hers. The pinched look and the lightness of the child didn't match the fineness of their clothes. And people on Pullman Palace cars didn't carry threadbare carpetbags. Ah, well. Whatever the mystery, *Mutti* would soon have the child feeling better. Thank God for Mutti and her way with people. . .and her gift for healing.

The minute Peter stepped inside, Mutti waved him toward her room. "Take her there. I get featherbed. In here we set up cot."

"Let me climb up and get the featherbed," Peter said, ducking into Mutti's room to deposit the sleeping child on her bed. He hesitated only long enough to pull the bottom half of a tied comforter up from the foot of the bed to cover her. It would keep her warm for the few minutes until Mutti had things arranged.

Intending to climb to the loft, he hurried back into the main room, but Mutti had already shed her cape and bonnet and mittens and was halfway up to the loft above. Peter knew better than to scold her. Mutti didn't appreciate reminders of her advancing age. She seemed to have read his mind though, as she shot him a warning glance. *Don't say it.* She was already to the top of the ladder before the child's mother had so much as unbuttoned her coat. When the woman hesitated, looking about the room, Peter pointed to the free hook next to Mutti's cape.

She hesitated. "But that's for your coat."

"I have to see to things outside," he said. "My Molly doesn't

take kindly to being made to stand in the cold once she's home."
When she looked confused, Peter smiled beneath his scarf. "The
horse. Her name is Molly, too."

They both started. Mutti had pushed the featherbed off the
ledge above. It landed with a thud at the base of the ladder. "If
lingering you are, Peter, let me hand down some quilts."

Mrs. McClure quickly removed her coat and hung it on the
hook Peter had indicated earlier. "I'll take them." She headed for
the ladder.

He couldn't help but notice the woman's narrow waist as she
limped across the room to where Mutti waited, a stack of quilts
just showing at the edge of the loft above her room. *The limp.* He'd
forgotten. Something about a sore knee. If he stayed inside to help,
he was going to have to unwrap the scarf and— He glanced up at
Mother and saw understanding—and with it, sadness in her eyes.

"You may go," she said, her voice gentle. "We will be fine here."

With a nod, he headed back into the cold world outside.

Jane held her hands above her head as, one by one, Mrs. Gruber
dropped three quilts and then sheets and two pillows down from
the loft. Finally Mrs. Gruber lowered a bundle that proved to be
a folding cot. As Jane bent to unfold it, she thanked Mrs. Gruber
again. "This is so kind of you."

The old woman backed her way down the ladder, but once her
feet were on solid ground, her wrinkled face folded into laugh lines
as she said, "To have guests makes blizzard into blessing." She put
her palm to her chest. "You must to call me Anna, please."

Jane nodded. "All right, Anna. And I'm Jane." She smiled. "I
understand your son's horse and my daughter share a name."

Anna chuckled. "Is good name, Molly. Fine horse, beautiful

child." Just then the Molly in the other room began another round of coughing. Anna followed Jane into the bedroom, where she bent down and pulled out what proved to be a trundle from beneath the bed. "We make this up for Molly"—she hesitated and pointed at Jane's knee—"or for you. Whichever is better. You decide."

Jane frowned as she glanced toward the middle room. "But we just—" She hesitated.

Anna nodded. "The cot is for me."

"I couldn't possibly—"

"You must," Anna insisted. "Your Molly needs rest and quiet. Peter is up very early. I must cook for him. Is better for all." She bustled into the other room.

Jane went to Molly's side, murmuring comfort as she helped her out of her coat. "You have a fever." She bent to make up the trundle and had just pulled Molly's nightgown out of her carpetbag when Anna appeared in the doorway.

She held up a huge shirt. "Please to put this on." She showed Jane the deep V at the front, explaining that the nightshirt was one of Peter's castoffs and would make things easier when it came time to apply the poultice she would cook in the next few minutes. "So," she said, "you make ready, and I make poultice and tea." Without waiting for Jane to answer, she retreated back to the main room.

With a grimace, Jane moved about the trundle, spreading a clean sheet across the featherbed. "I'll help you with the nightshirt, but you're going to have to climb down to the trundle yourself, sweetheart. I'm afraid I don't trust my knee to pick you up."

Molly sat up, blinking and putting her hand to her head. "My head hurts. It's too bright."

Jane turned to look out the window that was, now that Molly had mentioned it, letting in more light than she would have expected. The sun must have peeked through the clouds. Jane rose and went to the window to pull the plain muslin curtains closed, smiling as she noted the embroidered design on the simple fabric—a crane of some kind, from the long neck and storklike legs. As she reached up to draw the curtains closed, a shadow fell across the snow. Jane leaned forward just in time to catch sight of Peter Gruber leading his Molly around the rim of a mountain of snow that Jane realized must be hiding the barn. She smiled at the picture of the massive black horse following its owner like an overgrown dog.

When the mare stretched out her neck and nipped Mr. Gruber's shoulder, he batted her away. She dodged his hand, then lowered her head and butted him between the shoulders, sending him headlong into the snow. Jane could have sworn the horse was laughing as it stood, bobbing its head up and down as it watched Mr. Gruber flounder his way back to his feet. Gruber's booming laughter sounded through the window as he shook the snow off and bent to pick up his scarf.

With a sharp intake of breath, Jane stepped back from the window and dropped the curtain. She glanced back at Molly. Maybe she wouldn't notice. *Of course she'll notice. Unless he's only inside when it's dark, she'll notice. And ask all sorts of embarrassing questions. Children just do that. They don't mean anything by it, but—*

The poor man. Such terrible scars. Just the thought of the agonies he must have endured made Jane shiver. She would make certain to speak of it to Molly. In some way to prepare her to be polite. And kind. Wondering if it had been a mistake to come here after all, she limped back to the bed and finished helping Molly change.

☙

Peter's laughter died the instant he noticed movement at his mother's bedroom window. Snatching his hat out of the snow, he clamped it on his head, then grabbed Molly's bridle in mock anger. "Come along, you. Just look what you've done. They've only been here a few minutes, and you've managed to frighten our guests." His eyes stung from the cold. He turned his face away from the window. The woman had let go of the curtain, but maybe she was still in there. . .peering at him through that tiny crack where the curtains didn't quite meet the window frame.

He shook his head as he headed into the barn. Even after all this time, a little thing like a curtain moving brought everything back. Would he never escape it? He'd come here to do just that—to build a life away from the memory of rejection and from the pity he'd never asked for. Mutti called the scars his "Medal of Honor." He wouldn't mind them so much, if only a few more of the boys in his regiment had gotten up that hill behind him before the rebels realized there was a sharpshooter in the trees. All the while he was tending Molly, Peter fought the memories of the shouts. . .the rebel yells. . .and the searing pain of the minié ball that had changed everything. Forever.

Once Molly was unharnessed and standing in her stall, contentedly munching on the mash Peter had mixed for her, he pulled his scarf back up over his nose and ventured back to the house, keeping a wary eye on the bedroom curtain as he walked the shoveled path between the barn and the soddy. After he opened the front door, he leaned in just far enough to make certain his mother heard him call for her, keeping the scarred side of his face turned toward the door.

"Come in and close the door," she scolded as she looked up from where she stood at the stove, stirring something oniony. Mrs. McClure wasn't in the room. Still, Peter only stepped in far enough to pull the door closed against the cold. "I need to shovel a path to the necessary. Then I'll check the harness. And Molly seems a bit off her feed. I may stay out in the barn for a while to keep an eye on her. Don't worry if I don't come in right away."

"It's too cold for you to be outside for long."

"I've got that little stove in the tack room. I'll work in there. It'll be fine."

Mutti tilted her head and peered at him, a question in her eyes. She glanced at the room where the sick child and her mother must be resting, then looked back at him and shook her head.

He cleared his throat. "Do you need me to move the child?"

"She is settled in my room." Mutti pointed at the cot. "I sleep here."

Peter nodded, relieved that he wouldn't have to dance about trying to avoid guests bedded down in the main room. He could rise early and find things to keep him busy out in the barn until the train signaled its departure.

Mutti leaned over the pot to inspect the contents as she spoke. "As soon as I have seen to the poultice. . .and to Jane's knee. . .I start our supper." She ladled some of the concoction into a crockery bowl and reached for the squares of flannel on the table. "Go," she said, shooing him out the door. "Tend to things in the barn. But there will be a meal served at the usual time, and coming after you by lamplight I will not do."

He nodded. "Just light the lamp in the window. I'll come right in."

Chapter 5

Molly had just donned Peter Gruber's nightshirt and, with a little shiver, settled back beneath the covers when Anna bustled into the room, bowl in hand. "Please to make ready for poultice," she said to Jane, as she moved to the opposite side of the high bed.

It didn't make sense for Anna to have to stoop to tend Molly. "I'll sleep on the trundle," Jane said, then shoved it back beneath the bed with a grunt. She pulled Molly's covers down, unbuttoned the borrowed nightshirt, and held it open while Anna spread a gooey concoction across Molly's pale skin.

Molly made a face. "It stinks."

Anna nodded. "Ja. Is gut. And soon better you will be." She laid a double layer of soft flannel over the poultice, then nodded to Jane, who buttoned up the nightshirt. Anna pinned through the nightshirt to hold the flannel in place, and together the two women began to pile on the comforters.

"I'm hot," Molly protested.

"You have fever," Anna said. She produced a small bottle from her apron pocket and, pouring what looked like black sludge into a teaspoon, enticed Molly to take it. "This tastes not good," she said. "But it will help stop the coughing. You can rest while I make soup for our supper."

Molly shuddered as she swallowed. Her eyes opened wide. "It's awful," she croaked, and a tear slid out of the corner of one eye. She glanced over at Jane. "I want Katie."

Even as Jane searched both their carpetbags, she suspected the truth. "Oh, sweetheart. I'm so sorry. Katie's still on the train." Tears threatened to spill down the child's flushed cheeks. Jane rushed to reassure her. "I'm certain that kind porter, Henry—he has a little girl just about your age. He'll know how important a special doll is. He'll take good care of Katie."

Molly sniffled. "I don't want to go to Denver. I don't like Mr. Huggins, and I don't care about the department store windows and—and I want to go home." She began to cry. "Why can't Christmas be like always? Just you and me. . .and not some. . .*stranger*." She began to cough again.

Anna stepped in with another teaspoonful of the dark sludge, and although Molly protested taking it, once it was down, both the tears and the coughing quickly subsided. She closed her eyes, and when Jane was certain she'd fallen asleep, she followed Anna into the main room. Anna had set the poultice bowl on a battered worktable positioned against one whitewashed wall. A couple of shelves above the table were laden with an assortment of colorful tins, small boxes, and blue-tinted Mason jars with zinc lids. Anna reached for a green tin as she said, "Is gut for her to sleep." She pulled a chair out from the dining table and motioned for Jane to sit down.

For some reason, Jane felt the need to apologize for Molly's outburst. "What you must think."

Anna shrugged. "Is of no importance." She pointed at Jane's knee. "Please to show me."

When Jane hesitated, Anna glanced toward the door. "Peter will not come until he sees in the window the lighted lamp." Her voice sounded sad. "If he comes at all." She sighed. "He is. . .how do you say it. . .*shy*." She took the bottle of cough syrup out of her apron pocket and set it on the lower of the two shelves.

"I saw his face." Jane blurted it out, then hastened to explain when Anna turned back to her with a concerned frown. "Molly was complaining about the bright light in your room when the sun came out earlier, so I went to pull the curtains closed. The horse— Molly shoved him, and Mr. Gruber stumbled into a snowdrift. The scarf fell away." She took a deep breath. "It'll be all right. I won't let Molly be rude." She shook her head. "I can't imagine what he's been through."

Anna nodded. She glanced toward the barn, and her eyes filled with tears. "The worst wounds you cannot see." She seemed about to say more, but then she cleared her throat and motioned for Jane to lift her skirt while she retrieved a footstool. When she set it down, she patted the needlepoint surface.

With a grimace Jane lifted her foot onto the footstool and raised her skirt. When Anna touched a bit of the lace edging that had been one leg of Jane's bloomers, she felt herself blushing. "I. . .uh. . .had to make do on the train."

Anna chuckled. "Ja. That I see. Is gut." She headed into the room where Molly was resting and returned with a sewing basket in hand. "*Fräulein* Molly sleeps." She put one wrinkled hand to her bosom and inhaled deeply. "She breathes like so." Opening the sewing basket, she handed Jane a pair of scissors and motioned to the makeshift wrapping. "Snip and undo, please. I have many ointments, but I must see to know which is best."

Jane obeyed, snipping the makeshift wrap with trembling hands. Focusing on the knee seemed to make it hurt more. Or was she nervous about having mentioned Peter Gruber's scarred face? As Anna poked and prodded the swollen joint, Jane said, "I didn't mean to be rude. About Mr. Gruber. I only meant to say there's no reason for him to—" She broke off. "It's his home, after all. He shouldn't be out in the cold because of Molly and me."

Anna grasped Jane's ankle and, ever so gently, helped her straighten her leg. "He does not stay out because of you." Gently, she guided Jane to bend her knee. "He hides because of someone else." When Jane grimaced and let out a little moan, the older woman nodded and let her rest the leg. Rubbing her hands together, Anna cupped Jane's knee between her palms. The warmth felt wonderful, until Anna began to poke and prod. With each painful intake of breath or "Ouch!" Anna alternately nodded or apologized. Finally she let go and crossed the room to the shelf. Taking down a blue tin, she dipped two fingers in and spread something thick and golden over Jane's swollen knee. "My Peter is hero," she said as she worked. "Many men lived because of him. But he did not get away." Her voice wavered. She shook her head. "What they did to my beautiful boy."

"It must have been terrible," Jane said.

Anna nodded. "But worse was to come." She paused. "People don't see hero. They see only. . .what they see." She continued massaging Jane's knee. "He was beautiful man, my son. And he was to marry."

Jane sat quietly, no longer thinking about her sore knee.

"But after," Anna said, "she could not see that man she loved. She was like everyone else. Everyone who sees only with eyes."

Jane frowned. "She abandoned him?"

Nodding, Anna finished wrapping Jane's knee. "I only tell

you because—" She lowered her voice. "The child must not be frightened if she sees. He is good man. Only hiding inside. Like in folktale. What is seen hides truth. You understand, ja?"

Jane nodded. As Anna finished wrapping the knee, she said, "That's what I keep telling Molly about Mr. Huggins. That we mustn't judge by appearances. That he's kind." She paused. "We've been corresponding for some weeks now, and he sent tickets so that we could join him for Christmas. But Molly—" She broke off, took a deep breath. "I'm sure it'll be fine. She's just—we've had a bit of a hard time recently. Once she sees the possibilities—how much better things could be for her. . ." Jane's voice trailed off. Did she sound mercenary?

Anna's eyes shone with kindness. "Mothers do what is best for their *kinder*. Sometimes the kinder don't understand. But still, we try to do what is best."

Jane nodded. "Exactly. I'm only trying to do what's best for Molly." With a grimace, she rose to her feet. "My knee feels so much better. Please let me help you with supper." She smiled. "Working in the cold used to make Molly's father ravenous. I imagine Mr. Gruber is no different." While she helped Anna with supper, she spoke of Stephen. His battle scars, his plans, his dreams. . .and his death.

By the time the lighted lamp appeared in the window, Peter's stomach had stopped growling and begun to hurt. He'd shoveled the path to the outhouse first, then retreated to the barn, polishing the tack and brushing Molly until her coat shone. He'd combed her mane and tail until they rippled like corn silk, trimmed her hooves, fed the sow in the corner stall, shoveled out the chicken yard, and practically given himself a stiff neck hunkering in the henhouse to repair a couple of broken nesting boxes. He'd just begun to think about attacking the drift obscuring his bedroom window when the lighted lamp appeared. With a final look around the barn to make certain all was in order for the night, he made his way inside.

As quickly as possible, he shuttled into his room, laying coat, hat, scarf, and mittens across the foot of the narrow mattress. Taking a seat on the ladder-back chair by his bed, he pulled off his boots, sighing with relief as he pulled on fur-lined moccasins and wiggled his numb toes to get the circulation going again. That little stove in the barn wasn't nearly as efficient as he'd claimed it was.

He dipped his hands in the bowl atop the little washstand beside the door, swiping them across his face and shuddering before reaching for a towel to dry off. Reaching for his comb, he glanced in the mirror. Did he always do that? He hadn't noticed before, but did he always turn his head so that all he saw was what he wanted to forget? Odd that he chose to look at the bad side first.

He turned his head, almost surprised to see the unscarred side of his face. He remembered Priscilla's giggle. *"Why, Peter Gruber. You know why I had to have that dance. You were the handsomest man there, and I always dance with the handsomest man."* She'd laughed after saying it, and he'd told himself that silly talk was just the way girls were these days. Priscilla loved him. She was just—coy. That's all it was. Except that wasn't "all it was." He hadn't learned it until she'd come to the hospital. Mutti had been there for weeks. Priscilla, on the other hand. . .Priscilla had waited. And then. . .then she'd written the last letter.

Facing himself in the mirror, Peter compared sides and reminded himself to be thankful for Dr. Warren's skill with reconstruction. He hadn't been able to rebuild a cheekbone, but he'd done miracles nonetheless. Peter was luckier than a lot of men he'd seen during that long, nightmarish stay in the hospital. Movement in the doorway caught his attention, and Peter stepped back. Away. Dodging the light.

Mutti's voice was kind, but a note of something sounded beneath the kindness. Care. Wariness, even. "The child still sleeps," she said. "I have told Jane not to wake her. You come now." She held out her hand. "Join us." She turned back toward the main room. "I have put another lamp in the child's room. I will be able to see better in the night." She forced a chuckle. "We have only candles for supper. I hope you can see your way."

Dear Mutti, trying her best to make things easier for everyone. Lowering the light so he could hide. He peered into the room, ever mindful of keeping the wounded side of his face turned away. Mrs. McClure was already seated, her foot propped up on the footstool.

"She wouldn't let me help her," she complained, pointing to the footstool. "But she obviously didn't need help." She leaned down and inhaled the aroma of the bowl of soup before her. And then she looked up at him and smiled. "If you're like my Stephen always was, you're hungry enough to eat a bear." She paused. "I hope you won't let the presence of strangers chase you out of your own home, Mr. Gruber." Her voice wavered as she met his gaze. "You've been so kind. I don't know how Molly and I will ever repay you."

Peter sidestepped to hold Mutti's chair as she sat down between Mrs. McClure and him. Once she was seated, he slid into his own chair, careful to position it so that "the bad half" was at least in the shadows.

Mutti reached out, inviting Mrs. McClure and Peter to take her hands. When they did, she bowed her head, praying in German. Peter wondered if their guest knew what was being said, if she knew that Mutti was invoking God's healing hand on the sick child in the other room. It worried him a bit to hear how Mutti prayed. As if she was much more concerned about the child than she'd let on. He kept his head bowed, but finally managed a glance toward the other end of the table. Was Mrs. McClure taking the obvious opportunity to inspect his face?

She wasn't. In fact, Mrs. McClure seemed to be praying, too, moving those lovely full lips— He stopped midthought, scolding himself for noticing. He closed his eyes, waiting for the "Amen."

Chapter 6

Everything changed in the night. With a strangled cough, Molly began to sputter and cry, and Jane leaped to her feet, staggering momentarily on the trundle. She gazed at Molly, who lay wheezing, her eyes wide with fear as she struggled to breathe. Anna rushed into the room and turned the lamp up while Jane rolled the trundle out of the way. Leaning forward, Anna lifted Molly's chin so that the girl would look at her. "Calm, *mein liebling*," she said gently. "Stay calm for just a moment. Anna will make better soon."

When Anna patted Jane's shoulder and directed her to climb up and hold Molly, Jane felt steadied. She pulled Molly into her lap, and together they leaned against the high headboard. Jane stroked Molly's dark hair, whispering comfort. "Shhh. . .shhh. . .it's all right. Anna knows what to do." Molly's chest heaved with the effort to breathe while, out in the next room, Anna rattled about. She was stirring up the stove—Jane heard one of the round covers rattle as Anna slid it out of the way. And then Mr. Gruber's voice.

"What is it? What's wrong?"

Oh no. They'd awakened him. His deep voice sounded closer as he crossed the room to where his mother stood. "Here. Let me."

Jane didn't know what Mr. Gruber was doing, but at some point a cold blast of air indicated he'd opened the front door. "Is this enough?"

"Another washtub full," Anna replied. "Melt it all while I warm up the poultice." She paused. "A tent over the bed would be good."

"I'll get the old wagon cover."

The moments crawled by. Was it her imagination, or was Molly's breathing easing up a bit? *Please, God. . .please.*

"Mama. . ." Molly pulled her arm free. "Don't hold so tight. It hurts." The words came out clearly, but then another attack of sputtering and coughing wracked Molly's thin frame, and she began to cry. "It hurts. . .it hurts." She put her hand to her throat.

Jane began to rock back and forth in a vain attempt to comfort herself as much as Molly. "Show Mama where it hurts." Molly lifted her chin and touched a spot just beneath her jawline. Terror rising, Jane felt beneath Molly's chin and was nearly swallowed by dread. *Swollen glands. Sore throat. Croupy cough. Fever.* It might be nothing, she told herself. Just a cold. Admittedly a bad one, but not—that. She wouldn't let herself think the word. If she allowed the word into her conscious mind, she'd be of no use to Molly, because she'd be too terrified to think clearly. "Shhh. . .shhh. . . it won't be long now, and Anna will be here with more medicine. Remember how much better it made you feel?"

Molly nodded.

And Jane held on.

❧

Peter scaled the ladder leading up to the barn loft and dragged the old wagon cover out of the corner, hoping that once he got it down where he could take a look, it wouldn't be so covered with bird or mouse droppings that they didn't dare use it. Back down below, his hands trembled as he unfolded and spread it out in the darkened walkway before lighting a lamp so that he could look it over. Once he'd lit the lamp, he bent low to inspect the canvas, relieved that a good brushing was all it would take to make it usable.

When his Molly thrust her great head over her stall door, Peter patted her soft muzzle on his way to the tack room to retrieve a broom. He swept the canvas cover briskly, then turned it over and cleaned the other side. Finally, back outside, he did his best to shake the dust off, mimicking Mutti when she hung sheets on the clothesline between the house and the barn—the clothesline now buried in a pile of snow.

While he worked, Peter was surprised to find himself thinking about God. *Surely You didn't bring them to Mutti to have the child d— No.* He wouldn't even think it. He would string the wagon canvas from the rafters and create a tent. Steam would relieve the child's breathing, and she would get better. There was no need to be morbid. He would not think the word that had come to mind. He would not. And yet, as he remembered the sound of that cough, as he carried the wagon cover back inside, another word forced its way into his conscious mind. A word that represented a scourge to parents and, sometimes, to entire families. A word that had populated Buffalo County cemeteries with far too many children.

Diphtheria.

❧

When Jane moved to settle Molly in the bed so she could help put up the tent, Mr. Gruber shook his head. "You're doing what's best. No one comforts like a mother. Mutti and I will take care of this. You stay with the child."

So Jane remained beneath the covers, holding Molly, rocking her, humming, as Mr. Gruber positioned chairs around the bed. Anna helped him by standing on a chair and holding the canvas up while he rigged rope to the rafters above, and in moments Jane and Molly were surrounded by a stained canvas tent.

Anna ducked beneath it and into view, and while she directed him, Mr. Gruber positioned a small table on either side of the bed. "We will put pans of hot water here," Anna said. She made circling motions with both hands. "We need steam, but you must be very careful so that no one is burned, ja?"

Jane nodded, and Anna disappeared. When she returned with more of the poultice, Jane unbuttoned Molly's nightshirt while Anna applied more of the stinking concoction. This time Molly didn't complain about the smell. In fact, she struggled to inhale the aroma, coughing and sputtering but fighting less. Anna had her take two teaspoons of the stuff in the brown bottle and left again.

"I have the hot water." Mr. Gruber's voice sounded from the other side of the canvas.

"We're settled in," Jane said, wrapping her arms around Molly, thankful for the shadows in the darkened room. Even if Molly opened her eyes, she wouldn't notice the poor man's scars.

In moments, Mr. Gruber had positioned two pots of steaming water beneath the tent. And finally Molly took a deep breath without coughing—without that horrible, terrifying, strangling sound.

Molly stirred and croaked, "I want Katie."

"I know you do, sweetheart, but remember—"

"Who's Katie?"

Mr. Gruber's rumbling voice caught Jane off guard. "I didn't mean to eavesdrop," he said. "Mutti had me bring in another lamp."

Anna ducked beneath the tent, lamp in hand, and asked Molly to open wide.

Molly shook her head. "It hurts."

"Ja." Anna's voice was gentle. "This I know. If you let me see, I will know how to help it not hurt so much. Peter will hold the lamp high, and your Mutti can still hold you. Is gut, ja?"

Molly looked up at Jane. She nodded reassurance. With a sigh, Molly agreed.

Mr. Gruber appeared on the side of the bed where only the handsome side of his face would be reflected in the lamplight. Anna reached forward to cup Molly's face in her hands, then directed Molly to lift her chin while she inspected the swelling. Jane couldn't interpret the old woman's expression. She wasn't certain she wanted to. While Mr. Gruber held the lamp high, Anna produced a mirror. Molly opened her mouth wide, and Anna peered inside, all the while using the mirror to reflect light so that she could get a better view.

Red tonsils. Gray membrane. Dear God. . .don't let her see a gray membrane. . .please.

Anna put the mirror away and motioned for Mr. Gruber to withdraw. Jane thought her heart might pound out of her chest while she waited to hear what the old woman had to say.

Anna smiled down at Molly. "Red is why it hurts so much. And spots. You have spots."

Molly raised her hands, as if looking for spots on her skin.

"Nein," Anna said, and took Molly's hands in hers. "Not on skin. Inside. I can make it better, but that medicine tastes even worse. Still, you must take, ja?"

Molly swallowed, grimaced, and nodded.

Anna smiled then and looked at Jane. She brushed her own throat with the tips of her fingers. "You must to stay with us until Fräulein Molly is better."

Jane's voice wavered as she asked, "Did you see—is there—her throat. It's only red?"

Anna nodded and said something about God answering prayer and sparing them the worst. She also said that Molly needed at least a few days of bed rest before she and Jane continued on their journey.

Of course Anna was right, but still, Jane felt tears gathering. She hated feeling so helpless. It was one thing to accept overnight lodging when a blizzard stopped a train in the middle of nowhere, and quite another to impose on strangers for—how long? How long would it be until Molly could travel? And what of Mr. Huggins? Would he wait? Would he understand? And yet, what could she do? *Nothing.*

Anna put one hand on Jane's shoulder and gave it a little pat. "She sleeps," she said, and nodded at Molly.

Jane slid out of bed, and Anna helped her elevate Molly's head with pillows.

Putting her finger to her lips to indicate silence, Anna handed Jane a blanket to wrap up in and motioned for her to come out into the other room. Once there, she waved Jane into a chair and said, "I make tea."

"No, *I'll* make tea while *you* sit," Jane said, but just as she moved to lay the blanket aside, the door opened and Mr. Gruber appeared, bearing yet another huge tub of snow to melt atop the stove. Jane clutched the blanket around her nightgown and stayed put.

⁂

Ducking beneath the canvas tent, Peter replenished the steaming water and paused to look down at the sleeping child, thankful that her breathing seemed to have eased a bit. They would have to stay for at least a few days, of course. That would be awkward, especially once the child started feeling well enough to pay attention to— things. He reached up and traced the worst scar with his fingertips, wondering what it would have been like if he and Priscilla. . .if Priscilla hadn't— The child began to murmur in her sleep. She was dreaming, talking about something pleasant. She smiled and murmured the name *Katie*. Katie again. Who was Katie?

As Peter stood gazing down at the sleeping child, it hit him. He could have had a daughter just this age by now. Would she have had dark hair like his, or would it have been blond like Priscilla's? A shadow played across the surface of the tent around the bed, bringing Peter back to the moment. Mutti's voice sounded from the other side of the canvas. "Is everything all right?"

Peter ducked back into the room. "It's fine. She's dreaming. Murmured something about her friend Katie."

"Her doll," Mutti said. "Left on the train. Twice she has asked now."

Back in the other room, Peter avoided making eye contact with Mrs. McClure as he headed for his own room.

"We are having tea," Mutti called softly. "You should join us."

Peter shook his head. He didn't want to have tea with a beautiful woman tonight. Not when she was trapped and when good manners would require her to pretend that she wasn't revolted by the sight of him.

"Thank you," he said, "but I want to get an early start in the morning. I'll hitch the sleigh and head to the train first thing." He paused in the doorway, speaking over his shoulder. "If you'll write out a message, Mrs. McClure, I'll ask the porter to see that it's sent on to Denver as soon as they reach the next station. So your family won't worry. Just leave it on the table. I'll leave at first light." He didn't wait for her to answer. But once in his room and out of sight, he stood at the window for a while, looking out on the landscape, listening to her voice as Mrs. McClure and Mutti talked. Mutti reassured her that she didn't think they were fighting diphtheria, and that she and Peter counted it a blessing to help others.

A blessing to help others. Mutti said it with such conviction. Of course she believed it with all of her gentle, God-fearing heart. Peter had believed it once, too. Before the "blessing" of helping others had cost him the chance to build a life with Priscilla.

Chapter 7

In spite of Anna's reassurances and remedies, the night wore its way through one episode after another of Molly waking, coughing, crying, needing more steam and more of whatever it was in Anna's brown bottle, and finally, in the gray light of dawn, a newly prepared poultice. Weariness creased Anna's already-wrinkled face as she spread the warm goo. Jane began to worry for the old woman's well-being, but when she pleaded with Anna to please rest for a while and let Jane tend Molly, Anna shook her head.

"A mother should not be alone when her child suffers."

"At least sit down for a while," Jane pleaded. As soon as Molly was resting comfortably, she followed Anna into the main room, pleased when the older woman pulled her rocking chair close to the doorway and sat down with a sigh.

"Do not forget," Anna said, pointing to the table where a piece of paper and a pencil waited. "Peter will need your message for Mr. Huggins."

Anna leaned her head back and closed her eyes, and Jane settled at the table. Composing a telegram that displayed just the right sentiment proved difficult. She must not hint at the near-panic she felt when she wondered if Mr. Huggins's interest would wane if they didn't meet again soon. She wanted to show interest. But how to do so without appearing shamefully forward? Finally she wrote a letter across the top half of the page Anna had torn from her household ledger book, knowing that the process of writing it out would help her compose the shorter version Mr. Gruber would telegraph to Denver.

> *Dear Mr. Huggins,*
>
> *By now you have received word that the train is snowbound. We have been assured that all appropriate measures are to be taken to clear the tracks as soon as possible. Unfortunately, Molly has taken ill, and I am advised by the kind woman who has taken us in that she should not travel for a few days. While I at first feared diphtheria—just writing the word makes me shudder—Mrs. Gruber assures me that Molly's symptoms will continue to improve, and that we should be able to take up the journey in a few days.*
>
> *Please know that Molly and I are desperately disappointed at this unfortunate turn of events. We sincerely hope that the delay will not force a change in your plans. While we will miss the pleasure of spending Christmas in Denver, we hope that the idea of welcoming the New Year with us is anticipated with the same warmth displayed in your invitation for Christmas.*

Jane read the letter over and over again. If only she could send that. It sounded so much more positive in tone. Taking a deep breath, she underlined the essential information and ended up with the telegram.

MOLLY ILL *Stop* FEARED THE WORST BUT NURSE ASSURES
SHE WILL RECOVER SOON *Stop* HOPE TO ARRIVE IN A FEW
DAYS *Stop* ANTICIPATING OUR TIME TOGETHER *Stop*

Jane stared at the last line. Was it too forward? *Is it even true?* A twinge of guilt raised its head. *I am anticipating it. Just because it isn't a romantic anticipation doesn't mean it's a lie.* She decided to leave the last sentence. Next came the matter of how to sign the thing, and that caused more than a little consternation. Finally she decided to use her Christian name, hoping that Mr. Huggins would take note of that, too. He had yet to depart from addressing her as *Mrs. McClure.* Perhaps he needed permission. She would give it. *Jane.*

She set the pencil down and sat back, looking over at Anna and smiling at the image of the older woman fast asleep in the rocking chair. Rising with a soft grunt, Jane hobbled past Anna's sleeping form and into the bedroom. When Molly stirred and whimpered, Jane climbed up beside her. Beneath the pile of comforters, with her arms around Molly and the child's head on her shoulder, she closed her eyes and fell instantly asleep.

Jane woke with a start to the aromas of coffee and fresh-baked bread. Molly stirred when she slipped out of bed, then settled back into a deep sleep. When Jane put her palm to Molly's forehead, relief washed over her. She might still have a slight fever, but *slight* was a good word. And while rumbles and rattles still accompanied each breath, Molly wasn't struggling like she had in the night. Jane closed her eyes for a moment and listened, then sent a fleeting thanks toward heaven.

When she ducked beneath the canvas tent and looked out the

window, she realized that someone had put the lamp out. A band of gray light shone below the hem of the embroidered curtains. What time was it? Just as she reached for the blanket draped across the foot of the bed, she heard it. *The train whistle.* What could that mean? Surely a crew hadn't reached the train yet. They couldn't possibly be ready to leave.

The telegram! Clutching the blanket around her, Jane hurried into the other room. A blast of warm air greeted her as Anna opened the oven door. When Jane glanced at the table, Anna said, "The note Peter has taken to the train." She hoisted a loaf of bread out of the oven and inverted the pan over a plate. "The whistle is for to say all is well. He has delivered your message and is on his way back." Wrapping the fresh loaf of bread in a towel, she placed it on the open oven door. She crossed the room and donned her cape. "I go for eggs. Peter will be hungry when he returns." And with that, she hurried outside.

Jane got dressed, then returned to the main room where she set the table and sliced the warm bread, pausing often to step into the bedroom and listen for Molly. Finally, when she'd done everything she knew to help prepare for breakfast, she lingered in the doorway between the two rooms, noticing for the first time that the framed needlework above the table really was lovely, and wondering what it said. The only word she recognized was *Gott.* She knew that German word because one of Mrs. Abernathy's boarders had a penchant for profanity. She smiled in spite of herself, remembering the confrontation one day when Mrs. Abernathy stood, hands on hips, glaring up at the lumbering boarder and telling him in no uncertain terms that if he insisted on using the Lord's name in vain in *any* language, he could find another place to live.

The needlework featured what looked like a castle tower. Pink and burgundy flowers gathered along the base of the stone wall and then meandered around the edge of the sampler. Now that she thought about it, as Jane gazed around the room, she realized that the soddy epitomized the word *cozy*. It was so different from Mrs. Abernathy's drafty, two-story frame boardinghouse. Different, too, from the rooms Mr. Huggins had described over his mercantile store in Denver.

Anna returned in a swirl of cold air, her blue eyes bright as she produced several eggs from the pocket of her cape. "It snows more," she said, closing the door and scurrying over to stand by the stove while she took off her cape and mittens. She thanked Jane for setting the table and had just gone into the next room to check on Molly when Mr. Gruber returned. At least Jane thought it must be Mr. Gruber, although from all appearances it could have been anyone, so encased in crusted snow was the person who staggered in the door.

Jane glanced out the window. Another wall of white. "You drove into that?"

Mr. Gruber nodded once. He stepped closer to the stove but then hesitated and turned into his room instead.

"Wait," Jane said. When he looked back her way, she shrugged. "Please. You've been so kind to us. Stay by the stove where it's warm."

Anna bustled in and, grabbing her son's coat sleeve, pulled him closer to the stove, muttering like a hen clucking over a wounded chick. She dragged the rocking chair over, and as soon as Mr. Gruber had shrugged out of his coat, she directed him to sit down. Jane took her own coat off the hook and hung Mr. Gruber's where it would dry more quickly, then headed into the bedroom to deposit her coat over the sewing rocker by the bedroom window.

When she returned to the main room, Mr. Gruber was leaning toward the oven, soaking up the warmth as his mother unwrapped the stiff scarf wrapped around his head and neck. Once again he'd positioned himself so that only the handsome side of his face was in view. His cheeks were so red Jane wondered aloud at frostbite. She poured coffee. Mr. Gruber cupped the mug in his huge hands, then took a sip and sighed with pleasure.

"Sit back," Anna said, kneeling before him while she helped with his boots.

"They hope to be dug out by the end of the day," he said. "This round of snow shouldn't last long. There's a thin line of blue far to the west." He glanced up at Jane. "The porter promised to send the telegram as soon as they reach the next stop." He smiled down at his mother. "And they said to thank you for the meal." He paused. "I was in such a hurry to get inside, I left your baskets in the sleigh."

"Is no matter," Anna said as she set her son's boots on the open oven door. "Soon we have bread, eggs, and griddle cakes. Is gut, ja?" She moved to the rustic narrow table positioned beneath her medicine shelf and began to mix batter for griddle cakes.

Mr. Gruber stood up and stretched, then crossed the room in his stocking feet, talking to Jane over his shoulder as he reached inside his coat. "Your Molly talks in her sleep," he said and held up the rag doll he'd tucked in the inside pocket. "I heard mention of a Katie."

❦

The look on Jane McClure's face as she took Katie from his hands was something Peter would savor for some time to come. Somehow he got the courage to actually turn around and look at her. If he was testing her, she received high marks, because she looked him in the eye and smiled. A real smile, not one of those conjured expressions people managed out of a sense of duty to *not* notice.

She held his gaze for a moment before glancing down at the well-loved doll and then back up at him. "Thank you. So much."

She paused. "I've been dreading having to tell her that Katie was on her way to Denver without us. You have no idea how relieved I am that that won't be necessary. You're very kind to have remembered."

Kind. No one had said that of him for a long while. And for some reason, it made him want to retreat before the inevitable happened and she could no longer stomach looking him in the eye. He nodded and headed for his own room, pausing at the door just long enough to say, "The porter said that your Mr. Huggins would likely be reading the telegram by Christmas Day."

"Will they deliver a telegram on Christmas Day?"

"He seemed to think so, especially in light of the train getting stranded."

"Mama!"

All eyes looked toward the bedroom where Molly lay.

"I'm here," Jane called back, limping into the room, the doll in hand.

Mutti stood still for a moment, her head tilted. At the child's joyous exclamation over the doll, she smiled at Peter. He nodded at the room. "Go and see after her. I can fry griddle cakes." Mutti headed in to check on the child, and he slathered butter on a slice of bread, eating it while he used his free hand to flip griddle cakes, stack the finished ones on a plate, and pour out more batter.

The women were still in the other room when the cloud cover gave way and sunlight poured in through the window. The temperature might not be climbing, but the sunshine made it feel warmer. Mutti bustled back into the main room just long enough to snatch two bottles off her medicine shelf. She nodded at his unspoken question. "She is to be well. It takes time." She pointed at the stack of griddle cakes waiting on the table. "Eat. We will join you soon."

But they didn't. Mutti joined him, but Mrs. McClure stayed

in the other room with her child. Which was only to be expected. For many reasons. When he'd finished eating, Peter hauled in two more tubs of snow to once again make steam rise inside the canvas tent. The child thanked him for bringing Katie "home," speaking from the other side of the canvas wall in a raspy voice that ended in a sputtering cough.

"You're welcome," Peter said, then retreated to the main room where he helped Mutti wash the dishes. By the time Mrs. McClure emerged from the bedroom, he was donning his coat to retreat to the barn. He needed to retrieve the baskets from the sleigh, he said. And he had things to tend. Both were true, even if the real reason he wanted to escape was the desire to savor the first genuine smile he'd received from anyone but Mutti in a very long time.

Chapter 8

Molly finally asked for something to eat Thursday afternoon. Anna soft-boiled the egg she'd kept out of the flapjack batter, and Jane made toast and tea. Molly grimaced with the first swallow of toast and opted for the egg and tea. After eating, she settled back against the pillow and asked Jane to read more about Jo and Meg. While Anna heated up more water and sent more steam into the tent, Jane climbed up beside Molly and read until the child fell asleep. When she ducked back out from beneath the sheet of canvas, the sun had begun to set. Once again Anna lit the lamps in the windows. Then she asked to examine Jane's knee.

"It's much better," Jane said as she sat before the stove and unwrapped her leg.

Anna perched on the footstool at Jane's feet and repeated the poking and prodding, nodding with satisfaction when Jane only winced. "Is gut," she said, then reapplied ointment. When the front door opened abruptly, Jane started and stood up so that her skirt would fall back into place.

Mr. Gruber, his arms full of firewood, kicked the door closed behind him and crossed the room to the woodbox. He bent to deposit the wood, and by the time he'd turned back around, Jane had snatched the bandage off the floor and muttered something about checking on Molly.

"If all goes well tonight," Anna called after her, "Peter takes down tent tomorrow, ja?"

That night Molly held Katie close and slept so soundly that, midway through the night, Jane slipped out of bed, pulled out the trundle, and crawled beneath the pile of comforters with a sense of gratitude and a weariness borne of the ever-present concerns of recent days.

Moonlight spilled in the window as Jane lay listening to Molly's even breathing and trying to imagine where they would have been this night if Molly hadn't taken ill. She wondered at the kindness of Anna Gruber and her son. *Thank You. I haven't spoken to You in a while, but thank You for taking care of us. Thank You that Molly didn't have—* She still couldn't even think the word. *Thank You that she didn't have that.* She wondered at the tragedy that had ravaged Peter Gruber's handsome face and the heartbreak he'd endured. How could a woman turn her back on a man she loved? How many men had had that happen to them after the war? How terrible for Peter.

And he didn't look that horrible. Not really. If you looked past the scars and into those beautiful eyes— Thinking of Peter's dark eyes reminded Jane of the expression in them earlier this morning when finally he'd let her look him in the face. She'd caught a glimpse of caution. Wariness, as if he was testing her.

It made her think of that time she'd encountered a stray dog in the alley behind Mrs. Abernathy's. The poor thing had stood its ground over a ham bone, watching her. Wary, although now that she remembered, it hadn't bared its teeth. Not once. It had just watched her. And when she spoke kindly to it, it lowered itself to its haunches, the hambone between its front paws. Not exactly relaxed, but not so defensive either. When Jane said, "That's a good dog. I won't bother you," the dog had thumped the earth once with its tail. And never stopped watching her as she returned to hanging out the day's assortment of kitchen towels and linens.

Mr. Gruber's gaze earlier reminded her of that dog. Wary. Hoping for the best but accustomed to being kicked and chased off. She was so glad she hadn't looked away. So glad she'd concentrated on his kindness in bringing Katie back from the train and seen beyond the scars to those beautiful eyes. Stephen had had brown eyes, too, but not like Mr. Gruber's. Not that dark, not set beneath finely arched eyebrows, not separated by an aristocratic nose.

Molly muttered in her sleep. Jane tensed momentarily, then realized it wasn't anything to worry over. Her breathing was even, and she didn't cough or sputter. She must be dreaming. Jane rolled onto her side and burrowed into her pillow. Her last conscious thought was the somewhat troubling realization that she couldn't remember the color of Mr. Huggins's eyes.

❧

Peter woke with a start and sat up in bed, listening. Listening. Swearing softly under his breath at the realization that his campaign against unwanted residents in the house was about to begin again. He and Mutti had waged war on field mice after the first cold snap in the fall, setting traps in the loft and engaging in more than one chase involving brooms and the two of them in their nightclothes—chases that had ended in success and with them both out of breath and laughing at their ridiculous antics. Mutti wanted a cat. Peter agreed it was a good idea. He had word out to several of the neighbors in case any Christmas litters appeared in barn lofts nearby.

Another rustle out in the main room convinced him he'd better get up. He'd have to wake Mutti, but she wouldn't mind. She defended the soddy against unwanted invaders with the passion of a Prussian field marshal. Quietly, he slid out of bed and pulled on his pants. He padded to the doorway and peered into the main room, thankful for the faint moonlight reflecting off the whitewashed walls. What he saw made him smile.

The child had her back to him. She'd moved a kitchen chair over to the shelving on the far wall—that must have been what he heard—and was standing atop it, reaching for a biscuit tin. He stepped into the room, doing his best to move silently, lest he startle her and make her fall. The hem of the borrowed nightshirt she was wearing touched the seat of the chair. One of the sleeves had come unrolled. As she extended her arm to reach for the biscuit tin, several inches of sleeve dangled past her outstretched fingers.

When Peter was close enough to the chair to keep her from falling if she startled, he whispered softly, "It's good to see that you're hungry."

She didn't look his way, just stood with her hand stretched toward the biscuit tin. She was cradling her doll in the other arm.

"I'm afraid that's not what you think it is," he whispered, coming to her side. Still, she didn't answer. Her eyes were open, but— *Ah.* She was sleepwalking.

He reached to the higher shelf and a cracker tin that did, indeed, contain crackers. Opening it, he offered her one, shoving the dangling sleeve back up her arm to free her hand. She took the cracker, then stood motionless.

"Shall we give Katie a cracker as well?" She nodded, and Peter gently pried open her hand and put a second cracker in her palm.

"There," he said. "Ready to go back to bed?"

Again the child nodded. This time she looked toward the window.

"It's still nighttime. Tomorrow, when you wake up, you can have a nice breakfast. Katie, too. All right?"

He intended to help her down off the chair and walk her back to bed, but when he touched her arm, she tucked the doll between her upper arm and her body, put the crackers into that hand, and with her free arm, reached up, clearly intending for him to pick her up. When he did, she curled up in his arms and laid her head against his chest. She sighed, and he felt her relax in his arms. Sound asleep.

There was nothing to do but put her to bed. How he would explain it to Mrs. McClure if she awoke to find him standing over her, he didn't know, but as it turned out, she was sound asleep in the trundle. As he crept around the foot of the bed to the opposite side and ducked beneath the canvas curtain to put Molly back in bed, her mother didn't stir.

Peter settled the child back against the pillows and, pulling the covers up, tucked them beneath her chin. He crept into the main room, replacing the chair at the table and then pausing to put the lid back on the cracker tin and return it to the high shelf. He'd just headed back toward his own room when Mutti stirred.

"Vas ist?"

"It's nothing, Mutti," Peter said quietly. He stepped closer. "The child was up. Sleepwalking, I think. Hungry. I gave her some crackers and put her back to bed." He chuckled. "I heard a rustle. I thought we were going to have another war against mice."

He heard Mutti's low laugh. "Another dance with a broom, ja? Let us hope not, at least not until our guests depart."

"Let us hope," Peter agreed.

"She is pretty, ja?"

"She's a beautiful child. Those dark curls. Thank God she's going to be all right."

"I speak of Jane. She is pretty. And kind. It's nice having her here." Mutti sat up in bed. "We must to have special Christmas, ja? For the child."

"They might be gone by Saturday."

"Nein. Molly must rest a few days at least."

Peter sighed.

"She is child, Peter. She must have Christmas. A tree, ja? If you take the sleigh out to the river, you could find something."

He could almost hear Mutti's thoughts skittering about as she gathered ideas and made plans. He knew her so well. She was making a paper chain in her mind. Already tearing out another page of her ledger book to make *scherenschnitte* snowflakes. And making *springerle* cookies. How he loved springerle. He could almost smell them baking, imagine the aroma of anise oil in the air. Mutti was right. Why not give a sick child a happy moment? Why not, indeed. He didn't know about a tree though.

"It's only two days away, Mutti."

"And what? You have so much doing in this snow you can't take the sleigh to look for a little tree?"

She was right. Again. He chuckled. "You can't see my face, but I'm smiling. And yes. I'll drive out tomorrow and see what I can find. I'll keep it in the sleigh until you come out and approve it."

"That's my Peter," Mutti said. "It will be wonderful surprise. You will see."

Peter padded back to his room and slid beneath the covers, shivering when his bare feet touched the cold sheets.

❧

It was still dark when Jane woke—to the sound of Mr. Gruber

leaving the house, she realized. Probably headed out to feed the livestock. *Livestock. I wonder what they have in the way of livestock.* She hadn't paid much attention to the length of Mr. Gruber's absences from the house. In fact, she didn't really know very much about him except what Anna had said about his injury and subsequent heartache. She didn't know anything at all about Anna, except that she was Peter's mother and she'd apparently only come to live with him since he was injured. Where had she been before that?

Hearing Anna in the next room, Jane rose and dressed. "How can I be of use today? I feel like I've been something of a pampered guest, and I'd like it if there were a way to repay you for all your kindness."

Anna reached for a small basket hanging on a peg below the "medicine shelf." "Bundle up and gather eggs while I knead dough." Anna leaned into her kneading. "Inside the barn look to farthest wall. You will see the door to the chicken coop."

Unwilling to admit that she knew next to nothing about chickens and had never gathered eggs, Jane donned her coat and headed out to the barn by way of the trench Mr. Gruber had dug in the snow, which was nearly up to Jane's waist, thanks to the way the wind had drifted it between the house and barn. When she stepped inside the barn, the black horse thrust its head over a stall door—so suddenly that Jane dodged away.

"She's just saying hello," Mr. Gruber said. "She's very gentle. Never bites or kicks." He raised his head to glance at the horse. "Do you, Molly-girl? You never bite or kick?"

When the horse whickered, Jane laughed. "It's as if she's talking back."

"She talks back all the time," Mr. Gruber said. "She's a *she*, after all. Can't let a man have the last word." He glanced Jane's way, and his grin disappeared. "I do apologize, Mrs. McClure. I didn't mean anything by it."

Jane smiled his way. "That's perfectly all right, Mr. Gruber. I didn't take it to mean much of anything." As she made her way toward the door at the opposite end of the rows of stalls, she passed several pigs huddled together in the deep straw in one of the larger stalls, and a dun-colored cow obviously expecting a calf. In the next stall, Mr. Gruber sat milking a second dun-colored cow. He nodded at the basket in Jane's hand. "I see Mutti has put you to work."

"I offered," Jane said, nodding at the door just beyond the little room. "That opens into the chicken coop, right?"

Mr. Gruber nodded. As Jane walked past, he said, "Don't let Solomon worry you. He's all bluster and no fight."

Solomon? Jane didn't have to wonder long who Solomon was, for the instant she opened the door to the coop, a large bird began to flap its russet-colored wings and march toward her. How on earth could a chicken sound threatening? But this one did. Jane turned away from it and went to the four rows of nesting boxes to her left, all save one inhabited by a rust-colored hen, looking perfectly content and almost cozy. Jane hesitated. The blustery bird fluttered up off the earth, menacing enough that Jane ducked and raised her arm to shield her face.

"Stop that, Sol!" Mr. Gruber stepped into the coop, and the rooster settled and sauntered away. At least it seemed to Jane that he was sauntering.

"Thank you," she said primly, and turned once again to the nesting boxes. She hesitated. How did one get the hens to vacate the premises so their eggs could be collected?

"You've never gathered eggs before." He sounded surprised. Amused. Before she could respond, he brushed past her and slid his hand beneath one of the birds.

"No eggs," he said, but when he checked the next box, he withdrew an egg and, with a smile, handed it over.

So they don't bite. Jane followed Mr. Gruber's example, but the second she began to slide her hand beneath a hen, it clucked madly. Jane snatched her gloved hand away just in time to avoid being pecked. *Thank goodness for gloves.*

"You don't have to be afraid. They don't know you, is all. They're mostly bluster and very little bite." He paused. "But if you *are* afraid, just hand me the basket, and I'll take care of it. Mutti never has to know."

Was he teasing her? He'd said more since she'd come into the barn than he'd said the entire time she and Molly had been here. Jane lifted her chin. "I believe I can handle a few clucking hens, Mr. Gruber." She glanced toward the barn. "And besides, weren't you milking a cow?"

He nodded. "I was, and I apologize if I seemed to think you aren't up to handling the ladies." He nodded at the nesting boxes, then sidled around her, pausing at the door. "Just keep an eye on the rooster. He's been trained to attack if his ladies are threatened." He swallowed. "Killed a big bull snake once."

Jane glowered at him. "Are you teasing me, Mr. Gruber?"

He shrugged. "Well, something killed the bull snake. Maybe it was the dog."

"You don't have a dog."

"We did. It ran off. But I haven't seen a bull snake about, so you needn't worry about that."

"Just because I grew up in the city doesn't mean I'm afraid of snakes. And for your information, I am not. Unless, of course, they rattle."

"I'll still gather the eggs if you'd like."

By way of an answer, Jane slid her hand beneath another hen, ignored the creature's clucking and fussing, and was rewarded with not one, but two eggs. She glanced his way. "Anna said to tell you that breakfast will be ready soon." She quickly investigated the rest of the nesting boxes. She was tempted to glance back to see if Mr. Gruber was watching her but didn't want him to see her do so.

"Well, look at that," he finally said. Jane looked his way. He was pointing at the rooster, who'd settled on his perch. "You've won Solomon over." He retreated into the barn and bent to retrieve the milk pail. "Your Molly can have fresh milk if she feels up to it this morning."

Jane pulled the door to the coop closed behind her. "She had a good night. I have high hopes." Mr. Gruber swept his hand toward the house, like a gentleman showing a lady the way to a coach. With a smile and a nod, Jane led the way inside, hoping that the friendly man she'd just been joking with in the barn wouldn't go into hiding inside the house.

Chapter 9

Jane had just stepped inside and set the egg basket on the floor when Molly called out, "Look, Mama! I'm helping make biscuits!"

And indeed she was. Her nose smudged with flour, Molly—still in Mr. Gruber's nightshirt—stood at Anna's worktable near the warm stove, pressing a biscuit cutter into the sheet of flattened dough spread on the table before her.

"She is so hungry," Anna explained with a smile, as she crossed to where Mr. Gruber was standing. Taking the milk pail out of his hand, she called out to Molly, "And now Peter brings you fresh milk, just as Anna promised."

Molly had been concentrating on her biscuit-making, but at the mention of fresh milk, she looked up. And over at Mr. Gruber. And—

Jane hurried to get her gloves and coat off as she spoke. "Fresh milk, Molly. Isn't it wonderful?" Feeling a knot form in her midsection, she bustled over to where Molly stood and put a hand on her shoulder. *Please don't. Don't say anything.* But Molly said something. A word that made Jane cringe.

Her eyes round with surprise, Molly blurted out, "You're my monster!"

Mr. Gruber's hand went to his scars, and he turned away.

"Oh. . .Molly," Jane said under her breath.

"No. . .really, Mama." Molly put the biscuit cutter down. Mr. Gruber was headed into his room, but Molly called out, "I dreamed about a monster. A *good* monster."

Mr. Gruber stopped.

"He gave me a cracker." Molly turned to look up at Jane. "And Katie. He gave Katie a cracker, too." She pointed at Anna's medicine shelf. "Out of that."

Jane looked up. There was, indeed, a cracker tin on the shelf above the row of bottles.

Mr. Gruber turned back to face Molly. He dropped his hand from his cheek. "You were sleepwalking." He glanced at Jane. "I thought I heard a mouse skittering about in the night. Molly was up on a chair, reaching for"—he glanced meaningfully at his mother—"the wrong tin." He shrugged. "I gave her two crackers and carried her back to bed. That's all."

Molly nodded. "That's what I said. There was a good monster, and he helped me. In my dream." She frowned and looked at Mr. Gruber. "But it wasn't a dream?"

He shook his head. Swallowed. "No. The monster is. . .real."

Molly's brow furrowed as she inspected the man's face. "Does it hurt?"

He shook his head. "No. Not in the way you mean."

"What happened?"

"Molly—" Jane tried to stop it, but Mr. Gruber glanced her way. Shook his head.

"It's all right." He smiled at Molly. "The war. Do you know about the war?"

Molly nodded. "A lot of people got killed. And the slaves got free. But people still don't let them ride on the trolley car."

"You know a lot."

"Papa told me about it. Sometimes, when it rained, he limped. And he had a scar, but you couldn't see it. He showed me once. It was on his leg." She reached down and patted her shin. "He said I almost didn't get born because he almost didn't come back to Mama."

Jane spoke up. "One of Stephen's best friends saved his life. Keig was the best shot in the company, and one day they were taking heavy fire, but when the retreat sounded, Keig stayed behind." She looked into Peter's dark eyes, forcing herself to meet his gaze as she said, "He was very heroic. He gave his life saving several of the men in the company."

"Papa said Keig was why I got born."

Jane felt the heat rising in her cheeks. "I doubt that it comforted Keig's widow very much, but Molly's right. Because of him, Stephen came home." She cleared her throat. "In fact, I know of at least a dozen children who never would have existed if not for his sacrifice." Her voice wavered, even as she wondered how many children were alive thanks to Peter Gruber's scarred face.

For a moment, the room was quiet, and then Molly spoke again. "Can I touch it?"

There was nothing to do now but let it play itself out. To Jane's amazement, Peter Gruber motioned Molly over and knelt down. She put her palm to his ruined cheek and traced the scars. Finally she said, "I'm sorry you got hurt." She sniffed. "You're a *good* monster."

It seemed to take Peter a long while to respond. He blinked, but a tear escaped and trickled across the scars. He took Molly's hand and kissed it. "I'm glad you know you don't have to be afraid of me."

And then the spell was broken. Molly said she was cold and headed back toward the cookstove. Jane scurried into the bedroom to retrieve a blanket and settle her in Anna's rocking chair. Peter poured a mug of warm milk for her, then set the table for breakfast, while Anna finished cutting biscuits and slid them into the oven.

Soon they were gathered around the table eating breakfast together, like prisoners who'd inhabited cells alongside one another but never seen each other's faces. And now that they'd been set free, they could get acquainted and talk about normal things.

❧

As the morning wore on and Molly began to wilt, Mutti administered more tonic and Peter carried Molly back to bed for a nap.

"You have a nice house," Molly said, while Peter stepped up on chairs and untied the ropes that held the wagon cover up to the rafters.

"Thank you." Peter smiled down at her, then went back to untying the rope he'd looped through the iron hooks in the rafters above the bed. "Do you know about sod houses?"

Molly shook her head.

"I plowed up the prairie to make bricks. And then I stacked the bricks to make these walls."

Molly looked around the room. "It doesn't look like dirt."

"That's because I plastered the inside. If there wasn't so much snow, you would have seen the sod bricks when we drove up to the house."

"Won't it wash away when it rains?"

Peter paused. "That's a very astute question."

"What's a stoot?"

Peter chuckled. "*Astute* means you're perceptive. You ask good questions." He paused and moved the chair to take down the last rope. "And you're right. This house will eventually wash away, even though the eaves are wide to protect the walls from rain, and even though I have boards at the corners to keep cattle from rubbing against them. They like to do that. It's a way for them to scratch their own backs, and with so few trees growing on the prairie, the house is a constant temptation. However, I'll have a new house built long before this one is in danger of washing away. One more like the houses you're used to seeing in town."

"Where will you get the bricks?"

Peter shook his head as he looped the rope he'd used to tie up the wagon cover and laid it in Mutti's sewing rocker. "The new house won't be brick. I'll order lumber from the sawmill and hitch my Molly up to the farm wagon and haul it back here."

Jane grabbed one edge of the wagon cover, and together they folded it up.

"We had a brick house," Molly said. "But then my papa died. We had to sell it and move."

Peter hoisted the wagon cover over his shoulder. "I'm sorry to hear that."

"It's okay. The boardinghouse isn't so bad. Sometimes I miss Sonja though."

Jane spoke up. "It's time for you to settle in, young lady."

Molly burrowed deeper beneath the comforters. But she kept talking. "She was our housekeeper. But after Papa died, we couldn't keep Sonja anymore. She got another job with someone else. We do our own housework now. And Mama helps Mrs. Abernathy cook for everyone."

Jane's cheeks blazed scarlet. Peter wished Molly a good nap, gathered up the rope, and headed for the main room. He paused before heading back out to the barn with the wagon cover. With a glance behind him, he stepped closer and lowered his voice as he said, "I don't want you climbing that ladder again, Mutti. Think about what else you need to bring Christmas to Molly, and I'll retrieve it as soon as I get back inside."

☙

Christmas! Dismay colored over Jane's enjoyment of the last hour spent gathered around the table with Anna talking about life growing up in Germany—she'd worked the motto hanging over the table as a young wife before she came to America. *Ein' feste Burg is unser Gott,* it said. After translating the motto—it meant "Our God is a strong tower of defense"—Peter had waxed poetic about his mother's apple butter and talked about the three varieties of apple trees they'd planted behind the house.

"Will they survive the blizzard?" Jane asked.

"If they don't, we plant again," Anna said. "Someday we will have an orchard. Fields of wheat. Many cattle. And more horses."

Peter had reached over to squeeze his mother's hand and said, "You'll have to forgive Mutti. She seems to think we're going to work miracles out here on the prairie."

Anna pretended to be indignant. "Is not miracle. Is hard work and God's blessing. Both will come. You will see."

Anna's love for her son and her faith in God were both so strong. Jane wanted the moment of joy to last, but as Peter headed outside and she helped Anna clear the table, all she could think of was that she had nothing to give Molly for Christmas. Mr. Huggins had said they would all go Christmas shopping together in Denver. And here they were—snowbound.

Anna put her hand on Jane's shoulder. "Please don't be sad. To Denver you will soon go. As for Christmas—snow cannot keep the Christ child away."

"Of course not." Jane forced a smile. "It's just that we were supposed to go shopping in Denver. I don't have anything to give her."

Anna pondered for a moment, then said, "Perhaps we make new dress for Katie. Would Molly like such?"

"She'd love it. But do we have time?"

Anna headed into Peter's room, waving for Jane to follow her. Feeling like an intruder, Jane stood back while Anna rummaged in Peter's dresser drawers. Jane couldn't help noticing that Peter Gruber's bed was neatly made up. And he had plants growing on the wide windowsill. In fact, one was about ready to bloom. Jane was trying to decide what the flower might be when Anna held up a blue work shirt and said, "We make blue dress? I have small piece of lace in my sewing basket. With nice buttons—"

"But I can't let you cut up one of Peter's shirts for a doll dress," Jane protested.

"Is old shirt." Anna held up one sleeve and pointed out the frayed cuff. Without waiting for Jane to agree, she headed back to the main room. "Peter goes now to find Christmas tree." She laid the shirt aside. "And we make springerle. Later, we sew." When Jane repeated the word *springerle* as a question, Anna pointed to the two rectangles of carved wood hanging on either side of the framed motto. "Please to take those down, and I will show you." She smiled as she bustled about. "Put on apron, Jane. We have much work to do!"

❧

Peter squinted through the layers of his scarf as his horse pulled the sleigh toward the river. It was going to take a miracle to find a suitable anything to use as a Christmas tree in all this snow, but he was determined. Short of risking freezing to death, he'd find a way to make Molly smile on Christmas morning. He was, after all, a *good* monster. The idea made him smile briefly—until he remembered the other reason December was meaningful.

He'd proposed to Priscilla in December. And, as always, memories of Priscilla brought a flood of other emotions. Rejection. . .loss. . .grief. . .and loneliness. He frowned and willed himself to remember little Molly's voice saying, *"You're a good monster."* And thinking on that, Peter realized that he didn't want to wallow in the past anymore. Something about the way Jane McClure was able to smile and banter with him and the way Molly had touched his ruined cheek—something about all of it made him feel hopeful.

As his Molly plodded along, head up, ears alert, Peter replayed the scene in his mind, smiling beneath his scarf and savoring the idea that someone had finally said the word *monster* aloud and made it part of a memory he would treasure. At least for a little while today, what that minié ball had done to his face hadn't really mattered all that much. In fact, as they sat around the breakfast table listening to Mutti talk about life in Germany and God's goodness and her hopes for an orchard, it was as if it hadn't even happened.

That first night when he'd stood looking down at Molly, he'd wallowed in regret when he realized that he and Priscilla might have had a child her age by now. But today, Jane had spoken of another soldier whose sacrifice had played a part in precocious Molly McClure's existence. What children would never have been born if Peter Gruber hadn't stayed up in that tree? Would he wish them out of existence to melt his scars? Given another chance, would Keig have saved his own life and let his friends die? Peter shook his head. He knew the answer to that. In battle, some men stood their ground, and some ran. He'd been the first kind in battle that particular day. Funny that he'd spent so much time running ever since.

Molly pulled up abruptly, tossing her head and snorting. Peter looked about, realizing they'd come to the riverbank. He guided her to turn east. There was a low place not far ahead, and if he remembered right, a few small cedar trees grew along the edge of a low rise. Maybe, just maybe—yes. Exactly as he'd hoped. The wind had driven snow across the top of the rise, accumulating more slowly in deep drifts along the opposite side of the clump of trees. He could still see the tip of the tallest one. Now, if only he could manage to dig one out.

Suddenly he was floundering in waist-deep snow again, laughing and flailing with his arms, until he struck gold. Or green at least. A small cedar tree. He returned to the wagon for his ax, and in a few minutes, red-faced and breathing hard, he'd put the tree in the sleigh and headed home. About halfway there, he had an irresistible urge to sing.

"*Stille Nacht. . .heilige Nacht. . .*" Something broke inside when he got to the last verse and the line "*Da uns schlägt die rettende Stund. Redeeming grace. . .*" He hadn't felt like the recipient of grace in a long while. And yet, thanks to Molly McClure, he realized it had always been there. He'd missed it, ignored it, refused it. And yet God offered it. Even to monsters.

Peter began to talk to God.

Chapter 10

Molly woke from her nap, ravenous and thrilled with her first taste of springerle. But she was coughing a bit and said her throat felt "scratchy," so after a dose of Anna's tonic, the challenge became how to keep her quiet so she would let her body rest and recover.

"Tomorrow is Christmas," Anna said gently. "You must to rest so it can be special. We have surprises." She leaned close. "Even Peter has surprise."

When Molly looked at her with doubt in her eyes, Jane smiled. "Anna's right. We have all kinds of plans for you. In fact," she teased, "now that I think of it, you really should go to bed at once so that we have time to prepare."

But fueled by promises of surprises, Molly had no interest in retiring. She wanted to go out to the barn and see the animals. They managed to stave off that idea with the news that Peter had harnessed Molly to the sleigh and headed off on an errand.

Molly's expression was hopeful. "Is he telling Mr. Huggins we aren't coming?"

"Of course not," Jane replied. "Because we are going. As soon as Anna thinks you're well enough." She retrieved *Little Women* from the other room and proposed to read another chapter.

"'What in the world are you going to do now, Jo?' asked Meg one snowy afternoon, as her sister came tramping through the hall, in rubber boots, old sack, and hood, with a broom in one hand and a shovel in the other. 'Going out for exercise,' answered Jo with a mischievous twinkle in her eyes."

"That's what *I* want to do," Molly muttered, tossing Katie onto the table with a decidedly rebellious attitude and kicking her foot back and forth in a restive rhythm.

Jane pretended not to hear and kept reading. "'I should think two long walks this morning would have been enough! It's cold and dull out, and I advise you to stay warm and dry by the fire, as I do,' said Meg with a shiver.

"'Never take advice! Can't keep still all day, and not being a pussycat, I don't like to doze by the fire. I like adventures, and I'm going to find some.'"

Before Molly could comment on her obvious desire for adventure, Anna spoke up. "I am thinking poor Katie is cold with no blanket of her own." As she spoke, she laid some scraps of cloth alongside the doll. Smoothing them, she looked over at Molly. "What would you think if we make Katie a quilt of her own?"

Molly looked at the fabric. "I don't know how to sew except for buttons and hems."

"I'm afraid I haven't done my duty in that regard," Jane said quickly. "I—I just—"

Anna waved the explanation away. "Is no matter. Perhaps God knew that Molly would need. . .*diversion*. . .one day." She looked over at Molly. "What do you think? What colors for Katie?"

Molly leaned forward. She pointed to a tiny black-and-white check that reminded Jane of the apron Anna had loaned her earlier in the day.

Anna nodded. "Is gut." She rummaged in her sewing basket, then stood up. "One moment." She went into the bedroom. Jane heard the sound of scraping, as if something was being pulled out from beneath the bed, although of course only the trundle was beneath the bed. Anna returned with a bit of red cloth. "Is nice for accent, ja?"

"Red's my favorite color," Molly said.

"Then must be Katie's, too." Anna smiled. She laid two pasteboard squares atop the fabrics and handed Molly a pencil. "You must draw around square on fabric then cut on line. Are these colors gut?" Molly nodded. "Of little square, twenty-four dark, twenty-four medium. Of big square, you make six light."

"How do I know if it's dark or medium or light?" Molly frowned. "Some of them could be either one, couldn't they?"

Anna quickly sorted the bits of cloth into three piles. "Dark, medium, light. You see?"

Molly nodded and, taking up the pencil, began to trace. When Jane offered to help her, Molly shook her head. "I'd rather you read about Jo's adventure."

&

The sunlight was fading when Peter Gruber finally came through the door. He wasn't quite as frozen as he'd been after going to the snowbound train—or maybe he just didn't seem as cold, for the first thing he did was cross to the worktable where dozens of springerle cookies lay cooling. "There is no aroma on the earth better than this."

He inhaled with pleasure and had just reached out to take one when Molly said, "We aren't allowed." She turned around in her chair and looked over at him. "We have to wait until after supper."

"Is that right?" He unwound his scarf then and looked to Anna, pressing both his hands together as if in prayer. He said something in German that Jane didn't understand, but it made Anna laugh.

"All right, all right." She held up two fingers. "Two each for you and the little one. But only two."

With a wink in Molly's direction, Peter pulled off his mittens and immediately popped two cookies into his mouth.

"You didn't even look to see the designs!" Anna scolded.

"I know the designs," Peter said. "I made them. Ja, Mutti?" He scanned the cookies on the table and selected two, which he carried over to Molly. "Two flowers for a lovely girl."

Jane looked up at the carved molds she'd rinsed off and returned to their place of honor on either side of Anna's embroidered motto. "You carved these?" She reached up to trace the intricate design of a stag, then a prancing horse. "They're gorgeous."

He bowed. *"Danke."* Then he clomped across the floor to the stove and, sliding past it to the rear of the room where Anna's cot was set up, took off his coat and sat down on the cot. Once again, she helped him with his boots, insisting that he stay put while she hurried into his room to bring out his fur-lined moccasins. He slid into them with an audible sigh, murmuring something to Anna. He waited until Jane looked his way and nodded a yes as he gestured with his hands.

Jane realized he was telling her how tall the tree was. When Molly looked his way, he pretended to be scratching his ear. Jane suppressed a smile.

"Something's going on," Molly said.

"What could be going on?" Jane grinned.

Molly rolled her eyes. "Christmas."

Peter came to the table and sat down. "Would you like some help with that?"

"Men don't sew," Molly said.

"Men do so." Peter reached into his mother's sewing basket, pulled out a spool of thread and a needle book, and in no time he was stitching two squares of fabric together.

Jane didn't hide her amazement. "You sew, you carve—do you cook, too?"

"As long as it only requires flipping flapjacks." He finished stitching the squares of fabric together and showed Molly how to finger press along the seam.

Molly took a bite of her second cookie. She looked at Jane. "Mr. Huggins doesn't do anything," she said. "He just stands behind a counter and takes people's money."

Later that night, Jane hung the last snowflake atop the little tree Peter had dragged home from the river. She and Peter had worked half the night making paper chains and scherenschnitte snowflakes and tying calico bows on branches, while Anna fashioned a new dress for Katie out of Peter's worn blue shirt. When she finally held it up—with an apology that it wasn't nicer—tears sprang to Jane's eyes. "It's beautiful," she said, then looked back at the tree. "Everything is so beautiful."

Peter stifled a yawn. "If I feed the livestock now, I can sleep a bit longer."

"I'll help," Jane said. Peter looked surprised. "You said your horse doesn't bite, and I refuse to let that raging lunatic of a rooster intimidate me." She crossed the room and took down her coat and scarf.

"I will roll out the dough for cinnamon rolls," Anna said. "We have enough butter for a good batch."

"You should get some rest," Jane protested. "I can do that

when we come back in. I don't even want to think about how many hundreds of cinnamon rolls I've made in that boardinghouse kitchen in the past couple of years. I'm happy to do it—if you don't mind the sounds of someone else in your kitchen while you rest, that is."

Anna hesitated for only a moment then nodded. "Danke." She was in bed before Peter and Jane left the house.

Out in the barn, Jane inhaled the aroma of fresh—and not-so-fresh—straw, following Peter's lead as he moved from one stall to the next, cleaning out his Molly's stall, breaking the ice in her water tank, and tending to the other animals. When he settled on the milk stool to milk the cow, Jane headed into the chicken coop and gathered eggs, happy that Solomon had apparently decided she didn't present any threat to his harem.

It seemed that they were back inside the house in no time at all. They entered to the sounds of Anna's soft snoring. Jane smiled as she hung up her coat, donned an apron, and rinsed her hands in the bucket of water Anna kept beside the stove for washing. She dusted the worktable with flour and began to roll out the dough for their cinnamon rolls, then spread it with butter and sprinkled cinnamon and sugar over the entire surface. In only a few minutes, two pans of rolls were rising atop the warm stove. It wasn't until she'd cleaned off the worktable and rinsed her hands again that she realized Peter hadn't gone to bed after all.

He was standing in the doorway to his room, watching her with a look of—something—on his face that might have worried her if a new boarder had expressed it. At the moment, it only made her catch her breath.

"I didn't mean to startle you." He held up his coffee mug. "I thought I might steal another cookie and some coffee, if there is any."

Jane lifted the coffeepot to check. "A cup, anyway." She grasped the handle. Peter crossed to where she was standing, and she poured the coffee, blushing for some foolish reason.

"Danke," he said.

His tone made her look up at him. "I–I'm afraid I don't know how to say 'You're welcome' in German."

"*Bitte.*"

She nodded. "Bitte, then. Really, it's nothing."

"You're wrong about that," he said. "It's everything. To have a woman as beautiful as you look at me without wincing. To have a child see through this"—he touched the scars—"and call me a good monster."

"You're not a monster. You're a good man."

He nodded. "But I'd forgotten that. Until you and Molly came into our lives."

Anna coughed. Jane started and, with a little laugh, set the coffeepot back on the stovetop. She nodded toward Anna's cot. "I refuse to be responsible for her response if she catches you stealing her springerle." She reached behind her to untie the apron, and for a moment she thought perhaps he would put his arm around her and draw her close. For a moment, she wished he would. But instead, he grinned like a mischievous boy as he lifted the lid of the wooden box where Anna had stowed the springerle.

Anna's voice sounded in the darkness. "Only two, Peter."

Chapter 11

"Is it Christmas yet?"

Jane opened her eyes. Molly was leaning over the edge of the bed looking down at her.

With a groan, Jane glanced toward the window. Gray light. "I believe it is. But you have to wait here until things are ready. We were up very late—actually until early this morning. Peter and Anna may wish to sleep a little longer." When she pulled her stockings on beneath the covers, she was suddenly aware of her new ability to bend her knee. With a quick thanks to the heavens, she rose and wrapped herself in a blanket. She paused at the foot of the bed before heading into the kitchen. "Promise me you won't peek."

"I won't. But I might get dressed. Is that okay?"

Jane gathered up Molly's things and handed them over. "That's perfectly all right. I'll be back in a bit." She tiptoed into the main room, glad when it seemed that both Peter and Anna were still asleep. As quietly as she could, she stirred up the fire in the stove, grateful for the warmth that emanated into the room as she stood, transferring her weight from one foot to the other in an attempt to keep them from going numb with cold.

"It's too cold for stocking feet."

She jumped at the whispered comment. Peter held out a pair of fur-lined moccasins.

"But where—?"

"There's a pile of cured hides beneath my bed. I guessed at the size, but at least you won't freeze." He anticipated her protest. "It took all of twenty minutes to cut and stitch a pair. They're very primitive."

Jane slipped one on. "They're wonderful." And suddenly she was newly aware that beneath the blanket wrapped about her, she was in a nightgown. And her hair was down. She felt heat crawling up the back of her neck. "I just wanted to get the rolls in the oven. I–I'll get dressed now."

Molly called again. "Is Christmas ready?"

Peter smiled down at her. "I think Christmas had better get ready."

"I hate to wake Anna. She must be exhausted."

"Anna is fine," the old woman said with a chuckle. "She can nap later."

Jane looked over at Anna's cot. Only a pair of merry blue eyes were visible above the edge of the woman's comforters. She'd been pretending to sleep. And obviously enjoying whatever it was that was going on between her son and Jane.

Jane shrugged deeper into the blanket, holding on tight as she headed into the bedroom to get dressed. When she glanced back to see if Peter was watching her, he was.

❧

Almost.

As Peter lay in bed Christmas night, that was the word he finally landed on to describe the day. Almost perfect. Of course Molly had no intention of making Peter feel the way he did as he lay in the dark, trying to talk himself out of the emotion that had been born inside of him and grown steadily. Today had been the first day in years when he could simply be a man enjoying life without any need to hold himself apart in order to escape notice.

The aroma of Jane's cinnamon rolls had lingered all through the presentation of the tree and the new doll dress this morning. Molly had clapped her hands with joy over both. She said the tree was almost as big as the last one she remembered at their old house. When Mutti presented a tray of her springerle for an afternoon snack, Molly said that even Sonja couldn't make cookies as good as Anna. They were almost the best she'd ever eaten.

In the afternoon, Peter and Molly played checkers while Jane and Anna napped. And then, when Molly insisted that she was almost well and begged to see the animals, Peter bundled her up and carried her out to the barn. She loved every minute of it. Molly the horse's stall was almost as big as the stalls where Papa kept his team when they lived in the other house. That barn had been brick. And Molly didn't call it a barn. She called it a stable.

As the day went on, Mutti's stew bubbling on the stove filled the air with savory aromas, and while Jane made biscuits, Peter once again took up needle and thread and joined Mutti and Molly as they stitched some more pieces of the doll quilt together. After supper Peter read the Christmas story by lamplight, first from Mutti's German Bible and then from his own English Bible. And they sang carols—Mutti in German and the rest of them in English.

The day had been perfect. *Almost.* Except for Peter's realization that Jane McClure had known fine things and was likely hoping for fine things again, and that he, Peter Gruber, with his ruined face and sod house, could not give them.

Mutti was right to say that it had been a blessing to help the McClures through a difficult time. But as he lay thinking back over the day, Peter told himself that it was also good that Molly was feeling well enough for them to go. She and Jane deserved to be blessed by the generosity of a man who offered prosperity in a bustling city where Molly would get the best of schooling and Jane— Peter closed his eyes.

The memory of Jane McClure looking at him without revulsion would grace his life forever.

&

Standing beside the bed, Jane smiled down at Molly as the child said her prayers, thanking God for the tree and the doll dress, for springerle and cinnamon rolls, for Molly the horse and Solomon the rooster, and, it seemed to Jane, for everyone and everything in the sod house. In spite of the nap she and Anna had taken this afternoon, Jane was exhausted. Poor Anna had nodded off while Peter read the Christmas story from his English-language Bible this evening.

When Molly finally pronounced her "amen," Jane stopped fighting her own weariness. Molly settled beneath her covers with Katie at her side, and Jane quickly undressed and followed suit. She'd just closed her eyes when she heard Molly say, "And please make it snow again. A lot. So that we can't leave tomorrow."

It was quiet for a few minutes, and Jane had almost fallen asleep when Molly leaned over the edge of the bed. "Did you hear that last part, Mama?"

"I did."

"Do you think God heard it, too?"

"Of course."

"Do you think it made Him mad for me to ask for snow?"

"Why would it?"

"Because I want snow so I don't have to do what you want." She was quiet for a moment. "Did it make you mad?"

Jane took a deep breath. "No, Molly. I'm not angry. But we can't stay. Mr. Huggins is waiting."

"Do you like him better because he doesn't have scars?"

Jane took another deep breath and let it out slowly. What or who she liked didn't matter. Mr. Huggins was offering them—something. And for all his kindness and gentle ways, Peter Gruber was not. "Do you remember what I said on the train when we left Omaha?"

Silence. Finally, a muttered, "You mean about having to trust you about Mr. Huggins?"

"Yes."

"I remember."

Molly tossed and turned for a moment. When she'd finally settled down, Jane said, "I love you more than you can possibly know, Molly."

"I love you, too, Mama."

In spite of her weariness, Jane lay awake for a long while, trying her best to look forward to Denver.

❧

"Peter."

Peter woke with a start and sat up. Mutti sat on the edge of his bed trembling. His first thought was of Molly or Jane, but then Mutti put her hand to her chest. She covered her mouth with the other hand and coughed. "I am afraid that I am unwell."

He reached out to take her hand. She leaned in, and he felt her forehead.

She nodded. "Ja. Is fever." She coughed again. "I am so sorry."

"There's nothing to be sorry about." He slipped out of bed and guided her to lie down. "Rest. Everything will be fine. Do you need anything?"

"In the green tin," she croaked. "Make tea. And don't—don't tell Jane. She must not worry."

Peter paused. "I'll tell her you were tired, and I insisted on you resting in my room. She'll understand."

"I want to go to the train. To say good-bye."

"I'll bring the tea. We'll see how you feel in the morning."

Peter had commenced making the herb tea as quietly as possible when Jane appeared in the bedroom doorway. Obviously she'd expected to see Mutti bustling about. She hadn't bothered to wrap herself in a blanket. When she saw Peter, she took a step back.

Before she could ask, Peter said, "Mutti's worn herself out. I talked her into sleeping in my room and letting me bring her some tea to help her sleep." He looked away, but not before taking in the vision of Jane's thick hair cascading around her shoulders. "I'm sorry I woke you."

"It's all right. Can I do anything to help?"

He shook his head. "She'll be fine." He concentrated on pouring hot water into the waiting mug. When next he glanced up, Jane had retreated to bed.

Mutti protested when Peter insisted that he move the cot in where he would hear her if she needed anything, but he did it anyway, and he was glad. As night wore on, she began to cough more, although she smothered each cough with a pillow. Finally, when Peter insisted that there must be more he could do, she directed him to make a different kind of poultice.

"No onions," she croaked. "It will wake our guests."

And so he crept about, wincing with each sound, grateful that Jane didn't reappear in the doorway while he followed Mutti's instructions. She applied the poultice herself, tapping on the edge of the bowl when it was all right for him to retrieve it. Then she insisted he keep it on his own nightstand so there'd be no evidence of anything but tea-making out in the main room when Jane and Molly got up.

"Don't look so worried," she said as she leaned forward so that Peter could put more pillows behind her. "Is gut. I will be fine."

But she wasn't fine. She slipped into a heavy sleep, and her fever raged.

❧

Jane leaned down and lay the back of her hand against Anna's pale cheek, then looked up at Peter, standing next to her. "We can't leave. Not today. Not until we know she's better."

Molly's voice sounded from the doorway. "I didn't mean for it to happen this way." Her voice wavered and tears spilled down her cheeks. "When I prayed that we could stay, I didn't mean—"

Peter went to her. Crouching down so he could look into Molly's eyes, he said gently, "Of course you didn't. This isn't your fault. You mustn't think any such thing."

Molly's lower lip trembled, and she looked down at the floor. "I was sick. And she took care of me." A tear slid down her cheek. "Maybe I brought it."

"The only thing you brought into this house that matters, Molly McClure, is joy and laughter. Because of you, Mutti and I had the best Christmas we've had in years. Because of you—" He broke off. Tapped his ruined cheek with his forefinger. "Because of you, I won't let this keep me from having a good life." He took her in his arms and held her close while she cried. "You must believe me. Mutti is going to be all right. And this isn't your fault. People get sick. We're both so glad you came to us." He let her go. "Do you know what you could do to help Mutti get better?" Molly shook her head. "You could finish the doll quilt while your mama helps me take care of her. It will make her feel happy to know you like it so much that you really are going to finish it."

"I was always going to finish it," Molly said. "I just didn't have time."

"Well, now you do. Spread your things out on the table, and I'll light the lamp. And you and your mama can tend Mutti while I drive to the train and send another message." He glanced at Jane. "If you're sure—"

"I'm sure," Jane said. "We're staying."

She wrote another telegram. This time the words came easily.

FRIEND TAKEN ILL *Stop* MUST STAY TO HELP *Stop*
APPRECIATE YOUR UNDERSTANDING *Stop*

She hesitated again about the signature. If only she knew how Mr. Huggins had responded to the delay. Perhaps there would be a response waiting when Peter delivered this new message. Something that would give her a hint as to what he was thinking. But for now it was impossible to know. And so she signed the telegram *J. McClure*.

❧

Anna was still sleeping when Peter finally bundled up and headed off to deliver Jane's telegram to the train station. Molly begged to go with him, but when Jane sent a pleading glance his way, Peter seemed to understand.

"I would love nothing better than to take you for a ride. But we must take care that you don't relapse. Do you know what that word means?"

Molly sighed. "It means I have to stay here."

Peter smiled. "It means we don't want to take any chances that you would get chilled and get sick again. We need you to be healthy to help with Anna." He paused, then said, "Is gut, ja?"

Molly shrugged. "Is gut." She grimaced. "But not really."

Jane handed Peter the piece of paper with the message written out. He folded it without reading it and tucked it in his shirt pocket. Then he donned his coat and hat. "I wish we had at least two real bricks," she said. "I could heat them in the oven to keep your feet warm while you're gone."

"You know about such things?" He seemed genuinely surprised.

"Sonja used to do it for us," Molly said.

Peter nodded. "Of course. The servant."

Something about the way he said it made Jane feel odd. Why did mention of Sonja annoy him? She retrieved a couple of blankets from the cot in his room, rolled them up, lowered the oven door, and set them down. "These will warm up while you hitch up the sleigh. Give a shout when you're ready to leave, and I'll bring them out. You can put them under the lap robe—" She broke off. The way he was looking at her made her feel foolish. "I only meant, we can't have you taking a chill. One patient at a time is enough."

He nodded. "Danke."

When Jane heard Peter's voice calling, "Ready," she grabbed the warmed blankets and hurried outside. He'd driven the sleigh near the door. As she handed up the blankets, words tumbled out. She jabbered all the while Peter was wrapping his legs and pulling the lap robe around them. *Be careful. Hurry back. Thank you for doing this. I'm so sorry to be extra trouble. Be careful. Hurry back.*

Finally he interrupted. "Jane. It's all right. Of course I'll hurry. If your Mr. Huggins has sent a message, you'll be reading it before you know."

Chapter 12

Molly stitched, Anna slept, and Jane worried. What if something happened to Peter out there in the cold? She wouldn't have any idea what to do without him. What if Anna was truly, desperately ill? Henry, the porter on the train, had indicated that Elm Creek didn't have a doctor. How did people stand living in a place where they didn't have a doctor? And Mr. Huggins. How would he respond to the news that Molly was better, but they still weren't heading to Denver? Would he understand? Was Jane ruining her only chance to give Molly a better life by lingering?

"Mama!" Molly's frustrated tone drew Jane back to the moment.

She held out a bit of patchwork. "My thread knotted up, and I can't make it work."

Jane took the sewing into her own hands but went to the doorway leading into Peter's room to look in on Anna before checking Molly's sewing problem. Anna was still sleeping, so Jane retreated to the table. She unthreaded the needle and used it as a tool to loosen the knot in the thread. Problem solved, she rethreaded the needle and handed the patchwork back to Molly.

"You don't have to work on that every minute if you don't want to."

Molly didn't even look up. "I want to show Anna when she wakes up." She bent to the piecing. "Anna said to make the stitches small and to back a stitch every third or fourth one."

"It's called a 'backstitch,'" Jane said.

Molly ignored her. "Anna said it makes the seam hold better."

Jane nodded. "She'll be very pleased to see your progress. Are you certain you don't want any help?" Molly was certain, and so Jane rose and stirred up the fire, hesitating for a moment when she realized that she wasn't quite certain what to cook. She decided on potato soup when she found some shriveled potatoes in a crock along the back wall. And onions. Anna had quite a supply of onions, which was no surprise, seeing as how she had such a firm belief in smelly poultices. Jane set to peeling potatoes and peeking in on Anna and counting the minutes, all the while wondering when Peter would return and what would happen when Mr. Huggins heard the news.

❧

Jane stared down at the telegram Peter had brought back from the station.

REGRETS *Stop* PLANS ON HOLD *Stop* HOPE TO HEAR GOOD NEWS SOON *Stop*

He'd signed it *H. Huggins*, which made her regret the *Jane* she'd sent his way. Did he think that too forward of her? At least she'd signed today's differently. She thanked Peter and tucked the telegram in her apron pocket. He hung his coat and things up and hurried to Anna's bedside.

When Jane heard low voices, she went to the doorway and peered in. Peter sat on a chair leaning forward, clasping one of Anna's hands between his while she smiled at him. At the sight of Jane, she looked up, but when she opened her mouth to speak, she began to cough. Peter hurried into the other room and returned with a mug of water. Anna took a sip, grimaced with the effort of swallowing, and then spread one wrinkled hand across her chest as she explained what was needed to make another poultice—this one with onions.

"I know how to do it, Mutti," Peter said, patting her hand gently. "And you want the syrup in the green bottle—not the brown one, right?" Anna looked surprised, even as she nodded her head. Peter said he'd see to the tea as well, kissed her on the cheek, and motioned for Jane to follow him into the main room. Once there, he handed her the green bottle and a spoon. "If you'll get that down her—take a mug of water with you—I'll handle the poultice and the tea."

"Can I help?" Molly had set her sewing down and was watching them.

Peter smiled. "You may." He reached for a small washtub. "Step outside the door and fill this tub with clean snow and bring it back inside. Then you can help me make Mutti's special tea."

When Jane went back to Anna, the old woman waved the teaspoon away and took a sip directly from the green bottle, then grimaced and drank down the mug of water. "Don't look so sad," she said. "Grubers are strong people. I will be fine. Mostly I am only tired. And I have—" She lifted her chin and stroked her throat with her fingertips, then coughed.

"At least you don't sound like you're congested the way Molly was." Jane paused. "Do you think we should put another steam tent up?"

"Nein." Anna took a deep breath to prove that her lungs were clear. "I breathe good." She reached for Jane's hand and put Jane's palm to her forehead. "See? Is only little warm, ja?"

When Jane agreed, Anna settled back with a smile. "All will be better in a few days. Maybe a week. Maybe a little more. We will see." She motioned to the main room. "Now go. Help Peter."

෴

Peter had Molly cut a square of cheesecloth and spread it on the worktable. Next, he reached for the cracker tin on the medicine shelf. "This is what you were after in your sleep that night." He took the lid off and held it so Molly could see the contents. When she took a whiff of the herbs and made a face, he chuckled. "I agree. It makes a powerful tea, but it's not something to be savored as a midnight snack." He took a generous portion of the dried leaves and put them in the center of the cheesecloth, then directed Molly to get some of Mutti's strong thread and help him make a tea bag. "We steep this until the water is a horrible shade of green, and then we take it in to Mutti." While he talked, he was heating water on the stove.

Jane came out of Mutti's room, went to the onion bin, and came back to the worktable. "She said they don't need to be peeled. I don't honestly remember seeing her make the poultice for Molly, but somehow that doesn't seem right."

"I know, but that's how she does it." Peter reached for a knife. "If you'll mind the teapot, I'll do the honors."

They worked together for a few minutes, and finally Molly looked up from the mug of tea she'd been watching. "It looks pretty awful," she said, and leaned down to take a whiff. "And it smells worse."

Peter leaned over to take a look. He nodded. "Yes, I believe that's just about terrible enough to effect a cure."

"Can I take it in?" Molly asked as Jane lifted the herbs out of the cup and set the sack on a saucer.

"Of course." Peter nodded. "Thank you for helping."

As soon as Molly got to the doorway, Anna called out a greeting, followed by a few dry coughs.

"It doesn't sound too bad," Jane said. "I mentioned a steam tent while you were gone, but she said it wouldn't be necessary."

"She said as much to me," Peter agreed. "But I'm still going to bring the wagon cover back in and the ropes. Just in case she's proven wrong in the middle of the night."

Anna administered her own poultice as before, and when Peter coaxed her to eat a little supper, she proclaimed Jane's potato soup delicious. As evening wore on and Jane mentioned reading to Molly before bedtime, Anna asked if she would mind reading at the bedside so she could enjoy the story as well.

Peter brought Mutti's rocker in for Jane and set it by the window. He turned up the lamp so she could see to read. Mutti insisted that Molly climb up and sit at the foot of her bed. Peter was about to step into the other room when Mutti called for him to stay. "Get chair. Stay near." She paused. "Bring springerle for Molly." She forced a weak smile.

❧

After everyone had retired, Jane lay awake for a while. It struck her suddenly, right before she fell asleep. Mr. Huggins hadn't mentioned Molly in the telegram. She rose and went to the sewing rocker by the bedroom window where she'd put her day dress and the apron, then dug the telegram out of the pocket and held it up to the low-burning lamp. Of course telegrams were by nature brief and to the point. *Regrets*. It occurred to Jane that, while she hated the idea that Anna was sick, whatever she was feeling about not being able to catch the train today, *regret* did not apply. *Relieved* was a better word for how she felt when it came to not being able to leave for Denver.

Plans on hold. At least Mr. Huggins had made some plans and was still hoping they would be realized. That was reassuring. Wasn't it?

Hope to hear good news soon. Jane sat back in the chair and looked toward the bed where Molly lay asleep. *Good news.* Yes. It would be good news when Anna was feeling well—well enough for them to say good-bye.

Jane sat for quite a while in the dim light of the lamp, thinking. Staring out at the snow. Finally she rose. On her way back to bed, she folded the telegram and tucked it into the side pocket of her carpetbag.

It was three long days and three longer nights before Anna finally asked Peter to help her out of bed and into the main room to sit at the table with everyone for breakfast. Molly proved herself a willing and able nurse, making tea according to Peter's instructions, shuttling toast and medicine bottles to Anna's bedside, and sitting with Anna while Peter tended the livestock—except for the chickens. Jane had taken over the chickens, surprised to find that she enjoyed the chore. She admired Solomon's spectacular iridescent tail feathers and even named the hen that seemed particularly resistant to the idea of giving up her eggs to an interloper.

"The one with the gold eyes," Anna said, when Jane called the hen a "she-donkey."

"How did you know?"

Anna chuckled, although the laugh cost her a few minutes of

coughing and a grimace as she commented on how sore coughing made an old woman's ribs. She glanced toward the door before speaking and then motioned for Jane to come close. "I never have liked that hen. Maybe we have her for supper when I'm feeling better, ja?"

For all of Anna's pain and coughing, it appeared the old woman had been right and that her illness wasn't going to be serious. She never needed the steam tent. Jane was thankful, but as the days wore on and Anna stayed abed, she began to wonder again about Mr. Huggins. She could almost sense dark clouds gathering in the west and a storm about to break.

A week after Peter had gone to send the second telegram, Jane's imaginary dark clouds became real. A loud knock on the door made everyone jump. Anna, who'd joined them at the breakfast table, clutched her blanket close as Peter rose to answer the door.

"Sorry to bother," a voice said, "but I've a letter for a Mrs. McClure. It's marked urgent." Peter swung the door wide enough for the speaker to step inside.

Jane rose. "I'm Mrs. McClure."

The man rummaged inside the oversize fur coat he was wearing and finally withdrew an envelope. He held it out, speaking to Peter as he did so. "Hope it isn't bad news. The sender addressed it to the telegraph operator at Elm Creek and enclosed two dollars as incentive to get me to deliver it right away. Said I was to wait for a reply."

Jane opened the envelope with trembling hands.

Jane—I take the liberty of addressing you informally, in light of the telegram which brought such disappointing news. I

*have thought of little else but how to understand the situation
since receiving your brief notice. While I do not wish to appear
unsympathetic, it does seem that you have more than repaid the
kindness of strangers. It is my utmost hope that you will relieve
my nagging questions by directing the bearer of this letter to
respond with a telegram stating the time of your arrival—which
I think it reasonable to expect within the next two days. You said
you were looking forward to welcoming 1876 in my company.
We are several days into the new year. Have I been wrong to
think that you shared my hopes for a mutually beneficial future?*

Respectfully,
Howard H. Huggins

"It's from *him*." Molly was the first to speak, and she didn't try to hide her resentment.

"Is everything all right?" Peter's voice was gentle. Concerned.

Jane swept her hand across her forehead as she stared down at the letter. "Yes. Of course." She looked up. Forced a smile. "I think so." Her voice wavered. "I'm not sure."

"Not meaning to rush you, ma'am," the letter carrier said, "but I'd rather my team not stiffen up waiting in the cold."

Jane nodded. And then, quite suddenly, she felt weak in the knees and once again took her seat at the table.

"I'll get you a pencil and paper," Peter said, then offered the man waiting a cup of coffee. "I'll take it," he said, "but if you don't mind, I'll wait outside with the team." He grasped the mug Peter offered and spoke to Jane. "Try not to take too long, ma'am." And he was gone.

It seemed like all the joy had gone out of the room. Jane stared down at the letter. Cleared her throat. Took the pencil and paper Peter offered.

Anna sighed. "Peter," she said, "help me back to bed. I think—I think I have fever again." She sighed, grunting softly as Peter took her arm and helped her back to bed.

As soon as they were gone, Jane forced a smile as she said to Molly, "He wants us to come soon. He's—well, he's tired of waiting, and he wants us to come no later than day after tomorrow."

"But Anna's still sick," Molly said. "And I don't have my quilt finished. She has to tell me how to finish it."

Peter's voice sounded from the doorway. "You don't have to answer it now. I'll send the driver away. When you have an answer, I'll take it to Elm Creek."

"I can't ask you to—"

"You didn't ask," Peter said. "I offered."

Jane lay the pencil down. "Thank you."

He was out the door almost before she finished the second word. When he came back inside, Jane rose and picked up the letter. "If you don't mind, I think—" She looked toward the room she and Molly had been sharing.

Peter spoke to Molly. "How about you stop pricking those dainty fingers of yours and try to beat me at checkers?"

Molly shrugged. "I can't beat you."

"You did beat me, just last night."

"Only because you let me."

"You think I let you win?"

"I know you did."

"Why would I do a thing like that?"

"Because you're a good monster," Molly said. She looked over at Jane. "Mr. Huggins wouldn't ever let me win," she said. "He doesn't even *like* to play checkers." And with that, she jumped up and ran into the bedroom.

Anna called for Peter, and Jane was left alone with the letter.

Chapter 13

W hat is it, Mutti?" Peter hurried to the bedside. When he reached out to see if she had a fever, she waved his hand away.

"Is nothing," Mutti said. "I must rest." She hunkered down and turned her back on him.

"But you just called for me."

Mutti nodded her head. "Is small house. Jane must be alone for a while."

Peter sat down in the chair by the bed. Leaning forward to rest his forearms on his legs, he stared down at the floor, agonizing over what might happen if he didn't speak up, terrified to risk it.

Mutti turned over in bed. She pulled the covers down below her chin. "You are going to let them go?"

"Please don't worry," Peter said. He reached for her hand and gave it a squeeze. "I'll take good care of you."

She sighed. "For that I do not worry. I worry for you."

He frowned. "I'm not coming down with whatever it is. My throat's fine. My lungs are clear."

Mutti rolled her eyes. "Lungs clear. Brain clouded." She paused. "You love her. You think I don't see?"

He took a deep breath. "I have nothing to offer. She had a fine house with her first husband, and this Mr. Huggins will likely provide her with another."

"And what is a fine house without love?"

He met her gaze. "And what is life with a monster?" He stood up. Mutti opened her mouth to say more, but he held up his hand. "Please. You're going to say it doesn't matter. But it does." Surprised when tears threatened, he drew a ragged breath. Forced a smile. "Molly calls me a good monster, and I'll never forget that. Between the two of them, they've healed something I didn't think could ever be right again. Those are good memories. And I don't want them ruined by the memory of yet another beautiful woman looking away when I declare—when I ask—" He broke off. "Sleep well, Mutti. I love you very much."

There was no point in his trying to sleep. Peter didn't even try. Instead, he headed outside to the barn. He hung a lantern on a nail by Molly's stall and brushed her sleek coat until it shone. He mucked out stalls. Finally, when he ran out of work, when his feet felt like two blocks of ice, he headed into the little tack room. He closed the door behind him and started a small fire in the woodstove before perching on a bale of hay and propping his feet up on a crate.

He woke with a start to Solomon's crowing. With a groan, he stood up, stretching before opening the door to the tack room and peering across the way through the little window that faced the house. The snow was beginning to melt. The clothesline was no longer buried in a snowdrift. He left the door open to the tack room and made his way past the stalls and out into the fresh air. The sky was getting lighter in the east. In the west, it was still dark.

A sliver of moon hung low in the clear sky. If he was going to take Molly for a sleigh ride, he'd better get it done today. He'd bring her out after breakfast and— He gulped. Jane was lighting the lamp in the bedroom window. He looked back at the barn. And finally up to the sky. *I'm afraid. God. . . . I'm so afraid.*

He turned toward the house. He hadn't felt this way since that long-ago day when he perched in a tree and watched gray uniforms emerge from a cornfield. Everyone told him he'd been brave that day. Maybe he had. He'd wanted to defend his friends. What was a man worth if he wasn't willing to try just as hard to save himself? Taking a deep breath, Peter whispered, "Help," and headed inside.

It was still dark when Jane rose and lit the lamp in the window. Without bothering to do anything about her hair, she slid her bare feet into the moccasins Peter had made for her, then grabbed a blanket and headed into the other room. *Peter.* She'd heard him leave the house. He hadn't come back inside. The idea of him sleeping in the barn spoke volumes. Whatever flights of fancy she'd entertained, whatever she thought she'd read in his dark eyes, obviously she'd been wrong. He was avoiding her.

She laid Mr. Huggins's letter on the table, then lit another lamp and tiptoed to Peter's room to look in on Anna. The old woman was sleeping peacefully. Whatever vestiges of illness she was fighting off, it was obvious she no longer needed special care. Mr. Huggins was right. It was time to go.

Back in the main room, Jane heated water. She didn't want to disturb Anna by grinding coffee. She would settle for hot water until everyone was awake. Then they'd have a proper breakfast, and she'd tell Molly what she'd decided they must do.

She sat for a moment staring down at the letter, praying desperately for peace. Finally it came. Taking up the pencil, she wrote the letter that Peter would take to the depot today. Tears slid down her cheeks as she signed it, then folded it and slipped it into the envelope. Swiping them away, she clutched the mug of warm water between her palms and looked around the room. She gazed up at the sampler. For a moment, she closed her eyes. *Please be my strong tower today.*

Molly was going to be so angry about not having time to finish her doll quilt before they left. She would promise the child that they would have a cabinet photo taken of her with Katie and the finished doll quilt so that Anna could see it. Maybe that would help. Certainly Anna would enjoy a memento of their brief friendship.

The door opened, and Jane sprang to her feet. Peter moved slowly, unwrapping his scarf, removing his hat, hanging everything up before he said a word. When he did, it was to nod at the envelope on the table. "I was hoping. . ." He paused. "You've written your answer."

Jane nodded.

"I wanted to. . ." His voice trailed off again.

"You must be so cold." Jane set the mug of warm water down. "Did you sleep at all? Anna's resting. I haven't heard her cough once. I'll make coffee. And breakfast. Just let me get dressed." She headed for the bedroom.

"Don't go."

She turned to face him, afraid to say anything, afraid she'd heard what she wanted to hear, not what he'd actually said.

"Did you hear me, Jane? I said, 'Don't go.' "

"I heard."

He looked away. "I have a medal for bravery. For what I did that day." He drew his palm across the scarred cheek. "But I'm not brave. I'm terrified right now. Terrified to talk and afraid that if I don't I'll lose—" He closed his eyes, then finally looked her way. Shook his head. "Molly's right. I am a monster. I know that. Stephen McClure gave you so much. You had a servant, for goodness' sake. And this Huggins fellow? I can't compete with any of it." He took a deep breath. "But I love you, Jane. Heaven help me. I love you, and I love Molly. But if you can't love me back, I understand. Really, I do."

Jane swallowed. Couldn't he hear her heart beating? See her trembling? She nodded toward the letter. "I did my best to explain—to apologize. I never intended to mislead him. I just—I just wanted what was best for Molly." She paused. "We lost the house, Peter. Stephen made some terrible investments, and then he died, and we lost it. I had to sell it to pay all the people we owed money. I paid them, but—" She began to cry. "Things got hard. And I was so lonely. I answered an advertisement in the paper. And Mr. Huggins—" She gave a short, throaty laugh. Shook her head. "Poor Mr. Huggins. I told him we would be catching the train for Omaha."

"Omaha?" Peter frowned.

Jane nodded. "However desperate my situation, I could never marry one man when I was in love with another." Her voice wavered. "I didn't think you—" She cleared her throat. "You didn't kiss me. That night when you could have. You made a joke instead of kissing me."

"You wanted me to kiss you?"

She nodded. "I love you, too, Peter. I just—"

Whatever she was going to say slipped her mind as he pulled her into his arms.

❧

"Molly." Jane tickled the sleeping child's cheek. "It's time to get up. Breakfast is ready."

"I'm not hungry." She was lying with her back to Jane, and she didn't budge.

"Peter's taking us to post my letter to Mr. Huggins. He said you wanted a sleigh ride, and it's a beautiful day. He thought you'd want to go along."

Molly shrugged. "I want to stay here. With Anna. I want to finish Katie's quilt."

"I know. But you need to trust me—"

"—in the matter of Mr. Huggins," Molly groused. "I know." She finally rolled onto her back. And sat up. And looked from Jane to Peter and back again.

Jane leaned into Peter, and he put his arm around her as he said, "I have a question for you, Molly."

Molly grabbed Katie and held her close. "All right. Go ahead."

"I want to ask your mother to marry me. Is that all right with you?"

With a shout of joy, Molly launched herself into Peter's arms, wrapped her arms around his neck, and planted a kiss, first on his good cheek and then on the bad one.

Anna spoke from where she was standing in the doorway. "What am I seeing?"

Jane let go and went to her side. "You shouldn't be out of bed. Let me—"

Anna shooed her away. She glared at Peter. "You have asked?" Peter nodded. She looked at Jane. "And you have said yes?"

Jane nodded and glanced at Molly. "We both have."

Anna raised both hands to the heavens. "Praise be to Gott!" She smiled and shook her head. "So sick I was of being sick." She looked at Peter. "I thought never would you ask."

"Mutti," Peter scolded. "You were *pretending*?"

Anna shrugged. "Maybe a little." She forced a cough, then turned toward the kitchen, waving for everyone to follow her. "Come. We have springerle for breakfast today, ja?" She grinned at Peter. "All you want."

Discussion Questions

1. Share a favorite passage or scene from the story. Why did it resonate with you?

2. Did you learn something new, either about yourself, about the nineteenth century, or about God from this story?

3. Can you think of a time in your life (or a friend or family member's) when you/they wanted to hide from people? How do you think having Jane and Molly in his life will change Peter's feelings about interacting with others?

4. Have you experienced being snowbound? How did you pass the time?

5. Peter associates the aroma of springerle cookies with holidays. What scents make you think of Christmas? Do you have a special memory of a tradition that creates a sense of "home" and "family" for you? Have you ever had to celebrate Christmas away from home? What did you do to compensate?

6. Molly's outburst about Peter being a "monster" is used in a unique way in the story. Have you had an experience when a child innocently said something that made everyone uncomfortable? How did you handle it? What would you do differently?

7. Jane isn't really very comfortable with "farm chores" like gathering eggs. Have you ever experienced something similar? How did you react? How do you see Jane changing in years to come?

8. Brainstorm the sequel. Where do you think Peter and the family will be in five years? What would you want to see?

9. You are the casting director for the film version of *A Patchwork Love*. Who would you cast to play Jane? Peter? Anna? Molly? What about Mr. Huggins?

10. If you were in charge of writing epitaphs for these characters, what would you say about them?

Four Patch Doll Quilt

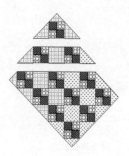

Finished Size   Quilt—15½" x 18¾"
Blocks—2½" x 2½"

Directions

The following instructions are for template-free method—using rotary cutter, seam allowances included.

Block Cutting:

2 (1¾" x 1¾") squares from each of the dark fabrics.

2 (1¾" x 1¾") squares from each of the medium fabrics

Setting Cutting:

6 (3" x 3") squares from background fabrics

3 (5⅛" x 5⅛") squares from assorted background fabrics, cut in half on the diagonal, twice (you will have two extra pieces) *these are cut slightly oversize

2 (3½" x 3½") squares cut in half in the diagonal for the corners *these are cut slightly oversize

Borders Cutting:

Inner

2 (1" x 14½") lengthwise cut strips for the sides
2 (1" x 12") lengthwise cut strips for the top and bottom

Outer
2 (2¼" x 15½") lengthwise cut strips for the sides
2 (2¼" x 15¼") lengthwise cut strips for the top and bottom

Make the Blocks

Arrange the squares to form the four patches for piecing.

Sew a medium square to a dark square, press seams toward the dark fabric. Repeat.

Pin the two segments together, matching seam intersections, then sew. Press this seam open. Square these blocks to measure 3" x 3".

Make the 12 Four Patch blocks.

Assemble the Quilt Top

Arrange the Four Patch blocks on point in rows of three across by four down. Be sure the dark squares are all going the same direction—vertical—and the medium colored squares the same direction—horizontal.

Position the assorted background fabric setting pieces.

Sew to make diagonal rows, pressing seams toward the alternate blocks.

Pin rows, matching seam intersections, then sew.

Using the Clipping Trick described below on the seam intersections, continue to press seams toward the alternate blocks; press the clipped intersections open. The top should measure 11" x 14½".

This is a nifty way to create less bulk at the seam intersections of machine stitched pieces, which will result in flatter blocks.

1. Clip up to the seam line through both layers of the seam allowance ¼" from each side of the seam intersection (the clips will be ½" apart).

2. Now you can press the seam allowance in the direction it would like to lie (or the direction indicated in the project instructions) to reduce the bulk. Press the clipped intersection open.

Add the Borders

Pin the two 1" x 14½" strips to the sides of the quilt top, then sew. Press seams toward the border.

Pin the two 1" x 12" strips to the top and bottom of the quilt top, then sew. Press seams toward the border.

Pin the two 2¼" x 15½" strips to the sides of the quilt top, then sew. Press seams toward the outer border.

Pin the two 2¼" x 15¼" strips to the top and bottom of the quilt top, then sew. Press seams toward the outer border.

Quilting

The quilting lines form a grid over the Four Patch blocks and produce an X in each square of the Four Patch. This same grid is repeated in the alternate blocks and setting triangles.

Quilt in continuous lines from inside inner border to opposite side inside the inner border. Inner border is quilted ⅛" from ditch. Outer border—the crosshatch quilting design is an extension of the Four Patch blocks.

Draw the quilting lines with a ruler and a chalk wheel fabric marker (use white). Since the chalk lines will disappear when quilting, you will only be able to mark one line and quilt it, mark a line and quilt it, etc. (Mark lightly!) I recommend single fold binding on all quilts from large to small, as that is what was done in the nineteenth century.

Springerlein

(German recipe adapted from a 1913 cookbook)

4 eggs
1 cup powdered sugar
Grated rind of 1 lemon
4 cups flour
½ teaspoon baking powder
Aniseed

Beat eggs thoroughly with sugar. Add lemon rind, flour, and baking powder sifted with flour, and mix quickly into loaf shape without much handling. Set in a cool place two hours. Flour a baking board and roll out dough to ¼-inch thick. Dust the mold* with flour, press the *springerlein* on it tightly but firmly, then turn it over and carefully remove the cakes. Cut off surplus dough, put in the remainder, and mold more. Use as little flour as possible in rolling out. Put a cloth on the table, sprinkle it with aniseed, lay cakes on it, and let it stand twelve hours in a cool room. Bake** in buttered pans.

*Springerlein molds are available through many Internet outlets and gourmet cooking shops.

**This original recipe doesn't indicate an oven temperature or a time, probably because the women were baking in woodstoves. Modern-day recipes vary in recommendations for oven temperatures from 255 degrees to 325 degrees and time from 10 to 15 minutes.

Filling for Graham Crackers

This recipe was handwritten at the bottom of an introductory page to The Horsford Cook Book *(1895) by Fannie Merritt Farmer. At the bottom of the title page, the publishers promise to "send a copy of this book, free, postpaid, on receipt of four labels from the bottom of the can of Horsford's Baking Powder."*

1 cup powdered sugar
1 tablespoon melted butter
2 teaspoons cocoa
3 teaspoons cold, mild coffee
1 teaspoon vanilla
Add a little cream if too thick

Stephanie Grace Whitson, bestselling author and two-time Christy finalist, pursues a full-time writing and speaking career from her home studio in southeast Nebraska. Her husband and blended family, her church, quilting, and Kitty—her motorcycle—all rank high on her list of "favorite things."

The Bridal Quilt

Nancy Moser

Dedication

To my dear friends Steph and Judy,
two women who live out their own place
in history with passion and character.

Chapter 1

New York City, November 1889

B ut Samuel, you *can't* leave me alone tonight." Ada stood within the warmth of his arms and fingered his diamond tie tack. "My evenings are empty when we're not together."

Samuel took her busy hands captive. "As are mine, dear lady. Your companionship is always my first choice."

"Then why—?"

"My friends know how devoted we are to each other. So much so, that they insist I pull myself away for a Friday evening in their company."

Ada knew the young men in their set didn't like how she'd plucked Samuel out of their circle. She imagined they were a bit uneasy to witness the effects of true love, especially when they would rather concentrate on flirtation, frivolity, and fun. They were mere boys, while her Samuel was a man.

Her man.

The clock on the parlor's mantel struck eight, prompting Samuel to press his lips to hers before gathering his hat and cloak.

"I'll call on you tomorrow at one. Would you like to go to the Met? We could dine afterward."

That sounded delightful. But Ada didn't want to let him off so easily. "Are you certain one is late enough after your night carousing with the boys?"

He volleyed her teasing right back at her. "One fifteen then." With a wink he left her.

The room was empty without him.

But before Ada could brood, she heard the tinkle of a bell coming from upstairs. Nana needed her.

Ada met her mother in the upper hallway. She was also on the way to answer the summons.

"I'll go, Mother."

"But Samuel. . ."

"He left." Mother looked taken aback, so Ada explained. "He had another engagement." When her mother's eyebrows rose, she added, "We aren't engaged yet, so Samuel is free to. . .to. . ."

"He's been so attentive, Ada. You must see to it this match is made. The Alcott banking fortune is huge and—"

"I wouldn't be marrying Samuel for his money. We love each other."

"All the better. But you really must—"

Her grandmother's bell saved her. "If you'll excuse me."

"Get him to propose, dear," Mother said. "Samuel Alcott is an excellent catch."

Ada was glad she was walking away so she could roll her eyes without fear of a reprimand. Yes, yes, she knew Samuel was an excellent catch, and yes, she would like nothing better than for him to propose. But her mother's words cheapened the feelings they had for each other. For this wasn't some arranged match; it was true love. Samuel could have been a peddler on the street and she wouldn't love him less. They were soul mates.

She cherished any time they spent together, whether it was going to the opera, enjoying dinner at the Vanderbilts', or sitting before the fire reading to each other. *How do I love thee? Let me count the ways. . . .*

Ada couldn't count the ways she loved Samuel. Each smile, each word, each wink, each touch left her feeling—*knowing*—that their love was a gift from God.

A proposal would come soon. Samuel had hinted at a special surprise he had planned for her at Christmas, which was just a month away. Marriage was inevitable, and a lifetime together was a dream that would come true.

Ada knocked softly on the door to her grandmother's room, then entered. The gas sconces were unlit, the only light coming from an oil lamp on the bedside table. Ada sought Nana's face. She could always tell how she was feeling by her expression. This evening there was an absence of discomfort, but her brow was furrowed. "What's wrong?" Ada asked, taking her hand. "You seem worried."

"I heard the front door open, then close in only thirty minutes' time. Why did Samuel leave you so soon?"

Ada smiled. Although loss of hearing was a normal result of age, Nana's hearing was finely tuned. Even though she often felt poorly, she knew the comings and goings in the Wallace household almost better than those who experienced them firsthand.

"Samuel's friends are jealous of the time he spends with me and insist he spend time with them tonight." Ada perched on the chair beside the bed, her bustle preventing her from sitting back.

"Can you blame them?" Nana said. "They know they're losing one of their own to the matrimonial yoke."

"That's a horrible term, Nana."

She shrugged. "To men it fits. To most men, anyway. They mourn the loss of their freedom, even as they seek marriage for its social advantages and the private. . .benefits."

Ada felt herself blush. Her mother would never even elude to the intimate side of marriage, so she was glad for Nana's more direct manner. "Samuel's not like that."

"Oh, I guarantee you, he is—and be glad for it. For without those advantages and benefits—especially the private ones—marriage is as shallow as a pond in a dry spell."

Ada was glad her mother wasn't in the room to cringe at Nana's down-home sayings. Nana had married well and had risen from her meager station to become a matriarch within New York society's "Four Hundred"—the elite of the elite. Mother seemed to have forgotten that fact, and that most of their friends—including the Vanderbilts and the Astors—had also started low and ended high after they came to America. Nana said that having dirt on your shoes didn't matter if you were on the right path.

Her proverbs always made Ada smile. Mother, on the other hand, wished there'd been an additional generation between their current wealth and Nana's humble beginnings.

Nana pointed to Ada's sewing basket. "Go gather your quilt-work and let's have a good talk."

"But didn't you need something?"

"I needed to have a good talk with *you*. Now go on. Idle hands are the devil's workshop."

Ada retrieved her sewing basket and took out the latest block of the crazy quilt she was making for her trousseau. She'd been working on it for six years, since she'd turned thirteen. Each fabric corresponded to a dress she'd worn and brought back memories of people and places and happy occasions. It was her bridal quilt, a map of her life she would bring to a marriage, detailing her life *before*. Once married, she would start a new quilt to chronicle that season of her life.

This particular square was nearly finished, with just some embroidery needed across the seemingly haphazard array of pieces. She threaded her needle with sage-green floss.

Nana pointed to the color. "That green against your mauve silk is a pretty choice. You do have an eye for such things."

"I take after you."

"Of course you do." Nana smoothed her gnarled hands over the lace edging on the sheet. "Now then. To the subject at hand. I won't ask if Samuel's proposed, because I know I'd be the first to know." She looked at Ada over her glasses, challenging her.

"Who else would I tell first?"

"Your mother."

Ada knew there was tension between Nana and Mother but tried not to take sides or play into it. "Mother will definitely be next."

"Hmm."

Ada changed the subject. "Samuel's taking me to the art museum tomorrow."

"Say hello to the paintings for me. Did you know you and I were there when it opened?"

"Yes, Nana." Ada had heard her grandmother's story of the first reception of the Metropolitan Museum of Art in 1870. How they'd hung the initial 174 paintings covering the walls from floor to ceiling, causing Nana to comment that obviously a woman needed stilts to see the paintings properly, eye to eye. Ada had only been a baby, but Nana had prided herself on starting her art education early. She'd always been the one to take Ada and her brother, John, on outings. Ada's fondest memories were of the times spent as the Three Musketeers, seeing New York through

Nana's eyes. How sad those times were over. Nana rarely ventured out of bed anymore, though her illnesses were often vague.

Ada's face must have revealed her wistfulness, but Nana guessed wrongly about the cause. "Don't you go worrying about Samuel going out with his friends. If you don't trust his character, you shouldn't consider marrying the man."

"Oh, I trust him. I just don't trust his friends."

"Now there, I can't help you. Let's say a prayer that God does the watching for us."

Amen.

❧

"Come on, Samuel. Don't tell us you've never gone slumming." Joseph yanked on his arm.

Samuel nearly tripped on the cobblestones, then righted himself and gently pushed his drunken friend away. It had been good to catch up on the news and latest gossip, but two hours and far too many drinks later on his friends' part, and Samuel was done with it. And now they wanted to go down to Five Points—to the immigrant slums? Nothing good could come of it.

But then Leo whistled for a hack and dragged Samuel inside while the other three shoved from behind.

"To the slums, driver! Show us how the other half lives!" Oscar was the last one in the carriage and virtually fell over Samuel on the way to his seat. When he muttered, "Sorry, old chum," his breath smelled of onions, garlic, and wine.

I gave up time with Ada for this? Samuel turned away from his friends to stare out the window. *Sweet, kind, bright, curious Ada.* How he loved her. Why hadn't he proposed yet? She was expecting it, and he wanted to oblige.

But something was holding him back.

There was no way he could explain his hesitation to her—he had trouble explaining it to himself. Was it the voice of God, or simply his own inability to make a decision? Maybe it wasn't anything to be concerned about. After all, didn't everyone feel apprehension when making a life-changing decision?

He closed his eyes a moment and said an oft-repeated prayer. *Show me Your will, O Lord.* Over the years he'd come to know this prayer covered everything. He could pray for specifics, spelling out exactly what *he* wanted, but in the end, it came down to preferring God's plan over his own. He couldn't pinpoint any monumental moment when he'd officially deferred to God's will, as the habit had evolved over a lifetime of being the son of parents who lived their faith. And a grandmother.

His parents had died when he was eleven, back on Christmas Day 1876. At least they'd been together. At least they'd been doing what they loved to do—attending the theater. That the theater had burned, killing nearly three hundred people, had been a horrific end to a happy day. But for a bad cough, Samuel would have been in the theater with them. "You were saved for something, Samuel," was a mantra often repeated by his dear grandmother, who, with Grandfather, had raised him. He felt it was his duty to find out exactly what that *something* was.

Grandmother had been gone four years now, but she'd always encouraged him by saying, "Listen for the Lord—whether it be a whisper or a shout."

Samuel had never heard God shout, but he'd come to believe the whispers in his mind were God's way of directing him to do the right thing. And so, until the *"Wait"* was replaced with a *"Now!"* Samuel would bide his time proposing to Ada.

Yet he sorely wished God would give him the go-ahead soon. How he longed to make her happy.

The carriage came to a stop, and Samuel's friends looked outside and loudly made the determination that they had, indeed, arrived in the slums.

Leo pressed some coins in the driver's hand and said, "Wait for us. We'll be back in a—"

The driver shook his head. "Pardon me, sir, but I ain't waiting 'ere for no man."

"Then how—?"

The driver pulled away, leaving them standing on the dark street.

Joseph laughed nervously. "Well then, chums. It appears we're on our own to explore."

"Explore some'ere else," came a voice.

They looked to the entrance of an alley and saw a man curled in a ball, trying to sleep on the ground.

He glared up at them with a toothless smile and pretended to doff his hat. "If yer don' mind, gen'lemen."

Oscar removed his own hat, swept it into an exaggerated bow, and addressed the man, his words slurred by the drink. "Anythin' you say, your majesty."

The man roused. " 'Ey there. No need to be rude."

No, there wasn't. Samuel pulled Oscar away. "Leave him be."

Oddly, the streets were full of people. It was after eleven, but people—mostly men—lollygagged around the stone steps leading to the front doors of dilapidated tenements, or were seen in the shadows, their hands in their pockets, watching Samuel and company like vultures eyeing their prey.

"I don't think this was a good idea," Joseph said under his breath. "We need to get out of here."

Oscar tipped his hat to the men, and Samuel pulled him forward even harder. "Stop it!" he whispered. "You'll get us all killed."

The sounds of an argument and more than one crying baby could be heard from the windows that looked down upon the narrow street. A dog ate some horse droppings just as someone heaved a pail of rubbish from an upper window.

It splattered on Oscar's shoes. "Ahh!" He looked upward. "What do you think you're doing?"

A woman appeared in the window and yelled something in Italian—complete with hand gestures—before shutting the window with a thud.

Samuel sidestepped around the rubbish—which appeared to be the leftovers of a meal.

A scantily dressed woman emerged from the shadows and locked onto Leo. She spoke in some Slavic language, her features exotic. Her hand brushed across Leo's chest, and suddenly, Leo took her wrist roughly. "Oh no, you don't! Let go of my wallet! And get away with you!" He pushed her away, and she smiled at him smugly, as if his rebuff meant little.

A group of four children suddenly swarmed around them, tugging at the men's clothes, their small hands hunting for some bounty.

"Off! Get away!" Joseph said.

The children scattered, but looking up the street was like viewing a gauntlet to be run. The young men's shouts—their very presence—were drawing too much attention. Samuel pointed back to the way they had come. "Men, we need to leave. Now. Perhaps we can catch a cab if we walk north—"

A child's screams cut through his words, and another kind of instinct took over. Samuel ran toward the scream into an alley. There, in the dim light of the moon, he saw a man hitting a little girl. Slapping her. Shaking her. Tossing her against the alley's debris only to pick her up again for more abuse.

Samuel ran forward. "Stop that! Stop that right now!"

The man paused in midslap. He glared at Samuel. "What's it to you?"

Before Samuel could answer, the girl made a run for it toward the street. Then, obviously spooked by the presence of Samuel's friends, she returned and took refuge behind Samuel. She pointed at the man and said something in another language.

The man picked up a piece of wood and slapped it against his palm. He strode forward slowly. "So this is the way it's gonna be. Don't make no never mind to me whether I hurt her or hurt you. 'Tis your choice, Mr. Fancypants."

"Samuel, come on." It was Oscar.

Samuel couldn't risk looking back to see exactly where his friends were, but by Oscar's voice, Samuel knew they had not followed him into the alley.

They were not supporting him.

"There's a cab at the next intersection!" Leo said. "I'll go hail it."

"Come on, Samuel," Joseph said. "Don't get between a father and his daughter."

"Er ist nicht mein Vater!" the girl said.

The man pointed his weapon at the girl. "You owe me, *Liebchen*, and you'll do as I say, *verstehe?*" He lunged toward her, forcing Samuel to step back, holding the girl in place behind him.

But the man was too quick. He reached around Samuel and grabbed the girl by the sleeve of her coat and yanked her back. He heaved her to the side of the alley where she bounced off the brick wall and fell to the ground in a crumpled heap.

Samuel had never witnessed such cruelty. He took a step toward the girl to help her, but the man moved between them.

"You leave 'er be," the man said. "She's mine!"

Samuel looked at the girl, then the man, then the girl. She

moaned and was not getting up.

Oscar called from the street. "Come on, Samuel! The cab's waiting."

Then he had an idea. He reached in his coat pocket where he'd placed the change from dinner and pulled out a handful of coins. It was only a few dollars, but it would have to do. Samuel held the money in his palm. "See here? I have over twenty dollars in coins. For your trouble."

"Now yer talkin'," the man said, taking a step forward.

Samuel flung the coins over the man's head, deeper in the alley where they clattered and scattered. A man who'd been sleeping in the shadows emerged and began scrambling after the money.

"Hey! Stop that! Those are mine!" The evil man raced back to claim his coins.

The distraction was just what Samuel needed. He rushed to the girl, scooped her into his arms, and ran toward the street.

At the mouth of the alley, he turned right and ran as fast as he could, feeling as if the hounds of Hades were nipping at his heels.

"Come on!" shouted Joseph from the cab a block ahead.

Behind him Samuel heard the man take chase.

"Come on! Hurry!"

Once at the cab, Samuel tossed the girl into the arms of his friends and dove in after her. The cab pulled away with his feet still hanging from the door. The sound of the horse's hooves replaced the footsteps of the man.

His friends helped him to a seat. The frightened girl sat on Oscar's lap. Blood glistened on her face, and Samuel retrieved a handkerchief.

As Samuel noticed the blood, so did Oscar. "Eeww. You take her!" He handed her off, then checked the cleanliness of his suit. "Why'd you bring her with you?"

Samuel carefully dabbed at a cut on the girl's forehead, hating to see her wince. She looked at him with wary eyes. What must she be thinking? Even though he'd saved her, she had no reason to trust him. To trust anyone. For all she knew, he was simply another kind of evil man. "I suppose you would have left her there?"

Oscar didn't answer.

"She smells awful," Joseph said, holding a handkerchief to his nose.

Samuel was appalled at their reactions. "What's wrong with you? Where is your compassion?"

"I left it in my other suit." Oscar laughed at his own joke.

Their laughter was like acid. Samuel had known these men his entire life—or at least he'd thought he'd known them. How could they be so cold and uncaring?

Finally Leo weighed in. "Chide them all you want, Samuel. The point remains: What are you going to do with her?"

Good question.

❧

Samuel would never forget the look on the butler's face when he entered his family's home carrying the girl.

"Mr. Samuel! What happened? Who—?"

"As you can see, Briggs, the girl is injured. I'm taking her to the green bedroom."

"I. . . Should I call for Dr. Brandeis?"

Although Samuel couldn't be sure, he didn't think the girl's injuries were life-threatening. "I don't think that's necessary—at least not yet. Please call Sally to come help."

"Very good, sir," Briggs said.

Samuel headed up the staircase and was pleased when the girl linked her hands around his neck.

"It will be all right," he said to her. "You're safe now."

❧

An hour later, Samuel tapped on the door of the green bedroom. Sally, the maid, told him to come in.

He found Sally tucking the girl into bed. She looked like a far different girl than the one he'd seen on the streets. Her hair was light brown, nearly blond, and her face was cleaned of dirt and blood—though bruises were forming on her cheeks.

"She's all clean, Mister Samuel," Sally said. "I even fed her some of our leftover dinner."

He motioned Sally aside. "What of her injuries?"

Sally kept her voice low. "She's been beaten more than once, with bruises on her limbs and body of every color from red to blue to yellow. But she doesn't seem to have any broken bones." She nodded toward the bed. "I gave her one of your grandmother's old nightgowns and sent her clothes down to be washed. Her coat is barely a coat. It's a wonder she didn't freeze out there. I hope I did right."

"You did well, Sally. You did everything you should have done."

"She doesn't seem to speak any English, sir, but she understands a bit. I think her name is Nusa," Sally said.

The girl nodded and pointed at herself. "Nusa. *Ja.*"

Samuel went to the bedside. "I'm Samuel."

Nusa let loose with a long discourse in what sounded like German. How he wished he knew the language. But then Nusa stopped talking and looked at the door.

Samuel's grandfather stood there in his dressing gown, taking it all in. "What's all this ruckus in the middle of the night?"

Oh dear. Samuel drew his grandfather into the hall and told him the story of finding the girl.

"So you plucked her off the street?"

"She was being beaten."

"Then save her. But don't bring her here. Where are her parents?"

Samuel realized how little he knew about her. "I don't know."

"Don't you think you'd better find out? They'll be worried about her."

As usual, his grandfather cut right to the chase. The entire series of events had transpired so quickly, Samuel hadn't thought it through. "I'll take her back tomorrow, and we'll find them."

"See that you do." With one more glance into the room, his grandfather added, "Is she wearing one of your grandmother's nightgowns?"

"Yes, sir. I—"

Grandfather turned and walked away. Samuel didn't have time to regret his grandfather's disapproval, for he heard Sally clear her throat. "She wants you, sir."

He'd worry about pleasing Grandfather another day.

Nusa needed him.

Chapter 2

"Careful now, John," Ada told her brother.

"Nana knows she's safe with me," John said as he helped their grandmother down the stairs to the parlor. "Or maybe she'd prefer to slide down the banister." He moved to lift Nana atop the heavy oak railing, but Nana flicked his ear.

"If my bones were a few decades younger, I'd take you up on that, Johnny."

Ada hurried ahead and got the pillows on the fainting couch ready. John helped Nana to her place, and Ada arranged the folds of her dressing gown, adding a velvet coverlet over her legs.

"There now," Nana said. "I'm snug as a bug in a rug."

"Can I get you anything?" John asked.

"Not a thing. When I have you and Ada in my presence, I am totally content."

The feelings were reciprocated. The world was a safe and even place with Nana around.

John checked his pocket watch. "I do have a little time before I need to leave for the Academy, so I'll stay and—"

Ada interrupted him. "But Samuel's coming over." She really didn't want to share Samuel with her brother. The two men were the same age, and when they got together they always ended up talking about how the Alcott banking empire was doing, or how John enjoyed his doctoring work as a Fellow with the New York Academy of Medicine.

"And why is that a problem?" he asked with a smile.

"You know how you two are. When you get together, you always end up talking about banking or doctoring."

"My, my, sister. How greedy you are, wanting Samuel all to yourself. I was merely—"

Nana interrupted. "Leave her alone, Johnny. If you had a sweetheart, you'd want time alone with her."

John acknowledged Nana with a bow. "Touché, Nana. In deference to you—and true love—once Samuel arrives, I'll make myself scarce." He turned to Ada. "When will he be here?"

"Anytime now. He was coming this afternoon to take me to the art museum but sent word he's eager to see me this morning."

"Eager is good," Nana said. "Very good."

"I like *eager*, too," John said with a grin and made himself comfortable in a chair.

Ada ignored him—which never worked but was her only recourse. She addressed Nana. "I wore my new dress today. I can hardly wait to add scraps from this dress to my bridal quilt. I don't have any aubergine."

"The deep purple will make a lovely addition, I'm sure."

"Absolutely *lovely*," John said, drawing out the word.

The knocker sounded on the front door.

"He's here," Nana said. "Smile prettily."

John showed Ada a toothy grin.

Waiting for Wilson to show him in, Ada started to sit, then

stood, knowing the drapery of her new day dress was at its best advantage while she was standing. She had just adjusted the drape of the train when she looked to the foyer and saw Samuel—with a little girl.

Samuel removed his hat and entered the parlor, urging the girl forward. "Good morning, Ada. Mrs. Bauer. And hello there, John. Nice to see you."

Ada was stunned into silence, her focus on the girl. She was seven or eight, and very skinny. She had a cut and horrible bruises on her face, and her coat was threadbare and torn. Ada's heart immediately went out to her. She moved close and put a hand on the girl's head. "Samuel. . .who's this?"

"Her name is Nusa, and last night—"

But before he could answer more fully, the girl tentatively touched the golden trim on Ada's dress. *"Recht,"* she said. *"Sehr recht."*

"She says your dress is very pretty," Nana said. Then she called out to the girl. *"Guten Morgen, liebes Mädchen. Sie sind deutsch?"*

The girl beamed. *"Ja. Sind sie?"*

"Ja!" Nana extended her hands, and Nusa went to Nana's side. The two of them talked back and forth in German.

Samuel moved toward Ada and John. "I didn't know your grandmother knew German."

"She immigrated from Germany when she was young," John said.

Ada couldn't take her eyes off the little girl chattering on with Nana as if they were already friends. "Nana tried to teach me German, but Mother insisted I learn French instead."

They all watched as Nana patted the foot of the chaise and Nusa sat at her feet. "They're getting along famously," Samuel said.

"So who is she, Samuel?" Ada asked. "Where did she come from?"

"The boys and I were at Five Points last night, and—"

"You weren't slumming it, were you?" John asked.

"I hate to admit, we were."

Ada didn't know what "slumming it" meant, but she did know that Five Points was the most notorious and treacherous area of all New York. "Way down there?" Ada asked. "Isn't that dangerous?"

"It was dangerous for Nusa. I saved her from being beaten by some hoodlum."

If this happened last night, it meant Samuel must have. . . "You took her home?"

"I couldn't leave her there. The man was vile. He might have killed her."

"I know the type," John said. "I've done some work down there with the Academy, and the poverty, violence, and disease are rampant."

Ada was proud of Samuel, yet to put himself in such a situation. . . It was then she noticed a cut on his hand. She took hold of it. "You're hurt."

He pulled his hand away. "Just a scratch, and nothing compared to the bruises Nusa has endured."

John stepped forward. "Would you like me to check her out?"

Samuel considered this a moment, then shook his head. "I truly believe her wounds are superficial—this time."

The German conversation paused, and Nana said, "She says her parents are dead, and the man who was beating her was the head of a gang of children he recruited to steal for him. She refused and. . .the rest you know."

"She has no parents?"

Nusa shook her head. *"Eltern. Nein."*

Samuel ran a hand through his hair. "I was going to take her back to Five Points this morning, to wherever she lived."

Nana nodded and asked Nusa a question. *"Wo leben Sie?"*

Nusa shrugged. Then she said something that seemed half German and half English.

Nana translated. "She sometimes stays at the Merciful Children Foundling Home. Otherwise, she sleeps on the street."

Nusa walked over to Samuel and took his hand. *"Ich bleibe mit Ihnen. Ja?"*

"She wants to stay with you," Nana said.

John let out a laugh, then stifled it. "It appears she's adopted you, Alcott."

"Are you keeping her, Samuel?" Ada asked. She thought of her childhood clothes up in the attic. Surely some of them would fit the girl until new ones could be made.

But before she could voice the offer. . .

"Grandfather says she has to go back," Samuel said. "That's where we're heading right now." He looked at Nana. "Please tell her I'd like to give her a home, but Grandfather. . . I just can't. Tell her I'll take her back to the foundling home. I'll see her safely there."

Nana motioned for Nusa to come close again and spoke to her. At first Nusa shook her head, but Nana persisted, and finally Nusa nodded.

"She understands."

Samuel offered her a bittersweet smile, and the girl ran to him, wrapping her arms around his waist. "I hate to send her back there. But I have no choice."

Ada was torn. Although her heart went out to the girl, she said, "Perhaps it *will* be for the best."

Samuel gave her a look that made her immediately regret her comment.

"I mean, she'll be with children of her own kind. . .people who speak German. . ." She looked to John and Nana for help.

"You can't dig yourself out of that one, sister," John said.

Nana chastised him. "Behave yourself, Johnny." To Ada she said, "You may be right, Ada, but being right doesn't equal being fair."

Samuel spoke to Nusa. "Are you ready to go?"

Nusa looked at Nana. *"Gehen?"*

Nana nodded. *"Gehen. Gott segnen Sie und halten Sie, liebes Mädchen."*

Nusa ran to Nana and embraced her. Everything was happening so fast. Samuel was leaving with the girl, taking her back to Five Points. . . .

"Can I come with you?" Ada asked.

Although Samuel looked pleased at her offer, he said, "Another day, Ada."

After they left, Ada sank onto a chair. She ran her fingers along the golden trim that had so impressed the little girl. Golden trim that seemed ridiculously frivolous when compared to the girl's ragged clothes. "I wish he would have let me go with him."

"Five Points is no place for a lady," John said.

"Or a child," she added. "He left so quickly. We have clothes we could give to her, and food. Has she eaten?"

Nana smiled. "I'm sure Samuel has fed her well." Then she beckoned Ada to sit at the foot of the chaise where Nusa had sat just moments before. "You have a good heart, child. As does your Samuel."

"His compassion is one of the reasons I love him."

"You are a good pair, the two of you," Nana said.

Ada nodded. A good pair, who were once again spending time apart.

చ

After asking directions multiple times, and getting lost twice, Samuel finally found the Merciful Children Foundling Home.

There was a small sign by the front door, but otherwise, the brick building blended into the line of tenements surrounding it. Nusa ran up the steps and opened the door, running inside as if she was truly home.

Samuel was more tentative, not wanting to be the intruder. He stepped inside and called out, "Hello?" He looked down the hall to the left of the staircase and saw a middle-aged woman pull Nusa into an embrace. "Nusa! We're so glad to have you back!"

Samuel was relieved at the warm reception. It would make it easier to leave her behind.

The woman stepped back and took a good look at Nusa's face. "Oh my dear child. How did you get these cuts and bruises?"

"Dieser Mann rettete mich."

The woman looked at Samuel with new appreciation. She walked toward him, extending her hand. "Thank you for saving her. Welcome, Mr.—?"

Samuel shook her hand. "Samuel Alcott."

"Eliza Hathaway. Please come in, Mr. Alcott."

She led him into a parlor crowded with mismatched chairs, all facing in one direction. It reminded him of a school room. She turned two chairs around. "Please. Sit."

He did so, resting his hat and gloves on his thigh. Nusa climbed onto Mrs. Hathaway's lap.

"Well now," the woman said. "Tell me how the two of you met."

Samuel gave the shortened version of their meeting.

"Nusa did not exaggerate. It appears you are a hero," Mrs. Hathaway said.

Samuel shrugged. "I'm just glad she's safely here."

There was a bang overhead, then a stampede of footfalls racing down the stairs. Nearly a dozen children burst into the parlor, ignored him, and ran to Nusa, hugging and exclaiming and loving her back into their presence.

He was moved by their obvious affection for the girl and felt good about his decision to bring her home. Being around people who showed their love overshadowed any *things* he might have been able to provide for her back at his grandfather's house, where Nusa would be alone all day but for the servants.

His presence was no longer needed, so he stood and removed a fold of money he'd prepared as a donation. "I'll be going now. I'm just glad Nusa is safely home. And I want to give you this. . .for the children." Mrs. Hathaway took the money and slipped it into the pocket of her apron. "We are appreciative, Mr. Alcott. But please don't leave so soon. I have soup on the stove and fresh bread in the oven. If the finicky stove behaves itself, it will be a good meal. Please join us. It's the least we can do to thank you."

He didn't want to take their food, which was probably a precious commodity, but when Nusa wiggled her way through the crowd of children and took his hand, he succumbed. "That would be very nice, Mrs. Hathaway. Thank you."

"I may be old, but it's Miss Hathaway, and you can save your thanks for after the meal when you decide whether you like my cooking."

❧

The soup was tasty—but secondary to Samuel's dining experience. What fed him more than the meal were the children.

They sat on benches on either side of a huge table in the kitchen, a stairstep of ages and a world of nationalities. They were polite and, for the most part, well mannered. When twelve-year-old Tito sloshed his soup over the side of the bowl, he was quick to say he was sorry, and Miss Hathaway was quick to forgive and help him clean up.

Samuel remembered his own boyhood spills. Grandmother had responded with the same kindness as Miss Hathaway. But Grandfather had always been quick to jump on Samuel's irresponsibility or rowdiness or clumsiness or rudeness or. . .

He shook the memory away with a shiver. He was still trying to please his grandfather.

With the meal finished, he took a toddler named Kristin to his lap, where she showed interest in his shiny brass buttons. When she smiled at him. . .he'd never felt such a warmth inside.

"You're a natural, Mr. Alcott."

"Excuse me?"

Miss Hathaway nodded at the little girl. "The children love you."

"They're very tolerant."

She shook her head adamantly. "Actually, they're not. Most of them have lived on the streets and are wary of strangers. Because they've fended for themselves, they have acute instincts about people. They know a compassionate man when they see one."

He'd never thought of himself in such a way. As an accountant in his grandfather's bank, he was used to dealing with numbers, facts, and ledgers.

"Don't shake your head no," Miss Hathaway said. "Whether you've had a chance to act on your compassion in the past, you've acted on it now, and once the door's open, there's no turning back."

He didn't know what she was implying.

He must have offered a befuddled expression, for she laughed. "Don't worry, Mr. Alcott. I'm not expecting you to move in and help me or sign over your fortune, but I do know how God got *me* here, and. . .well. . .let's just say I'm looking forward to seeing what happens next."

"Next?" Samuel was confused. One minute he was playing with

Kristin, and the next Miss Hathaway was talking about God and opened doors and the future.

Miss Hathaway was still chuckling when she brought him his coat and gloves and placed his hat upon his head. "It's time to go now, Mr. Alcott."

"You're kicking me out?"

"I'm nudging you forward. You have a lot of thinking to do."

He stepped over the bench, placed Kristin on the floor, and put on his coat. "I don't know what you're talking about, Miss Hathaway."

"You don't need to, because I'm not the one who's going to do the talking." She led him to the door. "Good day, Mr. Alcott. Until next time."

He found himself on the street. It was beginning to snow, a soft, cleansing snow that was turning the harsh street into something beautiful.

What had just happened?

He buttoned his coat against the cold, put on his gloves, and walked to an intersection to hail a cab. Once inside, he looked out the window and saw the Merciful Child Foundling Home fall from view.

And then he knew.

He *would* see it again.

He *would* be back.

Chapter 3

Mr. Alcott? Sir?"

Samuel looked up from his desk to find the head teller standing before him. "Yes, Mr. Taylor?"

Taylor asked him a banking question, and Samuel managed an answer. Not that the question was very difficult, but moving his thoughts from Nusa and the foundling home to banking took some effort.

He could not get the children off his mind.

Or Ada.

Or how the one could ever be connected to the other.

Ada was the woman he was going to marry. She was beautiful, talented, and kind, but was from a class far removed from Nusa's world. She'd offered to accompany him to Five Points, yet the thought of her in such an awful place made him cringe. Ada was innocent of such horrors. She worked with the other ladies of their set making items to sell in philanthropic fund-raising, but that was far different from walking the streets among rats who raced between piles of debris, or smelling the stench of garbage and worse, or seeing—and being seen by—rough men who would not treat her in the way she deserved.

He'd bowed out of their trip to the museum, and to Ada's credit she had not complained. So tonight he would make it up to her. He'd take her to a romantic dinner at Delmonico's. And if everything went as planned, perhaps on Christmas Day he would get down on one knee and propose to her. In fact, he hoped to go shopping at Tiffany's in the next week or so and buy an engagement ring. He'd been saving for months in order to have enough money for a ring that would show her exactly how much he loved her. Although his grandfather was wealthy, Samuel relied on wages and a monthly allowance. He was due to inherit a fortune, but until then Grandfather wanted to "test his mettle," which was fine with Samuel. He enjoyed the satisfaction of earning a living. It was how his grandfather and father had started out, so he was following in their footsteps.

But how much money did he have in his personal account?

Samuel took out his private ledger and looked at the bottom line. He had $212 saved for a ring. Surely that would be enough to buy Ada something beautiful.

He looked up when his grandfather came in his office, and he slid the ledger out of sight. "What can I do for you, Grandfather?"

The older man smiled—which was unlike him. Then he put a small red box on Samuel's desk. "I have a gift for you, or rather a gift for you to pass along. It's been in the safe here at the bank since your grandmother's death and. . ." He pointed to the box. "Open it."

Samuel opened the hinged box and saw a familiar topaz ring. "It's Grandmother's."

"It's her engagement ring. I thought you might want to give it to Ada. If you'd like. It's just a thought."

Samuel had never seen his grandfather so sentimental. And to give up his wife's ring—this was monumental.

Samuel removed the ring from the velvet box. It was too small for even his pinky finger, and the gold filigree work around the smoky-colored stone was delicate. "Ada will love it, especially since it was Grandmother's."

"When are you planning to propose?"

Samuel started to say "Christmas" but suddenly felt an inner stirring that stopped him.

"Why the hesitation?" Grandfather asked. "He who hesitates is lost, Samuel. You know that."

Samuel nodded. "I'll propose soon."

"Good. See that you do. Now. . .have you finished wading through the Morrison accounts?"

"Not yet."

"Get to work, then."

And he was gone.

Samuel sat looking at the ring, remembering it on his grandmother's finger. How he wished she were here now to help him deal with his confusion over the pull he felt from the children, and the pull he felt from Ada. "What should I do?" he said aloud. "You always taught me to think of others first, and I want to help the children. But how? I work, I spend time with Ada. . . . How can I help one without slighting the other?"

He put the ring back in its box and set it on top of the ledger.

The ledger.

He opened it and saw the $212 he'd saved for a ring. Now he had a ring. Now he had $212 he could spend on something else.

Someone else.

A plan came to mind. Tonight he would talk to Ada about the

money and the needs of the foundling home. Together they could come up with a way to spend it.

The children and Ada reconciled, Samuel got back to work.

৵

Samuel took a bite of his squab and smiled. "You look ravishing tonight, my love."

Ada felt ravishing. Her apple-green and cream evening dress boasted a heavily embroidered front edged with soutache braid. The short sleeves and side panels of the dress were decorated with rows of tasseled loops of Venetian pearl beads. She wore a rose and white aigrette of ostrich feathers in her hair and carried a matching feather fan. Her neck was adorned with the string of pearls her parents had given her for her coming-out three years ago.

She appreciated his compliment and looked around the restaurant. "I'm glad you got us a table away from the main dining room. I miss having time alone with you."

"And I with you. And since we are alone, I have something I'd like to discuss with you."

Ada's heart added an extra beat. Was he going to propose? The setting was romantic; the evening was going well. Was the moment she'd been waiting for about to become a reality? She set her fork down, wanting her hands to be free when he knelt beside her and placed a ring on her finger.

She managed to keep her voice even. "What would you like to discuss?"

But instead of pushing his chair back and kneeling before her, he simply moved his plate forward and leaned his forearms on the table. "This afternoon I had some unexpected money come my way, and since it's the Christmas season, I would like to use it to buy the children at the foundling home some presents. And Miss

Hathaway mentioned that her stove was finicky, and it *did* look to be on its last legs. So I would like—"

Unwittingly Ada put a hand to her chest and gasped.

"Ada? Are you all right?"

All her wishes, dreams, and expectations rushed forward like waves upon a shore, only to pull back, leaving nothing in their wake.

He reached his hand across the table. "Ada, you're worrying me."

It's your own fault, Ada. Why do you do this to yourself? Why do you create amazing romantic scenarios that can never be fulfilled?

She let her hand find its companion in her lap. She gripped them together, hoping to calm herself. "I'm sorry. You mentioned buying a stove?"

He sat back and studied her a moment. "And presents for the children. I thought we could go shopping together and bring them to the foundling home as a couple."

She reined in her disappointment and managed a smile. "That sounds wonderful, Samuel. I'd be happy to help."

She said the words. If only she fully meant them.

Obviously being kind and good was harder work than she thought.

❧

Ada checked on Nana before she went to bed. When she saw her grandmother was sleeping, she started to close the door, but Nana called after her.

"Come back, child. I'm awake. I want to hear about your evening."

In the time it took to walk from the bedroom door to Nana's bedside, Ada decided *not* to mention her dashed hopes for a proposal. She didn't want her grandmother to think she was one of those desperate girls who weren't content until they had a ring on their finger.

"Turn up the lamp," Nana said. "I want to see you better."

Ada did as she was told, then perched on the edge of the bed.

"You look beautiful, child. Stunning and. . .and sad. What happened?"

Ada let loose an exasperated sigh. "How do you do that? How do you always see what I really feel?"

Nana patted Ada's hand. "Because I love you so much." She pointed to the water carafe on the bedside table. "My throat is sore. Pour me some water; then tell me what happened."

Ada poured the water, then moved to the bedside chair and told Nana everything: her hopes and expectations, and the reality of Samuel's commitment to the foundling home. "I'm very willing to choose presents with him, even go there to distribute them, for I'd love to check on Nusa. But it *was* a disappointment."

"I thought you said you expected a proposal at Christmas."

"I did, but when he arranged this romantic dinner for two, I just thought—"

"You thought like a woman, like a girl. Do yourself a favor and stop trying to orchestrate events to fit your imagination. Do you truly believe Samuel will propose?"

"Yes."

"Then embrace that certainty and let it happen when it's going to happen."

"You're right, Nana. I know you're right."

"Of course I am." Nana leaned her head back, deeper in the pillows. She closed her eyes.

She was flushed and perspiring.

Ada rose and put a hand to her forehead. "Nana, you're on fire.

You have a fever."

"I'm not feeling very good right now, but it will pass."

Ada wasn't going to risk it. She ran to get her brother, the doctor.

Chapter 4

I t's influenza," John said.

During the night Nana's room filled with family as Mother and Father joined Ada in a bedside vigil. At the news, they all took a step back.

"That's contagious, isn't it?" Mother asked.

John nodded. "Yes, it is. And I would guess we've all been infected. I think it would be best if we avoid going out in public, so as not to spread it around."

Ada immediately thought of Samuel. "But I'm going with Samuel to the foundling home to distribute some gifts."

John shook his head vehemently. "Not anymore, you aren't. You don't want to risk infecting those children, do you?"

"But I feel fine."

He gave her a chiding look. "Samuel can survive without you for a few days."

"Days?"

Nana stirred, and Ada went to her. "I'm here, Nana."

"I'm sorry to be so much trouble."

"You're never trouble to me. Ever."

Samuel and the children would have to wait.

❧

Samuel paid the clerk $63.25. "Can you have it delivered today?"

The clerk put the money in a money box and made a face.

Since it was clear he was going to say no, Samuel added, "It's for an orphanage. They really need the stove as soon as possible." He handed the man five more dollars. "Will this help?"

The man slipped the fiver into his pocket. "Give me an address, and I'll send George out with it right away."

Samuel wrote down the address, feeling giddy at his accomplishment. He imagined Miss Hathaway's face when the stove arrived.

He wanted to do more than imagine. He wanted to be there. That being the case, he hurried off to Bloomingdale's shoe department to buy shoes for the children. He'd have to guess on sizes, but he hoped if he got an assortment, there would be a pair for everyone.

And some candy. . .when was the last time these children had candy?

The only cloud to the day was that Ada wasn't with him. He'd received her note and understood her need to stay with her grandmother and her desire not to pose a health risk to the children. He just hoped that *she* would stay well. That said, he still missed her being a part of this special task.

Until next time. For he knew there would be a next time.

❧

Money talked. For by the time Samuel finished his shopping and traveled to the foundling home, the new stove had arrived, and the old one was being carted away. Samuel slipped past the delivery men and followed the sounds to the kitchen.

The place was in an uproar, with the children gathered round the new stove, touching its chrome trim, removing its burner covers. As soon as he entered and set down his other gifts, Miss Hathaway saw him. She ran to him, encasing him in a bear hug. "Words cannot express, Mr. Alcott. Words cannot express. . . ."

Not knowing what else to say, he lifted the boxes of shoes, which were tied together with string. "I have something else for each of you."

The children swarmed around him, wanting to know what was in the boxes. Tito, one of the oldest, read the word on a box. "Shoes? Shoes! He brought us shoes!"

Miss Hathaway got scissors to cut the string, and the boxes tumbled to the floor. Samuel stepped back and let the children find shoes that fit.

"Shoes, too, Mr. Alcott?" Miss Hathaway said. "Most of these children have never had new shoes."

"I wasn't sure about size, and I didn't even know their ages. So when the clerk asked me, I had to guess, telling her there were three children this tall, two this tall, all the way down to the baby. I brought fifteen pairs, just to make sure."

The older children helped the younger, and Samuel ended up helping Nusa put on her button shoes. She walked in a circle, trying them out. *"Danke, Herr Alcott!"* She wrapped her arms around Samuel's neck, and at her example, all the other children followed suit.

Their gratitude was embarrassing. Never had there been a better use of his money.

But he had one more surprise. He reached into the inner pocket of his coat and removed sticks of candy. The children's eyes grew big.

"You've outdone yourself," Miss Hathaway said, shaking her head.

It was only the beginning.

ॐ

The children were in the parlor having a lesson given to them by a part-time volunteer named Lottie.

Samuel sat with Miss Hathaway in the kitchen, alone but for the baby, Dolly, who slept in her arms.

"Today I'd hoped to bring along my intended, Ada. But her grandmother—"

"You're engaged?" Miss Hathaway asked.

Samuel avoided the question. "Last night when I took her to dinner at Delmonico's, I asked her—"

"You proposed last night? How romantic. I've never been to Delmonico's, but I've heard how special it is. What a romantic setting for a proposal. It *was* romantic, wasn't it?"

She'd turned the conversation offtrack. "Yes, I suppose it was romantic, but I didn't propose. I asked her if she wanted to come with me to buy a stove and some gifts for the children."

Miss Hathaway stopped rocking the baby. "You're in a fancy restaurant, just the two of you, having a romantic dinner, and you ask her to help you buy a stove?"

She made it sound ridiculous. "Well, yes."

She laughed. "I'm sure she was thrilled with *that* proposal."

Samuel thought back. Ada hadn't been thrilled. In fact, she'd turned a bit quiet. "Do you really think she expected me to propose? I mean, I plan to do so soon, but I hadn't ever thought of asking her last night."

Miss Hathaway shook her head. "If the question looms *soon*, as you say, I'm sure she *had* considered last night could be the night."

Samuel felt like a fool. Poor Ada. She'd hoped for the stars, and he'd given her. . .

A stove.

"There, there now, Mr. Alcott," Miss Hathaway said. "I didn't mean to make you feel bad. Just go over to her house and make amends."

"I can't. There's sickness in the house. We can't see each other. But I suppose I could send her a note. . . ."

Miss Hathaway chewed on this a moment. "I know something better. Speak to her through flowers. Stop at Thorley's on the way home—isn't that where your set buys their flowers? Have some sent to her house. It's the least you can do."

The very least.

"I hate that I've kept you from spending time with Samuel," Nana said as Ada adjusted her pillows.

"Hush now. I'm where I'm supposed to be."

Nana touched her hand. "I do like your company. If only I felt better. . ."

Ada was worried about her grandmother. Because she was already frail, this new illness was dangerous. Even if John had not forbidden Ada from leaving the house, she would have stayed.

Once Nana was settled, Ada returned to her bridal quilt. She'd brought the entire quilt in the room because she was adding three finished quilt blocks to the larger piece.

Nana must have been watching her, for she said, "It's quite a feat, that quilt. A chronicle of your life."

Ada stretched the bulk of the quilt over her lap and stroked it. "It's my life's work."

"Until you marry. Then what will you do?"

"I'll start another quilt, a marriage quilt."

"A family quilt," Nana said. "A big family."

"If you're wanting me to blush, you're going to be disappointed," Ada said. "I agree with you. I want many, many children, and I'll make them each a quilt of their own."

Nana laughed. "You're going to be very busy."

The talk of children made Ada think of Nusa. Was she safe? Had Samuel purchased a stove yet? What else would he buy for them?

"How many blocks do you have left to finish your quilt?" Nana asked.

Ada turned her thoughts back to her work. "I have the scraps from my Christmas dress ready to use in a block commemorating my engagement, which will start the last row that will culminate in a block that will include scraps from my wedding dress."

"You have it all figured out."

The door opened and John entered carrying a bouquet of blue violets. "I come bearing gifts," he said.

"For me?" Nana asked.

"Actually, no. They're for Ada."

She read the note: *I love you. I miss you. And I hope your grandmother gets better soon. . .Samuel.*

"From Samuel?" Nana asked.

She nodded. "But blue violets. . . What's the symbolism?"

"Get the book," Nana said.

John sat at the foot of Nana's bed, shaking his head. "You women and your language of flowers. As if Samuel even knows what blue violets mean."

"Thorley's House of Flowers knows. Just wait. . ." Ada hurried to her room and brought back *The Language of Flowers*, a must for any girl of marriageable age.

She looked under the V section. "Violets—Blue: faithfulness."

"That's lovely," Nana said.

"That's boring," John said.

Ada had to admit she was a bit disappointed in the flower choice. . . If only Samuel had sent her red roses or chrysanthemums, which were symbols of romantic love.

She was being petty. Flowers were flowers.

She wasn't given the chance to discuss it further, as John attended to Nana, his patient.

It was just as well.

Chapter 5

T here," Samuel said, righting the stool with its repaired leg. "Four chairs and a stool, all fixed."

Eliza—for they called each other by their first names now—was at her new stove, stirring a pot of potatoes. "I had no idea you were a carpenter, Samuel."

"Neither did I."

"You like this, don't you?"

"I do enjoy fixing things."

She shook her head. "You like *this*. All of this, working with the children, making them safe and happy."

He sat on the stool to test its stability. Two-year-old Bertie toddled into the room, dragging a blanket behind him, and Samuel took him on his knee. "I do like it. During these past two weeks I've never felt more fulfilled or of more worth to the world."

"You do have worth here, and I'm not just talking about the new stove, or the shoes, or the new window in the boys' room, or the stack of wood over there."

He was embarrassed by the praise, but it stirred an issue that had been on his mind. "I have worth *here*," he said. "Only here."

"I'm sure that's not true," Eliza said. "Not true at all."

"It feels true."

"In a few days it's Christmas, and you're proposing to Ada. You will find your worth in your new wife and in your new life together."

Instead of affirming Eliza's words, he found himself shaking his head. "I don't know what to do. I love Ada deeply, and until coming here, marriage *was* the next step."

Eliza stopped stirring and took a deep breath, as if needing extra air to fuel her words. "But now your heart has expanded to include. . ." She pointed at little Bertie, who was sticking his fingers through the buttonholes in Samuel's vest.

He nodded.

As did she. Then she sat on the bench facing him. "That's how it happened with me, Samuel. I was the nanny to a wealthy family in England. But when the girl grew too old, I suddenly had a life of my own. And so I came here, to New York City. I met a man on the boat, and during our voyage, we fell in love and began to talk of a life together." She looked at her lap.

"What happened?" Bertie stopped his playing and cuddled against Samuel's chest. Samuel cupped his head with a hand.

"We ended up at Five Points, along with a million other immigrants. Once here, I saw the children in need and knew I had to do something to save them. And so I used what little money I had and rented this place and took them in, trusting God to provide contributions and food and clothing enough to keep us open."

"And the man?"

She shrugged. "He had other plans that did not involve raising other people's children." She retrieved the lap quilt Bertie had dragged into the room and helped Samuel wrap it around the toddler.

"I'm sorry," he said, tucking Bertie in.

"I'm not." She went to check the potatoes. "I sacrificed one kind of love for another." She glanced over her shoulder at him. "Perhaps Miss Wallace could join you in your work here?"

He laughed, then felt guilty for it. His attention was drawn to the quilt around Bertie. He fingered the faded blue cottons. "You should see the bridal quilt Ada's making, full of velvets and satins, embellished with all sorts of embroidery. Not practical at all. She's not practical."

"She's had no reason to be. Perhaps you give her too little credit. If she loves you, she'll join you in your work. For isn't marriage a partnership?"

Samuel remembered that Ada *had* offered to come with him to take Nusa home. He'd been the one to tell her no, because Five Points was no place for a lady.

No place for Ada.

Looking around the room—even though he'd grown fond of this place and enjoyed using his allowance to provide for some of its needs—he had a hard time imagining Ada here. How could he ask a princess to visit a slum?

Eliza stopped her work and looked at him. "Forgive an old woman for stirring things up. You and Ada have your whole lives ahead of you. Relish each other and the time you have together."

"But you gave up your love and your time together."

"What's right for one is not right for all."

And yet. . .

As Samuel rocked little Bertie to sleep, the subject haunted him.

❧

Samuel sat at his desk at the bank—a desk that had been vacant too many days, as he'd given much of his time to the foundling home.

He felt disconnected, as if he was returning to another life.

For that's what it was. In the bank, he was Samuel T. Alcott, heir to the Alcott fortune. At the Merciful Children Foundling Home, he was Papa Samuel, a colleague, and a member of a family.

And then there was his life with Ada. Because of the influenza, they hadn't seen each other in weeks. They'd communicated through notes, but notes were far from enough.

He felt her slipping away—and knew it was his fault, that he was the one backing up and putting distance between them.

Samuel's grandfather entered his office, his face stern.

"Good morning, Grandfather."

The elder Alcott skipped the pleasantries and pointed a finger toward Samuel's desk. "Get out your personal ledger."

Samuel's stomach flipped. He knew what was going to happen and had dreaded the moment. But there was no escape.

He pulled out the ledger and handed it over. His grandfather opened it, ran a finger along the columns, and jabbed at the final number.

"What's this here? I see you've gone through all your allowance this month—and then some."

"I've had a few expenses of late."

"I never thought Ada was such a demanding girl. After you marry, you'll have to put her on a budget."

Samuel hated that Ada had taken the blame. "The money hasn't gone to Ada."

His grandfather hesitated. "You haven't been gambling, have you?"

"Of course not." He might as well say it. "I've been working down at Five Points, at a foundling home. They've needed some repairs and supplies, and I've used my money for that."

Grandfather paused, but only for an instant. "It's that orphan girl you brought home, isn't it? She's the cause of all this."

"She was the impetus that opened my eyes to their need."

"Charity is fine, Samuel—it's even commendable—but there is a limit."

Samuel found the statement odd. "Is there?"

His grandfather's eyebrows rose. "So you wish to give all your money to the poor."

"Isn't that what Jesus told the rich man to do?"

"What are you talking about?"

It was a Bible story his grandmother had taught him, a story forgotten until lately. "A rich man approaches Jesus and asks what he must do to gain eternal life. Jesus tells him he needs to be willing to give up everything, distribute it to the poor, and follow Him."

Grandfather stood there aghast, which made Samuel panic.

"We have so much, Grandfather, and they need so much. In fact, I thought it would be wonderful if we could build them a better place, perhaps in a safer neighborhood, and—"

Grandfather planted a finger on the desk, leaning forward. His voice was a harsh whisper. "*I* have so much. You have nothing without me. And if you continue with this folly, I will make sure you get nothing *from* me. Not a penny."

Samuel couldn't believe what he was hearing. How could his grandfather threaten to disinherit him? How had his simple acts of kindness come to this?

His anger pushed him to standing—but his legs were weak. "Then there it is. We're in agreement. You want to give nothing, and I want to receive nothing." On impulse, Samuel grabbed his coat and hat from the rack.

"Where are you going?"

"To a place where I'm truly needed."

His grandfather's voice softened. "Whoa now, boy. You're needed here, Samuel. And I do admire your altruistic heart. But God also wants us to be wise, and to be strong and do the work."

"But the important work is not here at the bank."

Grandfather shook his head. "There, you are wrong. For without the investment of this bank's money, dozens of businesses would not exist. Hundreds—if not thousands—of people would not be employed in those businesses, and all those families would be hungry and in need. You must find balance, boy. It does not have to be all or nothing. You need to find a compromise."

Samuel knew what his grandfather was saying was wise and prudent. But he was weary of straddling both worlds. "I'm being torn in two. Or three."

"Then mend yourself together again." Grandfather moved to leave the office, then turned one last time. "I don't discount your situation, Samuel, but enough is enough. Your work here, your life here, deserves more than you're giving it."

"Perhaps it's more than I have to give."

Grandfather was taken aback. "What are you saying?"

Samuel wasn't sure—until he heard his own words. "I'm done here. I'm done with this life. I choose to go where I'm truly needed, to the place where God has led me."

"Don't be ridiculous. God's put you right here, and it's time you set aside this other nonsense and get to—"

Samuel felt as if he would burst. "I'm sorry, but I can't. I just can't." He brushed past his grandfather and left the office.

Grandfather called after him. "If you leave this building, you're giving up your job *and* your home. You'll be on your own, Samuel. Completely on your own!"

Samuel's heart beat wildly in his throat as he raced through the bank and out onto the street. He strode down the sidewalk, his head low, his coat flowing behind him. With each step he repeated an admonition. *What have I done? What have I done?*

Then suddenly, he stopped. *I know exactly what I've done. And I know exactly where I need to go.*

He walked on.

❧

Ada poured Nana some tea. "I'm so glad you're feeling well enough to come down to the parlor. I'm sure you're ready for a change of scenery."

"I'm ready to feel well. I'm weaker than a newborn foal."

Ada was not surprised. Nana had eaten little but soup and Carr's crackers for weeks. "What if I ask Cook to make you some toast?"

"With apple butter?"

Ada smiled. "If I have to make it myself." She pulled the bell pull, summoned the maid, and made her request. Then she settled in with her proposal quilt block, readying the scraps of her Christmas dress for application. The red and green plaid was festive and joyful—as she would be on that happy day—just two days away.

They heard someone at the door, and Ada stood, ready to receive their visitor.

Wilson answered it, and Ada was thrilled to see Samuel come in. She rushed into the foyer, ready to encase him in an embrace. It had been so long—too long.

But something about his stance made her hold back.

"I'm sorry to come unannounced," he said, "and I wasn't sure if you were seeing visitors yet, but I. . .I. . ."

His face was drawn, his forehead furrowed. Something was terribly wrong. "I'm glad you came. I've missed you terribly. Please come in. Today Nana has come downstairs for the first time."

After Wilson took his coat and hat, Samuel ran a hand through his hair. Then he followed Ada into the parlor. "Mrs. Bauer. How good to see you up and around."

"How good to be up and around," she said. "Please sit, Samuel, and tell us what's happened in the world during the weeks of my confinement."

He took a seat but seemed baffled by her question. This was not like Samuel, who was always at ease talking about any subject. "I'm afraid I haven't been out in the world much lately. I've been busy with. . ." He looked to Ada. "Ada, pardon me, but may I speak to you in private, please?"

From the tone of his voice, that was the last thing she wanted, but Nana gave her permission, saying, "Go on now, children. I'm ready to take a little doze. Go have your discussion in the morning room."

Ada kissed her then led Samuel to her mother's study. Sunlight streamed through the east windows, warming the room. She closed the doors.

He motioned toward the settee, and she took a place at one end while he sat at the other. He seemed totally exhausted, and nervous, and. . .

"You're scaring me, Samuel."

"I'm sorry. I don't mean to, but. . ." He took a fresh breath and the words came out in a rush. "My grandfather and I had an argument, and I'm disinherited. I've also lost my job and am not welcome in my home—his home."

Ada had no idea what to say but finally managed, "Why?"

"Because of the foundling home. I've been spending some of my—most of my—time and money there, repairing things and buying them much-needed supplies, and he doesn't approve. He's cut me off and turned me out."

A thousand thoughts pummeled Ada's mind. She wanted to

support him, but he was foolish to alienate his grandfather and lose everything. Surely some compromise could be made. "I appreciate your heart for the poor. And I applaud your generosity. But must it be all or nothing?"

He sat silent a moment, his breathing heavy, his eyes locked on the air between them. "I feel called to help them. It's as if this is what I was born to do. It's my destiny."

Her empathy weakened. "I thought being married to me was your destiny. You've told me as much."

"I know." His eyes met hers, and a wave of panic flowed through her until she felt ready to drown. "I believed that. But I don't know how to reconcile my love for you with this *purpose* I feel compelled to fulfill."

"I thought we were getting engaged. You said you were giving me something special at Christmas. This isn't what I had in mind."

"Nor is it what I had in mind."

She took his hands. "Then don't do it. Help the children, but marry me."

He shook his head back and forth, back and forth. "I have no home, no job, and no income. I have nothing to offer you."

She put a hand upon his heart. "Offer me this. I only want your heart, Samuel. You know you already have mine."

He stood, causing her hands to fall away. "I can't marry you, Ada. I can't make you suffer for my choice."

"But I choose you and all that you are, and all that you do." A new thought surfaced. "I'll go with you and help you with your work. We can do it together."

His face turned wistful. "God called *me* to this. It's not for everyone. It's not for you."

"But how do you know? How do I know? You're not giving me a chance."

He stood. "I have to leave."

"Samuel!"

Ada ran after him, through the wide hallway and into the foyer where Wilson hurriedly gathered Samuel's coat and hat.

"Samuel, you can't do this to me. To us."

"I'm so sorry, Ada. I'm so sorry."

The sound of the closing door echoed in Ada's ears.

"Ada?"

It was Nana. Ada hated that she'd witnessed their parting. As had the butler. Soon the entire household would know of her rejection, her shame. For buried within Samuel's rejection was the fact that he didn't trust her heart or her capabilities.

Ada stumbled into the parlor, not daring to meet Nana's eyes.

"What happened?"

She couldn't talk now. She couldn't explain the unexplainable.

Instead, she gathered the scraps of her Christmas dress—the dress she was going to wear on the day of her proposal—and took them to the hearth.

Where they met a fiery death.

Chapter 6

Nearly a year later

Mother stood next to the desk, watching Ada address an invitation. When Ada was finished, she nudged the envelope to her left, waiting for her mother's approval. "Does this look all right?"

Mother took up the envelope for a better look. "Your *M*'s are a bit compressed for my taste, but it will do. What was our final count?"

"If everyone comes, there will be seventy-four."

"Very good," Mother said. "Fewer than fifty and a Christmas ball is a mere dance, and too near to one hundred seems overly grand for the season." Mother returned the envelope to the pile. "Do your very best, Ada. This party is essential to your future."

"How's that?"

Mother gave her a look of frustration. "Because most of your friends are betrothed by now."

By now was a decided dig. And though her mother's mention of betrothals in relation to the upcoming Christmas party might seem odd to the uninformed, Ada knew her mother hoped that a certain Owen Reed would be so overcome by the festivities that he'd propose that very night.

As far as Ada's hopes? They were less detailed and had a lot to do with simply wanting the whole issue of marriage to be *done*.

"Continue on, Ada. I must consult Mrs. Newly regarding the menu."

Whatever. The intricacies of etiquette made Ada weary. This entire Christmas ball had been her mother's idea. It would be a celebration of the season, but more than that, Ada knew Mother wished it to be a way to show New York society that the Wallaces—and especially Ada—had left the unhappiness of last Christmas behind them.

Last Christmas had been a humiliation, as the news of Ada's rejection spread. That Samuel Alcott, heir to the Alcott banking fortune, had shunned Ada *and* his inheritance in order to play do-gooder in the slums was the topic of conversation through all of last Christmas, well into the 1890 opera season, not to be overshadowed until the death of New York mogul John Jacob Astor III, and the subsequent squabbling of his family over *his* inheritance.

Ada didn't remember much about last Christmas or the parties and operas that rang in the new year. The few she'd attended, that is. To put it candidly, the Wallace family had been shunned for the social season as punishment for not securing a happily-ever-after ending to her romance. How embarrassing.

Ada had moved through the dark months of ostracism as if asleep, yet without the ability to happily awaken and discover that she and Samuel were still the loves of each other's lives.

She'd only received one note from him over the past year—an apology note. As if a few words could mend the tear in her heart. There had been no return address and no clue as to the exact location or name of the foundling home. Ada remembered Nusa telling Nana the name of it, but neither one of them could retrieve the exact memory.

In an effort to find him, Ada had even contacted Samuel's grandfather, hoping that he had more information. But Mr. Alcott was also in the dark. Samuel had vanished into the bowels of New York City, unbound and unfound.

In her desperation, Ada had even begged John to help her find him. But John had refused, saying what was done was done. And what would Ada do if she found him? Samuel had broken ties with *her*. And even if he had changed his mind, was Ada willing to give up the life she knew for some bizarre life *he'd* chosen?

She'd told herself yes, she was willing. But Ada also knew that words were cheap and the price of a wrong choice was costly. And so her sorrow, which had turned to desperation, evolved into anger. For even after a healthy dose of self-analysis, she couldn't think of a single thing she'd done to cause the drastic change in Samuel. The fact he'd chosen to exclude her from his decision was unfair. He'd never given her a chance. She had no idea if she would have risen to the challenge, but to be denied the opportunity. . .

None of it made sense.

Until the breakup, Ada felt as if God had brought them together. But if that were true, then why had He allowed them to be split apart? Her inability to rectify this question caused her faith to suffer and made her doubt her own inner compass for what was genuine and what was false.

Until Owen Reed came into her life.

Owen had saved her from drowning in a sea of emotion. He was a member of their set and was gentle and kind. It didn't really matter that he was on the shortish side, or that he was an ember to Samuel's fire. That Owen was content with quiet conversations about music or the arts or his latest book of interest was a blessing. He didn't require much effort on Ada's part.

Ada found it appropriate that Owen had saved her at Easter— redeemed her. He'd accosted her after Easter service, and his attention had opened a door, allowing Ada readmittance into New York society.

Her sentence was commuted, and Owen did everything society proclaimed a beau should do. He was her companion to any event she desired to attend, was an able dancer, was conscious of her needs, whether it be getting her a glass of punch the moment she was thirsty or offering her his arm as they negotiated the marble stairs at the opera. He gave and she took, and though she recognized the disparity in their relationship, she was relieved that he seemed content in it.

As was she. As much as she could be.

For with Samuel's departure from her life, so had gone Ada's passion. Not only the physical passion, but also her desire for living, for enjoying the moment, and for thinking of the future with anticipation. Though Owen's presence smoothed over the rawness of her pain, it still hid just below the surface, making Ada fear that feeling too much one way or the other might set it free.

Ada's parents wanted Owen to be the *one*. They appreciated how he *had* been the one to finally break her out of her haze. And above all, his attention saved Ada's mother from a fate worse than death and allowed the Wallace family to step free of their societal banishment. His family was suitable—being *the* Reeds of the Reed shipping fortune. But so far at least, Ada had felt no spark in his presence, no inner tug indicating he was God's choice just for her.

Nana was the only one who understood the limbo she was in, the uncertainty, and the confusion that assaulted her each morning and clung to her dreams each night.

Ada was surprised to see that she'd completed a dozen more envelopes without conscious thought. If only she could complete all tasks in such a way.

"Psst!"

She looked to the doorway of the morning room and saw her brother.

"How would you like to go shopping?" John asked.

She was surprised that the idea *did* pique her interest. But then she looked back to the invitations. "I'd better not. Mother wants to mail these tomorrow. She's obsessed with this party. It's going to change my life, you know."

He plucked an envelope from the pile. "Your *M*'s are too broad."

She snatched it back from him. "What do you need to buy?"

"Mother says all my gloves are a disgrace, and she will not let me ask a single girl to dance at the ball until I rectify the matter. I am therefore off to Macy's, and was thinking that surely you need some new gloves, a bit of lace, or perhaps some other bit of feminine fluffery?"

She loved how he made her smile. "I suppose I could think of something I need."

He clapped his hands. "Then get your bonnet and cape and let's be off. McCoy is bringing the carriage around."

Shopping. Why not?

❧

The carriage stopped with a jerk, causing Ada to lurch forward toward her brother. John took her hands, helping to set her aright.

"Sorry," Ada said.

"I wonder what's going on." John reached behind his head and opened the sliding window in order to speak to the driver. "Careful there, McCoy. We nearly ended up in each other's laps."

"I apologize, Dr. Wallace. But there seems to be some commotion ahead. All traffic is stopped."

"Can you see what it is?"

"Not yet, sir."

Ada knew they were still a long way from Macy's. The sidewalks were busy with people walking hurriedly amid the December cold, their shoulders raised toward their ears, the distance between couples testing propriety as they sought each other's warmth while they braved the weather to travel from here to there. The path of each person was marked by the puffs of their breath.

McCoy tapped on the window. "Excuse me, sir, but there appears to be an accident of some sort in the next block. No one's moving. I'm sorry. There's not much I can do but wait."

Waiting was not Ada's strong suit. She looked out both sides of the carriage to make her own assessment of the situation. *Actually, there—what if we went. . . ?*

"How about there," she said, pointing to a street to their left. "Could McCoy go around the carriage in front of us, turn onto that street, and find a different way?"

John did his own looking, agreed, then told McCoy the plan.

By cajoling the horses and getting the hack in front of him to move up just a bit, McCoy maneuvered their carriage onto a side street.

"I knew it would work," Ada said.

But as they tried to go around the block, various obstructions forced them to continue farther south and east, into neighborhoods that seemed foreign—not just in their unfamiliarity, but in their ethnic roots. Ada saw bearded men with ringlets on each side of their faces, wearing long black coats and flat-topped hats, and signage on shops that was written with an alphabet far beyond the ABCs.

"Well now," John said. "We've wandered into the Jewish area of town. We're way off course."

Ada knew her father had business dealings with Jewish people, and Arthur Wyndym had even bought his fiancée a diamond from a jeweler in this area. But Ada didn't think she'd ever seen a Jewish person.

A little boy ran to catch up with his father, taking his hand. He, too, had the long ringlets. *Jesus was a Jew.* . . .

Had Jesus looked like these men?

But as the carriage moved south, the neighborhood changed as if they had traveled from one country to the next. The buildings were similar, but even in the cold, these had laundry hanging on lines strung between windows. The people were dressed in earthen tones, their hair dark and silky, and their skin slightly darker, as if tanned by the sun. Only there was little sun here. The streets were bathed in shadow, with only a slice of sky showing above. The going was narrow as the street was occupied with a myriad of pushcarts, each with a vocal owner lauding their wares. Bread, apples, baskets. . .

"Pane, pane fresco!"

"Mele deliziose!"

"Bei cestini!"

"You were curious about Five Points, sister? Take a look."

Ada looked around with new eyes. "Samuel lives here. . . ."

"Well, yes, technically, I guess he does, but—"

Suddenly Ada felt an overwhelming need to find him, to be out of the carriage, to look for him, and to see what he saw every day. Since they were stopped, she opened the carriage door. "I'm getting out."

"You can't do that. Ada. . ."

Ada ignored her brother's words and his touch and stepped onto the street.

McCoy called down to her. "Miss Wallace! Please. You must get back in the carriage."

She scanned the crowd, desperately looking for the one face that was always in her thoughts. *Samuel! Please, God. Let me find Samuel.*

But as she stepped away from the carriage, she was overrun with children, their faces grimy and pitiful, their hands outstretched, pulling at her arms and her skirt.

"*Signora graziosa. Per favore. Aiuto.*"

"*Una moneta?*"

Some held up a piece of paper or chunk of wood, as if trying to sell it to her.

"*Compri la mia carta.*"

"*Compri questa parte di legno.*"

One held up a piece of coal. "Coal, lady? Keep you warm?"

She was appalled yet moved. Were these Samuel's charges? She wanted to push them away even as she wanted to hold them close to comfort them. Their dark eyes were so beautiful, their grimy angelic faces pulled with pleading.

"I'm sorry. I don't have any money."

John appeared at her side, offering them a few coins. "Get on with you now. Away! Shoo! Leave her alone!"

They ran off, scattering in the crowded street and around the pushcarts.

The congestion on the street had become an issue. A horse and cart coming toward them couldn't go any farther. The driver yelled at McCoy in Italian.

"In the carriage, Miss Wallace. Dr. Wallace. I must insist."

"Come now, Ada," John said. "We must get back inside."

With a glance, Ada knew they were right. Commotion swirled around her. The chance to find Samuel was tinged with the menace of the unknown. Ada returned to the carriage, and John started to help her inside. She was just raising her skirt in order to negotiate the step when. . .

The driver of the cart yelled at McCoy even louder, his hands gesturing wildly.

McCoy yelled back, and in the ruckus the horses lurched forward. Ada let out a yelp as she lost her footing, stumbled, and fell to the ground.

John rushed to help her up, but the horses. . .and the carriage. . . and the cart. Pushcarts, people, running children, and—

Just as Ada regained her footing, she saw the cart's horse panic and rear up.

She spotted the coal boy in harm's way and yelled, "The boy!"

Ada saw a flash of blue as a man burst out of the crowd and shoved the boy to safety.

The horse came down on the man.

There was an awful thud of hooves against flesh.

Screams.

"Inside!" McCoy demanded, his manners gone. "Now! We must back up and—"

But Ada didn't move. Mesmerized, she watched as a swell of people rushed to the man's aid. In the back of her mind was the accusation: *I caused all this.*

"Ada!" John said. "Get in the carriage. I'm going to help."

She was tempted. For inside the carriage she could hide away and pretend none of this had happened. She could draw the curtains on the windows and close her eyes and wait until McCoy got them to safety.

But the memory of the little boy's eyes assailed her, and the sound of a man being hurt. Added was the knowledge that good medical care was probably a rarity in such a neighborhood.

There was only one thing to do.

She pushed through the crowd until she saw her brother. "John!

John! Bring the man to the carriage. Take him away from here."

John looked up from his work on the man, his face a mixture of surprise, diligence, and questions. Then he nodded. "Men, help me. *Aiutilo!*" He pointed to the carriage. "To the carriage. *Veicolo!*"

Enough men understood to do as he asked. Ada rushed back, leading the way. The men got the hero into the carriage, where he fell upon the free seat, unconscious.

John rushed in last. He banged on the side of the carriage. "Go, McCoy. Get us home!"

Somehow, by the grace of God, a path opened and the carriage moved.

John knelt beside the man, pressing a bloody handkerchief to his face.

"Will he be all right?" she asked.

John looked up at her, hesitated, then said, "Ada. . .it's Samuel. Samuel Alcott."

What? She nudged John to the side in order to see the man's face.

"Samuel!"

Samuel opened his eyes for but a moment and whispered one word.

"Ada?"

"Oh, Samuel! I'm so glad we found you. I—"

But Samuel closed his eyes, and his head fell to one side.

Ada's heart stopped. "No! John. . .no. He's not dead, is he?"

John put his fingers to Samuel's neck, then shook his head. "He's alive, but barely so. He saved the boy, but the horse came down on him."

Ada's head shook *no, no, no.* She couldn't lose him now. "Faster, McCoy! Faster!" she yelled.

And then she prayed.

Chapter 7

Once home, John was no longer Ada's brother, but became Dr. Wallace. He gave orders to the servants and directed Samuel to be taken upstairs to a guest room. Their mother met the commotion with a hundred questions, which John dismissed, his attention wholly on his patient.

Then John asked Ada, "I need help, but I can't have you go squeamish on me. Are you up to it?"

Was she? Helping Nana when she was sick and helping John attend an injured man were far different.

"Well? I need to know."

"Yes, yes, I'll help." *Of course I'll help. It's Samuel.*

"Then get in here."

☙

Ada did not have time to feel squeamish or to think about the fact that Samuel was in their house. In the need of the moment, he became a generic man in trouble. She surprised herself by being able to separate her emotions from the work, assisting John as he cleaned the open wounds and tried to determine the extent of the deeper injuries.

"He has multiple bruises and contusions, but I don't see any broken bones," John said.

Ada moved to the far side of the bed and helped wrap a bandage around Samuel's arm, keeping the fabric flat and smooth.

"Gentle now," John said.

Only after they were finished did Ada allow her gaze to fall upon Samuel's face. With the blood cleaned away, and his hair swept back. . .

He'd lost weight, but he was still her Samuel. His high cheekbones, his strong brow. She put a hand on his forehead. "Samuel," she whispered, "I'm here."

John cleaned up his instruments and put them in his doctor bag. "I doubt he can hear you. He has a concussion—a blow to the head. As you've seen, he fades in and out of consciousness and is very disoriented. He doesn't understand where he is, and he's delirious."

"Will he be all right?"

"The cuts and bruises will heal, but his internal injuries are unknown."

Ada wanted to place her hands on his wounds and will him to health. She pulled a chair close to the bed. "I'll sit with him."

John put a hand on her shoulder. "You did very well, sister. I didn't know you had it in you."

"Nor did I. I'm just glad I could help."

John looked at her, then at Samuel, then at Ada again. "But please remember this. Just because you found Samuel doesn't mean he's yours again. He left you. He's made no effort to contact you. He's moved on, and so have you."

His directness surprised her. "I know."

And she did know. But. . .she couldn't deny that his presence seemed an answer to prayer.

Chapter 8

The next day Mother appeared in the doorway of Samuel's room and summoned Ada away from his bedside into the hall. "You heard John's orders that Samuel must stay here with us for a while?"

"Is that all right with you?"

Her gaze strayed toward the bed where Samuel lay motionless. "It's obviously a complication."

That was not a word Ada would choose. "Helping someone in need is not a complication. Would you rather we left Samuel injured on the street?"

"Don't get huffy with me, daughter. I'm simply stating the obvious, that with you on the cusp of being engaged to Owen, the sudden presence of your old beau is awkward."

She was right, of course, and that *rightness* annoyed Ada. "Be that as it may, I'm willing to deal with the awkwardness in order to do the right thing. Owen is a kind man. He'll understand."

"Are you sure?"

"Absolutely," Ada said, though she was *not* sure. Owen was a dear, but would he be put off by the situation?

Yet why would it be a problem? Samuel had spurned her, humiliated her by choosing his calling over her love and by not trusting her to be a part of it. No one understood how he could choose poverty over a privileged life. She also assumed that most people thought he left her because she simply wasn't enough for him. But now. . .the Wallaces had chosen to help the man who'd wounded her so badly, and were doctoring him and nursing him back to health. Wouldn't that cause her society friends to look at her family with respect? Wasn't it proof they'd risen above the pain?

It wasn't as if she was still in love with him.

☙

In spite of her protests, Mother insisted Ada go with Owen to Carrie Astor's party that evening. On the carriage ride there, she considered telling Owen about Samuel, but since he was in such a jolly mood—talking about a new shipment his family's business had received from China—she'd been content to let him ramble on.

Once in the midst of the party, she decided a group announcement might be the easiest. She *did* have to say something, for if word got out otherwise—and servants *did* talk—the gossip would be far worse than the reality.

And so, after they'd taken turns playing the piano and entertaining each other with witticisms and song, she told a small group of her friends. "I had an exciting day yesterday."

"Do tell," Carrie said. "For lately, the most exciting thing to happen to me was finding a blue ribbon I thought I'd lost."

Ada scanned the faces of the group, ending with Owen, standing beside her. She told them of her shopping expedition gone awry—leaving out Samuel's identity. For now.

"So you have that man at your house? Sleeping in one of your beds?"

"The accident *was* partially my fault," she explained. "John and I couldn't very well leave him on the street."

David Gould shook his head. "Five Points, you say? I wouldn't let my worst enemy visit that area."

Because Samuel lived there, she downplayed its worst qualities. "It's run-down, for certain, but there were a lot of people selling their wares in pushcarts, and—"

Maribelle Morgan made a face. "You didn't buy anything from them, did you? I mean, who would want to touch such things?"

"No, I didn't get around to buying anything." She thought of the children who'd swarmed around her. "I will admit it was sad to see the children trying to earn a few pennies by selling scraps of coal or wood. They were so desperate."

"Where are their parents?" Carrie asked. "And shouldn't they be in school?"

"I'm not sure they have parents," Ada said. "Or a school to go to."

Thomas Fairfield removed a piece of lint from his trousers and let it fall to its death on the carpet. "Then they should get jobs. The garment industry employs children. Let them earn their keep." He dismissed the subject of the children with a flip of his hand. "Enough of them. When can you be rid of the man?"

Ada hated their attitude. Surely they wouldn't have left an injured man on the street.

"I think it's marvelous you took him in," Owen said, with a hand on her arm. "We are to give generously to the poor and help the helpless. You and John are Good Samaritans."

Maribelle wasn't satisfied. "But a stranger in your house. . ."

It was time for the whole truth. "Actually. . .the man is not a stranger."

Oscar laughed. "*You* know someone in Five Points?"

"I know Samuel Alcott." She turned to Owen, offering him her full attention. "Samuel is recuperating in our house."

It took them a moment to react. "The man who was hurt is Samuel? Your Samuel?" Carrie asked.

Owen's eyes locked on Ada's, obviously needing reassurance. "But he's not her Samuel anymore."

"No, he's not," she told him quietly.

"No, of course he's not," Carrie said. "Silly me. But it *is* Samuel?"

"One and the same." She was glad to break her gaze with Owen. He *did* care that it was Samuel. Oh dear.

Maribelle fanned herself, as if wanting the whole notion to flutter far, far away. "But Samuel hurt you so horribly, Ada. How can you bring him into your home?"

The respect she'd yearned for was obviously not going to be offered.

"How the mighty have fallen," David said, shaking his head.

"He hasn't fallen," Ada said. "Samuel is a good man who simply chose a way of life that's beyond our understanding."

"But he hurt you," Carrie said. "Surely you haven't forgiven him?"

Ada felt her heart start to race. Had she forgiven him?

Her own doubt caused her ire to rise even more. "Instead of focusing on the past, I thought you'd focus on the present, on the needs of a friend. I guess I was mistaken."

"Come now, Ada," Thomas said. "You must admit the entire situation is rather odd and a bit. . ."

"Scandalous," Maribelle said. When no one responded, she scanned the group, ending with Thomas. "Don't look at me like that. Isn't that what you were going to say?"

"I was going to say 'unfortunate.'"

Maribelle's fan fluttered furiously. "My statement stands. Not that Samuel Alcott would care whether he caused a scandal or not. He's already shown a total disregard for society and propriety by abandoning his birthright, disregarding his grandfather's wishes, and breaking the heart of my friend. What goes around comes around."

Ada was fuming inside. "Are you implying he deserved to get hurt?"

Maribelle reddened. "I. . .I'm just saying he put himself in that horrible neighborhood, so what did he expect?"

"He did not expect my family's carriage to detour onto a busy street and cause congestion, upheaval, and injury." She handed her champagne glass to a nearby footman. "Now, if you'll excuse me, I need to go home to see if there is some way I can repair the damage I've caused."

With that, she moved to the front door with Owen rushing after her.

❧

"I'm sorry for cutting our evening short," Ada told Owen when they were in the carriage.

"No apologies necessary. But in our friends' defense. . .they were simply surprised at your news." He paused a moment, then added, "As was I."

She took his gloved hand in hers. "I should have told you in private. Forgive me."

He shrugged. "So what does Samuel have to say for himself? Where has he been this past year? What has he been doing?"

"I don't know. We haven't spoken. He's sleeping most of the time, and when he awakens, he's delirious."

"Oh. That's too bad."

But by the tone of Owen's voice, Ada could tell he was relieved.

❧

Once home, Ada went to Samuel's room, knocked gently, and, receiving no answer, went inside. The lamp was still burning beside the bed, and John was asleep in a chair.

She stood over Samuel and watched his chest rise and fall. If only he would awaken and know her.

But what would she say to him? How would she greet him?

As a friend?

Or. . .as something more?

She kissed her fingers and pressed them to his hair, leaving the answer to another day.

Chapter 9

"But why doesn't he know us?" Ada asked her brother.

Nana stood beside her and nodded, making it her question, too.

John took hold of Samuel's wrist, then looked at his pocket watch.

Ada remained quiet while John checked his pulse.

His mission complete, he set Samuel's hand on the covers. "His heart rate is strong, and it's good he *is* waking on occasion and is cognizant enough to take broth and medicine and tend to other functions." He nodded at the footman Patrick, who helped with Samuel's more personal needs. "His realization of where he is and who we are will come."

"What can we do to help?" Ada asked.

He nodded toward the door. "I'll ask a maid to sit with him when either you or I can't be here, but—"

Nana raised a hand. "I can sit with him, too."

Nana rarely got out of bed, and if she did, *she* was the one attended.

"Well, I can," she said. "I can sit in here just as well as I can sit in my room. I always liked Samuel. Let me help."

Moved by her offer, Ada kissed her cheek.

"Your help is accepted," John said. "But I'd feel better if he has a real nurse on hand full-time. At least for these first critical days."

Critical days. Ada didn't like the sound of that. She'd fully expected Samuel to awaken and know her, and be pleased to see her. Was there a chance that he'd never be completely with them?

Nana must have sensed her fear, for she took her hand. "And to do our part, we will increase the intensity of our prayers for his full recovery."

Tenfold. One hundredfold. "Can you arrange for a nurse?" Ada asked.

"I can and will. But I'm sure it will be afternoon before one can come. Can you handle it until then?"

"Of course."

"Me, too," Nana said.

John kissed his grandmother on her other cheek. "You are a constant surprise, Nana. I've never seen you so strong."

"Perhaps the presence of someone who needs more help than myself has been the shoe to boot me out of bed."

Mother came in as John was leaving, and they exchanged pleasantries. Then she joined Nana and Ada bedside, though she kept her distance as though Samuel were contagious.

"I hear John's sending over a nurse," Mother said. "Your father will not appreciate the expense."

Nana threw up her hands. "Gracious sakes, daughter, if Horace won't pay the money, I will. Sometimes you two act as cheap as a chicken."

"Shouldn't you be back in your own bed, Mother?"

Nana firmed her grip on Ada's hand. "I'm doing fine right here, thank you."

Then Ada brought up something that had been on her mind. "I wish we could contact the foundling home where Samuel's been living, to tell them where he is—that he's being cared for."

"Do you really think that's necessary?" Mother said.

"Winifred Grace!" Nana said. "Not only are your purse strings tied in a knot, but your heartstrings, too? Think of those worrying. They need to know what's happened."

Even though Ada appreciated Nana's defense, she intervened on her mother's behalf. "I wish we could contact them, but I don't know the name of the home. Samuel only sent the one letter and didn't say."

"He probably didn't want to be found," Mother said. "So that's that, then."

Ada had another task to suggest. "This afternoon I plan to go to Mr. Alcott's to tell him Samuel is here, and he's hurt—before he hears it from someone else." She thought of Carrie Astor, David, Maribelle, and all the rest at the party last night. The speed of the society gossip mill was unparalleled—especially when bad news was involved.

Mother turned up her nose. "*If* Alcott's even around anymore. I haven't heard hide nor hair of him since Samuel ruined his life."

Ada closed her eyes against her mother's barbs. "I must try. You'd want to know if I was hurt, wouldn't you?"

"Don't be silly." Mother turned to leave. "John said you volunteered to sit with Samuel until the nurse arrives?"

"I did."

She nodded, then said, "Perhaps you should get out your bridal quilt and work on it again. It's been a year, Ada. You've always called it a map of your life. You must catch up and create the squares to commemorate your happy times with Owen."

Ada had not even allowed herself to look at the quilt since she'd put it away on the evening Samuel left her. Adding any new square with fabrics and embroidery symbolizing her relationship with Owen would force her to create and stitch a new route to her life's map—one that detoured and traveled down roads she hadn't fully accepted. And if she allowed herself to be honest, roads she wasn't sure she wanted to travel.

She shook her head. "When I'm here I want to give Samuel my full attention."

Mother was persistent. "But when you and Owen become engaged, don't you want to take the quilt into your marriage as you planned?"

Nothing was as she'd planned. "Mother, I said no."

Mother shuffled her shoulders. "It was just a suggestion. The quilt is your prized possession, and it doesn't seem right you've abandoned it because of a little heartache. Things are finally back to normal. Life goes on."

A little *heartache? Life goes on?* It wasn't that simple. Surely Mother knew it wasn't that simple.

To avoid an argument, Ada moved toward the door. "I think it's best if Samuel rests in silence right now. If you don't mind."

Mother walked into the hallway but offered one last barb. "Watch yourself, Ada."

It took all of Ada's restraint not to slam the door. "Argghhh!"

"Now, now," Nana said. "As much as my daughter and I don't agree, she does have a point about the quilt—your life quilt. In spite of what you believe, your life did not end when Samuel left."

There it was again: *Life goes on.*

Nana slipped her hand around Ada's arm. "Besides, he's back, isn't he?"

"What do you mean by that?"

But Nana only put a finger to her lips and smiled.

❧

Ada sent a note to Samuel's grandfather, asking if she might visit him that evening after he got home from work. Soon after the hired nurse arrived, she received word she should come at three. The early hour surprised her, but she was also grateful, for it would prevent her from being out after dark.

A gentle snow was falling—a Christmas snow as Ada liked to call it, for it fell gently, as if covering the city in a heavenly mantle.

The Alcott butler greeted her and took her coat and bonnet, the snowflakes already melted on the warm fabric. "Nice to see you again, Miss Wallace," Briggs said. "We've missed you."

How very kind of him. "I've missed you, too, Briggs. Is Mr. Alcott ready to see me?"

There was a moment of hesitation, and Briggs looked nervously to the floor.

"What's wrong?"

"He's much changed, miss."

"How so?"

"You'll see." The butler led her back to a room she had never entered. "He's in there, miss. He's always in there." Briggs knocked, then opened the door and let her in, closing it behind her.

The room was a study with dark paneling and floor-to-ceiling shelves filled with books. A fire was in the grate, but other than its light and two gas wall sconces turned low, the room was dark. It smelled of lemon oil, leather—and grief.

Ada looked toward the massive desk, expecting to find Mr. Alcott there. But the desk chair was empty. Perhaps he was going to join her in a few minutes. She moved to wait in one of the chairs facing the fireplace, but pulled up short when she saw one was occupied.

"Oh. Sir. Mr. Alcott. I didn't see you there."

He didn't rise, but looked up at her over his spectacles. "That's because I'm not here. Not anywhere." He pointed to the other chair, but it seemed the effort to raise his arm was nearly too much. "There. Sit there."

She sat in the other wing chair, adjusting her bustle against the cushions. "I'm so glad you agreed to see me," she said. "And that you were home from work so the meeting could be early."

He snickered. "Work. What does work matter? What does anything matter without my grandson?"

Ada sucked in a breath. Briggs was right. Mr. Alcott had changed much. Gone was the vibrant—if not domineering—man who ran a banking empire as well as his grandson's life. In his place was this lump of a man with tousled hair, an unruly beard, and rumpled clothes.

She spotted a pillow and blanket on the couch nearby. Was he sleeping in here, too? Had this room become his world?

He looked at her with rheumy eyes. "I always liked you, Ada. I wanted you as my granddaughter, I really did. Since Emma died. . .this family needs a woman's touch."

"Thank you, sir. I wanted to be a part of this family."

"Until Samuel rejected you. And rejected me," he said. "All my life's work was not enough for him. And what is any of it worth without him? When I lost my son in the fire, Samuel became my everything. I may not have shown it well, but that truth remains. And I never thought he'd turn his back on all this—on me. I didn't mean it when I gave him the ultimatum." His voice cracked with emotion. "I didn't mean it."

Her heart went out to him. To feel like such a failure. *Please, God, give me the right words to help him.* Ada reached out to touch his knee. "Mr. Alcott, Samuel's choice had nothing to do with your life's work, or your success, or the legacy you worked so hard to build."

"Then why?"

She searched for a mingling of truth and discretion. "Samuel has a heart unlike any other. He sees when others look away; he feels what others wish to ignore. God called him to do special work, work that demanded sacrifice. You and I are a part of that sacrifice." She took a cleansing breath, then continued. "I, for one, don't like that role. And sometimes I sit and think and pray that I would hear such a call. Yet I fear that even if God called, I wouldn't have the strength to go. Samuel had that strength."

"But he left us behind."

Ada realized that in answering the question for Mr. Alcott, she had answered an unasked question in herself. She fumbled in her pocket for a handkerchief. "I'm sorry. As you see, it still affects me, too."

He plucked his own handkerchief from a pocket, removed his spectacles, and dabbed at his eyes. "We are quite a pair, Miss Wallace, for we have both lost our Samuel."

Suddenly Ada remembered why she had come. "But he's not lost, Mr. Alcott. I found him. And he's at our house."

She filled in the blanks, telling him the complete story.

His eyes cleared, and his face became animated. When she was finished, he surprised her by rising to his feet. "We must go. Now! I must see Samuel!" He hobbled to the door and thrust it open. "Briggs! Come help me. I have to go out!"

❧

Samuel's grandfather entered the Wallace household like a hurricane. Not two steps into the foyer, he called out, "Where's Samuel? Where's my grandson?"

Mother rushed out from the parlor, her hand to her chest, clearly concerned about the barbarian who'd invaded her house.

Ada didn't know who to calm first. She chose Mr. Alcott, because it was clear he was unrestrainable. She led him up the stairs, calling down to her mother. "Forgive him. He's just excited."

Mother fumbled some reply, which thankfully Ada couldn't hear.

"Down this way, Mr. Alcott."

But before he could fling the door to Samuel's room open, Ada barred the door. "Now stop. You must contain yourself."

The old man's breathing was labored from the stairs and his zeal. He put a hand to his chest and forced himself to calm down.

"That's better," Ada said.

He nodded, and when he'd fully gotten himself under control, he took Ada's hand and kissed it. "How can I ever thank you, dear girl?"

Get Samuel to fully awaken.

"Are you ready?" she asked.

"I am."

She opened the door. The hired nurse stood near the door, clearly alerted to the uproar outside. Ada tried to reassure her. "This is Mr. Alcott's grandfather. He's very eager to see him."

The nurse raised an eyebrow. "There will be no agitation, no dramatics. Is that understood?"

Mr. Alcott lifted his right hand as if taking an oath.

"Very well then." The nurse stepped aside.

Ada let Mr. Alcott proceed to the bedside alone. She whispered to the nurse, "Any change?"

"None."

Ada had warned Mr. Alcott of Samuel's condition, but seeing his grandson immobile and bandaged. . . He put a hand to his mouth, and Ada heard a moan escape.

She moved to his side to provide support. "See?" she said, trying to sound positive. "He's really here."

Mr. Alcott nodded, and Ada heard him sniff. He was crying.

She linked her arm through his, and together they watched Samuel sleep.

❧

Ada left Mr. Alcott sitting at Samuel's bedside and headed to her room to change from her suit to a day dress.

Passing Nana's room, she heard all sorts of commotion inside. She let herself in.

Nana was sitting at her dressing table. Two maids fluttered around her, one doing her hair and another brushing off a dress.

"What's going on?" Ada asked.

Nana turned around on the bench. "Shame on you for not telling me we have a guest, Ada."

Ada was confused. "You mean Mr. Alcott?"

"Of course I mean Mr. Alcott. Who could help but hear him?" She pointed at the burgundy moire dress. "Do you think this will be appropriate for dinner?"

"Dinner?" Nana had not joined the family for dinner in years.

"I assume he's staying for dinner."

Ada had lost all track of time. It was nearly the dinner hour. "I suppose he could. I haven't asked him."

"Where are your manners, child? Go invite him to stay, and leave me to my toilette."

Ada met the eyes of the maids, and they both shrugged as if they didn't know any more than she did.

There was a story behind all this. . . .

❧

There had been much scrambling behind the scenes to set two extra places for dinner and alert the kitchen of the additional guests, not for the quantity—there was always enough food—but for their identity. The invalid Mrs. Bauer had actually dressed for dinner, and the other diner was the grandfather of the injured man upstairs—who used to be Miss Ada's beau. . . . The servants' grapevine would lose its leaves tonight.

Ada saw her grandmother walk into the dining room on the arm of Mr. Alcott. "Look at her," she whispered to her brother.

"Look at them," John said.

They were seated, and the dinner service began. Mother looked peeved, but Ada's father was positively jolly. "My, my, Nathaniel Alcott, how good to see you. And Mother Bauer. . .you light up the room."

"Why, thank you," Nana said.

Mr. Alcott smiled at Nana. "The last time I saw you look so lovely was the first of August, 1832."

Nana blushed—she actually blushed! Ada had never seen pink on her cheeks.

And they knew each other?

"It was a Wednesday, Nate. And if I remember correctly—which I do—you looked quite dashing yourself."

Mother's soup spoon clattered onto the table. "Mother! You're a married woman."

"I'm a widow, and Nathaniel is a widower. And in 1832 neither one of us was married."

Mr. Alcott laughed. "We weren't married, and we didn't have more than a nickel in our pockets. We'd just arrived in New York City."

"We met on the voyage over," Nana said. "Nathaniel and I had quite the shipboard romance."

"Why haven't we heard any of this before?" Ada asked. "Especially since I was going to. . ."

Mother's head was shaking so vehemently, Ada feared for her neck. "This is totally inappropriate dinner-table talk. I want—"

Father interrupted. "It's fascinating dinner-table talk, my dear. And I want to hear the answer to Ada's question myself."

Nana and Mr. Alcott exchanged glances, and suddenly their wrinkles fell away and Ada could imagine them as twentysomething youths with America at their feet.

Mr. Alcott continued the story. "Our ship arrived in New York City on August second, so there was a party on board the evening before." He grinned. "Hildegard and I danced until the soles of our shoes begged for relief."

"We danced out of desperation. Our families had divergent plans in America. We didn't know if we'd ever see each other again," Nana said. "And we didn't—for ten years."

"Which was after I married my Emma."

"And after I married my Herbert."

Ada was entranced. To think that her grandmother and Samuel's grandfather had known each other, and loved each other. . .

Mr. Alcott took a spoonful of squash soup and dabbed his mouth with a napkin. "Even Samuel doesn't know of our connection. I planned on sharing all of this with him and your family, but then. . ." He looked around the table, making sure he gave each diner a look. "I must apologize for last year. I'm devastated that Samuel's choice brought such pain to so many."

Ada's father answered. "We appreciate how hard it was on you, too, Nathaniel. I'm just pleased you've had a chance to be reunited—though the conditions are less than ideal."

John piped in. "I do believe Samuel will recover."

"You do?" Ada and Mr. Alcott asked at the same time.

"I do. His body is taking care of first things first, which is resting in order to repair itself."

Ada was glad for John's words.

Then Mother said, "Ada is nearly betrothed to Owen Reed. The Reeds make their fortune in shipping."

Ada was appalled. "Mother! I am not engaged to Owen yet."

"You will be. Mark my words."

"Good for you," Mr. Alcott said. "Do you love him?"

Mother gasped, but Nana nodded, also wanting an answer.

"Forgive me for being so forthright," Mr. Alcott said. "I've wasted too many months holding my tongue. But now that I'm released from my self-imposed prison, I realize there are only so many words left to say, so I shouldn't waste time being coy or subtle."

Nana nodded. "As I always knew, you're a man after my own heart, Nathaniel Alcott."

After an awkward silence, Father turned to John. "Now then. Tell us how things are progressing over at the Academy, son."

The discussion shifted.

Thank you, Father.

❧

After dinner Ada stood beside Samuel's bed. Mr. Alcott had gone home but would return tomorrow. Her mother had retired with a headache. And Nana. . . Her grandmother's room was Ada's next stop before retiring for the night.

Ada had given the nurse a break so she could go have some dinner, but mostly because Ada needed this time alone with Samuel. With the story about Nana and Mr. Alcott. . .

Everything had changed.

It wasn't a monumental transformation, but knowing that their grandparents had once loved each other caused a shift in Ada's thinking. When she and Samuel had been together, they'd often shared a common belief that God had brought them together—which had made their split especially painful. *What God has joined together, let no man put asunder.* But now. . .who would have thought a traffic jam and a rearing horse could have been instrumental in bringing Ada and Samuel back into each other's lives? It was an astounding coincidence.

Or not. Perhaps there was no such thing.

Perhaps it was God. Who but the Almighty could have arranged it? And on that very outing, hadn't Ada prayed that she would find Samuel? Perhaps God wasn't through with them yet.

Suddenly Samuel breathed deeper, a long, controlled in and out.

Ada leaned over him, touching his forehead. "Samuel? It's Ada. Please wake up and know me. *Please.*"

But Samuel slept on.

For now.

&

"Come in."

Ada entered Nana's bedroom and found her in her usual spot in bed, leaning against a mountain of pillows. Yet tonight there was something different about the scene.

"You're positively glowing, Nana."

Nana put her palms to her cheeks. "Am I?"

Ada sat on the edge of the bed. "You had quite a surprise for us this evening."

"My, that was fun," she said. "And the look on my daughter's face. . ."

"So Mother didn't know? Any of it?"

Nana shook her head. "When you and Samuel started courting, I crossed paths with Nate as our families began to socialize. But his wife had recently died, and the focus needed to be on you two lovebirds. We occasionally discussed telling the families of our connection but decided we would wait until after you were betrothed." She shrugged, then smiled. "He's still quite a handsome man, don't you think?"

Ada laughed. "I suppose he is."

Nana snuggled down under the covers. "Turn off the light, child. I'm looking forward to happy dreams."

Chapter 10

Mr. Alcott spent most of his days by his grandson's bedside, and though Samuel occasionally stirred and even spoke a few incoherent words, he did not fully awaken.

Ada tried to be patient, and she renewed her prayers, thinking that if God saw that she had pulled aside the curtain she'd drawn between herself and the Almighty since last Christmas, He might hear her pleas and fully bring Samuel back to her.

Nana spent her days keeping Mr. Alcott company. Ada often paused at the door to Samuel's room and listened to their happy voices and laughter. They sounded like young people, eager in each other's company. Not at all like a sickly octogenarian or a broken, rumpled man, hidden away in his study. What had changed them?

Love.

Though Ada dared not mention that word in front of her mother—who could not hide her annoyance toward the two—Ada knew love *was* the reason for their transformation. And it gave her hope. If she loved Samuel enough, and if he still loved her. . .

Anything was possible.

But first things first. Tonight was her family's Christmas party. The Wallace household would be teeming with seventy-some guests, all dressed in their holiday best. There would be a seven-course meal, Christmas caroling, and even some dancing to a string quartet hired for the occasion. Yet in spite of the merriment, Ada wished she could spend the evening in Samuel's room with Nana and Mr. Alcott. Although they were obviously invited to the party, they had declined for the sake of propriety. Having Samuel ensconced in the Wallace home had created enough brouhaha among their set. Knowing Nana and Mr. Alcott's past—and present—relationship would have been too much for society to bear.

Sadie pinned a sprig of holly in Ada's hair. "There. How do you like it?"

It was very pretty—and Ada said so. The problem was her heart wasn't in the evening.

Especially since there was the chance that tonight Owen would propose. She knew it was her mother's fervent wish. And as such, it was Ada's fervent fear. For even though she loved Owen—in a way—with Samuel back in her life. . .she couldn't become engaged to Owen. She just couldn't.

And yet, with Samuel still out of commission, with no words exchanged between them, she couldn't be certain he still loved *her*. What if Owen proposed and she declined, and then Samuel woke up and *he* declined? To enter another Christmas having lost two beaus—one of them twice?

Yet wouldn't it be worse to marry the wrong man?

"Does your head hurt, miss?" Sadie asked, looking at Ada's reflection. "Would you like me to get you some headache powder?"

Ada nodded. It was not a good way to begin a party.

❧

"You look very pretty tonight, Ada," Owen said, kissing her cheek. "Merry Christmas."

"Merry Christmas." She forced a smile, hating her mood, knowing Owen didn't deserve her brooding.

"How is Samuel?" he asked.

"He still hasn't fully awakened."

"I'm sorry to hear that."

A few other friends asked after Samuel, but Ada could tell their interest was more prurient in nature than a true concern for his health. They wanted him well so he could talk and add to the gossip by giving details of where he'd been for the past year. They wanted him well so they could shun him.

But as the festivities began, the guests forgot Samuel Alcott was in the house. They mingled and laughed, ate heartily from the mountain of holiday delicacies, sang carols, and danced to the string quartet. Ada went through the motions. She smiled at the appropriate times, offered the appropriate verbal response to every question, and danced with her usual ease, but her heart was elsewhere.

Upstairs. Close, but so very far away.

Ada's mother seemed to be the only one who sensed something was wrong, because the more Ada felt detached from the party, the more frenzied her mother became, flitting from this couple to that one, talking too loudly, laughing too forcibly, and being too much the hostess.

Ada looked toward the stairs longingly. If only she could make a discreet exit.

But then Owen stepped forward among the crowd and clinked a fork against a glass. "Attention, friends! Attention, please."

The musicians ceased, and the room grew quiet as everyone drew close.

"I have an announcement to make."

At first, Ada, wrapped up in her if-only thoughts, felt no premonition of what was to come. But when she saw the beaming face of her mother, she knew a specific plan had been hatched and was about to play out.

No! No, Owen. Don't do it!

But Owen continued. "In this season of love and goodwill, I would like to ask Miss Ada Wallace to be my wife." He took her hand, got down on one knee, and repeated the question. "Ada, would you marry me?"

It was as though Ada were removed from the moment, as if she floated near the coffered ceiling and looked down upon the scene. *Owen's proposing in public? Now?*

Before she could gather herself to figure out if there *was* a way to politely decline, her mother rushed forward and said, "Yes! Of course, Owen! How wonderful!" She held out her glass. "Come, everyone. Toast the happy couple!"

Awkwardly, the guests gained a glass. Owen stood, but his eyes were on Ada, the question still on his face.

But she couldn't say yes. And with seventy guests ready to toast their betrothal, she couldn't say no. Not here. He deserved an explanation, and that wasn't possible here.

"To Owen and Ada!" someone said.

"Hear, hear!"

Hugs and congratulations followed.

What had just happened?

❧

The party was over, and thankfully the house was quiet. The guests and Mr. Alcott had returned home. Ada felt wrung out inside, yet she could not retire until she talked with Nana. She found her seated at the dressing table, a maid braiding her waist-length hair in preparation for bed.

"How was the party, child? Tell me all about it."

Ada took over for the maid and waited until she was gone before speaking. "Long ago I promised that you would be the first to know."

It only took Nana a few seconds to understand. She stopped Ada's braiding by facing her. "You're engaged?"

Ada nodded.

"To Owen."

"Of course to Owen. It's not like Samuel has suddenly awakened and proposed."

Nana's shoulders slumped, her forehead strained in deep thought. "You didn't have to say yes."

"And I didn't! Not really." Ada explained what had happened. "And afterward, on more than one occasion, I tried to pull Owen aside to set him straight. But each and every time I had him alone, Mother appeared and pulled us back with the others. It's very clear she instigated the entire proposal. I don't doubt she even assured Owen I would accept, for I can't imagine him proposing in public unless he was sure of my answer."

"What Winifred wants, Winifred gets."

Ada nodded. "Mother was so strong. She just stepped in and—"

"Made it happen."

Ada nodded. "So how can it be fixed?"

Nana put a hand on Ada's, quieting her. "There's only one question that needs to be asked."

"What's that?"

"What do *you* want?"

Immediately Ada's mind became congested with words and thoughts. "I. . .I—"

Nana held up a hand and shook her head. "Shh. Don't say anything now. Life-changing decisions are like tea; they need to steep in hot water in order to develop their full flavor."

"But I'm already in hot water. I'm engaged!"

Nana moved to the bed and snuggled into the pillows. "Turn down the light, child, and bring me some tea in the morning."

❧

Ada sat at her dressing table in her nightgown, brushing and rebrushing her hair.

I'm engaged.

Nana's question returned: *What do* you *want?*

She closed her eyes but found Owen's face there—his smile broad as he stood at the door and kissed her cheek good night. "We can choose a ring together, Ada. Your mother thought. . ." He'd finished the evening with a declaration. "I'll make you happy, Ada. I promise."

"No!" Ada threw her brush on the dressing table, knocking over a perfume bottle.

The smell of honeysuckle wafted toward her as she righted it. But it was the only thing that could be righted. . . .

She had no doubt Owen would try to make her happy. He was a good man, a kind man, and up until very recently, she'd thought he was the right man.

And all logic said that was still true. In fact, she'd hoped for a night like this, a festive night where he would propose.

That is, until Samuel came back into her life.

The fact she'd never told Owen yes seemed of little import to her friends, to her family, or to Owen. To them the deed was done, the betrothal made. Ada leaned her head on her hands.

She started when her mother entered unannounced, her arms

outstretched, her face glowing with gladness. "Ada, my dear daughter. You did it! You really did it."

Before Mother could make contact, Ada turned around on the bench and glared at her. "I didn't do anything, Mother. I didn't even say yes."

Mother took a step back, her hand to her chest. "Of course you did."

"Of course *you* did. *You* stepped in and agreed for me. You didn't give me the chance to answer him—nor to make things right."

"I have no idea what you're talking—"

Ada stood to face her. "You have every idea. In fact, I suspect every detail of this evening was your idea."

Mother tried to veil a smile but was only partially successful. "I'm not going to argue with you, Ada. If, as you say, I answered for you, it's because someone had to take charge and move you forward on your proper path."

"The path *you* think is proper."

"Absolutely. I've seen the look in your eyes since Samuel came back. He spurned you once, Ada. Are you truly waiting for him to awaken so he can spurn you again? Nothing has changed. You might as well live in separate countries for the expanse of class and philosophy that divides you. Owen is one of us. He loves you. And if you'd snap out of your fog, you'd see he's the best thing that's happened to you."

Ada did appreciate Owen for being instrumental in lifting her family out of the pit of society's oblivion. And her mother was right about the fact that nothing had changed in Samuel's situation. As far as she knew, he was still married to his work. But what if his work could also be *her* work? Somehow. Some way.

Mother's face softened, and she took Ada's hands. "Be honest with yourself, daughter. You *do* want to marry Owen Reed, and all this protest is ridiculous. I know your heart has been touched by Samuel, and even by the ridiculous pairing of my mother and Mr. Alcott. But compassion is not passion. Samuel came into your life, and you're helping him. You—"

"He's helped me."

Mother looked skeptical. "He is not of our world. And as soon as he's able, he will return to his world. And you. . .you must let him go."

"But—"

Mother's eyes grew hard. "Listen here. I've worked my entire life to get the Wallace family firmly ensconced into the Four Hundred. Samuel Alcott nearly ruined that for us, and Owen Reed rectified Samuel's mistake. Our mistake. Do you understand?"

Ada had no argument.

No stand.

No way out.

Chapter 11

The day after Ada's engagement dawned, and the sun came up. And though she'd always imagined such a day would seem extraordinary and full of anticipation for the future, with this morning came confusion, desperation, and even anger.

She was engaged to a wonderful man, but she resented it.

She was in love with an injured, unresponsive man who might *not* be in love with her, a man who lived and worked in a world set apart from her own.

Ada felt as if she were walking on a rope stretched across a cavern. One false move and she would fall into nothingness, with no hope of surviving unscathed. Yet to stay the course and make it to the other side. . . What waited for her there?

Sadie helped her get dressed, but breakfast was difficult as Mother insisted on talking about the wedding. Invitations, dinner menus, flowers. . .

"And your dress should be covered in Belgian lace. Perhaps we could have Worth in Paris design it."

"Sounds expensive," her father said.

"Of course it does," Mother said. "Of course it *is*. Ada is our only daughter. We only get to do this once."

Nana looked directly at Ada. "Indeed. You only get to do this once."

Once. I only get to marry once. I must make the right choice.

"I suppose you'll be wanting a European tour for your honeymoon?" Father asked.

Mother answered for her. "I'll miss having you gone six months, but it is a must."

And there it was. The tipping point, the one comment that made everything fall into place.

A European honeymoon. . .

The idea of being away from Samuel for six months was unbearable. She couldn't marry Owen and leave. Not when her heart belonged to Samuel.

Ada dropped her fork against the plate and scooted her chair back. "I'm sorry. If you'll excuse me?"

"Excuse you?" Mother said. "We're in the middle of a discussion about your wedding."

She wanted to tell them of her revelation, but she had someone else to tell first. Whether Samuel awakened or not, whether he could hear her or not, she had to declare her love to him.

As Ada moved to the doorway of the dining room, Nana asked, "So the tea is brewed and hot, child?"

Ada paused and nodded. "The tea is steaming and full of flavor."

As she hurried up the stairs, she heard Nana's laughter.

"Tea?" her mother said. "What's all this talk about tea?"

❧

Ada burst into Samuel's room and set the nurse free to get her own breakfast.

She rushed to Samuel's side, took his hand, and gave the words release. "I love you, Samuel. I don't know if you love me, but I have never stopped loving you, and—"

He moaned.

Ada leaned close and stroked his cheek. "Samuel? It's Ada. Come on now. Open your eyes. Wake up. All the way now. Talk to me, Samuel."

As if her wish was his command, Samuel's eyelids fluttered, then opened. He looked at Ada, blinked slowly, then looked again. "Ada? It *is* you."

Ada began to cry. "It is me."

The world was right and good again.

Thank You, God! Thank You!

She'd made her choice not to marry Owen without knowing how Samuel felt—an all-or-nothing decision. But now, since he was awake, what if he. . .

Ada shook away the thought. The fact was, whether Samuel still loved her or not, her own feelings wouldn't change.

The tea was brewed, and her heart was warm with love.

Neither could be undone.

❧

Samuel couldn't take his eyes off her. Ada was more beautiful than he remembered. He could only guess at the extent of the pain he'd caused her during the past year. Yet her smile still had the ability to melt his heart.

He was content to let her explain how he happened to be at the Wallaces'. He had little memory of the accident and certainly had no memory of all that had come after but for seeing her face and saying her name, once, before falling into the abyss of his injuries.

Yet he *had* seen her before that. "I saw you," he said, after she explained the accident. "I saw you on the street."

"I didn't see you," she said. "Or rather, I saw a man save a little boy but didn't know it was you until you were in the carriage."

"I'd prayed for the chance to see you again," he said.

Her eyes widened. "I prayed to see you, too, on that very outing."

He squeezed her hand, relishing the softness of her skin and the elegant length of her fingers. "It seems clear that God brought us together again."

Her eyes filled with tears, and she cupped his face in her palm. "He did, didn't He?"

Their reunion was interrupted when the door opened and Samuel's grandfather walked in. "Good morning, Ada. How's our patient do—?"

He pulled up short.

"Morning, Grandfather."

The old man rushed toward him, fluttering and flubbering his greetings. Samuel was surprised at his tears and extinguished one as it slid down his grandfather's cheek. "I'm so glad to see you."

"Oh, Samuel, my boy, you'll never know how glad I am to see you."

Ada relinquished her place. "I'll leave you to your celebration. I must spread the good news."

Samuel was reluctant to see her go but took solace in knowing she would return.

If he had his way, they would never be separated again.

๛

Ada caught up with her parents in the entry foyer as Wilson helped her father don his coat to go to work. She rushed down the stairs.

"He's awake!" she said. "Samuel's fully awake!"

They all froze for a moment, her father with his arm halfway in the coat's sleeve. Then he said, "Well, good for him. It shows he's on the mend."

Mother's head shook back and forth as if trying to let the news percolate through the soil of her brain. "Yes, good. He can go home now."

Ada felt her jaw drop. "Mother!"

Father adjusted the coat at his shoulders as Wilson stood by with his hat, gloves, and walking stick. "Winifred, really."

Mother reddened but did not change her stance. "I don't mean this very minute, but since he's awake, I'm sure he'd rather go back to his home. After all, Christmas is just a few days away and—"

Her mother's brash words gave Ada the courage to share her own. "I'm not going to marry Owen. I want to marry Samuel."

Father bobbled his hat, and it was recovered by the butler. "You just became engaged to Owen."

"But I've never stopped loving Samuel, and now that he's fully back—"

"He is not back," Mother said. "He is here only because of his injuries. He still lives in some hovel down in the slums. He is still penniless."

Father cocked his head. "I wouldn't count on that anymore, Winifred. From what I've seen of Nathaniel, the fences between grandfather and grandson have been mended."

"Be that as it may," Mother said, "we will not have you shame this family again, daughter. It's bad enough to have one man reject you, but to break it off with yet another man who is actually your fiancé? Our reputation cannot endure it."

Ada turned to her father for support, but he said, "Your mother's right, Ada. Do you honestly want to put your family through another year like the last?"

No, but. . .

"And this time there may not be an Owen Reed to pull you out of it," Mother said. "Owen is your last chance in society."

"But what if I don't want to be in society anymore?"

Her parents looked as though she'd announced she wanted to die. Father's voice became stern. "You've made a commitment to Owen in front of friends and family. You must follow through. You will follow through."

"But *I* didn't make the commitment—Mother did!"

Father looked from his daughter to his wife, then clinched the entire conversation by putting on his gloves. "You are engaged to Owen Reed. I do business with his father. His family and ours will be bound through your union. Samuel Alcott is a man from your past. Do not confuse sympathy and empathy for love."

"But I do love him."

Father tapped the top of his hat with the brass tip of his walking stick. "I will hear no more of it, Ada. We've done our duty by Samuel. He is awake, and when able, he should return to his life and leave you to yours."

"But Father—"

He left the house, the situation sealed with the closing of the door.

"You see, your father agrees with me," Mother said. "You see, I'm right."

Ada swept past her and ran up the stairs to Samuel.

To her Samuel.

As she passed her grandmother's room, Nana was coming out. "My, my, what's wrong, child?"

Ada burst into tears and let Nana usher her inside.

❧

Samuel reveled in the company of his grandfather. Gone was the gruff man who'd raised him, the man who rarely uttered a kind or encouraging word. The man before him wore his heart on his sleeve, and his heart revealed his love for his grandson. Samuel mourned the deeper wrinkles in his grandfather's face and knew he was their cause. But the glint in the old man's eyes made up for the extra creases and furrows, revealing a light and life that Samuel had never seen before.

Their reunion was interrupted by the entrance of Mrs. Wallace. Grandfather stood. "Do you see, Winifred? The dead have come back to life!"

"I see," she said, though her face showed no joy in the fact. "If you don't mind, Mr. Alcott, I would like a few words with your grandson—in private."

Grandfather hesitated and looked to Samuel, who said, "Go on. Perhaps you could see if I might have something to eat. I'm feeling hungry."

His grandfather jumped at the chance to help and left Samuel alone with Ada's mother.

Samuel was glad for the chance to offer his appreciation. "I'm glad to talk with you, Mrs. Wallace. I want to thank you for taking me in and looking after me while I—"

She stood a goodly length away from the bed, her hands clasped in front of her. "I want you gone, Mr. Alcott."

"What?"

"You've hurt our family once, and you will not hurt us again. I'm glad you're all right, but now it's time to leave. Go away, Samuel Alcott. You must, for Ada's sake. Because she's engaged."

"Engaged?"

"To Owen Reed, a fine, upstanding man of breeding and society, who will love her, cherish her, and care for her in a way you cannot."

"I. . .I didn't know."

"Well, now you do."

With that, she made her exit.

Samuel was left speechless. The joy that had filled him to overflowing at seeing Ada and his grandfather was dashed. But why hadn't Ada said something? Her attentiveness and smile had given him every indication she still loved him as much as he loved her.

For he *did* still love her. Had never stopped loving her.

The past year had been excruciating for him. Although he felt satisfaction in helping the children, he often wondered at the price he'd paid. Had he misread God's leading when he thought God had said *"Wait"* in regard to their engagement?

His own heartache had tested his decision, and when his grandfather had cut him off and they'd become estranged. . . How could so much heartache be God's will? He wasn't the only person who could work with the children—he was never so arrogant as to think that. So had he given up everything for a calling that was *not* his own? And why hadn't he given Ada the chance to join him in his work? She'd offered, but he'd judged her offer as impulsive and unfeasible. He'd virtually deemed her willingness to sacrifice her lifestyle for a life together as insincere.

Who was he to judge her in such a way? To limit her?

But by the time he'd realized the arrogance of his mistake, he'd seen the society pages in a newspaper that mentioned Ada attending a dinner at the Vanderbilts' with Owen Reed—of the Reed shipping fortune.

He'd let her go, and she had moved on without him. And now she was to be Mrs. Owen Reed.

It was too late. He'd experienced true love but had tossed it aside, unmindful of its value. *"Who can find a virtuous woman? for her price is far above rubies."* Samuel had found such a woman but had not been willing to pay the price to keep her.

He stared into the fire, letting the flicker of the flames take his mind back to the days before the accident. Ada had been on his mind more than usual. As he'd gone about his work, trying to make some wooden toys for the children for Christmas, trying to keep the foundling home supplied with firewood and food, his thoughts had returned to Ada. They always returned to Ada. Her face. Her smile. Her loving eyes. Her soft skin, and the completeness he felt when she was in his arms.

And when he'd seen her alight from the carriage in Five Points, it was as if an angel had touched down in a dark world—his dark world. The children, the horse, the screams, the pain. . .he would suffer them all again if it would bring her back into his life.

But to have found her, only to lose her?

His thoughts burned away in the flames, leaving the images of Ada in the ashes.

❧

After telling Nana about all that had transpired, Ada let her grandmother's arms enfold her. "You always know how to comfort me, Nana."

"It's my job, child."

Ada sat upright. "So what should I do? I chose Samuel, and now he's awake. But Father says—"

"You are to honor your parents."

It was not what Ada wanted to hear. "Even if they're wrong?"

"They are not *wrong*. Owen is a wonderful man, and in spite of your feelings, your father has laid down his decision."

"What about brewing tea? What about coming to my own life-changing decision?"

"Ultimately, whether you like it or not, you are under your father's authority."

Ada stood, her frustration requiring movement. "If I have no power, then why did you urge me to make my own choice?"

Nana put a hand to her forehead, rubbing the space between her eyes. "Perhaps I was wrong to offer you an option where there was none. Perhaps I was caught up in the fantasy of true love and happy endings."

"Fantasy? So my feelings aren't real? And it doesn't matter what I choose?"

"In the end, probably not."

"But that's not fair!" Ada knew she sounded like a petulant child but didn't care.

"Life isn't fair, child. Was it fair that Nathaniel and I lost track of each other and were directed to marry others? I think not."

Ada was surprised by her grandmother's admission. "So you regret marrying Grandfather?"

" 'Tis better to have loved and lost, than never to have loved at all.' " That said, Nana shook her head. "Regrets have sharp teeth, child. And I *did* grow to love your grandfather." She put her hand beneath Ada's chin. "Without him I would not have you."

"But what if. . . ?"

Nana shook her head. "A life can drown in what-ifs. After seeking God's counsel and guidance, we must make the best decisions we can amid the barriers that exist around us. Beyond that, we must look forward instead of back."

"But you've found Mr. Alcott again. You're getting a second chance."

Decades fell from Nana's face. "God is good—all the time. And

He's often full of surprises."

"If God brought Mr. Alcott back into your life to love, doesn't it follow that He brought Samuel back into my life to love?"

"Time will tell."

But time was the problem. Her mother would see to it that Samuel left as soon as possible.

Time was running out.

Or was the hourglass already empty?

❧

By the time Ada returned to Samuel's room, he was sitting up and his grandfather was feeding him some soup.

"Look, Ada. He's eating," Mr. Alcott said.

"I told him I could do it myself, but he insists."

Ada's smile seemed wistful. Almost distant. Had something happened to upset her?

"You've grown weak," she said. "We fed you when we could, but you were asleep more than awake, and often delirious."

"Until this morning when I awakened and saw you." He smiled, then looked away. He had to be careful not to be too familiar. She was not his anymore. "I'm going home tomorrow."

Ada hesitated, her face tormented. Then she nodded. "I'm sure they're worried about you. I would have sent word, but I never knew exactly where you were."

He'd kept the location and name of the foundling home a secret from her—and his grandfather. It had seemed right at the time. He hadn't wanted either to seek him out and make his decision harder, but now he thought of Eliza and the children. What must they be thinking since he hadn't returned?

Mr. Alcott handed Samuel a napkin to wipe his chin. "I think leaving tomorrow is being hasty, Samuel. Dr. Wallace hasn't even seen you yet. He may say you can't go."

Samuel found Ada's eyes and held her gaze. "I must go."

Her forehead furrowed. Samuel wasn't sure if Ada was aware that he knew of her engagement. His visit from Mrs. Wallace had seemed clandestine, as if Ada's mother had wanted him to know Ada was promised to another—because she guessed Ada wouldn't tell him herself. He wished Ada *would* tell him. For until he heard the words from her mouth, he would always cling to a glimmer of hope. And until he heard the words, he could *not* declare his love.

His need for the air to be cleared took over. "Is there something you'd like to tell me, Ada?"

He watched her eyes flicker, as if matching the fire of her thoughts.

Tell me. If you love another, set me free. If not. . .tell me you love me and let me soar.

She finally said, "I'm going to miss you, Samuel. It was so wonderful seeing you again."

Samuel dissected her words. Did her omission of the facts mean she didn't consider herself truly engaged? Or perhaps she was trying to be kind, thinking that her betrothal would hurt him.

"This going-home business," Grandfather said. "If anything, you should come home with me. You need more care. And I—"

Samuel put a hand on his grandfather's, stopping his words. "I need to return to the place where I belong."

"But I just got you back. You can't leave me again."

"I must." Samuel's throat tightened. He would have liked nothing better than to stay in the company of these people he loved. But he'd strayed beyond the boundaries of his domain, and it was time to return to it.

Lord, please help me do this.

Chapter 12

I'm going home today.

Samuel looked around the guest room for the last time. He would miss the people who had visited him here. Ada and Grandfather, Mrs. Bauer, and John.

Not Mrs. Wallace.

He couldn't get the image of Ada's mother out of his mind. Or her command: *"Go away, Samuel Alcott."*

He understood why she hated him. In many ways he hated himself.

But Ada. . . He doubted he would ever love again. Not in that way. He loved the children as his own, and loved Eliza as the big sister he'd never had, but he knew that the part of his heart reserved for a wife, a partner, and a soul mate was closed. Whether by God's design or his own folly, the door was locked, the key misplaced.

With a hand to his sore ribs, he stood and held the bedpost for support. He'd done a good job of convincing John he was well enough to return to Five Points. But the truth was far less certain.

He hated to be a burden to Eliza, but he had to leave here and stop this torture.

He thought back to the carriage, to the first time he'd opened his eyes and had seen Ada looking back at him. In his delirium during the days that followed, he'd heard her voice. She'd been the one to guide him through his haze into clarity. He'd even felt her touch and had taken comfort in it. If only he could hold her one more time, kiss her—

Stop it! She belongs to another man. You rejected her. You caused all this. You. . .

Are a fool.

❧

Getting Samuel home became a production. John was going along as a doctor—to help Samuel negotiate the carriage and to inform those on the other end as to Samuel's medical needs.

Mr. Alcott had insisted on going, for he wanted to see this foundling home that had stolen his grandson's loyalty.

And Nana, who hadn't been out of the house in over two years, was going along because Mr. Alcott was going. Plus, she'd always had a soft heart for children.

And finally Ada, who had never imagined seeing Samuel to his destination, became a part of the farewell party—in spite of her mother's protests. This—at least she could have this.

The seating arrangement in the carriage was exactly to Ada's preferences. John sat outside with the coachman, leaving room for Mr. Alcott and Samuel with their backs to the horses and the ladies facing them. Although Ada would have liked to feel Samuel's arm against hers, to be able to see him, knowing within a short time she might never see him again. . .

It was bittersweet, but better than nothing.

She looked at the two men sitting across from her. They were members of the same family tree, a tree with wealthy roots. Yet they had ventured onto two very different branches, each with its own distinct purpose and reach.

The world needed both of them. Mr. Alcott's entrepreneurship was the sap that made America grow and flourish. He created jobs. And as a banker he loaned other entrepreneurs money to go after their dreams. Without this type of ingenuity and risk-taking, the working class would all fall into poverty.

Poverty. Five Points. Children without a home.

Ada looked at Samuel and received a wistful smile. Samuel had chosen an upper branch, one not often touched by human hands. But were the fruits of his labors any less important simply because they were less seen? To take care of children, to help them trust again, to help them feel of worth, was a fruit that could reap riches beyond measure. Who knew what those children would do or be when they grew up? Would one of them become president? Or create some invention that would change the world? Or fall in love and marry and have a houseful of children of their own?

This last bounty was priceless yet harder to measure than the success that revealed itself on ledger sheets. Ada was going to marry Owen. They would have children. The parade of generations would go on. To be fair, she knew she should tell Samuel about her betrothal, but she couldn't bring herself to do it. To tell him the truth would forever separate them.

Distance would accomplish that of its own accord.

"What's got you thinking so deeply, Miss Wallace?" Mr. Alcott asked.

"Oh, nothing."

Oh, everything.

❧

Samuel led the way up the steps of the foundling home. He was nervous. How would Ada and Grandfather react to it? Would they be repulsed by what they'd see? Or would their hearts be softened? He knew it didn't really matter, but he still wanted them to understand why he had given them up.

"This is it," he said, leading the group inside. He nearly made apologies in advance but stopped himself. There were no apologies to be made. It was what it was.

Eliza came into the small entry foyer from the kitchen, wiping her hands on an apron. "Samuel!"

She ran toward him and encased him in a rocking embrace that caused him pain—which he disguised. "Where have you been? Are you all right?" she asked. She gently touched a cut on his face.

"I had an accident with a horse. The Wallaces took me in and cared for me." He didn't go into more details. There was plenty of time for that.

The children heard the ruckus and came rushing from all corners of the house, hugging his legs and wrapping their arms around his waist. "Papa Samuel! You're back!"

"Ich verfehlte Sie."

"Sono felice che siete bene."

Samuel put his hands on their heads and told them he'd missed them, too. Home. He was home. There was nothing like it.

"Back, children. Back," Eliza said. "Give him room to breathe." Eliza finally gave her attention to the others. "And who have we here?"

Mr. Alcott removed his hat and gave her a bow. "Good day, ma'am. I am Nathaniel Alcott, Samuel's grandfather."

Eliza bobbed a curtsy. "Very nice to meet you, I'm sure."

Samuel took over the introductions, taking Ada's arm and moving her close. "Eliza Hathaway, this is Ada Wallace."

Eliza's eyes grew large, and she looked to Samuel for confirmation that this was *the* Ada Wallace. Samuel nodded.

"Very nice to meet you, Miss Wallace. I've heard so many wonderful things about you."

Samuel checked Ada's reaction. She seemed perplexed, as if she couldn't imagine Samuel saying anything nice about her. That made him sad.

Mrs. Bauer stepped forward. "And I am Ada's grandmother, and this"—she drew John forward—"this is my grandson, John. Dr. John Wallace. He's been caring for Samuel."

John offered a bow. "Nice to meet you, ma'am."

"Glad to meet all of you."

"You have quite a gaggle there," John said, pointing to the children.

Samuel looked to Ada as he answered. "These are my children."

"Plus one," Eliza said, nodding to a little girl who stood away from the others on the bottom stair. "I found her yesterday, hiding under the stairs in the alley. Her name is Francesca. She's Italian."

Samuel nudged his way through the children and went to sit on the bottom step. He didn't move to hug her, knowing that many of these children were wary of contact. *"Ciao, Francesca. Il mio nome è Samuel. Il felice voi sono qui."*

"My goodness," Ada said. "You know Italian?"

Once again Eliza answered for him. "Living where we do, we've both had to learn a little Italian, German, French, Russian—"

"And Yiddish," Samuel said. "I learn enough to make the children feel welcome. But they are doing the hard work. All of them are learning English."

"I admire your ear for languages," Mr. Alcott said. "I can barely order from a French menu. I have no talent for it at all."

"Neither did I," Samuel said. "Until I had no choice." He patted the stair, inviting Francesca to sit next to him. She did so, and he touched her raven-black hair. It was as soft as silk.

Eliza clapped her hands. "Come, children. Time for your English lesson with Mama Lottie." The children ran into the parlor nearby, and Ada could see rows of mismatched chairs, all facing in one direction. A young woman stood at the front with a chalkboard in hand. Little Francesca left Samuel's side to join the others.

"Would you like some coffee?" Eliza asked.

"That would be wonderful," John said.

"And I'd like a tour," Mr. Alcott said. "Show us around, Samuel. I want to see everything."

Samuel was surprised by his grandfather's interest but glad for it. "Come. I'll show you where the children sleep."

As they headed upstairs, Mrs. Bauer took the railing with one hand and Mr. Alcott's arm with the other. "Are you coming, Ada?"

"Of course."

&

Samuel swept an arm toward the hallway. "We have four bedrooms on this floor, and there are two rooms in the attic, one for children and one for me. Eliza stays in a room off the kitchen, and Lottie is married and lives elsewhere. That's the extent of our operation. Nothing fancy."

Ada walked by doorways that revealed small but neat rooms crowded with cots, beds, and bedrolls, three to a room.

"Very nice," she said, though *nice* was an exaggeration. She saw rags shoved between the window sash and sill. A child had drawn a face in the frost on the inside of the glass. It was starting to snow. "This room has nice light."

"A few rooms don't have any windows at all, so this one is prized." Samuel moved to the end of the hall. "Let me show you the attic. Some of the girls have spruced up their room with bits of tin."

"Tin?"

"Come. I'll show you."

Samuel led the way up a narrow staircase. Among the eaves there were two rooms, one on either side. He pointed to the left. "See there? The girls have taken it upon themselves to make their room prettier. They find bits of metal and old cans on the street, flatten them, and punch designs in the tin."

One wall was their gallery, showcasing their odd art. It was an admirable attempt to create beauty where none had been before.

"And this is my room," he said, pointing to the room on the other side of the small landing. "It's small and unadorned. Hardly a place for. . ." He looked to the floor and let the sentence die.

He'd deemed the room unworthy of *her*.

Ada took a step inside the room. The space was smaller than the girls' portion of the attic, the furniture scuffed and in need of paint. A dresser, bed, bedside table, washbasin and pitcher, and chair. The room was the size of her bathroom back home.

She didn't dare ask about those facilities—if there were any.

"I suppose this is very disappointing to all of you," he said. "And incomprehensible."

Ada wasn't sure what to say. For *this* he'd given her up, given up his own family, his inheritance, and his way of life.

"You are one in a thousand men, Samuel Alcott," Nana said.

"Among thousands of children who need my help. If only we could help them all."

With Mr. Alcott's help, Nana sat on the one chair. " 'Suffer the little children to come unto me, and forbid them not: for of such is the kingdom of God.' "

Samuel smiled. "Exactly."

His grandfather took a deep breath. "I smell coffee. Shall we?"

As they had to descend the attic stairs in single file, Ada purposely held back in order to have a moment with Samuel. "I'm glad you showed me all this," she said when they were alone.

"So you understand?"

She couldn't honestly answer him in the affirmative. She understood the need; she saw the good they were doing. But the sacrifice. . .

He touched her arm. "Ada? Do you understand why I gave up everything to be here?"

She touched his hand with her gloved fingers. "I'm trying to."

❧

Samuel followed Ada downstairs. He was glad she'd come but was dismayed that she still didn't understand his choice, that his rejection of her was because of something bigger than them both. And that even though he loved her, he'd made the right choice.

Because the foundling home was no place for Ada.

As they descended the main staircase to the first floor, he fought this statement. Who was he to say such a thing? God had a purpose in mind for Ada, just as He'd led Samuel to *his* destiny. Now that she'd seen the home, seen the need, seen the children, the seed had been planted.

But she's going to be married to a wealthy man. She's going to live the life she's always known.

The entire issue was too much for Samuel to dissect.

It was up to Ada to water the seed or let it perish.

Lord, guide her.

❧

"Well now," Eliza said as Ada and Samuel came into the parlor. "There you are. Did you enjoy your tour?"

"Very much."

Eliza responded, but Ada didn't hear because she was enraptured by the sight of Nana starting a game of cat's cradle with a little girl.

"I see you've met Nusa again," Samuel said.

"Shh!" Nana said as she carefully pinched the right strings to continue the game. "I haven't done this in years. . . ." She successfully completed the transfer, and it was Nusa's turn.

Nusa. The little girl saved by Samuel a year ago. The little girl who'd opened his eyes to the needs of all children. The little girl who'd been instrumental in the destruction of Ada's future with the man she loved.

Ada suffered a shiver. It was too coincidental. Only somehow it wasn't.

"Ohhh! *Ich ließ es fallen!*" Nana dropped the cat's cradle, and Nusa laughed.

Ada's thoughts swam. Everyone seemed so at ease here, as if they'd come a hundred times before.

She felt no ease, only confusion. And the need to leave. Immediately.

"We should go," she said.

Eliza held forth a cup. "But you haven't had your coffee."

Ada shook her head, feeling claustrophobic. "I need air." She apologized and rushed outside.

Samuel followed her. A gentle snow fell, dotting their shoulders.

"Ada, why are you upset?"

How could she explain the complexity of her thoughts? "I'm thrilled to have seen you again, Samuel. And I admire the work you're doing here. As Nana said, you are one man in a thousand."

He reached forward and touched her hand. "But I am still just a man. And I. . ." He took a fresh breath. "I wish you every future happiness, Ada."

With that, he returned inside. The visit cut short, the others passed him on their way out, calling their good-byes.

The coachman helped Ada into the carriage. She wanted to be quickly gone. Away from this place. From him. To leave would cause pain, but to linger. . .

As the carriage moved away from the curb, she felt all eyes on her. "You were rude, child," Nana said. "What got into you?"

She shook her head and looked out the window.

"I, for one, was very impressed," Mr. Alcott said. "Yes, the conditions are minimal and bare, but the children seem happy."

"And healthy," John said. "I offered Miss Hathaway my services if there is ever a need."

Their acceptance and good opinions only added to Ada's inner turmoil.

෬

After dropping Mr. Alcott at his home and John at the Academy, Ada helped Nana upstairs.

"I've tackled more stairs in this one day than I've tackled in a year," Nana said, gripping the massive walnut railing.

"To think that until recently you rarely came down."

"Silly me. Learn from my mistakes, child. If you give up on life, life will give up on you."

It was the perfect segue. "Giving up on life. . .that's what I need to talk to you about."

At the landing, Nana paused, her eyebrows high. "The visit today affected you?"

"How could it not? Let's talk in your room."

Once there, Ada shut the door, poked the fire to life, and placed a blanket over her grandmother's legs as she sat by the fire. Ada took a seat in a facing chair and plunged ahead.

"It was hard seeing the foundling home," Ada said.

"A fact you made perfectly clear. Rushing out of there as if the entire place was below your dignity. . . Really, Ada."

"But it wasn't that."

"Oh, wasn't it?"

Fine. She'd deal with her reservations first. "They had rags stuffed in the windows and frost on the inside."

Nana pointed to her own bedroom windows. "Go over there. If you move aside the draperies, what do you see?"

Ada pulled aside the massive brocade. "There's frost on the windows."

"Glass is glass, child. *We* have draperies to block the draft. They have rags. Your next objection?"

"They're not objections, Nana. Just observations."

"Such as. . . ?"

"The beds. . .many of them are mere cots with only a thin blanket as a covering."

"And. . . ?"

"And Samuel's room up in the attic—it was tiny. There aren't even proper walls. Just open beams and studs and—"

Nana rolled her eyes. "Did you only see what they didn't have and not see what they *did* have?"

Ada hated that Nana thought badly of her. "Of course I saw what they have. They have each other, and I know love trumps all the not-haves I can name."

Nana seemed to relax. "Now that's a proper observation."

"I tried to think of myself there—for a year ago I *had* offered

354

to go with him."

"And?"

This is where it got difficult. "I actually think I would have grown used to the simpler conditions. If I would have been with Samuel, I'm not sure much of that would have mattered."

"Good for you." She studied Ada's face. "But something else is bothering you."

"I don't know anything about children."

"What's to know? Children are simple creatures. They need food in their stomachs, a roof over their heads, and clothes on their bodies. But most of all, they need attention and love."

She made it sound so simple. Ada fingered the braid on her skirt and moved on to the next issue. "After seeing it all. . .I do think I understand why Samuel chose that life. In fact, I'm kind of jealous."

"Now there's an unexpected twist."

"I know. It surprised me, too," Ada said. "What struck me is that Samuel lives a life full of deep emotions. He felt called by God to this purpose. He felt it so deeply he gave up everything." She cocked her head, her cheeks warming. "I'd like to feel things so deeply. I don't want to give up on life. I don't want to settle. And I'd like God to call me to some purpose."

Nana leaned forward and patted Ada's hand. "Maybe He just has."

Really?

Ada was glad there was a back to her chair. "But Father and Mother insist I marry Owen."

"The way I see it, the call of the heavenly Father usurps any earthly one."

Ada was shocked by Nana's turnaround. "So you want me to disobey them?"

"I want you to take a breath, calm down, and pray about it. Ask God to show you His plan."

Her mind swam with possibilities. And yet there was one hitch. . . . "Samuel never told me he still loves me."

"Did you tell him you still love him?"

Ada scrolled through their conversations since he'd awakened. "After the engagement I realized I did love him, and I made my choice. I wanted to be with Samuel, and I marched into his room to tell him—asleep or no. And I did tell him I love him. But then he woke up, and I worried about what he felt toward me, and then my parents ordered me to marry Owen, and Mother insisted he leave, and. . .it all happened so fast."

"Then slow it down, child. Ask God the questions, and give Him time to arrange the answers."

"Arrange the answers?"

" 'God works in mysterious ways, His wonders to perform.' "

Ada could hear the music of the familiar hymn in her head. An excitement stirred inside her. To anticipate God's leading. . .

She suddenly stood. "I have to go."

Nana smiled "And. . . ?"

"I'll let you know what He says."

Chapter 13

It was just a few days before Christmas, and Ada's time was spent in a whirl. Praying and looking for God's answers consumed her thoughts, even as life went on.

There were Christmas parties to attend, and a caroling excursion. She'd even taken out her bridal quilt, hoping that by looking at its evidence of her life's journey, God would give her some direction. Should she finish the last row of blocks with scraps from the dress she wore the night Owen proposed, or the dress she was wearing on the day of Samuel's accident?

Knowing there was no answer—yet—she decided to use her energy to make a crazy quilt pillow with the appropriate scraps—the dress from the accident, the dress she wore to see the foundling home, and even scraps from the torn shirt Samuel had worn when he'd been injured. She worked on it in secret, feeling joy in each stitch.

Surely that meant something. Was it a sign from God?

It was certainly a start. But time was ticking by, and life was moving on around her.

Unless God gave her immediate direction, she needed to buy Owen a gift for Christmas. She took a trip to Bloomingdale's, where she looked at pocketknives, pipes, a brass match safe, and pocket watches. Nothing seemed quite right. The idea of a pipe was rejected because she'd never seen Owen smoke. The match safe—although pretty—was a bit utilitarian, and the pocket watch too intimate. And so she had the pocketknife monogrammed. It was the least she could do.

It was the most she could do.

Ada sat in the parlor and finished stitching a small gift bag for the knife. Her brother was in the foyer, dressing up warmly to venture over to the Medical Academy. But before he could leave, there was a knock on the door. Wilson answered it and received a note.

Ada set her stitching aside. Her stomach executed a small flip, as if God. . . "Who's it for?" she asked.

But by then the butler had handed the note to John. "It's for me, sister," he said, unfolding it. He read the note, then looked at her. "It's from Samuel."

Ada's stomach flipped a second time, and she hurried to his side. "What does he say? What does he want?"

John read the note aloud. " 'Dear John, Some of the children are sick. We would greatly appreciate your medical help as soon as possible. Sincerely, Samuel.' "

"Sick children? You're going, aren't you?" she asked.

He donned his hat and began to put on his gloves. "How can I *not* go?"

How can you *not go?*

Ada obeyed the inner nudge. "I'm going with you."

"I can't let you do that. They're sick."

"I've helped with Nana for years, and wasn't I a help to you when you treated Samuel?"

John paused a moment, scrutinizing her. "There's a risk, Ada."

"I'm healthy. I can handle—"

"The risk I was talking about has nothing to do with your health."

So her struggle in regard to Samuel was not a secret. She stepped closer to her brother, speaking low, for his ears alone. "I want to go there again, John. I need to go."

He searched her eyes, then nodded. "I hope you know what you're doing."

God knew. And that was enough.

❧

Eliza spooned out oatmeal. She filled three bowls on a tray and handed it to Samuel to take to the sick children upstairs.

"Do you think Dr. Wallace is coming?" she asked him.

"I hope so."

"The children aren't *that* sick, Samuel. . . ."

"I just want to make sure." He turned toward the front hall and the stairs.

But Eliza called after him, "Do you think Ada will come, too?"

Samuel pretended not to hear.

❧

"Would you please stop pacing?" Eliza asked. "I'm trying to give the children a lesson, and you're distracting them."

Samuel stopped in place and looked at the children being taught their alphabet. All eyes were on him instead of on their teacher.

"Sorry." He moved his pacing to the hall beside the stairway. This waiting was a complete waste of his time, for he had no idea if the note had even reached John, or if he'd had time to divert his day to include Five Points, or whether Ada would even know about the note at all. What if John got the note and left immediately, not even telling his sister of his destination? What if John didn't come? What if John did come but came alone?

"Why didn't I just send Ada a note?"

Hearing his words said aloud caused his pacing to stop. "What have I done? What was I thinking?"

He sank onto the stairs, put his head in his hands, and questioned the whole thing. Ada was on his mind—constantly. The need to see her again was a gaping hole that remained unfilled. So when three of the children had taken sick, he'd concocted the scheme to get her here. Hopefully.

But even if she comes, it doesn't mean she'll stay, or that she'll return your love. She's still engaged to be married. Until that changes, none of your feelings matter.

Samuel raked his fingers through his hair. This is how his thoughts had been since Ada had left, a cacophony of hopes and admonitions rattling against each other, never still.

He prayed under his breath. "Lord, forgive me for taking matters into my own hands. But I love her so. I just want to be with her."

A still, small voice broke through the mental chaos. *"Now. Now, Samuel."*

He sat upright. He dared not make a sound, expel a breath, or move a muscle. *Now?* he prayed.

"Now."

The knock on the door made him jump. His heart beat wildly. He stood and moved his hand toward the door handle. If he opened the door and it was Ada. . .

And there she was, her cheeks flushed from the cold and the journey, her golden curls contained by a gray wool bonnet adorned with a sprig of holly.

"You came," he managed.

"I came," she said.

John cleared his throat. "I came, too. You sent for a doctor?"

Samuel felt himself redden. "Yes, thank you. I'm so glad. Come in and examine the children."

Samuel's thoughts continued to spin—with gratitude. *Thank You, God. Thank You for. . .now.*

&

"They should be fine," John said, latching his medical bag. "Give them plenty of fluids and rest, and keep the other children away as much as possible."

"Thank you, Doctor," Samuel said. "I'm much relieved." He turned to Ada. "And thank you, Ada, for coming to assist."

Ada accepted his thanks, even though she hadn't done much. To make herself feel useful, she smoothed the covers around the oldest boy, Tito, and stroked his hair away from his forehead.

"*Grazie, signorina,*" he said.

Ada melted. "You're welcome, Tito."

"Sleep, children," Samuel told them. "I'll be up to check on you in a little while."

As they went downstairs, John said, "Send me a note again if you need me. But honestly, I think they'll be much improved even by tomorrow."

Suddenly Ada panicked. Their mission was complete. They were leaving. But they'd just arrived—*she'd* just arrived.

She couldn't leave yet.

Couldn't.

Wouldn't.

In the foyer she made her declaration. "I want to stay and

help—if it's all right with Samuel and Eliza, of course."

Samuel beamed, and Eliza came out of the kitchen. "Did I hear an offer to help?"

Ada could have kissed her. "I offered to stay, if you could use me."

Eliza put a finger to her chin and looked to the ceiling. "Let me see. . .thirteen children, three sick in bed, with rooms to rearrange so others won't get sick, and bread to make, and Christmas two days away. . ." She looked at Ada and smiled. "I would much appreciate your help. In fact, how are you in the kitchen?"

"I guess we'll see." Ada kissed her brother on the cheek. "I'm needed here, John."

But before she could escape, he pulled her into the parlor and spoke for her ears alone. "Come home, Ada."

"I can't come home. There's work to be done. Samuel needs me. The children need me."

"Owen needs you. Mother needs you. At home." He glanced at Eliza, who was wiping the nose of a little girl. "Home, Ada. Not here, playing nanny and nursemaid."

"I'm not needed at home and you know it. If I go home right now, how would I spend my day? Reading a book? Listening to Mother press me for ideas about my wedding?"

"You've waited a lifetime for such a wedding."

She had. From the time she'd been old enough to consider the opposite sex more interesting than annoying, she'd daydreamed about a big wedding, marrying an important man of breeding and station.

Yet recently she'd been praying for God's direction. . . .

Ada looked to the foyer. Samuel held a little girl who was playing with his collar. The sight of him was like an answer to her prayer. "Come get me Christmas Day, John. Until then, I want to be here where I'm needed."

"Ada, do you know what you're doing?" he asked.

The answer was no, but she left him to ponder the question on his own. She hurried to the foyer, nudging Eliza toward the kitchen. "Teach me how to make bread, Eliza. I'd love to learn."

Her heart beat in her throat and did not relax until she heard the front door close.

Samuel came into the kitchen. Was he going to argue with her decision?

But he just stood there looking at her.

Say something. Please say something.

"I'm glad you're here," he finally said. "Very glad."

Eliza stepped between them, handing Ada an apron. "Get off with you, Samuel, or I'll find an apron for you, too. If I'm not mistaken, we need more firewood."

He smiled and took up the wood sling. "I'll be back soon."

They were wonderful words, full of promise.

❧

Samuel strode down the street, grinning like a madman, his open coat flapping against the wind, his face enveloped by the puffs of his breath in the cold.

Cold he did not feel.

For he was warm inside, glowing and on fire with happiness. Ada was staying! She'd volunteered to stay!

God was good! God was amazing!

He added a joyful jig to his step, receiving a laugh from Mrs. O'Connor, who was selling tin cups in a pushcart nearby. "What's made you so happy today, Samuel Alcott?"

"Christmas," he said. "Merry Christmas!"

☙

"You're glowing, Miss Wallace," Eliza said.

Ada wiped the back of her hand across her forehead, trying to rid it of loose hairs. "I'm not glowing; I'm just plain hot. And please call me Ada."

Ada ladled another bowl of stew and handed it down the row of children seated around the table. Older children held younger ones on their laps and blew on each spoonful before helping it reach an eager mouth.

Eliza pulled a pan of baking powder biscuits from the oven. The smell of hot bread was enticing, and Ada's stomach growled.

But her own hunger could wait. The children came first. And oddly. . .she didn't mind.

Which was a revelation of sorts. She couldn't remember the last time she'd felt a hunger pang, or when she'd truly needed something. She also couldn't remember the last time she'd perspired because of exertion rather than the weather.

A *whoosh* of cold air blew in, and she heard the front door close and snow being stomped off boots. She stopped her spooning to look to the hall, eager to see Samuel.

He entered the kitchen with a sling full of wood. His eyes sought hers, and he smiled as though the sight of her truly pleased him. His cheeks were bitten by the cold, and once he set the new wood by the stove, he stood over it, warming his hands. Ada waited for him to say something.

But he didn't.

And she didn't. She wasn't sure what to say. She was in his world; she'd invited herself in. Partly. But Samuel had been the one to send for her brother. Had he wanted her to come along, or was her appearance a surprise?

Did he want her here? He'd said as much, but were they merely polite words? Samuel was usually talkative. They'd never had trouble making conversation before.

Eliza glanced at him, then at Ada. "Gracious sakes, Samuel. Cat got your tongue? Say something nice to our new volunteer—who's just made biscuits for the very first time."

His eyes skimmed over the bread but landed on Ada. "She's full of surprises."

Now he was being ridiculous. Ada spooned out the last bowl of soup and, nudged past him, and replaced the pot on the stove. "They're just biscuits, Samuel. And the surprise might be that you like them."

He plucked one from the pan and took an enormous bite, all the while having his eyes locked on hers. "Mmm, good," he said, with crumbs falling to his chin.

Ada brushed a crumb away, then took a seat at the table. On a whim, she reached for a toddler who was sitting on the lap of an older girl, then took up a spoonful of stew, blew on it, and fed it to the child. *See? I can fit in here. I'm up to the challenge.*

Samuel merely laughed and sat at the opposite end of the table.

Eliza shook her head. "My oh my. Life just got interesting."

Indeed.

&

"I hope you don't mind sharing the bed with me," Eliza said. "The good news is I tend to sleep like a corpse with my hands clasped over my chest, so you won't have to nudge me over to my side."

Ada stood before the narrow bed, swimming in one of Eliza's nightdresses. "I told you I could sleep on the settee in the parlor."

"Nonsense. A proper bed brings a proper sleep." Eliza gathered two bricks by the fire with tongs and wrapped them in pieces of flannel. She carried them to the bed and slid them down to the foot end. "There," Eliza said. "That'll take the chill off the sheets. Get in now, and I'll blow out the light."

Once they were settled, once Ada's eyes had adjusted to the moonlight and the low embers of the fire, Eliza said, "Care to pray with me?"

"Of course," Ada said. *Absolutely.*

"Our Father, who art in heaven, hallowed be Thy name. Thy kingdom come. . ."

Thy will be done.

❧

Samuel tucked in the last of the children. It was a nightly ritual that never grew old. To see each one safely in bed, their angelic faces nestled against the pillows, gave him a satisfaction that was full and warm and complete.

Well, not entirely complete. For tonight when he returned to the house and saw Ada there, helping the children, at ease and hard at work, he'd felt his usual satisfaction swell to a new level. It had taken all his self-control not to drop the wood with a thud and a thump, rush to her, and take her in his arms—where he would never let her go.

That's why he'd been so tongue-tied; he'd feared his surge of emotions would envelop them both and scare her away. God had been very generous in bringing her back to him. Samuel didn't want to ruin things by moving too fast.

But you only have two days. . . .

"Patience is a virtue," he whispered to himself.

"What you say, Papa Samuel?" Nusa asked.

He shook his head and smiled at the girl who'd started him on this journey. Then he kissed her forehead. "Sleep well, Nusa. God bless you."

God bless us all.

❧

Ada's eyes shot open. Then she flinched as she saw the eyes of a child at bed level, staring at her. She remembered the little girl's name. "Sara Christine? What's wrong?"

"I had a bad dream."

Ada opened the covers. "Everything will be all right. Come in here with us."

The little girl climbed in bed but quickly crawled over Ada to the center spot between Ada and Eliza. Ada turned over and saw Eliza's eyes gleaming in the moonlight. "Welcome to my world," she whispered.

As Sara Christine snuggled her head onto Ada's pillow, Ada pulled the child close and reveled in her warmth. She felt her throat grow tight at the perfection of the moment, of holding another person close, of providing comfort, of. . .of. . .

Of offering love and feeling loved in return.

Chapter 14

"Y ou're a good bed-maker, Mama Ada."

Ada mitered the final corner and stood. She stared at her helper, twelve-year-old Brigid. "Mama Ada?"

Brigid shrugged. "You don' mind, do ya? That's what the kids is calling ya."

Ada shook her head no. Yet back with her family *she* was the child.

Back home *she* didn't have to work.

Ada handed Brigid a stack of sheets. "Take these to the next room. I'll be with you in a minute." Once alone, she sank onto the bed.

It was all very confusing. She'd been at the children's home less than a day, helping to take care of the children, helping the children learn to take care of themselves. Both Samuel and Eliza had told her she didn't have to help so much, but she'd wanted to. She'd needed to.

And yet *she'd* had to be taught how to make a bed, to do the wash, to make bread to sell in a pushcart on the street along with some wooden toys that Samuel whittled. Two older boys did the actual selling, so at least there wasn't *that* task. She'd learned how to change diapers, and this afternoon she was going to learn how to teach the alphabet and arithmetic. Eliza had told her the children loved to sing all eight verses of "Mary Had a Little Lamb." Eight verses?

Ada rubbed her right shoulder, feeling muscles she'd never felt before.

She was feeling a lot of things she'd never felt before. And not just physically.

Being around Samuel was a balm. At breakfast he'd read from the Bible, and the sound of his mellow voice soothed her and made her happy. They hadn't had a chance to talk in private, yet every time they saw each other, their eyes met and spoke words their mouths couldn't voice.

Ada had purposely stayed behind to help because she wanted time with him. God had opened the door, and she felt good about walking through it. She knew if she went home, *that* world would consume her, and she might melt away like a pat of butter in a hot pan. Plus, if she went back, she would have to endure the pressure to marry Owen.

But if she stayed here?

Not once had Samuel said he loved her or wanted to marry her, or that he wanted her to stay forever. She knew it had only been a day, but time was short. Tonight was Christmas Eve. Tomorrow John would come fetch her, and she would go home and. . .

Ada was drawn from her thoughts when she heard Samuel's boots on the stairs. They needed to talk privately. Now.

She met him in the hallway. "Good afternoon, Ada," he said.

"Samuel."

He held a tray of broth and bread for the sick children. "I heard they're hungry. 'Tis a good sign."

"Yes, it is." She ached to pull him aside and speak with him, to ask him bold questions that would determine her future. But nothing more came out. And he moved on down the hall.

Ada stomped her foot, angry at herself for her own inaction. She looked heavenward. "Please help us. Help me do what *You* want me to do."

Samuel came out of the sickroom. "Ada? Did you say something?"

He'd heard her?

Good.

"I was just praying that God would help us," she said.

He came close. "Help us do what?"

She looked at him, willing him to say something that would reveal his intent. "Tonight is Christmas Eve. I go home tomorrow."

He seemed to struggle to find the words. "I only wish. . ."

"You only wish. . . ?" *Say it plain, Samuel. Please say what I need to hear. Demand that I stay here and marry you. Don't leave me hanging like this.*

"I only wish that you would—"

"Samuel? Is that your voice I hear? I need some help down here."

He answered Eliza's call from the top of the stairs. "Coming."

Suddenly weak at his exit, Ada leaned a shoulder against the doorjamb.

Lord, please help us! Please.

❧

Samuel was bursting with words—words he wanted to say, declarations of love he longed to share. With Ada so close, it was heaven.

And it was hell.

Because every time he wanted to speak, he had to hold back because she was betrothed to another.

And yet. . . If that was the case, why wasn't she back home with Owen Reed? If you loved someone, you ached to be with them; you didn't want to miss a moment together. He kept waiting for her to mention Owen. To talk of her engagement—or to talk of a broken engagement.

Something. Anything.

But Ada said nothing. So Samuel could say nothing.

Oh, that she were free! Free to be his wife.

He watched Ada drape popcorn strings around the parlor, knowing that back home her family's Christmas tree was heavy with glass ornaments and lit by a myriad of candles. She sang a carol as she worked, teaching it to the children, one line at a time.

" 'Hark! the herald, angels sing. . .' "

They repeated the line back to her.

"The word's 'sing,' Teddy," she corrected. "Not 'ring.' "

Teddy sang the last word again, making it right.

" 'Glory to the newborn King. . . .' "

Samuel joined in.

Ada beamed.

He committed her face to memory, needing to remember all of this, just in case it was their one and only Christmas together.

❧

On Christmas Eve it was time to go to church. Ada helped the children button their coats, none of which fit particularly well, and all of which were tattered hand-me-downs. She noticed Nusa didn't even have a coat, but only a shawl. "No coat?" she asked her.

"I grew too big. This fine," Nusa said and draped it over her head. "See?"

Ada didn't see, but before she could think more about it Samuel clapped his hands. "All ready, children? Everyone hold hands."

They ventured outside to walk to church. A soft snow fell, the perfect accompaniment to the sacred day.

They walked hand in hand, three adults with children in hand or in arms, the oldest children doing their part by taking custody of those younger. The little ones skipped along, their joy overflowing.

Neighbor families came out of their tenements to join the throng, the pleasure of the evening evident on every face.

"Gledelig Jul!"

"Buon Natale!"

"Fröhliche Weihnachten."

"Happy Christmas!"

"Nollaig Shona Dhaoibh."

The greetings in languages understood and foreign added to Ada's happiness. It was as though the entire world were coming together in celebration of Christ's birth.

Outside the church there was a gathering. "What's going on?" Ada asked Samuel.

"They display a nativity scene and place the baby Jesus in the manger on Christmas Eve. Hurry, so the children can see."

They rushed forward, and the little ones pushed to the front to see a pastor in a black robe reverently place a carved baby Jesus in a small trough blanketed with straw. Wooden statues of Jesus' father, Joseph, and mother, Mary, looked on. As soon as the baby was settled, the pastor turned with a finger held to his lips. "Shhh. The Christ child is sleeping."

The men removed their hats, and one began to sing, "'Silent night, holy night. . .'"

Everyone joined in, some singing the song in their native tongue. *"Alles schläft; einsam wacht. . ."*

"Tu che i Vati da lungi sognar, Tu che angeliche voci nunziar. . ."
"Sov i himmelsæl ro! Sov i himmelsæl ro!"

Ada felt her heart would burst. She'd never experienced such a feeling of unity, nor had she thought much about Jesus belonging to *all*.

In her arms, Francesca ran a finger along the track of Ada's tears. Her little face showed concern. Ada smiled and sang with the crowd. *Help me to always remember this night, Lord. Bless these people. Bless us all.*

Then she spotted Nusa walking out of the crowd toward the manger. The little girl removed her shawl and placed it over the baby Jesus, tucking him in, wiping the snowflakes from Jesus' face.

Nusa returned to Samuel's side, and Samuel pulled her beneath the warmth of his own coat.

Samuel's eyes found Ada's, and he leaned toward her. "She's giving her best to Jesus."

The final verse finished around them.

Jesus, Lord, at Thy birth.
Jesus, Lord, at Thy birth.

❧

"She's giving her best to Jesus."

The Christmas Eve service swelled around Ada, yet it was Samuel's words that played over and over in her head.

An eight-year-old little girl who owned nothing of value *but* the shawl, had given that same shawl away.

Ada was moved and humbled, and by Nusa's example began to measure her own heart.

I'm a loving person, a giving person, an empathetic person.

At least she'd thought she was. But until now, had Ada's love, generosity, or empathy ever been truly tested?

Her reverie was interrupted as the offering plate came down the pew. She opened her reticule to gather a donation but was ashamed to see she only had a few coins. She put them all in the plate as it passed by but knew her "all" was a pittance.

She rationalized that she never carried money. Any item she wished to purchase was bought on the credit of her father's good name. If she was honest, she had little knowledge of the prices of the things she purchased. If she wanted something, she bought it.

Ada looked down at the gold bracelet on her wrist. Impulsively, she pulled it off and leaned over Nusa and Samuel to toss it in the offering plate.

She felt better for it but avoided their eyes. Yes, the bracelet was worth a goodly amount, but still the sacrifice had cost her nothing. Her life would not be changed for the giving of the bracelet—or the keeping of it.

Ada closed her eyes, trying to hold back tears of frustration. She wanted to be a good person. She wanted to do the right thing with the right motives from a loving and grateful heart. She wanted to give her best to Jesus.

Suddenly she thought of her family, at this same moment sitting across town in St. Patrick's Cathedral, dressed in their Christmas finery. She'd sat beside them in church all her life, and yet not once had she thought about putting something in the offering plate when it came by; not once had she thought about sacrificing anything of value. In truth, during the sermon her mind usually strayed to thoughts about how she'd spend Christmas Day, or the new dress she was wanting, or the New Year's Eve party she would attend the coming week.

Frivolous nothings, worth nothing.

I've never given my best to anyone or anything.

She bowed her head, her tears having their way.

Samuel's handkerchief came into view, and she took it, then risked a glance.

"Are you all right?" he whispered.

She started to nod, then gave in to the truth.

"No," she said.

And more than that, she feared she would never be right again.

❧

No? She's not all right?

Samuel hated seeing Ada cry. If Nusa weren't sitting between them, he would have put his arm around her shoulders, offering her comfort. He felt so helpless.

Nusa looked up at him with questioning eyes.

Samuel could only smile and nod, suggesting that Ada would be fine.

But would she?

He wasn't sure why she was so upset. The day had gone well, filled with the merriment of the children as they decorated the house, the Christmas Eve dinner of roasted duck and plum pudding, and the happy stroll through the neighborhood to church.

Ada had been happy, too, smiling and offering greetings along the way.

But everything had changed with Nusa's offering of her shawl.

He heard Ada sniff. He ached to talk to her, to understand what had made her so sad.

But until he had that chance, he prayed that God would give her the comfort that he could not.

❧

Ada was a good actress. After church she put on a happy face and tucked the children into bed. But the fact that it was her last night here loomed large and heavy.

As soon as she smoothed the covers around Nusa, the little girl asked, "Are you mad I gave shawl?"

"Of course not. It was your shawl to give."

Her brown eyes warmed the room. "I not leave Jesus *kalt*. Not when I have shawl."

Ada looked down at her, so innocent, so giving, so unassuming—all traits *she* should aspire to. A question loomed: Could *she* leave Jesus cold in the snow?

Could she give up what was fine in her life? Could she sacrifice her comfort? Her possessions, her blessings?

"Mama Ada, you all right?"

Ada stroked her cheek. "You humble me, young lady."

Nusa's forehead tightened. She didn't understand.

Ada kissed her forehead and said a prayer for her own understanding.

❧

Eliza blew out the lamp and settled onto the bed beside Ada. "You go home tomorrow."

"Yes."

"We're going to miss you."

"And I will miss you."

A swath of silence hung between them. "Christmas blessings, Ada."

"The same to you."

Ada did not sleep well that night as the notion of blessings and sacrifice danced in her head.

Chapter 15

The children wiggled and bumped into one another, each trying to find a place to sit at Samuel's feet. In his arms was a huge basket covered with a cloth.

Eliza pointed at Enoch. "Children who shove do not get a Christmas present."

Enoch sat perfectly still—which Samuel knew was quite a feat.

When they were finally settled, Samuel made a show of peeking under the cloth. "Now, what do we have here. . . ?"

He pulled out a carved wooden doll and handed it to Sara Christine. "Mama Eliza made a dress and some hair out of yarn," he said. The doll's arms and legs were tied to the body with a piece of leather, allowing them to move.

The girl touched the doll's face with a mother's tenderness. "Thank you, Papa Samuel."

Next he pulled out a cart and horse. "This is for Siggie."

Siggie spun the wheels. "They work!"

"Of course they work. What good is a cart that can't move?"

"What do you say?" Eliza prodded.

"Thank you, Papa Samuel!"

The rest of the gifts were distributed: a musical clapper for Nusa, a set of wooden blocks for Francesca, a train, some farm animals, another doll, a duck pull toy, a top, a game of nine-pins, a Jacob's ladder, a cup and ball game. . .

Then Samuel gave Eliza her gift. She untied the string holding its towel wrapping. "It's a pot rack to put on the wall."

"It's beautiful, Samuel," she said.

Samuel looked to Ada. He felt bad for not having a gift for her. "I wish I would have known you were going to be here. I would have made you something."

She sat beside Anthony and helped him spin the top. "No need at all. I had no idea you were so talented. I've never seen toys as fine as these. Ever."

"You're too kind. I—"

There was a knock on the door. Samuel and Ada exchanged a look. Was it John, come to take Ada home? Could Samuel bar the door? Or tell the children to be quiet and pretend no one was home?

"I'll get it," Ada said. She went to the door slowly, as if dreading the task. She paused and took a deep breath; then she opened it. "John. And Owen. I. . .I. . ."

It was clear she hadn't expected Owen. The tone of her voice as she said his name. . . His sudden appearance seemed to distress her.

Distress her? He was her fiancé. She should be happy to see him.

The men stepped in, carrying gifts of holiday food: a ham, spritz cookies, fruit cake, and nuts. Upon recognizing John as the doctor who'd come to help, the children ran to him, showing off their toys. "My, my," he said. "What treasures you have."

As John was drawn away from the door and Eliza took possession of the food, Ada was left with Owen.

Seeing them together, Samuel felt a swell of panic. But he stepped forward to greet him. "Owen Reed. Merry Christmas to you."

They shook hands. "Samuel Alcott." Owen looked around the room. "So this is where you ended up."

Samuel guessed the comment was not meant as a compliment but acted otherwise. "We're very proud of the home here. And Miss Wallace has been ever so helpful."

Owen looked at Ada. "I'm very proud of Ada for her charitable nature."

"It's more than charity," she said. "I love helping the children. I love the—"

"I'm sure they'll miss you when you're gone," Owen said.

An awkward silence hung over the room.

Samuel rushed to fill it, to ease Ada's discomfort. "Congratulations on your upcoming marriage, Owen," he said.

"Thank you," Owen said. "We're both looking forward to it, aren't we, Ada?"

Ada was staring at Samuel, her face distraught. She looked as if she wanted him to save her. And more than anything he wanted to save her, to pull her into his arms and say, "You can't marry her. *I'm* going to marry her!"

But then John interrupted and retrieved Ada's wool cape from a hook by the door. "Come now, sister. Our parents are waiting for your return so we can celebrate our own Christmas."

Although Owen leaned close to Ada and spoke in a whisper, Samuel heard his words. "I've bought you the most lavish present."

And there it was. Owen could offer Ada a life full of lavish presents. And here, today, Samuel had had nothing to give her for Christmas.

In a flurry of activity, Ada's coat was helped on, her bonnet tied, and the children kissed. As the door opened, Samuel panicked. For once she went through that door, she would be gone to him forever.

He stepped through the crowd of children. "Ada? Miss Wallace?"

She turned to him, her eyes frightened and confused. "Yes, Samuel?"

"I. . ." He didn't know how to say what needed to be said.

Owen took her hand. "Come, Ada. The carriage is waiting."

With one last look, she turned and left him.

The door closed, shutting her off from him forever.

❧

The carriage ride home was accompanied by much talking—by her brother and Owen. Ada heard a phrase here and there, and even responded in a fashion, but her mind was absorbed with one thought: Samuel knew that she and Owen were engaged?

How did he know about the engagement?

How long had he known?

Although she would have liked to know the details, the point remained that he *did* know. And with her knowledge of *his* knowledge came new eyes regarding Samuel's recent behavior: his reserve, his awful politeness, and their limited snippets of personal connection.

If only he'd said something to her earlier. If only he'd congratulated her on her engagement or mentioned it in some way, she could have told him the whole awkward story of her betrothal.

Yet by telling him the truth, she would have virtually been asking him. . .suggesting to him that they. . .

Did Samuel want to marry her?

John's voice intruded. "You should see the spread Mother has planned for Christmas dinner. Goose and turkey, yams and hard rolls, cranberry relish, minced meat *and* pecan pies."

Ada put a hand to her mouth. The thought of eating disturbed more than enticed.

"Aren't you feeling well?" Owen asked.

Perhaps if she feigned illness, once she got home she could escape to her room and wallow in her thoughts and memories of Samuel. And she needed time to pray, to talk to God, to ask Him if this was really what He wanted. How could this be His plan for her life when it made her feel so dreadful?

"Oh, Ada's fine," John said. "When she sees the Christmas tree and has a cup of wassail, she'll be her old self again."

But Ada didn't want to be her old self.

❧

"Papa Samuel, will you read?" Nusa held a copy of *Hans Brinker and the Silver Skates*.

Eliza rushed forward to shoo the girl away. "Leave Samuel alone, Nusa. He needs some time to himself."

Samuel was glad for the intervention. Since Ada's departure, he'd been tormented by a bevy of should-have-saids and should-have-dones. His first inclination had been to run after the carriage, calling, "Ada! Come back! Come back!"

Nusa stood before Samuel, studying him.

"Please, Nusa. . ."

"Why you not stop Mama Ada from going?"

Good question. "She's supposed to marry Mr. Reed."

Nusa shook her head. "She supposed to marry you. Marry us."

And there it was. The truth laid out as fact.

"Now, Samuel. Now."

God's words. He'd heard them before and had only partially followed through. But God didn't want partial obedience. Partial faith. He wanted people to step out boldly, to trust Him completely.

Samuel had asked for guidance. *Had* God spoken to him?

There was only one way to know for sure.

He stood.

"You go get her?" Nusa asked.

Could he do that? Could he rush to the Wallace house, knock on the door, and claim Ada as his own?

"Should I?" Samuel asked, even though he knew the answer.

"Of course," Nusa said, in that simple way of children. "God brought her here. To us. He want her here."

Samuel smiled. "He does?"

Nusa's nod was strong. Then she ran to get Samuel's coat. "Can I go, too?"

"Not this time, Nusa. This, I have to do alone."

But not alone. For finally, at this moment, Samuel was certain God had been with him—had been with both of them—since the first moment he and Ada had met. Each happenstance since had been set in place by their heavenly Father. Though both he and Ada had been offered choices along the way, with this final choice made, Samuel felt as though he was finally and firmly rooted in the Almighty's plan.

Which, as always, was the best plan.

Ada sat in the drawing room of her family's home, an immense Christmas tree decorated in the corner, the candles making it glow like the stars in a Bethlehem sky. A fire roared in the fireplace, and the smell of spiced cider and pine boughs filled the room.

Nana untied the ribbon around a quilted bed jacket Ada had made for her. She held the item close, inspecting the stitches. "You are so talented at quilting and embroidery, child. It's beautiful."

Ada's mother chimed in. "Now that you're quilting again, once you choose the fabric for your wedding gown, you'll be able to finally finish your bridal quilt."

Ada thought about the unfinished quilt. The satin of a wedding dress she'd wear to marry Owen did not fit with the rest of the quilt, which chronicled her life before Samuel, and finally with him. What came after Samuel had no place on the quilt, no right to be there. Just as the quilt had stopped, so had her life. It was as though there'd been a gap in time. The months and days since Samuel had left her last Christmas until he'd come back to her a few weeks ago were a blur, as if she'd been sleepwalking, waiting to be awakened.

But now she *was* fully awake. In this clarity, she knew what needed to be done and prayed she had the strength to do it.

Owen stood and handed her a gift. "This is from me," he said.

He was clearly excited to see her open it, yet that was the last thing she wanted to do. To open it would add another slice of time to her Owen-life.

"Ada," Father said. "Don't keep Owen waiting."

She had no choice but to untie the ribbon and open the velvet box.

"They're emeralds," Owen said proudly. "The set belonged to my mother, but she—but I—want you to have it."

Ada touched the largest stone at the climax of the substantial necklace. There were three-stone drop earrings and a matching bracelet.

Mother came to her side to admire it. "Oh, Owen. This is exquisite."

"It's only the beginning. Although I wanted to give you family jewels for this first Christmas together, I promise to have some modern pieces made for you in the future. We'll go to Tiffany's together, and you can choose whatever stones and setting you like."

"You are too generous," Mother said. "Come now, Ada, you must try it on."

Ada didn't want the emeralds to touch her skin. For once they did, she felt as if she would be branded: forever Owen's. The emeralds would sear into her skin and—

I'm not Owen's. I'm Samuel's. With my entire being I belong to Samuel! Lord, please give me the strength to do what I must do.

There was a knock on the door.

Ada's heart jumped to her throat. She gave her mother possession of the emeralds and stood.

"Who would come calling on Christmas?" her father asked.

Is it. . . ? Could it be. . . ? Please let it be. . .

Ada took a step toward the foyer, but Mother put a hand on her arm and kept her back. "Wilson will get it, dear. Come now, and let's put on the necklace."

Ada heard a man's voice talking to the butler. And then the butler led him in.

"Mr. Alcott, sir. Ma'am," Wilson announced.

And suddenly her family was gone from the room. Gone from the world. Only two people existed: Ada and her Samuel.

She ran to him and pulled him close. "Oh, Samuel, I prayed you'd come."

He whispered in her ear. "I never should have let you go."

Ada's mother was in a panic. "Ada! What are you doing? Let go of him! Come back here with your family."

Ada released Samuel but for an arm around his waist. "Samuel is my family, Mother."

"He most certainly is not. Don't be ridiculous." She turned to the others in the drawing room, who stood staring at the scene. "Horace. John. Owen. Mother. Stop her."

"Ada seems to know her own mind," Nana said softly.

Mother looked aghast and turned to Owen. "Owen, please. She's to be your wife."

Owen looked uneasy but took a step forward. "Is she?" He looked at Ada, his brow furrowed. "Are you, Ada? Are you going to be my wife?"

This was the hard part. To choose one man, she must hurt another. Reluctantly she left Samuel and took Owen's hand in hers. "Owen, you are a wonderful man and will make someone very happy."

"I want to make you very happy."

She shook her head. "But I would not make *you* happy. You deserve a wife who will adore and cherish you. I am not that woman."

For the first time, Ada's father spoke up. "This is ridiculous, daughter. You can't break your engagement to Owen. His father and I agreed—"

Mother interrupted. "His mother and I agreed. And wedding arrangements have begun."

"Hush, both of you," Nana said. "None of that matters."

"Of course it matters," Mother said.

Ada agreed with Nana. It was time to focus on what *did* matter.

Suddenly an image of Nusa offering her best to the baby Jesus came to her mind. *"What will you offer Me? What is your best?"*

Where was Ada at her best? Where were the best parts of her— her giving nature, her compassion, and her ability to love—allowed to flourish?

It was not here, in the lush drawing room of a mansion on Fifth Avenue.

"Surrender yourself as you are, and I will help you be your best."

Ada pulled in a breath, the thoughts, the inner voice vivid in her mind. For her Christmas gift Nusa had given Jesus all she had. For Ada's Christmas gift. . .

She closed her eyes, needing to concentrate on this very important offering. *I give You my life, Lord. I offer my life to You, for You to do with as You will.*

And suddenly she felt a calling from God. And with it came the knowledge that it had always been there, an unopened gift, waiting for her to unwrap His glorious will.

"Ada?" Mother said. "Don't just stand there with your eyes closed. Do something."

Ada opened her eyes and smiled, knowing that she *had* done something, *the* something that would change everything.

A wave of peace passed over her, letting her know that God had accepted her offering—and approved. "Please forgive me," she said to Owen and her family. "But everything has changed. I'm not who I used to be, nor am I the woman I'm going to be. I only know that God has opened a door, and I'm walking through it."

"Door?" her father said. "What door?"

She looked to Samuel. "The door that leads me to Samuel."

Oddly, it was Owen who spoke next. "Do you love him, Ada?"

Ada's eyes remained on Samuel. She hated that the first time she'd say the words she was across the room from him. But perhaps it was necessary. She held her ground but kept her eyes on his. "Oh yes."

He beamed and held out his hand.

She crossed the room, leaving one man's hand to take up another's. And once again, they were alone in the world.

Samuel beamed down at her. "Remember how I said I had nothing to offer you this Christmas? Actually, I do. I give you my hands to provide for you, my arms to hold you and keep you safe, my eyes to see who you really are, my ears to listen to your thoughts and desires, my lips to say I love you, and my heart to swell with joy at your presence. I give you all of myself. And so. . ." He got down on one knee. "Ada, my love, will you be my wife?"

Ada spoke with utter confidence. "Yes, oh yes."

She fell into his arms.

Where she belonged.

Epilogue

One year later

Nusa! You're eating more popcorn than you're stringing," Ada said as she and the children sat around the kitchen table making Christmas garlands.

Nusa merely smiled and put a garland around Ada's neck. "A Christmas necklace," she said. "And you can eat it, too."

The children laughed, and Ada found their laughter more precious than jewels.

Then she heard Samuel and his grandfather coming down the stairs, talking about the just completed addition to the foundling home. She moved to join them. "I'll see if I can get a couple more oak dressers sent over from Macy's," Mr. Alcott said. "One for the older boys' room and one for the new baby."

"That's very generous of you, Grandfather," Samuel said. "Generous again. Buying the building next door and helping us expand. . ." He looked at his wife. "And I know for a fact that both Ada and I are much appreciative of having our own apartment there."

"I readily admit it's better than the attic room," Ada said with a laugh.

"I still wish you would have agreed to turn my home into an orphanage," Mr. Alcott said. "All those empty bedrooms going to waste."

Ada kissed him on the cheek. "Your offer was extremely generous, but we need to be down here in Five Points so the children can find us."

A little three-year-old tugged on Mr. Alcott's coat. He picked her up. "Yes, well. . .there is that."

"And don't offer up our house so quickly," Nana said as she came down the stairs. "As your wife, I have plans to use that space for charity fund-raisers and women's suffrage rallies and—"

"You'll drive me to drink, dear woman," Mr. Alcott said.

She reached the foyer and flicked the tip of his nose. "I drive you to *think*. And you love it."

"That I do," he said.

Ada found a place beneath Samuel's arm and rested a hand on her ample belly. She felt the baby move, low and heavy. With any luck, it could still be a Christmas baby. So many events of their lives linked to Christmas. . . .

Eliza appeared at the top of the stairs and called down to Ada. "Your surprise is ready. You can send the children up now."

Finally. After months of work, her Christmas present was complete.

Ada went back to the kitchen to gather the children. "Are you ready for your Christmas gifts?"

"Yes!"

"Yay!"

Ada crooked a finger at them. "Follow me."

They scrambled around her, a thundering herd following her

up the stairs. Once on the landing, she set them loose to scatter to the bedrooms.

Exclamations, shouts, and laughter erupted. Ada was joined by the other adults, and they walked from room to room. The children came and went between them, excited about their gifts.

Her brother, John, came out of the boys' bedroom, laughing at the melee. "Mother will be appalled you cut it up."

"She knows, and she *was* appalled. But she came to understand. For what better use of my bridal quilt than to embellish the coverlets of my children. By the way, brother, are you coming over for Christmas dinner tomorrow? Mother and Father are coming around one."

John nodded, and they all watched as the children examined their new coverlets that were each adorned by a portion of her quilt, the quilt that showcased the costumes of Ada's life, the gowns and dresses that had once seemed so important to her. Many coverlets made from one. Ada loved the symbolism of it. She had been one girl, concerned with only herself. And now, through love, her life had expanded a hundredfold.

Ada had one more surprise and, from behind a door, pulled out a pillow that highlighted a very important part of her quilt. She handed it to Samuel.

"This is for you. I started it last year, but now it's finally finished."

He ran his fingers along a patch of rough cloth, its textures intermixed with the finer silks and brocades. "These are from my shirt," he said. "The one I was wearing on the day of the accident."

Ada nodded and continued his tour. "And this is from the dress I wore that first day I saw you in Five Points, and this, from the dress I wore when we brought you home, and this green is from the dress I wore when I came back to help the sick children, and—"

"And this red velvet is from the dress you were wearing when I came to your house and proposed."

"And I said yes." They kissed across the pillow.

So many days. So many memories. But as they looked at the joyful children bustling around them and their happy grandparents reunited in love, Ada knew that the waiting had been worth it.

For *now* was the most wonderful time of the year.

Discussion Questions

1. Ada is very close to her grandmother. Nona is someone she can confide in and be herself with. Who fills these needs in your life?

2. Ada's quilt is a chronicle of her life. Do you do anything to chronicle your life? A diary, scrapbooks? What other ways could you record the moments of your life?

3. Samuel is drawn into going down to Five Points to go "slumming" with his friends. What situation have your friends drawn you into? What are ways you could have told them no?

4. Samuel feels an inner voice directing him, and he takes this voice to be God giving him direction. How does God speak to you?

5. Samuel takes a huge risk saving Nusa *and* bringing her home. The choice changed his life completely. When has your life been changed by an act of kindness—from you or done for you?

6. Samuel feels an instant connection when he's at the Merciful Children Foundling Home. When have you felt a strong connection to a place, an organization, or a group of people? Why?

7. Samuel sees a need at the Foundling Home but has no money to spare until his grandfather gives him a ring, freeing up Samuel's money. When has God provided finances to you at just the right time?

8. Do you agree with Samuel's decision to break up with Ada? How do you think the story would have ended if he'd stayed with her the first time?

9. You are the casting director for the film version of *The Bridal Quilt*. Who would you cast to play Ada? Samuel? Eliza? Owen?

10. If you were in charge of writing epitaphs for these characters, what would you say about them?

Crazy Quilt Ornaments

Crazy quilts use random odd-shaped pieces that are embellished with bits of trim of embroidery.

Step 1: Choose your shapes—simple shapes. Cookie cutters are a good source, or children's coloring books or workbooks. The size should be about 3". Once you choose a shape, trace it on a piece of muslin or solid-color cotton with a permanent marker (you want it to bleed through). This is your base fabric and will not show in the final ornament. For illustration, a stocking shape is used.

Since these are so small, don't use a sewing machine. Just hand-stitch the pieces together (as described in the following steps) using a simple running stitch.

Step 2: Place your first fabric, right side up, over a large portion of your muslin pattern. Stitch ¼" from the edge on top and bottom of piece. Note: any piece of fabric that extends over edge of pattern should do so by ¼" to provide future seam allowance.

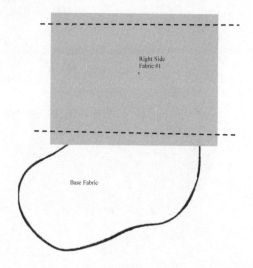

Right Side
Fabric #1

Base Fabric

Step 3: Place your second fabric, right side down over a corner of the basic shape, covering a bit of the existing fabric, edge to edge. Stitch ¼" from the edge. When done, flip Fabric #2 over along stitching line and press.

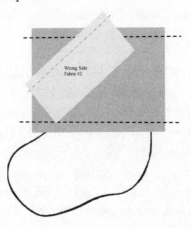

Step 4: Add Fabrics #3 and #4, repeating process in Step 3. It helps to baste the shape outline through all the fabrics to help keep them in place while you move on to the next step: embroidery and embellishment.

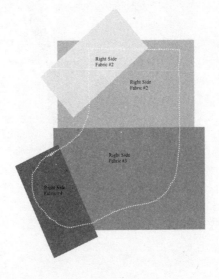

Step 5: Once the ornament is pressed, you're ready to embellish it with embroidery stitches, beads, or bits of lace. There are many online sites with directions for stitches. Here's one: http://www.embroiderersguild.com/stitch/stitches/

Step 6, Lining: When you're done making the ornament fancy, cut ¼" from the outline of the basic shape. Cut a piece of backing fabric—something pretty, not muslin. Choose a piece of ribbon for the hanger. Making a loop, put hanger in place between the right side of the ornament and the right side of the lining. Pin. Then pin right sides of ornament and lining together. Stitch around the shape outline, leaving an opening of about 1½". Trim the corners and the curves so it's not bulky when you turn it. Turn the ornament right side out and press. Blind-stitch the 1½" opening shut.

To see a color photo of the ornament, go to Nancy's website: http://nancymoser.com/updates.html

Grandma Lillie's Raisin Bars

1½ cups raisins
1½ cups water
1½ cups brown sugar
1 cup shortening
2 eggs
1½ teaspoons baking soda
1 teaspoon salt
1 teaspoon vanilla
3½ cups flour

GLAZE:
1½ cups powdered sugar
4 tablespoons milk

Boil raisins in water for 3 minutes until plumped up—do not drain. Mix together all other ingredients and add undrained raisins. Spread on greased, *sided* cookie sheet. Dough will be about ½" thick. Bake at 350 degrees for 17 to 19 minutes. Cool. Spread glaze over bars.

Nancy Moser is an award-winning author of over twenty novels that share a common message: we each have a unique purpose—the trick is to find out what it is. Her genres include contemporary and historical novels including *An Unlikely Suitor*, *Mozart's Sister*, and the Christy Award-winning *Time Lottery*. She is a fan of anything antique—humans included. www.nancymoser.com.

Are You an eBook Reader?—Check Out...

A Basket Brigade Christmas by Judith Miller, Nancy Moser, and Stephanie Grace Whitson

In 1862, with the country embroiled in civil war, the women of Decatur, Illinois, launched a campaign to minister to Union soldiers being transferred from the overflowing hospitals in the South to more northern locations. Known as the "Basket Brigade," a committee of thirty women boarded every evening train for more than nine months, offering fried chicken, pickled peaches, pound cake and other "dainties" to men who hadn't had a home-cooked meal since enlisting. *A Basket Brigade Christmas* was inspired by the true story of the women of Decatur, Illinois, who eventually served nearly two thousand meals to wounded warriors. The three novellas are based on the real words written by the women who organized and participated in relief efforts during the Civil War.

Includes:
A Stitch in Time by Stephanie Grace Whitson
A Pinch of Love by Judith Miller
Endless Melody by Nancy Moser

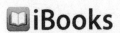

JOIN
US
ONLINE!

Christian Fiction for Women

Christian Fiction for Women is your online home for the latest in Christian fiction.

Check us out online for:

- Giveaways
- Recipes
- Info about Upcoming Releases
- Book Trailers
- News and More!

Find Christian Fiction for Women at Your Favorite Social Media Site:

 Search "Christian Fiction for Women"

 @fictionforwomen